GOODNIGHT!

ALSO BY ABRAM TERTZ (ANDREI SINYAVSKY)

For Freedom of Imagination
The Makepeace Experiment
Fantastic Stories
The Trial Begins
On Socialist Realism
A Voice from the Chorus

GOODNIGHT!

A Novel

ABRAM TERTZ
(ANDREI SINYAVSKY)

Translated and with an Introduction
by Richard Lourie

VIKING

VIKING
Published by the Penguin Group
Viking Penguin, a division of Penguin Books USA Inc.,
40 West 23rd Street, New York, New York 10010, U.S.A.
Penguin Books Ltd, 27 Wrights Lane, London W8 5TZ, England
Penguin Books Australia Ltd, Ringwood, Victoria, Australia
Penguin Books Canada Ltd, 2801 John Street,
Markham, Ontario, Canada L3R 1B4
Penguin Books (N.Z.) Ltd, 182–190 Wairau Road,
Auckland 10, New Zealand

Penguin Books Ltd, Registered Offices:
Harmondsworth, Middlesex, England

First published in 1989 by Viking Penguin,
a division of Penguin Books USA Inc.

3 5 7 9 10 8 6 4 2

Originally published in Russian under the pseudonym Abram Tertz
by Syntaxis, France, 1984.

LIBRARY OF CONGRESS CATALOGING IN PUBLICATION DATA
Terts, Abram, 1925–
[Spokoĭnoĭ nochi. English]
Goodnight! : a novel / Abram Tertz (Andrei Sinyavsky).
p. cm.
Translation of: Spokoĭnoĭ nochi.
ISBN 0-670-80165-8
1. Terts, Abram, 1925–   in fiction, drama, poetry, etc.
I. Title.
PG3476.S539S613   1989
891.73'44—dc20   89-40049

Printed in the United States of America
Set in Sabon

Contents

v

Introduction

In an unreal time, autobiography is necessarily fiction. And no epoch was more bizarrely unreal and all-too-brutally real than that of Joseph Stalin. His reign began sometime in the late twenties and came to an end sometime in early March 1953. Ambiguity clings to both Stalin's rise and his demise, appropriate for a man who, as an up-and-coming revolutionary, was once described as a "gray blur." Andrei Sinyavsky is a son of the Stalin years. He was born in 1925, the year after the death of Lenin, when Stalin was already busy ensuring his own ultimate succession. By the time Andrei was four, Stalin was securely in power; his fiftieth birthday was celebrated with megalomaniacal splendor, launching the cult of the personality. Sinyavsky's childhood and youth coincided with collectivization and the great terror, both of which are echoed in this book. He came to manhood and the crisis that made him an artist during the final flowering of Stalinism. As that growth withered in a final, poisonous bloom, the key events in Sinyavsky's life took place.

The first shock came in 1948, when the secret police began summoning Sinyavsky, seeking to enlist his aid "as a good Soviet" in a plot against a friend of his, Hélène Peltier-Zamoyska, the daughter of the French naval attaché in Moscow. Sinyavsky says that this "may have been the most serious crisis in my life, after which it was emotionally impossible for me to return to the ranks of moral and political unity with the Soviet people and Soviet society." In 1951 his father was arrested. The year 1953 opened with the "Doctors' Plot"—a group of doctors, mostly Jews, were accused of planning to kill Stalin. In fact, this was the end of one phase of official anti-Semitism and the prelude to a new wave of terror. But even a tyrant's dreams don't always come true; this campaign was cut short by Stalin's death two months later. By 1956 Khrushchev was denouncing Stalin, and Andrei Sinyavsky, former Young Communist League member and devoted revolutionary, had metamorphosed into Abram Tertz, a daring writer who used a variety of forms—essay, novel, aphorism—to effect his spiritual liberation.

Those works were smuggled out to the West, where they were first published in 1959. Since Tertz was clearly a pseudonym, a guessing game began as to the author's real identity. That game ended in 1965 with the arrest of Andrei Sinyavsky, a Soviet literary critic known for his work on the poetry of the early years of the revolution, Pasternak, Babel, and who lectured at the prestigious Gorky Institute of World Literature, in Moscow.

Sinyavsky never had any doubt he'd be caught. He predicted both the fact and the circumstances of his own arrest in his first novel, *The Trial Begins*, whose hero is arrested in the same year the novel was written, 1956. Sinyavsky knew that he was in danger from the moment he conceived his book, not to mention sending the completed version to the West. It was just a matter of time. In fact it was nine years, during which he produced a series of remarkable works: the furiously ironic essay *On Socialist Realism* and its embodiment in fictional form, *The Trial Begins*, were both written in 1956; the *Fantastic Stories*—the grit of reality whirling in a suspension of pure imagination—were produced between 1955 and 1961; the merry dystopian novel *The Makepeace Experiment* was completed in 1962, and the jagged, sparkling aphorisms *Thought Unaware* in 1963. Sinyavsky was at work on *Earth and Heaven*, an analysis of the Russian view of life as expressed in ancient works of art, especially icons, when he was arrested in September 1965. And it is with that arrest—"They grabbed me near Nikitsky Gate"—that this novel, the culmination of everything he has so far written, begins.

Fiction and nonfiction have strikingly different powers when it comes to diluting each other. A few drops of fiction in a work of history or biography is enough to taint the mixture and render it suspect. Fiction, on the other hand, can absorb great quantities of fact and still retain its essence of fable. This is particularly true of *Goodnight!*, which is clearly a work of art even though it is built out of slabs and slivers of reality. Nearly all of the book's contents describe actual events, except for the obvious flights of fantasy and the literary essays and plays inlaid within the text. But everything is arranged and held in a vision originating in the imagination.

Besides, how could the relationship between fact and fiction, life and literature, be anything but tentative for Andrei Sinyavsky, the first Soviet writer to be convicted for the opinions voiced by imaginary characters. Officially, he was charged with a violation of Section 1 of Article 70 of the Criminal Code of the Russian Republic—"Agitation or propaganda carried out with the purpose of subverting or weakening the Soviet system or in order to commit particularly dangerous crimes against the state." However, both in the courtroom and in the Soviet press, he was tried and vilified for his fictions. Sentenced to seven years in a camp, he would serve somewhat less than six. He was to do real time, hard labor, for works of the imagination, an example of the seriousness with which Russians take literature's being carried a bit far.

Though the grotesqueness of the situation was not lost on him, Sinyavsky had always known that he was going to have to pay for his words, and accepted his fate with a peculiarly Russian blend of resignation, sorrow, and gladful pride. Fortunately, he had his alter ego, Tertz, along to remind him that any other trial would have been somehow asymmetrical to his nature and his vision of the world.

Sinyavsky really had two codefendants at the trial—Yuli Daniel, friend, fellow clandestine author, best known for *This Is Moscow Speaking* under the pen name Nikolai Arzhak; and Abram Tertz. Himself a fictional creation, the hero of songs sung by the thieves of Odessa, Tertz is the crook as heretic, the imagination as outlaw. Tertz, as literature itself, was also in the dock. Tertz is everything the plodding, helpless Russian intellectual Sinyavsky isn't—savvy, brash, quick on his feet, and a Jew. Sinyavsky may have identified the persecution of the Jews with the arrest of his father, more or less concurrent events, but it probably runs deeper than that. When the guessing game was still on, one observer, the Polish poet Aleksander Wat, whose memoirs, *My Century*, can stand with Nadezhda Mandelstam's *Hope Against Hope*, saw a mixture of typically Russian and Jewish elements in Tertz: "Jewish mutterwitz as well as truly Muscovite sarcasm, and Jewish hysteria side by side with muzhik coarseness." And Wat was right, but on the level of psychology, not genealogy. Sinyavsky's works continue to reflect an affection and respect for Jews, tinged with the good-natured derision that comes of true knowledge, that is rare in Russian literature.

The writing in *Goodnight!* is jumpy; it interrupts itself and proceeds by digression, a Slavic jazz solo on sax. But free-form though its dynamic and outline may be, the work has a definite musical arrangement; each of its five chapters is a movement with its own dominant theme. The first is arrest, interrogation, trial, and transport to the camps, those stations of the cross for every Russian writer worth his salt. But, a short way into the narrative, Sinyavsky is already describing his release, out of a profound conviction that the "past cannot be grasped in sequence."

The second chapter concerns the camp itself, the cozy hell of the Gulag. Prisoners, Zeks, were more likely, however, to refer to their camp as the "zone" and, with their typical sardonic wit, called the greater society the "big zone." It is in this chapter that Sinyavsky says: "I am happy to be in a camp." Similar remarks dumbfounded otherwise astute Western correspondents when Sinyavsky visited Moscow in 1989. As no other sentence in this book, it epitomizes a mentality, a humor, a sensibility that is essential to the understanding of this work and of Russians in general. For many the camps were not only an ordeal but a revelation. There human nature is stripped bare, and the exact weight of evil and virtue is taken.

In the third movement, both the clearest and the warmest, Sinyavsky comes to terms with his father—an aristocrat, a revolutionary, a failure, a great man. His father had been a member of the Socialist Revolutionaries (the SRs), who had won a plurality in the free elections after the October Revolution; they received 40 percent to the Bolsheviks' 24 percent, sufficient cause to doom them. This chapter is a miniature Soviet *Fathers and Sons*, though Turgenev could never have foreseen what would bring fathers and sons together, and set them at odds, in the Russia of the twentieth century. Sinyavsky's father was arrested away from home, but Sinyavsky was present at the search of the family apartment. It was a key night in his life. As he wrote in *The Trial Begins*: "The doorbell rings. Surname? Christian name? Date of birth? This is when you begin to write." So that even those proceedings should not be devoid of those twists of Russian fate which give rise to the twists of Russian humor, one of the plainclothesmen inadvertently supplied Sinyavsky with the idea for his book *On Socialist Realism*. The KGB as muse.

It is only in the fourth chapter/movement that Joseph Stalin makes his appearance—after his death, as seen in a clairvoyant's vision, a tale told to Sinyavsky and retold by him. Stalin is also seen as a poster, a distinctive dot on top of Lenin's tomb, the star of apocryphal and sometimes scabrous legend. But, more than anything, Stalin is the very air one breathes, the charge in the atmosphere, the medium in which the madness occurs. Sinyavsky says straight out: "I'm afraid of writing about him." Yet that's nearly all he writes about—Stalin the magic, Stalin the system, Stalin the ism. Sinyavsky is not interested in the man ("What does it matter who Stalin actually is?"), but in Stalin as image, impact, consequence. In fact, the realistic portraits of Stalin—Solzheni-tsyn's *The First Circle* and Rybakov's *Children of the Arbat*—do not deliver the person behind the personality cult. (The best glimpses of Stalin are still those in Milovan Djilas's *Conversations with Stalin* and in Stalin's daughter Svetlana's *Twenty Letters to a Friend*—he was an indulgent papa, her mother was the strict one.) On the days preceding the announcement of Stalin's death, Sinyavsky sought refuge in the library, in ancient texts. He uses the same method in his portrayal of Stalin, capturing his subject by avoiding it.

In the fifth and last chapter we get to the "belly of the whale," the heart of the matter. This chapter flows from a central irony—Sinyavsky defends his accuser and accuses the defendant, himself. The accuser is his brilliant childhood friend Seryozha, who Sin-yavsky believes has had a hand in betraying him and Daniel. But a second, even more perverse irony comes into play here—the more Sinyavsky defends this philosophical stoolie, the more loathsome he appears.

Sinyavsky's indictment of himself is even more convoluted. Sifted out and rearranged, the facts seem to be these: in 1948 the KGB enlisted Sinyavsky in a complex intrigue. He was to try to win the affections of Hélène Peltier-Zamoyska with the probable goal of compromising her father, the French naval attaché, in some way. The KGB had used this approach before—the way to Trots-ky's skull had led through his lovelorn secretary's heart. The KGB as Cupid.

This involvement lasted until 1952, when Sinyavsky was dis-patched to Vienna with two operatives in a scheme that was as nebulous as it was nefarious. It was never clear to Sinyavsky what the KGB was up to in all this, for two very good reasons. First, as Mariya, Sinyavsky's wife, put it: "The hunter doesn't consult with the decoy"; and second, by definition, there is no way a normal person can fathom the psychology of the KGB. Many times in *Goodnight!* Sinyavsky poses the perfectly human question: How can they be that way?

Sinyavsky confesses his complicity. He is not only the child of his era, not only its victim and witness, but an accomplice in its crimes. Needless to say, he played his role with maximum dishonesty vis à vis the KGB, constantly warning Hélène of the danger. But as in the Russian Orthodox religion, confession brings deliverance from sin. In fact, the spirit, if not the letter, of Russian Orthodoxy pervades this book; it is the smile of forgiveness which plays over nearly every page.

The final paradox in a book that crackles with them is that Sinyavsky's crowning vision of what he found most "superb" in life, his vision of beauty and joy, takes place when he is essentially a prisoner. But what better image for the distinctly Russian concept of "inner freedom" than a man's being liberated from Stalinism, history, time itself, as he hurtles back to Russia under guard. The book's very structure defies time and logic—it begins in 1965 with arrest and ends in 1952 with liberation.

Since 1973 Sinyavsky has been living outside Paris and teaching at the Sorbonne. Before completing *Goodnight!*, he produced several important critical works, including *Strolls with Pushkin* and *In Gogol's Shadow*, as well as *A Voice from the Chorus*, a collage assembled from the letters he wrote home from the camp.

He visited the Soviet Union in January 1989 to attend the funeral of Yuli Daniel, but because of bureaucratic ineptitude or malice, he did not receive his Soviet visa in time and arrived in Moscow the day after the funeral. In 1960 he and Daniel had been pallbearers at the funeral of Boris Pasternak, for them the symbol of Russian literature unbowed, uncorrupted. By then they, too, had assumed the burden, risk, and glory of that calling. Now Daniel was dead and Sinyavsky was a visitor from distant Paris, to which he had every intention of returning. Though eager to discuss perestroika ("Can you rebuild a pyramid into the Parthenon?"), Sinyavsky was irked by journalists who wanted to know if he was considering moving back to Moscow. "Why, for example, when the English writer Graham Greene moved to France, didn't anyone ask him whether or not he was planning to return to England?

Who cares where Graham Greene lives—in England or in France? And Hemingway, he lived quite peacefully in Cuba (can you imagine! on an island!) and didn't hurry back to his Great Homeland." Though belonging utterly to Russia, Sinyavsky, as a free man, a free artist, reserves that same right for himself.

Among works of modern literature *Goodnight!* is remarkably good-natured. Ultimately, it has no ax to grind, no point to prove, no score to settle. Subjective to the point where author, narrator, and hero are one, the book can still hold the tonnage of history. And the shape the narrative takes is unique, as is always the case with freedom in motion.

—*Richard Lourie*

GOODNIGHT!

I
• • •

The Turncoat

They grabbed me near Nikitsky Gate. Late for my lecture at a Moscow Art Theatre workshop, I was waiting at a bus stop, keeping an eye out for my bus, when suddenly from behind me came a voice that sounded familiar, asking, "Andrei Donatovich?!"

As if he doubted it was really me but still was delighted by the off chance that it might be. Having turned obligingly around and, to my surprise, seeing no one who would have called me by name so distinctly and so fondly, I continued to swivel on my heel and lost my balance. Then I was propelled by a gentle yet precise movement into the open door of a car that sped away, as if on command, the instant I was shoved inside. No one on the street caught so much as a glimpse of what had happened. Two bruisers with huge faces held me by the arm, one on either side. They were both thick-set, middle-aged. Macho, black hair streamed out from their short-sleeve shirts, running down to the phalanges of their fingers, tenacious as handcuffs. One's swirled into an indecent overgrowth like goat hair at the barrier of his metal wrist band, no doubt the source of the comparison with handcuffs that had occurred to me. The car glided soundless as an arrow. I hadn't expected it all to be carried out with such fabulous speed. But, taking a breath, I thought I had better make some inquiries, so that those two did not begin to find my resignation suspicious in itself.

"What's going on here? Am I under arrest, is that it? On what grounds?" I said, uttering the words without confidence, my tone forced, my voice lacking the proper indignation. "Let me see the warrant. . . ."

My father had been arrested at one time, and so I had enough experience to know that the law requires a warrant in such situations.

"If there's a need for you to see it, then you'll see it!" growled the one on the right, clearly in charge, without looking at me.

Even as they held me by the arms, both my bodyguards seemed strangely detached from me, preoccupied with calculations of their own, their minds racing ahead, as if their withering gaze were clearing a path down Mokhovaya Street and the hubbub of midday Moscow. One might have thought them waging a relentless battle against some invisible enemy concealed on our route. It was much like what I'd described ten years before my arrest in the novella *The Trail Begins*. Now, in the back seat, a plainclothesman on either side of me, I could savor the full irony of the situation, and delight to my heart's content in my fiendishly penetrating insight. Still, I must admit, I had a great deal to learn. How quick and masterful they were at seizing a person, in broad daylight and in full view, leaving no loose ends, no evidence! The dense crowd at Nikitsky Gate had not even noticed them arresting me. . . .

And—as if again confirming my second sight—when we pulled up to the building on Lubyanka Square, the car did not drive in through the armored gate and into the courtyard, but came modestly to a halt by the curb; I was taken out by the arm and ferried toward the front door, openly, in full view of the passers-by, though no show was made of it either—they only held me by the elbows. It all seemed somehow purposeful, done to make a point— how sure they were of themselves, how unconstrained, and to what degree my feigned composure paled in comparison with the reality of theirs! Once again no one noticed either the prisoner or the escort. . . .

Could I have started shouting, shown some fight at that moment? Made a scene? Appealed to my fellow citizens? Torn free and tried to escape? . . . Thieves always do. . . . A ridiculous intellectual, my only thought was how to behave with as much decency and dignity as possible. If, back at the bus stop, they had handed me a calling card and politely invited me to follow them to the address on the card, immediately but not under guard, I would have obliged, after first requesting permission to phone the workshop and have my class canceled due to a sudden illness. The two hairy gangsters who had seized me so unceremoniously, as if fearing armed resistance, had probably done so, I guessed later, as a preliminary means of instilling in their prisoner a sense of utter helplessness. It was important that I be shaken up good right from the start.

In prison it's often hard to tell where theatre ends and reality begins, especially for a first-timer grabbed warm, on the fly, in mid-air, and drawn into the intrigue of an investigation with its dazzling play of chiaroscuro. The stylized, exaggeratedly decorative gloom of the casemate where you have landed grows denser and denser but still leaves your mind a ray of light—the door to the investigator's office, open a crack, from which a guiding light, severe in its restraint, reaches even you. Late in the evening of that same day, September 8, 1965, after I had been questioned and was on my way to solitary, an old guard, looking like a lanky adolescent but also like a man with plenty of experience, ordered me to undress and squat down, and then, listlessly frisking my underwear, muttered encouragingly, "Don't worry, it'll be all right. They might let you go yet." At the time I wasn't sure—and I still have my doubts as to whether he was trying to bolster my spirits with a kind word, at no great cost to himself, or to smooth over his own awkward role, or whether he had been trained to make those encouraging remarks as part of the prison system, a measure designed to play on the prisoner's nerves. Forgive me, old man, if I have wronged you!

I don't think that the universe of prison can be grasped except by projecting its walls into other sources and symbols—those of the theatre—the realm of the stage's conventions, inaccessible to us as tangible reality, and existing only in the form of a writer's fantasies. Sometimes a writer is free to disregard the facts in order to elucidate them more fully and lend them greater power, but he must always present disclaimers for these rare incursions of the creative will into the natural order. Later on, in my rough drafts for the play "The Mirror," which is still unfinished, I undertook a similar sort of exalted attempt to interpret what had happened to me. Please do not confuse that with the actual story of my arrest, which I shall be telling at the same time.

"The Mirror," a fairy-tale play in five scenes, begins with extensive stage directions:

The curtain rises. The first scene (and all the others) takes place in the investigator's office. It seems—at first—a vast, bright room. There are five, seven, perhaps fifteen people in civilian and military dress in the room. They are all in a state of great excitement. Sunbeams flutter like butterflies across the designs on the frosted window, creating an impression of life, silent but tumultuous, on the other side of the glass. On one side of the wall is a plywood first-aid chest marked with a small red cross. A safe. Above the desk with its two telephones, and counterbalancing the entire office, is the Mirror, elegant, with a tendency to enlarge; set in a Baroque gold frame, the Mirror on occasion emits incense, which trails up to the ceiling. The crackle and glare of an arc lamp, small and reassuring, are perceptible; a muffled backstage racket, hollow, distant cries.

The scene opens with a pantomime accompanied by a tune on a record player, a song like "The Spray of Champagne" or the fox trot "Rio Rita," which were popular at the end of the 1930s in the provinces. Just before I appear on stage, the civilians and military people gesture uncertainly, in a trance, showing one another things of importance either in their hands or their notebooks, glancing at their watches and at the door through which I will soon be brought—it all resembles a wedding, a festival, the dancers freezing for a moment, staring through their mad masks at the hospital-white door.

Suddenly the phonograph music dies in mid-note and, in a quick mimetic rhythm, the group of operatives breaks into its component parts, assuming the tranquillity of the noble Gobelin that has been hanging on that lordly wall for generations. Closed in a harmonious circle dance, the extras now scatter like birds about the office, each assuming the pose of casual boredom he had prepared in advance. One examines his fingernails, another the ceiling. The chief investigator, until then indistinguishable from the rest of the merry band, now springs like a tiger to the chair at his desk beneath the Mirror and, whistling a melancholy tune, thumbs through his papers. The prevailing atmosphere is that of a sophisticated, uninhibited get-together. Only the alarming sunbeams, electric butterflies zigzagging throughout the room, continue the interrupted dance. As often happens in the summertime, fiery dust particles whirl and dance in a gray column of sunlight, a reminder of eternity and the rebellious freedom outside the windows of the world.

Then the action requires that I be brought in, a forty-year-old man carrying a briefcase, wearing a baggy suit. Insignificant-looking, in low spirits.

HE (absorbed in his papers, not raising his eyes to me, dry and businesslike): Sit down.
I: Excuse me, I . . .
HE (casually, benevolently, as if speaking to one of his own people): Have a seat, Andrei Donatovich. . . .
I: But I . . .
AN OPERATIVE (previously looking out the window, through which

nothing can be seen, now turning abruptly): You heard him, sit down! (He turns away again.)

HE (frowning wearily; it's unclear whether he's addressing me or the operative, whose back is now turned): Why did you say that?

I (sitting down on the stool indicated): Will you finally explain . . . (To the people standing around) What's so funny? Why are they laughing? (As I say this, everyone begins laughing and grinning.)

In fact, to this day, I still cannot understand the mechanism that caused those State Security people to experience a shrill yet sincere mirth at the sight of a person scared witless as he first appears in their midst. What is this? Yet another demonstration of proletarian optimism? Inscrutable insolence? Their power over life and death? Or is this the savage's genuine delight in catching an edible louse? But these people are supposed to be professionals! . . . During the first few days, I kept thinking in horror: Why are they always laughing? What crude force is concealed within them, behind them, what sort of mental health, what sort of moral and physical tempering is required to make them able to laugh like that? Later on, when I had seen my share of the bitter and sour faces of the people who hold such positions, I began to incline toward the view that their primal, uncontrollable laughter—at the sight of extreme confusion in someone who has landed in trouble—also served them as a form of self-protection, a psychological barrier in a job that is harmful, even dangerous to a living creature who is obliged day after day to engage in a complex, refined psychological cruelty that is unacceptable and contrary to human nature. Children sometimes laugh that way when they are frightened.

People of experience, who were well versed in such matters (and were later to suffer themselves), explained to me that an investigator's laugh is—like an actor's mastery of his craft—the product of years of labor and practice in front of a mirror, a part of the curriculum in his practical training. That laughter serves to plunge the prisoner into an abyss where the authorities are omnipotent and he counts for nothing. At the same time, that laughter comes easy, is entirely natural, and is like ours when, with no regard for his feelings, we laugh at some sad sack who's lost his pants or fallen into a puddle. All the same, in response to my impassioned questions, the connoisseurs did not deny another possibility—that the laughter was a means of concealment, a way of saving face (don't we cover our face with our hands when we cry?); laughter as preventive medicine and therapy for mental disorders, for the troubling feelings of shame and sorrow that are natural under such conditions. . . . Oh, Chekists, cure yourselves of madness—with laughter!

Ha-ha-ha-ha! Ha-ha-ha-ha! He got caught?! . . .

The large office in Lubyanka to which I was brought upon my arrival, without even having been searched, was full of people. They seemed to be awaiting me as an honored guest, or else had just gathered to see what sort of creature would be led in through the door.

The first question, as I recall, came from someone at a distance: "What do you think, Andrei Donatovich, why are you here? Why here?"

Although I did not realize it at the time, this was precisely the sort of question asked as an opener, to feel someone out; it would be asked, by the book, to anyone new to that situation. Perhaps it was a sign of some special favor or trust, as if to say: Get all your sins off your chest, as if at confession, before it's too late. Whatever the case may be, you immediately feel foolish and uncomfortable, in the ambiguous position of a schoolboy caught in the act; it isn't clear exactly which act, but you feel caught all the same, and for something serious. Ultimately, would they arrest you without having some special reason? And the eyes of so many inspectors are fixed intently on you from every side, along the radii, the diagonals. "Please answer the question!" Now you're in the frying pan of your own "secret."

"Think of it, Andrei Donatovich, you, a Ph.D., a step away from being a professor, a member of the Writers' Union, a literary critic who publishes in *Novy Mir*—and suddenly one fine morning you end up here. What do you take this to mean?"

They all chortled when I forced out the words to say that they probably had a better idea why I was there. They laughed collectively.

"No, you try to find the reason yourself. . . ."

"Try to guess. . . ."

I didn't want to try.

The game went on until someone stopped laughing and drawled insinuatingly, "Does the name 'Abram Tertz' mean anything to you?"

Aha, so that was it! . . . I won't go into my pointless and humiliating denials here. For several days I kept on listlessly repeating, "I don't know anything about it," while they continued to hound me, chuckling as they caught me in one lie after another. In fact, they could not have had a clearer picture of my offense. However, it was not evidence that mattered at this point but the logic that dictated the course the questioning was to follow. According to that logic, the more I denied I was Abram Tertz, the more guilt I would experience. Otherwise, why did I resist identifying myself to them, getting a grip on myself, and finally acting like a man? "What do you have to hide, Andrei Donatovich?" . . . They did not raise their voices. Only Major Krasilnikov, the leader of the group, flared up for some reason and shouted, "Don't you play the fool here! I'm an old Chekist!"

I wonder how far back he went—to Yezhov's time, to Yagoda's, or to the era of the master himself, Dzerzhinsky, whose penetrating eyes gazed sadly and reproachfully at me from a painting on the wall. "Once upon a time there lived a poor knight. . . ."

The KGB stopped beating people some time ago; these days, when they have the facts in hand they use dirty tricks, deceit, threats, but, above all else, logic—logic!—to drive a prisoner onto the path of redemption, which he must tread with his own two feet all the way to the greedily gaping jaws of the trial. Later on, when I was already in the West, hairsplitting specialists would ask me how I had been fortunate enough to avoid repenting, confessing the usual mistakes, making the usual statement of regret, and how, once convicted, I managed not to accept the coal-black guilt ensured by the Soviet Criminal Code, covering the soul like a gravestone of logic. Was I better than the others? Braver? Stronger? Not in the least. Once burned, that's all. A great many things from the past proved helpful, came in handy, as I shall, with your kind permission, recount later on. But, for the time being, I will begin by expressing my gratitude to Abram Tertz, my shady double, who may yet be the death of me but who kept me out of trouble back then, me, Sinyavsky the brain, shamefully snatched and delivered to Lubyanka.

I can see him as if it were just yesterday—a crook, a cardshark, a real son of a bitch, his hands in his pants pockets, his mustache stringy, his cap snapped down over his eyes, walking with a light step, shuffling his feet a little, tender obscenities on his chapped lips, his body honed by years of polemics and stylistic contradictions. A trim man, gruff, he pulls his knife out at the drop of a hat. He'll steal, but he'll croak before he'll squeal. All business. A good man with a pen—and, my dear children, in underworld slang "pen" means "knife." That's right, "knife."

For some reason certain people, even some I know well, like Andrei Sinyavsky and dislike Abram Tertz. I'm used to it—so let me keep Sinyavsky as a stand-in for Tertz, a touched-up version, a sort of ad. In this life we all need to appear modest and noble. And if the two of us hadn't been linked together back then—one and the same person, caught *in flagrante*, which I deeply regret to this day—we would have cohabited peacefully, disturbing no one, each of us practicing his own profession, never surfacing, tucked away in Soviet oblivion, sealed up in a semibasement apartment on Khlebny Street. And you can be sure that Abram Tertz, the brazen and legendary Abram Tertz, would have gone to no extremes while Sinyavsky was still alive, and done nothing to distort or darken the humdrum story of Sinyavsky's life. That wiseguy Tertz would have taken a secret delight in the piquancy of the plot, deriving his satisfaction from one thing alone—that he, the inveterate thief and outlaw, shared quarters, like one of the family, with an honest intellectual inclined to compromise and the solitary, contemplative life, who, to cure an inferiority complex that had grown inflamed in his psyche—God only knew what kind of complex it was or when it would be cured—had concocted that acerbic villain nicknamed Abram Tertz, that weasel, that clown, that rogue in the bazaar of literature to whom I'd once said: "Get out of here! Otherwise, there's no telling what I might do! . . ."

In the course of the play we may pause again to consider the causes of the type of split personality that occurs when it isn't engineers but surgeons of the human soul who set to work on the psyche and, having bared all its malignant abscesses and aberrations, present the obliging and esteemed Andrei Donatovich with a memo to the effect that he is to be called by his first name and patronymic solely through the courtesy and goodness of our security agencies, who for a long time now, since the 20th Party Congress, have not been beating people; he, the double-dealing turncoat and imperialist hireling, should realize that he is not in the least esteemed and no Andrei, no Donatovich, but the sworn and proven traitor Abram Tertz.

To go back a few hours, I should add that, when I was in the car on my way to this decisive confrontation with myself, I had no one to help me—neither my wife, who was home in our apartment, which I suspected was already being searched (as bad luck would have it, she and I never found the time to prepare for that eventuality), nor my friends, whose names I recited to myself, ticking them off on my fingers, those who would also be grabbed, and those who, God willing, would give the police the slip, or deny everything, and those who had perhaps already spilled the beans; nor could I count on Sinyavsky, who, once shoved into the car with a single flourish, could be written off as a total loss. But only he, my shadowy hero—to compound the absurdity, or just for the fun of it, or in fact to make things more interesting and comical right from the start—my hero, whom I gave the simple first name of "Abram" and the grating last name of "Tertz," he alone whispered to me that everything was going fine, the way things had to go, according to the outline of a plot that needed only to be resolved, as is often the case in literature, brought to a close that revealed the final truth of all those similes and metaphors for which, needless to say, an author should pay with his head. . . .

Have you ever heard applause for a sentence passed on you, passed down on you? In a jolly frenzy, the people in the courtroom bring down the rafters with applause for the charges that will bury you, pitiful you, who in a moment will be taken under guard from the courtroom, as prescribed by law; but until you've been led out, taken away, and while you are still there in the flesh, the audience in the courtroom will clap their hands with all the gusto of the well-fed, as a sign that they approve of your punishment, and they give you one send-off after another with bursts of applause, right to your face, delighted to see you swept off and justly sentenced to five years, seven, fifteen, capital punishment—with no chance of wriggling out of it. No matter what crime you may have committed at some point, no matter what transgressions of yours have been exposed, you will rejoice, I assure you, even while shuddering within; you will rejoice that there are people worse than you ever imagined, far lower than you, if they dare to celebrate a person's suffering so frankly, with such human openness. After that lesson I understood and I adopted the contempt that those who are to be executed have for their executioners. Unwittingly, the latter shift the sentence passed on the poor sinner onto themselves; the blame is now laid at their door. Perhaps the only reason history continues to make progress is that from the gallows we remorselessly send telegrams—salutations from the victims—on and on into the future.

And mentally you will begin to refer to yourself in the third person, and feel purged of everything reptilian about you, having redeemed yourself in the crucible of that court, while they applaud like fools without rhyme or reason except for the dubious pleasure of baring their guts in public, they who become the leaders, the killers. In the crucible of that applause, the defendant grasps in a single inner leap that he was right to do everything he has been accused of—because they had it coming. By the way, that's the reason I now support capital punishment: *they* have it coming!

Sitting in the front row and clapping his hands louder than anyone was Leonid Sobolev, a literary boss (I recognized his bloated, ruddy face from photographs), the author of *Major Repairs*, whose denunciations were said to have sunk many a ship. Now this seagoing literary Tsushima of ours, too big for his chair, quivering, his heart fatally adipose, was beaming not only up to his ears but down to his shoulders, his legs spread like a woman's. His springy boxing-glove-brown cheeks bobbed out of sync with his hands.

Now I can consider all this calmly and can feel what those who applauded were feeling, for, ultimately, they too can be understood. But at the time? At the time, having seemingly foreseen it all in my feverish imagination, I shrank from a thought that cut too close and for that reason was unbearable. How dare these laymen—even if they viewed my codefendant Yuli Daniel and me as accomplices of Satan himself—how dare they abandon themselves with such immodesty to that incestuous orgy right before our eyes? I was of course aware that this was hardly the worst possible variation. I knew about the executions of the 1930s, and that writers had applauded them, including the most humane, like Feuchtwanger and Dreiser. . . . And the "Doctors' Plot"? I grew up on that! And . . .

"Why are you playing the offended party?" asked Abram Tertz all of a sudden and in a tone of voice that was somehow cynical. "They've got it coming! Let them celebrate. Feast your eyes on it! This is what you were searching for, getting ready for—to go under for the last time. You conjured it all up and brought it down on yourself with all the fantasy in those stories of yours!"

"Yes, yes," I answered distractedly, drinking in everything that was happening in the courtroom, at the same time flinching from it like a burn. "Yes, it's true, I did write. . . . But who would ever have thought it was all so real? That people would reveal themselves so nakedly? It's indecent. . . ."

The applause was not dying down. The applause was mounting. By applauding, the courtroom was voiding its indignation on me, wreaking vengeance on me because all that I had written was true, though far from the whole truth. And that can get to you. . . . Another minute and I'd have been applauding the appropriateness of the sentence passed on me and Daniel. Appropriate in relation to all humankind, and, in the end, to life itself. In general . . . As is its wont, reality had overdone its hyperboles, reminding me once again that there are times when a person must protect himself against it—reality.

"Mankind? Indecent?" hissed Abram Tertz. "Wasn't it you, goddamn your eyes, who wrote that mankind was washed up a long time ago? Didn't you make the sign of the cross over mankind with the devil's own hand?"

Tertz, that lowlife, was referring to the story "Tenants," in which I am alleged to have cast slurs on honest Soviet people by comparing them to the powers of darkness. . . .

"I can't understand how they can do it. Do you hear them? They're applauding again!"

"Why not—for gladiators?"

What did gladiators have to do with anything? I was puzzled. It was only much later, in the camp, that it came to me: Giovanniolli's novel *Spartacus,* which I read as a little boy. Do you remember that when reading *Spartacus* we were always on the side of the slaves and were horrified by the Romans' right to give thumbs down as a sign that the loser should be finished off in the arena? And we wondered: How could they?! But they could. They had their own normal, Roman life, not a whit worse than ours, and they had rules for killing or not killing the loser, thumbs up or thumbs down, according to what the public asked for. And the public would ask for death if it felt like it. That was democratic. But what about the slaves? Just imagine! Aesop was a slave. And

Plato was also rumored to have been sold into slavery by someone who wanted to buy, say, a horse. . . . It was not until a respected merchant from distant Riga was sent by Studebaker on business to Mordovia, to pick up a consignment (we made car axles there), which we'd done a good job of loading, and, learning that I was Sinyavsky, the same writer who had been castigated in the newspapers, slipped me a pack of Surf cigarettes, feeling both proud and embarrassed—it was not until then that I had any sense of what sort of writer I was or in what century our encounter was taking place. I knew none of that until, proud of myself, I slipped the pack of cigarettes inside my shirt.

Blurring past us, history becomes a blur. As if history does not exist and never did. We don't believe in history very much—how seriously can you take it? "But that's . . . history!" said Investigator Pakhomov in surprise, as if referring to fairy tales, when I mentioned something about the Roman Empire, which had also, despite everything, collapsed. . . . And, really, what does history have to do with anything as long as we're still alive? In time, history will cancel us out as well. Orphaned, spectral, we will enter history and ask: Is this really real, can it be? What slaves? Why gladiators? But that was something I came to later on. The courtroom, Judge Smirnov, Pakhomov, General Gromov, and the danger of ending up in the Dubrovlag labor camp brought me, speck of dust that I am, to a closer understanding of the universal picture to which, despite all our exertions, we are still connected, and which is not at all that far from Giovannioli's novel *Spartacus* and old Octavian. Until you have been touched by history's wings, its pointed swallow's wing, you will never understand how wingèd history is and how it can connect to a pack of Surf cigarettes slipped into your pocket when you're out of smokes. There are no boundaries between us; two thousand years have passed since then, or four years. . . .

God, my head is splitting! Gromov, commander of the camps in Mordovia, whose name inspired terror and who is lodged like a bullet in history; General Gromov, who started out as a dog trainer in those very same timber-rich regions and shot zeks like dogs; Gromov, who—when Stalin died and campfuls of zeks began chanting to dampen the atmosphere further, "The mustache croaked! The mustache croaked!," exhaling on the word "croaked" as if performing artificial respiration, the words rolling on through forests and marshes, "The mustache croaked! The mustache croaked!," followed, echoed, by the newspaper reports of Beria's execution and Dubrovlag, a gigantic generalissimo of a continent, was sent reeling—solemnly and in full parade dress, proud, immense, already a colonel then and so good-looking it would have been a shame to kill him, Gromov came out onto a platform surrounded by a gray, seething sea of prison jackets. By all accounts, he knew how to handle himself.

"Comrades!"

The camp grew still. Had they really heard that right? Could it be that everything was forgiven and everyone pardoned, comrades, and that they'd be going back home, to the place where they were born and had started out? This wasn't the first time that sort of thing had happened. The same idea had occurred to Comrade Stalin, who, when the country had been attacked by the Germans, had addressed us as "Brothers and sisters!" Gromov's old dog-trainer instincts told him the only way to save his skin now was to use a word that had once bound them all together, and so the director of Dubrovlag called the zeks assembled before him "Comrades!"

The dog! How long ago had it been that, upon hearing a new prisoner make a slip of the tongue and say, "Comrade Sergeant," "Comrade Lieutenant," or "Comrade Colonel," Gromov, close to shooting the man, would snarl, "A Bryansk wolf is your comrade!"? How long ago had it been that my father, in Butyrki Prison, complained to the doctor, a grown woman who combined Soviet indifference with a touch of liberalism, "Comrade Doctor, my heart's giving me trouble"? And, her face darkening, the doctor had drawn herself up, as women will, and cut him off with the words: "I am no comrade of yours!" They were so afraid of soiling themselves! And suddenly it's like your childhood all over again, the days of "all power to the Soviets":

"Comrades!"

But that's the truth! That's the way the revolution itself began. The tsar, the lords, and the generals had all been made equal by one brotherly word, "comrades." . . . What crap! In my day we called each other "sir" in the camps. Seriously—"sir"! "Mister," "*pan,*" "buddy," "my fellow this or that"—anything, as long as it wasn't "comrade"! "Comrade" was their word; let them eat their own words. We'd had enough! Bryansk wolves are their comrades!

But what I'm recounting here came even earlier, in 1953, and was just the very beginning. The camp grew still.

"Comrades! I, Gromov, am here. . . ."

"Gromov, Gromov"—the cry thundered through the camps. Was there anyone who didn't know who he was, the boa constrictor? He expanded his medal-covered chest as if offering it up to a firing squad. He must have really been scared shitless by the fall of that snake Beria to risk saying: "I, Gromov, am here! Gromov! The same Gromov who tortured you, comrades, yes, tortured you! On orders from the criminal gang of Ryumin, Abakumov, and Beria! . . ."

He paused to let the weight of those words sink in.

"But, comrades, this is not the same Gromov you knew yesterday! This is a new Gromov!"

Then he swore on his party card, his honor as an officer, the life of his daughter, and so forth that it would never happen again. And he kept addressing them as "comrades"! He was suffering. Though radiant as a messiah, he did not lose his self-control. He was aware what his name meant, the weight it carried, and he did not surrender his rank. He spoke in measured terms, firmly, with authority, taking all the sins on himself and redeeming them in one fell swoop. "Comrades"! He could just as well have been calling on the dead as his witness, and with that same self-possession. The "comrades' " minds were boggled; they couldn't believe what they were hearing. Covered by machine guns, Gromov had allowed himself a bit of bravado, and the camp was entranced. The camp never forgot Colonel Gromov's speech. It was passed on for many years by word of mouth, like a folk tale.

"This is not the same Gromov you knew yesterday! This is a different Gromov! Oh-ho-ho! A different Gromov! The same but different!"—the words raced through the camps.

Sixteen years after that unforgettable speech passed on by the old zeks, I saw Gromov, who was still in Mordovia. By my time he was already a general. So handsome in his sheepskin cap it would be a pity to kill him, Gromov had ordered us lined up in front of the platform; brandishing his fists, he roared as he had in the old days: "You just wait and see! You'll have a new Beria over you yet! . . ."

And once again words went thundering through the forests and the marshes: "Gromov! The same Gromov! Our own Beria! . . ."

"You'll have a new Beria over you yet"—that was said by General Gromov, who started out as a dog trainer and was now a part of the Roman Empire. . . .

I can see that my narration is bounding away from me like a kangaroo, then returning to hit the ground at my feet like a boomerang. That must be the nature of this story, this effort of memory to bring hero and author into a significant unity, to bind a variety of parts into a harmonious chain of causality where real time is not too binding. When soul-searching our past, don't we all hopscotch back and forth trying to encompass in a single glance the stretch allotted each person, along with a few points in a life that is still in motion? Don't our thoughts return to events, friends, enemies, ourselves, and to dreams that are always new yet always addressed to the same person? The past cannot be grasped in sequence. It slips through our fingers the minute we begin building monuments to it. In our desire to tell our story in chronological order, year by year, day by day, to speak of everything that befell us in our life, we unintentionally distort the greater truth, which, under the circumstances, is best adhered to. Especially when those circumstances are somewhat out of the ordinary . . . In my own defense, I should add that all this hopping about in telling the story of my life is not the result of a weakness for diversion or an innate penchant for chaos, but, on the contrary, stems from an unquenchable desire to write as precisely, austerely, and soberly as possible. Reconstructing one's own literary destiny is an experiment that requires that its author practice what in science is termed precision and purity of analysis. Though not promising a linear and consecutive narrative, I will all the same attempt not to deviate one iota from the actual pattern made by the events and collisions that reality bestowed upon me.

On June 8, 1971, nearly six years after my arrest, I was on my way home to freedom, feeling probably no less helpless and stunned than when the entire circus tour had just begun. My wife, who had met me by the prison gate at Potma Station, and I boarded a first-class car on the Chelyabinsk-Moscow train, an exotic couple, an amusing sight. Drunk with joy, we paid no attention to the sidelong glances from the woman conductor and the bored passengers; perhaps we were exacting a bit of unconscious revenge, flaunting a social contrast that was not of our choosing. My wife, lively and quite pretty, wore glasses, a rose-colored blouse, and pants with a European cut, and looked like an elegant vase beside me, an plague-stricken old man, rank with weariness and malnutrition, wearing oil-stained pants (I was taken straight from work), a long prison jacket, and a grimy zek forage cap with a ridiculous peak that had supposedly become part of the uniform when there were German POWs in the camps, and whose unnatural shape had earned it the nickname of "fag cap." The two engineers in their pajamas playing chess in our compartment gave us a very friendly welcome and helped me lift my unwieldy and, if not for their strong arms, unliftable homemade wooden trunk up to the baggage rack. My entrance and that of the young lady accompanying me whetted their curiosity, and no sooner had my wife gone to wash than they struck up a conversation.

"Was it a problem getting tickets at your station?"

It was abundantly clear that I was out of place there and that, were it not for some special circumstance, I would not be sharing their pleasant company in a first-class compartment. But I wasn't on my high horse. I was enjoying talking straightforwardly and on an equal footing with these "civilians" who didn't know which end was up. Smoking an Ocean Liner cigarette, I kept the conversation going:

"No, no problem. We didn't have to stand in line. Anyone leaving a camp gets his ticket without waiting in line. They don't want you hanging around when you're leaving a camp. . . ."

And that was the truth. To avoid trouble, people released from Potma were quickly dispatched to their place of parole. Sometimes a zek, vacillating in anguish about whether to cross the sacred boundary, would immediately go get drunk and then, at the train station, make a scandalous speech in praise of those he had left behind the barbed wire. Once, standing behind a stack of iron and lumber, we watched a young man who had just been released but was unable to walk any distance from the checkpoint and kept dashing back to the gate; each time, the cursing guards drove him away. Then once again he would stumble off toward the station, sit down on the road, and start crying, while we shouted to him from behind the pile, "Go! Move it!" He would rise unsteadily to his feet, make the sign of the cross to us, and break into tears, before dashing back like a madman toward the checkpoint. . . . And here were two engineers asking me an utterly idiotic question about problems getting train tickets. I had a foretaste of how I might cut them down if they dared continue to associate with a shady character like me, who still had the stink of the camp on him.

"From a camp?" echoed the engineers.

"That's right. Camps are located all along this line. You mean you didn't know?"

And, like an old-timer, I pointed to the dense forest passing the window.

"So," asked one of the engineers with respectful compassion, clearly not wishing to offend me, "is cutting trees hard work?"

I did look fairly ravaged. Or were they trying to make a quick association between two points in our country's past—the camps and lumberjacking? I quickly considered how best to eliminate that mental time-lag of theirs. It's been a long time since zeks were taken out to fell trees. All work is done within the zone now, to ensure our perfect isolation. Particularly those classified as "especially dangerous state criminals" . . .

"Especially dangerous?! State?! Criminals?!"

"That's right! The same people who used to be called 'politicals' . . ."

They were dumbfounded, saucer-eyed! I was a first for them. To tell the truth, I felt like bullying them, insulting them, to wake them up a little. But they weren't intimidated, and I began to wonder why they weren't, what they knew about us, and what they thought.

Back in the settlement and while on the platform waiting for the train, I had begun leisurely observing this new, mysterious tribe—my fellow citizens who had grown up at liberty with their bellies full. The country had definitely changed in my absence. Young people had started to dress up. Influenced by the West, men's fashions now included feminine curls, mustaches of various sorts, and pointy sideburns. I could accept the hairstyles and frankly welcomed the mustaches, but I detested those curved muttonchops that seemed transplanted from another peninsula to a garden bed soft as felt boots. My mind whirled with a new problem: how had sideburns come to old Russia? And the names that sprang immediately to mind were Chichikov, Manilov, Dobchinsky-Bobchinsky; that must have been the influence of Gogol, on whom I was intending to write. The engineers also had sideburns. . . .

"And were you in the camp a long time?"

"No, not long. Five years, nine months."

From the way my words reverberated, I could tell they thought this an enormous length of time.

"It must have been for religion, right?"

Their eye had of course been caught by my unkempt beard. They were being careful and delicate with me, walking on eggs. In their eyes, religion was a dark and devilish world, and that, to some degree, fitted in with my appearing suddenly and mysteriously among them. Sectarians, fanatics, and savages might still be tried for religion. . . .

"No, not for religion—for literature."

"For literature?! . . ."

At that moment my wife returned from the washroom, and the conversation petered out by itself. For them literature was still hidden under seven seals. What did literature have to do with anything? Literature was something that was taught in school, printed in magazines. . . . All this was too much for the minds of our fine traveling companions, and they began yawning un-self-consciously, as little children do when you speak to them too long about abstract things. It's hard for us all to pay attention to things we know are not real.

All the same, there was progress to be observed. There had been no squeamish fear at the sight of a "political." They had not shunned me, disdained me, avoided me. Stalin's Russia was a thing of the past now and not relevant to the present. The engineers rather sympathized with me, as a man who had suffered. Sympathy was no longer a punishable offense. But that was the extent of it. Utterly modern, they were indifferent to anything that didn't apply to reality. They had no use for prison or for fiction. . . . Yes, they'd read about the trials, seen something about them in the papers. But what did any of that have to do with their life, or with Moscow, which they were so excited about reaching, traveling on business from that mudhole Chelyabinsk? However, if I could give them a lead on where to find Italian raincoats . . . ! The vast world of the camps from whose smoky cloud I had just emerged did not exist for them. . . .

There was no talk the next day, as we approached Moscow. The engineers were busy now and ceased paying us any attention;

preoccupied with their suitcases, neckties, cuff links, they thought only of their upcoming meetings with their exacting superiors in Moscow. Not to sully the moment for them, my wife and I went out to the corridor and found a window where no one else was standing. I too wanted to lay eyes on Moscow with no strangers around.

It's odd, but in the past, when entering the city, I would often—no, always—experience a surge of joy just from reading the passing names of its simple suburbs—Udelnoe, Taininskaya, Mytishchi, Veshnyaki—and I had only to be away for a month to be impatient, on fire, picturing it looming up any moment beside the tracks and enveloping me in its heat—Moscow! Now, pressed to the window, I was intently studying the familiar mountains of trash by the tracks, increasing as we approached the city, peering at that heady mix of dachas with decors borrowed from the opera *The Golden Cockerel,* those pump houses, rolling stock, cisterns, and train yards strewn with heaps of rusted barricades that say nothing to the heart. My native city came crashing down on my shorn, defenseless head, and, unaccustomed to it all, I staggered as if slapped in the face whenever a sudden juncture of weaving tracks would hurl a semaphore, a pump, or the painted base of a high-voltage tower in front of my window.

Take this, take that! A right to the jaw! A left to the stomach! Another one to the jaw! The eye! The head! A semaphore! A stretch of red brick! A pump! To the solar plexus! A platform! What are you looking at now, you maggot?! A right to the ear! A left to the teeth! A right to your stupid bloody face! Your howling mouth! A semaphore! Another one in the teeth! A post!! . . . Then a bone-crunching landslide of sheer oblivion—a pitch-black tunnel . . .

I narrowed my eyes, lurching, then—oof—we came flying out from under the ground.

A long time ago, right after the war, I dreamed several nights in a row that the Germans had taken Moscow. I had the amazing feeling that I could be seen wherever I was. Lanes that curved like ears, courtyard passageways where I'd run since my childhood, the garbage cans, the back alleys, none of them were any good for hiding now: they'd find me! And now, with my own eyes, I observed a similar transformation of my hometown into something of a Berlin. . . . No, Moscow wasn't to blame for my estrangement. And, besides, my thinking hadn't changed at all: I was a full-grown man when I entered prison. The world where I had once lived had changed its relationship to me; the world to which I was now being returned ticking with anguish like a time bomb. Perhaps that was because they had released me before my sentence was up, with no warning, the same way they had arrested me. I did not have time to adjust to the new situation; freedom came hard to me. Oh, a cap of invisibility, my good old Abram Tertz mask, would have come in very handy here! But my buddy Tertz had been arrested, and the cap had been confiscated. . . .

The pavilions at the outskirts of Moscow rose up like the walls and towers of another labor camp. It was there to receive a transport composed of a single prisoner, me, the uninvited guest in the capital city, whose turnpikes and slogans radiated twenty-five miles beyond the city limits. I knew all that by heart, knew how bold Moscow was about stamping its mark on everything around it. But what had amused and excited me before, now inspired me to hold back and keep a sharp eye on that beast, which had assumed an air, if not of contempt, then of cold and predatory indifference, as it swallowed us in its jaws of stone. The six-story buildings were already dancing out, with their stunted modern windows and their concrete balconies that resembled the shields over cell windows. A department-store ad flashed me a quick glance, the first tram car went by, and, at that very instant, the train's radio, silent until then, filled every car with song: "Cool and fresh, the morning greets us! . . ." But it was another melody that struck you in the face from the loudspeakers in the station: "Teeming, mighty, invincible, Moscow!" Moscow! After so many epochs and nations—Moscow again!

At some point during this final stage, my eyesight began to fail me. As supporting information I include the following sketch of an unimportant incident, chiefly useful as a reiteration of the above—with a different twist, or a somewhat different edge to it. Perhaps its exaggerated precision will finally allow me to grasp the elusive thread of meaning that one so fears losing in all of life's embittering imbroglios. Here goes.

THE EYEGLASSES

I don't know how I lost my eyesight. The facts are these. I was being shipped from one camp to another in a Stolypin train car when suddenly, without any explanation, I was thrown into a local transit prison, where I had to kill a day or two under lock and key before being tossed out onto shore, freedom. All told, the whole process took about thirty or forty hours. Not so very long, considering that, late the next afternoon, I found myself a free prison rat at that filthy station Potma.

But, before moving on to this new phase in my life story, I should go back to the beginning, to the solitary-confinement cell in the Potma Transit Prison into which I had been thrown and where I spent some happy hours, not suspecting why they had brought me there. With no idea that Moscow was soon to loom in my life again, I began making myself at home, as the old-timers do when in transit, by banging on the food slot and shouting, "Hey, chief! I need food bad! It's mealtime! And when are you finally going to get me to the latrine?"

The head guard, an aging, rosy-cheeked sergeant, and no stranger to zeks, resembled Marshal Budenny but was fatter and shorter, with a gray mustache twisted up to eyebrow level; not in charge of the entire casemate but only of that lower floor, he responded at once, jovially threatening me with a punishment cell if I didn't stop yelling; I had no hot food coming that day, the paperwork on me hadn't been done, and no one even knew who I was yet. By nightfall he took pity on me and, escorting me to the latrine himself, on his own authority, and without so much as a look at me, he thrust me an evening bread ration and a metal mug of tasteless, lukewarm water. I could see that he was not a bad man, not dangerous, a man used to prison. He threatened and cursed more than he enforced the rules. And I accepted it all.

His stunning and improbable remark that they had no idea what to do with me or where to send me, that I did not exist, belonged to no one, and was seemingly beyond the law, struck me as such a frivolous and seductive piece of news—me, who had grown used to working under guard, dragging one goddamn crate after another—that I submitted inwardly to that blessing from above, not to think about tomorrow, not to know what would become of me, to live in obedience to the wave that had flung me, an old, rotten fish, into the deep, still backwater of the Potma Transit Prison. No, I did not delude myself with hopes of freedom. I had but a single desire—not to have to do physical labor that left me dead at the end of the day. To spend a few days—maybe a week, if I was lucky—in peaceful solitary at that crossroad, and not to be working, seemed an undeserved and unexpected smile of fate, as unwarranted as winning the lottery by mistake. Not only my heart, my very bones were pierced by a sense of pure and supernatural suspense. Whatever happens, happens; meanwhile let's have a smoke!

Frowning, I examined my new abode. The dwelling God had granted me was severe and frank. The plank beds reached to the door, and when I sat down I could rest my knees against the door's iron paneling. It was cold, and the light from the bulb, encased in a metal grill to keep it out of the long reach of the real criminals, added little in the way of warmth. Here electricity seemed not to dispel the darkness but to reveal it. Screwed into a socket blackened by time and numerous short circuits, the bulb seemed to be emitting fumes, quivering like the soul of a person facing death; it was a paltry needle, an unclean thread, a conscience ossified in remorse.

Then, almost as a matter of course, I inspected all four walls, figuring on reading the usual encrusted inscriptions left by those who had preceded me in that hole, before being shipped on to their next destination. I was to marvel at the somber art of those who had built the place; though not conceiving a hatred for them, I rejected their art with fury and impatience, from the heart. From top to bottom the cell had been corroded into a fine relief, as if it had been flooded by a sea of petrified, cresting stone waves. It was impossible to write on that crust. Its sharp, flinty ridges would break any pencil, devour all drawings and symbols. A person couldn't inscribe a cross or a curse there, or his name, or the date he thought he'd be leaving, or be executed. . . .

Then I took out a slate pencil that I'd had the foresight to sew into the lining of my prison jacket and an old copy of *Izvestiya* that I, as a diehard smoker, had fought to keep when being frisked by a stern sergeant on arriving there. On the newspaper, or, more precisely, on the margins and in the space between the headlines, never letting the round peephole in the door and the thick cavelike deposits on the wall out of my sight, I began making fugitive marks in an uneven hand. I did a little writing, well aware that this was no way to write, that it all was pointless, that the plank bed on which I was perched awaited other prisoners, possibly worthier men more skilled in writing, and that it would help them put their jolly tales on paper as well. But I had no pity then, either for my remote fellow zeks who had yet to walk the twisting paths of Russia's prisons, or, thank God, for myself.

I no longer remember what I wrote; there's little likelihood that anything serious could have issued from my slate pencil. I was too exasperated and spellbound by that impossible wall. What can it be compared to, what sort of architecture? That wall precluded the slightest sign of human presence. The cement floor, stained by moisture and dried spit, was simpler and more obliging. If it ever once occurred to a basalt rock, disgorged like lava, to speak of our fate in the netherworld after death, I suppose it would take the form of that wall, that sea of undulant, demonic, furious stone. I seemed to have landed in the very hell I had dreamed of and joked about when working an emergency shift in the camp—blinded by searchlights, loading iron in a cruel rain, losing my foothold on the ladder, in danger of having my stomach ripped open, my back dislocated and broken by loads beyond the strength of both mind and muscle, I nevertheless, feeling cocky and bold, winked at the other guys, who were furious, and said, "We're not in hell yet—this is purgatory, tops." And so, in that cell, hell seemed to have finally caught up with me, discharging up through earth, scratched until it bled, and mixed with sulfuric and hydrochloric acids.

But meanwhile the prison had been living a fuller and more inspired life than we live, than the one you live at home. From the outside, prison would appear to be despair, inertia, and silence incarnate. In reality, it's not like that at all. And the peristalsis that moves the prisoners along is a hundred times more intense than all Europe's effete passions, highways, airlines, hockey and soccer matches, your postal system, cinema, and telegraph. Later, many years later, when entering Parisian basement dives, mingling with the crowds at Italian carnivals, attending *corridas* in Madrid, or contemplating the arrogant erections of office towers and skyscrapers in America, I never again encountered the style, rhythm, and vital stimulus that make prison so terrifying, magnetic, consoling.

The ephemeral cardboard walls of my cell shuddered. With my passion for writing, I was like a little boy in comparison to the mighty, thousand-tongued echo that reverberated on that cathedral's resonant arches, even if it wasn't as famous as Lefortovo and Lubyanka, and didn't crackle like Sailors' Haven Prison, where burst after burst of prisoners arrived at night. But there, in solitary, in that godforsaken transit prison, I already thought of myself as one cell, one molecule in an enormous leviathan sailing off into the distance of history, with no lights along its starboard or leeward side, but lit from within, by the hold that carried the mobs of prisoners, devoured, swallowed, but still exultant. Women screeching, laughing, singing, starting to banter with the men; the men quick to return it and make voice contact with a girlfriend for an instant, the memory of skirts flashing irretrievably through their minds; the swearing and the roar of a game or a fistfight starting up to which our sergeant rushed like a lion to its dinner, first to check out the situation, then to punish the wet, grappling tangle of brawlers, and to prevent fatalities—all this merged into a light, measured tremor skimming along the stone as if it were the skin of some monstrous beast. As far as I could tell, it was only on the second floor that some madman whipped his groans and howls into articulate speech as he slammed what must

have been his entire body against his iron cage, attempting to prove—
to the laughter of all—that he was not guilty of anything. I recall that
he demanded to see a doctor and the prosecuting attorney immediately,
that very minute. Or else he would hang himself! I kept making notes
and more notes. . . .

When I came crashing back into Moscow, it was, to my regret, a
bright and sunny day. As if nothing unusual were taking place, all those
nonzeks were strolling around in the open air and doing as they pleased.
Had the weather been bad, had there been fewer people about, the
city might not have so impressed me with its glaring light, made all the
more intense by the clean faces, the smiles, the decorations in the
display windows, the suits. I regretted not having sunglasses. I could
not hear the din and clamor of the city, but my field of vision was so
saturated with Moscow's festive colors that I grew dizzy and wanted
to pass quickly and unnoticed through that kingdom of idlers, and take
cover in some dark gateway. I lowered my eyes to the sidewalk so as
not to see those people, but was drawn against my will to look at
those tropical birds, butterflies, flowers, those men and women flitting
down pavement polished to a parquet luster by tires, their images
multiplied in the mirrors of store and car windows. A pretty girl with
the proud face of an American Indian pranced by on gently clicking high
heels; she wore a short purple skirt that barely covered her hips; her
black pony tail beat time to her step. All that was missing was a spear
in her slender, swarthy hand. She must have been hurrying to a date,
bearing her torso through the entire city like a regimental banner; she
even seemed to be holding it a bit in front of and above herself. In
theory, I considered how dearly we'd pay for a sight like that in a camp,
just to see her walk by as un-self-consciously and independently as she
was walking past me now.

Back home, I rushed to my bookcase, which I had missed so terribly
during the years I was away on business. It was not so much that I felt
like reading; no, I just wanted to be back with my books again. I picked
one up and opened it, knowing that the place to which I opened would
have some prophetic significance for me in my new, uneasy life. And
it was only then that I realized that my eyes were shot, that I could

not make out the most ordinary letters, even though I had been reading and writing without any apparent effort the day before. I walked a yard away from the book, a yard and a half; only at a great distance could I just barely make out lines that struck me as inappropriate, a witless mockery for a person in my situation. The lines, by Lermontov, imprinted themselves on my mind:

> Oh, Hussar! Jolly and devil-may-care,
> Having donned your jacket of red . . .

Failing eyesight was undoubtedly no great loss, particularly when compared with the gift of freedom I had been granted. All people my age have trouble with their eyes, and how I kept from going blind that long is beyond me. But I racked my brains, ransacked my memory, for some reason dying to know at precisely what moment my eyesight had failed. Was it during my last night in the transit prison, when I was scribbling with my slate pencil on the newspaper, hoping to outshout and at the same time to immortalize the abstract voices on the wall, or was it a little later, when I saw Moscow's crowds, too bright and joyful for my dimmed vision? Or could it have been during those five or ten minutes filled with fear, confusion, and malicious delight when I was read the order for my early release that had come down from above, an order that I both believed and disbelieved, taking it for a new dirty trick, a new chess problem—our masters were generous with both.

> Oh, Hussar! Jolly and devil-may-care,
> Having donned your jacket of red . . .

I started crying, not over my blindness, which, I repeat, was no cause for alarm. And not over my lost youth, which, to tell the truth, was not that great a loss either. But I wept for the barrier—the "saddle," as I called it—that had suddenly arisen in my mind, dividing me in two, into before and after leaving the barbed wire—as if in a premonition of how hard it was going to be to return to the world of regular people, and what an abyss there was between us and them. I wept and saw the "saddle" assume the form of the eyeglasses that I would wear as

a sign of that impassable border, in memory of the gaseous wall streaming with hieroglyphics, forever crying out for the sea, the sea. . . .

And in fact those eyeglasses did evidently mark a passage in my life,
my entry into the realm of the deficient and abnormal; I could no longer
apprehend by sight or by mind anything that I possessed either within
or without. The eyeglasses caused an uproar at home. "Glasses! Eyeglasses!" shouted my wife on the phone to an old friend of ours who
lived in Donetsk and who had connections in London, imploring him
in the name of friendship to use those connections to have precise
English optics ground for me. Failing to understand her, our friend grew
alarmed and kept asking her questions, while my wife shouted: "Eyeglasses! I'll spell it for you: 'e' as in 'Evgeny,' 'y' as in 'Yakov,' 'e' as in
'Evgeny,' 'g' as in 'Grigory,' 'l' as in 'Lubyanka,' 'a' as in 'Anna,' 's' as in
'Sergei,' 's' as in 'Sergei,' 'e' as in 'Evgeny,' 's' as in 'Sergei'!"

At first I used other people's glasses, borrowing them from friends;
for reading, I employed the sort of magnifying glass children use to
examine butterflies and postage stamps. I got the idea from my late
grandfather on my mother's side, Ivan Makarovich Torkhov, a semi-
literate peasant who devoted the final years of his old age to solitary
prayer and the rereading of Scripture with the aid of a magnifying glass
that I, a child at the time, had given him as a present one summer. I
can still see him in his village, a kindly old man barely able to put one
foot in front of the other who, when solemnly seated on the porch,
would cheerfully inch his way from one letter to the next and, syllable
by syllable, whisper the beautiful names that to me, atheist that I was,
sounded like some abracadabra:

"Abraham begat Isaac; and Isaac begat Jacob; and Jacob begat Judas
and his brethren; And Judas begat Phares and Zara of Thamar. . . . And
Ezekias begat Manasses; and Manasses begat Amon; and Amon begat
Josias; And Josias begat Jechonias and his brethren, about the time they
were carried away to Babylon. . . ."

Anyway, it was no great task for my grandfather to read and reread
those dense and ornamented Slavic characters, since, as I now realize,
he knew the Gospels by heart and kept the book in front of his eyes

more out of respect than anything else, for physical as well as spiritual contact. I, on the contrary, found that the glasses that soon arrived from England posed an obstacle between me and books. When I read or write, I am at my most open; my usual mask is off, and, amiably inclined to the text, I bare myself mentally. Now, however, I was forced to place that helpful obstacle in front of my eyes, which distanced me from the page, from thought, from language. I began to notice that I was reading less and less, and writing only rarely.

Still, the eyeglasses did have a certain hidden virtue—it was enough to place those little hurdles on my nose for me instantly to disconnect from the life flowing all around me. I was inaccessible in my old-fashioned diving suit. Sometimes you put on your glasses and you're totally gone, in another world. It's as if glasses make us invisible. I was even tempted to try sleeping with my glasses on. But usually I just sat in a chair with all my armor and my visored helmet on, not thinking about anything, and with no intention of taking pen in hand. Seen through the thick lenses designed for reading or examining insects, my room, furniture and all, began to drift like the formless algae that grow wild in aquariums. I could barely make out the wave of the cupboard, the wave of the couch, table, and the two and a half museum-piece chairs which had no idea how they had ended up there, until one day I nearly fractured my knee on the corner of something and was doubled over into a dwarf by the pain: "What the hell good are they? I still can't see anything!"

I don't know whether the English optician had ground them improperly, having misinterpreted the miserable dioptics in my prescription, or whether my eyes, unused to glasses, had failed to align along the glasses' sight line, making everything appear double, a disconcerting distortion. I used my right eye to look for my cigarette lighter, which was forever getting lost, blending in with the nap of the rug that covered the couch. And I used my left eye . . . But do I need to go into detail about what I thought I was seeing with my left eye? Laughter, singing, women bantering with men, the ossified lime deposits on walls from which I had been torn, cast out, and flung from my beloved menagerie into the world like a godless gob of spit, like a wild dog's excrement . . . So, to sum up, I carried on the legacy I had received from my grandfather, my mother, my father, Abraham and Isaac. . . .

After speeches by the chief prosecutor and two eager beavers from the party co-opted by the KGB to represent outraged literary public opinion, all of which met with unremitting applause, I dragged myself back to the small holding cell at the rear of the courtroom, behind the raised section where the three judges sit.

A knockout! Another knockout! . . . For the last three days, my lawyer had been pale in the face as he ran over to me like a trainer during the recesses, restraining me from making outbursts, from replying to Judge L. N. Smirnov, imploring me not to pick fights. He kept assuring me that Smirnov had a reputation as a liberal in progressive Western circles and therefore would not wish to tarnish his image in Europe by playing the role of an ordinary Stalinist hangman, especially since such hangmen were no longer in fashion over there. Our case—tricky, literary—was clearly not to the liking of the godlike Smirnov, chairman of the Supreme Court of the Russian Soviet Federated Socialist Republic, and clashed with his image as an authority on the theory of international law, a field in which he had been steadily rising since the Nuremburg Trials. To me this was all nonsense. I could see no difference among those people, whereas my lawyer had a hunch that the Judge was in fact heart, soul, and career on Daniel's and my side and, since he was playing for popularity in the West, should not, the theory went, raise the stakes of our punishment too high. No matter how much KGB pressure he was under, Judge Smirnov was a mover and shaker himself, with connections in the Central Committee, the Moscow Party Committee, the Presidium—do you understand— the Presidium! And who the hell knows where else, in the State Planning Commission, the General Staff! . . . As I understood it, our defense was to be based on Smirnov's connections.

To my superficial, unenlightened view, the judge was more dangerous to us than any of the prosecutors, and was after our hides as soon as the guards had snapped to attention, their guns cocked, ready to fire, crying out, "The trial begins!" ("The trial begins! The trial begins!" echoed down the corridors, and I shuddered. Now it was for real: "The trial begins! . . .")

My lawyer tried to set my mind at rest: "You've been imagining things! He's no animal, that's just how he looks! He travels abroad! A forum a year! He's a vicepres! . . . ternationalgressofists! Of broad Eurolture! Eoretician! An iberal! Do you hear me, an iberal! Gressive, tive, umanist, eading udge! . . ."

All the same, I would not have believed a word he said if at the very start my Investigator of Cases of Special Importance, Lieutenant Colonel Pakhomov, had not reviled my lawyer in a fit of temper: "What kind of lawyer is he? Where did that wife of yours, Mariya Vasilevna, dig up such a . . . such a . . . ?" He struggled for the right word, grimacing eloquently. "Does he have any access to people? No one knows him . . . in legal circles. He's unpopular. He should be checked out some more. And just between the two of us, what do you need another Jew for? To my taste . . . it would be better if you and I put our heads together, gave the matter some thought, and found you another lawyer, a real one. What do you say?"

An excellent sign. A recommendation. If the KGB doesn't like someone, that's the very one to take. My mistakes had already taught me a little something about lawyers. . . . Lawyers? What do they have to do with it? . . . Oh, yes, I was with my lawyer on the eve of the trial, at one of our rare one-on-one meetings at twilight when it wasn't clear who was more afraid of whom, I of the lawyer or the lawyer of me. We finally seemed to have come to terms—I would plead not guilty, as I had during the investigation. That left me with a silver coin, but at first he could not even bring himself to touch that coin and kept insisting on using his paltry kopecks until I took a stand and angrily declared that I'd be better off refusing his defense if it came to that. Then, seeming to wilt, he agreed with me at once. Naturally, at the trial he could not so much as mention that his client was not guilty; nor could he enter an evaluation or analysis of the defendant's works, which would have put him in danger of ending up in the dock himself; he was, however, able to avoid just bumping and grinding to the tune of the accusation, as was the custom here long ago, and, not arguing with anyone, but, all alone in the lawyer's despised art of the dance, he used his hands to try to back up his bloodless, conflicted face. I have no complaints. . . .

I have just one bone to pick with my lawyer. I learned a few days belatedly that the press was carrying running coverage of our trial; for some reason my lawyer had not said a word to me about it in all that time. Could he have signed an agreement to that effect, and was he apprehensive about our conversations' being bugged? But, after all, there was no question of my being given any support, any sympathetic response from outside those stone walls, that island where everything grows distorted, when refracted through the prophetic Investigator of Cases of Special Importance. This was the Soviet press, available to everyone, where we were being treated like shit, and so why, I wonder, did my lawyer keep that from me?

The guards had stopped giving out newspapers during the trial itself: irregularities in the mail. I did not suspect that this was routine and that it was not the post office but Pakhomov who, as part of his job, had cut off all information capable of exciting the defendant. He, Pakhomov, already had a little experience with newspapers, in connection with Eremin's article "The Turncoats" in *Izvestiya*, a month before the trial. During one interrogation, Pakhomov had smilingly pushed the newspaper over to me as if by chance, the issue containing that made-to-order article with the usual educational aim—crushing you.

"By the way, Andrei Donatovich, you should see what *Izvestiya* has to say about you," he said with a look of curiosity. . . . But after I'd waded through all that dense manure, my spirits perked up for some reason: "They were wrong about Pasternak too," I said. "As I recall, Semichastny compared Pasternak's poetry to a frog croaking in a fetid swamp. And when Kornely Zelinsky returned from a trip abroad, he gave a lecture at the Writers' Union and said that in the West the mere mention of Pasternak's name is, you'll excuse the expression, tantamount to 'passing wind' at the table in civilized company. That's what he called it—'passing wind.' . . ."

"That was a mistake," grunted the lieutenant colonel.

"You mean the Pasternak business?" I asked joyfully.

"No, it was a mistake to let you read that," he said, suddenly direct, honest, and somehow very human. "It was too soon for that. . . ."

And so during the trial we were cut off from newspapers. I can understand why the Supreme Court needs to conceal from the defendants the snarling teeth it has already bared in the press—so that we would not snarl back, and so we would not lodge a protest with that same Supreme Court, a protest against its violations of impartiality. But what about my lawyer? What was he thinking of? Was he still nourishing some hope? Or did he fear that the newspapers might make me so desperate that I would have fought the defense as he had conceived and structured it? Sincerely wishing to save me, he bound my hands and did not let me defend myself.

"You did not answer the judge properly again! That's a point for the other side. Didn't I keep telling you not to argue with Smirnov? Argue with the prosecutor Tyomyshkin if you want to. You have the right to do that. There's no risk in that. But leave the judge alone, don't irritate him!"

None of it made any sense to me. It simply must be that we were pursuing different goals and, estranged from each other in that game of judicial tennis, never genuinely communicating, my lawyer and I would flounder in words, becoming oblivious to the world. Moreover, he had promised to meet with me just before the trial and then seemed to disappear. Now, during the intermissions, he would pop up like an educated Pierrot, wring his hands, and say: "You're dooming yourself with the judge! Dooming yourself! Our goal is four years, five at the most—no more than five. You'll come under the amnesty. The anniversary, the fiftieth anniversary of the revolution. In 1967 they'll let out everyone with a sentence of less than five years. There'll have to be an amnesty. Another year and a half, two, two and a half, three . . ."

And then he disappeared again. But because he kept extending the length of my possible sentence from one day to the next, and because he was being vague, mysterious, and wanly helpless with me, I guessed that something had gone awry behind the scenes. Something was afoot, something was being concocted amid inscrutable abstractions in Judge Smirnov's delirium. Planes had been dispatched to find an additional collaborator, a witness who lived in Central Asia. People were on the phone. Radiograms were being sent, arrangements made. A slow horror rose in my lawyer's ashen eyes. Breaking the rules of the game, he walked the razor's edge of the law, craftily avoiding the question of his client's guilt, and this silence offended the court. His voice barely audible, he subtly constructed what seemed a polemic with himself alone, as to whether or not it had been my intent to publish in the West. By then Chief Judge Smirnov was snarling at him. And the prosecutor did not deign to pay my lawyer any attention whatsoever. No, given the times and our hopeless case, my lawyer behaved stoically. The only question is, why did he conceal the press coverage of the trial? . . .

All of them—the lawyer, the prosecutor, the judge—rose up before me as if wearing masks, something out of *Sorochinsky Fair*. They all had one thing in common—reality disappeared when they were around. Now, at night, I have only to close my eyes and I hear their voices, which are not their own, natural, God-given voices. It's like a wax museum—you're not sure if it's all for fun or for the express purpose of putting a scare into you.

I won't dwell on the prosecutor. Simple enough in appearance. He wore a black suit and had jet-black hair; as sometimes happens with people who have genuinely black hair, his skin was quite white, and he shaved so close it acquired a blue tint; his hair gleaming with hair oil, his cuff links catching the light, he looked like an undertaker, or a torchbearer in a funeral procession. He had chosen an assistant prosecutor to match his own dark-haired look, though the assistant was a shorter man who I don't think opened his mouth once during the entire ceremony. Nature itself had cut him out for his part, and it required no effort of mind or psychology for him to fit fully and entirely into the Procrustean bed of his decorative function. That, however, could not in the least be said of Judge Smirnov, who, in a crowning irony, had the same first name and patronymic as Tolstoy, Lev Nikolàevich. He looked like a kindly boar. Fat, like all kindly people, he breathed heavily, as if being scratched behind the ear, when reading our files, and would then suddenly rush tooth and nail to the prosecutor's aid before we, the defendants, had a chance to object. The blows he dealt us from the bench were well aimed—direct hits. He simply would not allow us to reply, haranguing us, in complete disregard of the Criminal Code of Procedure. Then, having finished trampling us, he would halt the attack with equal ease and suddenness, regain his delirious composure, and magnanimously invite the prosecutor to continue with his cross-examination.

His reputation as a liberal melted away before our very eyes. That must have been his intent: he must have been putting his money on something more reliable than a European reputation. Of course, we were hardly his principal concern during those days of battle, nor was he actually doing battle with us. That we were doomed was as obvious to him as the date on the calendar, our sentences having been determined in advance. I suppose Lev Nikolaevich had other things on his mind. He was fighting his rivals, his enemies, on the Presidium, on Olympus, who out of jealousy had stuck him with this lousy little case. All right, Mr. Theoretician, let's see you put your achievements in international law into practice! Let the whole country see what kind of liberal you are. . . . Smirnov justified the trust placed in him and emerged the victor. A seat on the Soviet Supreme Court awaited him.

Soon after the trial, at a social get-together for writers and Chekists at the Writers' Club, Smirnov delivered a scholarly talk in which he summed up the operation: "The defendants were both educated men, and so, as chairman of the court, I gave the prosecutor a hand! . . ."

As we can see, my lawyer had not been mistaken: it was Lev Nikolaevich's European reputation as a liberal that was the key element. . . .

Is it, however, worth it to inhale all the poisonous chemical dust of a court trial, if the exalted magistrates only pass in front of you in a spectral dance and are able to confound the inexperienced observer, especially in a case as extreme as ours? But even the most bloodthirsty mask conceals a living soul, one not in the least callous, softer and more tremulous than might seem at first glance, a soul with all the usual human dreams, the full gamut of the mind's hierarchical complexities. At home, or with friends, no one could be a more pleasant and sensitive partner in conversation than they; none of us could hold a candle to them. Even the taciturn Trayan, the warden of Lefortovo Prison, under whose personal supervision we were brought to court, was unable to restrain himself after learning the charges against us; leafing through the press accounts, he confided to his better half:

"I would have been glad to shoot them myself! It's enough to make you weep!"

"And you do know," Trayan's loving wife would invariably add at those cultivated gatherings where they were welcome, "you do know that my Alexander Andreevich wouldn't hurt a fly!"

In support of this hypothesis concerning the basic goodheartedness of those who punish us, I cite the first scene of the fairy-tale play "The Mirror," even though I must admit that I have had no dealings with any investigator of that particular sort and have resorted to a certain amount of conjecture, based on eyewitness accounts.

HE (spreading his hands in a conciliatory gesture): This one knows everything! He's tops in everything! He has a doctorate! He's on the staff of the Institute of World Literature! . . . And so how about it, Andrei Donatovich, will you testify or not?

I: Testify? Testify to what?! . . . Gentlemen! Excuse me, I mean: Citizens! You've mixed me up with someone else! I've been slandered! It's a misunderstanding! A mistake! A terrible mistake! I have to give a lecture at the Sorbonne (I glance at my watch) in ten minutes! Think of it—at the Sorbonne! In ten minutes. I can't be late. . . . And this can't be any good for détente either. And, excuse me for saying so, but my wife will be worried. Her heart, her nerves. If . . . if I stay here any longer with you . . . You know we have a young child. I must let her know . . . even if only by phone . . . through friends. . . . (They all laugh.)

HE (suddenly serious): Everyone who needs to know has already been informed. There's no point in getting upset. As the old saying goes, "Long goodbyes bring more tears to your eyes." Do you read Dahl's *Dictionary*? Yes, yes, the Russian language is rich in folk sayings. . . . And, besides, it's all up to you. Go home to your wife. Go give your lecture. That's legal, that's allowed. We'll have you there in four minutes, if you like. . . . But what have you gone and done to yourself, Andrei Donatovich? Why have you ruined your young life?! . . .

(The light dims. The office fills with a brief moment of sympathy for me. At a sign from the investigator, all present tiptoe from the room. The soft strains of the tango "The Spray of Champagne" are heard, reminiscent of the opening section. The last operative to dart from the room returns quickly for a telephone book he has left on the floor. When he is gone, the light reacquires its harsh, white incandescence.)

HE: Oh, Andrei Donatovich! Andrei Donatovich! Don't you think we're human? (Wiping his mouth on his sleeve) Do you think this doesn't hurt us? I have a little child myself. Just a bit older than yours. Her name's Natalya. You know how it is. In the morning or the evening you go to her little bed. 'Natasha,' I say, 'Natasha, Papa's home from work.' And she laughs and jumps up and down on her little feet. She reaches out for me. Hasn't cut teeth yet, but she's already reaching out for me. 'Papa!' she says. 'Papa!' (He weeps, letting his head fall to the table. Then, the sobbing past, he begins singing in a thin, high voice.) Tap, tap, tap, the boy taps his feet! The boy taps his feet! . . . (Sobs.)

I: Yes, yes, I understand. . . . We have to talk it all through. . . . This is bad for me, but it's tough on you too. . . . It's tough all around. I can see that you're an intellectual person. You've read Chekhov, Gogol. *The Cherry Orchard, Uncle Vanya* . . .

HE (raising his tear-stained face): And so are we going to talk further, Andrei Donatovich?

I: Further in what sense?

HE: Are we going to testify? Or aren't we? (He drums his fingers on the desk, but with more force now.) Tap, tap, tap, the boy taps his feet! . . . Are we going to testify?! . . .

As a matter of fact, in our camp we had a Major Postnikov, a KGB supervisor, whose outbursts took a similar form. He's probably still there. Postnikov was fond of weeping during an interrogation or when inflicting punishment. At first, when the other guys told me of Postnikov's odd habit, I wondered if he was in his right mind, if that line of work drove a person crazy after a while. Or was this endless deceit, camouflage, the result of special training in manipulating people's emotions in order to throw them off balance? Over the years, however, I learned to take a more indulgent view, and was willing to admit that this veteran camp supervisor's crocodile tears—a rare event, but one that nevertheless did occur from time to time—were, like his laughter, the result of his soul's need to protect itself from his unhealthy profession. Weeping, he would appeal to us: "You must understand. Look at me. In my heart of hearts I'm a kind and compassionate person, and not the beast you make me out to be in your anti-Soviet conversations!" That may also have been a way of reminding himself that he was a human being, or a way of maintaining his reputation. . . . Appearances . . . It was only much later that I began to discern that those puzzling tears were not a means of self-defense but the sincere and genuine impulse of a heart whose better feelings had been offended. It was not he who was cruel but we who were cruel to him, we suspects, we convicts, who tortured our guardian with our malicious machinations, our orneriness, our ingratitude. In his suffering eyes, we, we are the hangmen; his conscience clean, and certain of his own kindness, he takes offense and bewails the injustice done him. . . .

HE: I remember now—childhood, youth, as Gorky put it. . . . You were lucky, Andrei Donatovich; we know that you were born and grew up in an urban, educated family. And what about me, I ask you, me? I had no father: he was killed at the front. He left five children alone in the world. Just between you and me, I came from the town of Borisoglebsk. . . .

I: Is that so? Borisoglebsk?!

HE: Yes. And there was only one pair of felt boots for the five of us.

I: One pair?!

HE: That's right. But we went to school, and we learned to read and write. Just between you and me, Andrei Donatovich, those were hard years. Chaos, collectivization. All that takes its toll. . . . (Grows thoughtful.)

I: It certainly does! Don't I know! And I didn't expect this of you, you know. Do you have a university degree? Two? . . . You've read Chekhov, Gorky. . . .

HE: Yes . . . My poor mother! Our poor mama! After all, you had a mother too, Andrei Donatovich. No matter what you write in your "works," and "works" is putting it mildly. You had a mother too, whatever she may have been like. You're a human being too. You did have a mother?

I: I did. . . .

HE: So, will you testify? Will you testify, I'm asking you? Or have you lost all shame and all conscience? . . .

No, it's not for me to vie in morality with the champions of order and authority, who are armored with an ethical code stronger than any of my haphazard and dubious thoughts on the subject. Continuing my own defense, I said to myself: You're a writer, and nothing else matters! To hell with everything. Be yourself, Abram Tertz. Don't argue with them about ethics or politics, or, God help you, about philosophy or sociology, which you don't know a damn thing about. You'll turn to dust, vanish in the earth, disappear once and for all, but bring in your harvest while you're still alive. And if your humanity is trampled, retreat into writing, for good, for keeps, no turning back this time. And take your stand there. . . .

It's embarrassing to admit, but this entire imaginary conversation, ranging from the investigation to the trial, and this entire novel, if I may call it that, composed in the entr'actes to give me a breathing spell while awaiting sentence, was undertaken solely to prove that I am a writer. I am a writer! . . . Damn you to hell, you vultures! Get out of here! . . . Have all the fun you want. Sling your mud. I'm a traitor? An enemy of the people? A Smerdyakov? Scum of the earth? A Judas? An anti-Semite? A Russophobe? A kike?! A kike?! Sure, sure, why not . . .

When pelted by curses, I somehow become diminished, I fade, I fade. I lose sight of myself. None of it seems to have anything to do with me any more: "necrophile," "subversive" . . . Terrible. I'm adlibbing now. I'm shaking in my boots. Bah, to hell with it. They've got nothing left now, because once they have declared me a matricide (as they will again) with no one to stand up for me, what's left for them to say? If I'm ever asked, "Who are you? What did you do? What's your name?" I'll whisper from the grave,

"I'm a wr-wr-wr-wr-writer. . . . Give me some paper and I'll write something! . . ."

HE: A little humility, please, Andrei Donatovich! What kind of writer are you? What's that supposed to mean? Judge for yourself. Any page I turn to in your opuses, if I may use that word, any page makes me sick. The language! Nothing but filth!

I: Perhaps you and I simply have different tastes in literature. . . .

HE: Aha, you mean I have bad taste? Let's say I do. But we've sought expert opinion. Scholars, writers . . . Sergei Antonov, Idashkin, Academician Vinogradov. Respected names. And they all agree (reads from his papers): "Patently anti-Soviet writing, half-veiled pornography, formalism devoid of ideological content"!

I: Well, I don't consider Idashkin a writer. . . .

HE (with malice): And what about Chekhov? Do you consider Chekhov a writer?

I: Chekhov? What does he have to do with it? In general, Chekhov . . . I . . .

HE: There, you see—"in general"! In general you have a negative attitude toward Chekhov. Is that something that started a long time ago? Is this class hatred? Personal envy? Or could it be the influence of foreign radio broadcasts? Confess, Andrei Donatovich! You'll feel better right away. I assure you, you'll feel better right away.

I: I've always respected that Chekhov of yours. Chekhov, *Uncle Vanya* . . .

HE: There, you see, "that Chekhov of yours"! Does that mean that Chekhov is ours and not yours? Ours, yours? There's nothing left to be said! You'll pardon my harsh choice of words, but we've reared a snake in the bosom of the Institute of World Literature. (Rises.) Yes, Andrei Donatovich, yes! You are right! Chekhov is ours. We love Chekhov. And we won't allow anyone to trample our Chekhov underfoot! The people will not allow it, Andrei Donatovich! The people are watching you! The people!

I: I never said anything against Chekhov.

HE: Have you no shame? And what's this, then? (Rummages in his papers.) Please, listen to your libelous lampoon "Graphomaniacs." With your own subtitle: "A Story from My Life." And what do we see: "I'd like to grab that Chekhov by his scraggly little beard. . . ." How could you bring yourself to say something like that? And after that you dare to call yourself a writer? . . . I'm surprised. (Reaches into his desk drawer.) Let's draw up a statement. . . . (Something glimmers in the Mirror above the investigator's head. Pale-blue streams of smoke rise with a hiss. A cry of "Stretcher! Stretcher!" is heard. Neither I nor the investigator pays this any attention.)

I: That's all wrong! That's not fair! It's out of context! That's not me! . . .

HE: What do you mean it isn't? It's right there in black and white. "A Story from My Life."

I: That's just a device, it's "my" in quotes, it's an artistic device.

HE (darkly): It's a well-known device, and a very, very artistic one—terrorism!

I: But his last name is different from mine! It's not my name! Look! He's the one talking about Chekhov, not me, not the author! . . .

HE (laughing): Come on, you're a master at changing names. You can turn anything inside out, wriggle out of anything. . . .

I: But, after all, I condemn that person, that poor character of mine, that miserable graphomaniac. . . . Anyone can see that! (Jumping up) In the first place . . .

HE: There, there, there. Don't be in such a hurry. And sit down on your chair. You're in no hurry to go anywhere. (Laughs.) You've got a lot of free time ahead of you. You know the old saying, "Haste makes waste." Have you studied Dahl? You haven't? You should, you must. Folk sayings are the pride of the Russian language. . . . You can't do everything at once. Let's go point by point. There's no other choice; it's bureaucracy, you know. Paperwork. "A stitch in time saves nine." And so, point one: you condemn your terroristic intent. . . .

I: Not mine! My hero's! And why terroristic?

HE: There, you see—your hero's. Let's put a finer point on it. You repent the incitement to terrorism which you camouflaged by putting it in your hero's mouth. Have I understood you correctly? (Makes a note.)

I: Good lord, I'm telling you he's not my hero, he's a negative figure, I don't share his views, I . . .

HE: "I'm not me and the horse isn't mine." Is that it? (Laughs.) Your hero isn't your hero. So, then, let's ask ourselves just who is your positive hero. Where's your constructive, your, so to speak, caring view of Chekhov? And whose views do you share, Rosenberg's?

I: Who's Rosenberg?

HE: Alfred Rosenberg, Adolf Hitler's ideologist and comrade in arms.

I: Are you out of your mind?! . . .

HE (calmly): No insults, please. You're being spoken to in a civilized manner. You're being asked to explain your illegal activities in a civilized manner. And you're acting like a hooligan. I'm warning you. All your attacks on officials will go into the record, and you'll be putting your signature to it right here. As it says in Dahl, "The cat pays dear for the mouse's tear."

I (turning away): I won't sign anything. You sign for your own terrorism. And don't forget to quote Dahl's "No mercy for mad dogs."

HE: A little humility, please, Andrei Donatovich! Did I hurt your feelings? I haven't written you off yet! That's just my way of speaking; I like to quote from Dahl. It's something you fall into when you're dealing with a writer. "Live and learn." "Birds of a feather"—heh-heh!—"flock together." . . . God forbid you were under the impression that I was trying to exert any sort of pressure on you. Judge for yourself! Where was the pressure? What kind? Am I threatening you? Trying to intimidate you? Do I seem about to beat you?

I: I've heard there's no telling what to expect from you. . . .

HE: No! Impossible! You—you!—really thought that? You could think that? I don't believe it. What, don't you think we're human here, Andrei Donatovich?! . . . By the way, do you feel like smoking? (Walks over, offers me a pack of cigarettes, raises his lighter. I take a drag warily.)

I: It's not so much that I thought that. But, you see, you, how should I put it, your commissariat has had a bad reputation for a long time now. At first I was pleasantly surprised. . . .

HE: Pleasantly surprised?

I: Yes, that you don't beat people any more. You used to, you know. And not just beatings—torture . . .

HE: Used to when?

I: Well, under Stalin.

HE: What Stalin was that?

I: What are you talking about? Under Stalin you beat people here. Everyone knows. Even that *Pravda* of yours wrote about it!

HE (reproachfully): There you go again! "Your Chekhov," "your" *Pravda.* That's not good, not good at all. It's unworthy of you. (Paces the office. Assumes a dignified air.) Andrei Donatovich, *Pravda* is an official newspaper. A central-government publication, and no one argues with it. But that's not enough for you; you need to have your opinion too! It's time you had the proper opinion, Andrei Donatovich! . . . And who put all that nonsense about beatings and torture into your head? You have a completely wrong and biased idea of us. Is anyone beating you here?

I: Are you saying that there was no torture under Stalin? Do you think there were no violations of legality during the period of the personality cult?

HE: I don't know, I don't know. I didn't work here then, and so I don't know. . . . It's all been blown out of proportion. Exaggerated by our ideological enemies, and not only the ideological ones, Andrei Donatovich. But how could you believe such nonsense, and how can you still believe it? That's what I can't understand. You are one of us, aren't you, Andrei Donatovich?!

I: What does that mean?

HE: It's clear enough. You're one of us. You don't consider yourself an enemy of our Motherland, do you?

I: No, I don't.

HE: There, you see. We agree on something. And, just between the two of us, we don't consider you one either. Do you really think that if you were our enemy, a genuine enemy, we'd sit here and talk nicely and calmly to you, like one intelligent person to another? Do you think we'd chat with you about things like art, literature? . . . Would you like some mineral water? Or perhaps you'd prefer tea? Or coffee?

I: Tea, if it's possible.

HE: One second. (Picks up the phone.) Who's this, the duty man? Tea, office 333, immediately! (To me) Do you prefer it strong?

I: Strong, if it's possible.

HE (into the phone): Strong tea! (To me) With lemon? Cream? English-style?

I: No, no. Just strong.

HE (into the phone): Just strong! And some chocolate candy, first-class! And sugar! Pastry! Jam! Cigarettes! (To me) What do you smoke?

I: Belomors, if it's possible. Or Liners.

HE (into the phone): Two packs of Liners and two Belomors! And matches! Move it! Make it snappy! . . . What do you mean, you don't have Liners? Borrow some from the lunchroom. What?! So, then, run to the store! There's no one to send? Send Chekhov! All he does is dick around there anyway. You're telling me he can't do it? You can tell him for me that we'll retire him if he doesn't. Move! (Hangs up.) And so what was in the second place?

I: In the second place?

HE (looking through his papers): In the first place, you confirmed that you condemn your previous slanderous statements about Chekhov, which were a call to violence against Russian culture. And in the second place?

I: That's not true! That's a distortion! I said . . .

HE: Agreed! I'll grant you anything, Andrei Donatovich! But you can't deny that, in your heart of hearts, you underestimated Chekhov, to put it mildly. I swear to you that this desk drawer contains accurate, verified information about you. So, then, why are you now compounding your crime by forcing us to arrest your own friends for giving false testimony? And, by the way, those witnesses include your students. Where is your heart, Andrei Donatovich? Your humanity? Open up! Confess! I assure you, it'll be a load off your chest. . . . (He turns to the door, though no knock was heard.) Yes, yes, come in! (A column of operatives enters, the same men as before, all in civilian clothes now, though some still have their boots on while another, in his haste, has stuck the company's light-blue service cap on his head. The one in front carries a tray with a glass of tea, the next man a sugar bowl, the third man a jar of jam, and so forth. The last man, the smallest and most flustered, claps the packs of cigarettes against each other. To the soft strains of the martial air "Our armor's strong, our tanks are swift, our people full of courage!" the operatives walk in solemn procession around the stage.)

SECOND OPERATIVE (carrying the sugar bowl, separates from the group and clicks his heels): Comrade Lieutenant Colonel, the colonel says that we've run out of first-class chocolate candy. And so instead . . . (The investigator makes a gesture of annoyance and, as he does, he and his desk plunge into near darkness, such that the operatives' gestures and words are addressed to me alone.)

FIRST OPERATIVE (confidentially, secretively, while handing me the glass of tea): I recommend that you behave as carefully as you can with our lieutenant colonel, Comrade Sinyavsky. He's a tough bastard! Do you know who he interrogated? He interrogated Penkovsky. And he personally executed Abakumov! Stay on your toes!

SECOND OPERATIVE (with the sugar bowl): Your best friend on the outside—I won't mention any names here, you know who I mean—asked me to tell you in the utmost secrecy that it's time to give up. And he also asked me to tell you, his words were, "They know everything about us, everything!"

THIRD OPERATIVE (with the jam): Your family is in danger!

FOURTH OPERATIVE (holding something or other): Prepare yourself for the worst. . . .

FIRST (interrupting): You'll be released tomorrow! Just use your head. . . .

SECOND: Fat chance . . .

THIRD: No one gets out of here. . . .

FIFTH: They can do anything!

SIXTH (the smallest man, with the cigarettes, in a whisper): I've been through it myself. Regards from Chekhov. Don't put up too much of a fight—that's his advice too. They'll throw away the key!

I: Regards from Chekhov? *The* Anton Pavlovich Chekhov?!

SIXTH: That's a secret! A big secret! But Chekhov advises you not to put up too much of a fight. Good luck!

(The procession recedes, to the accompaniment of the same music. Back in the light, the investigator rubs his eyes, as if waking up.)

HE: Come to your senses, Andrei Donatovich! Shed all the inhibitions that are keeping you from being fully open! Be Human with a capital "H"! You'll feel better right away. . . . "We'll rest, Uncle Vanya, we'll rest!"

I: I see! Chekhov again! Dear old Chekhov! If he knew . . . Do you know, Citizen Investigator . . .

HE (gently): My name is Nikolai Ivanovich. . . .

I: You know, Nikolai Ivanovich, apparently I really hadn't fully appreciated Chekhov's plays until now. . . . (He makes a quick note.) I regret it, but those things do happen. Taste can take a variety of forms, and some of them may even be mistaken, subjective. One person likes Chekhov, another prefers Gogol. But is that a crime? Didn't you ever experience anything of the sort, Nikolai Ivanovich?

HE: Be more concrete, more concrete! What is it you mean? What political conclusions do you want to draw from your errors?

I: Well, let's suppose you like one work of art but you're not very fond of another. Did you ever experience anything like that?

HE (with restrained fury): I've experienced that. I've experienced everything. I even fought at the front, my dear Andrei Donatovich. And when I left the front I fought outlaw gangs in the Ukraine. In Lithuania. In Hungary . . .

I: That's not what I meant. You are accusing me of undervaluing Chekhov. But whom do you personally prefer, Nikolai Ivanovich— Chekhov or Gogol?

HE: I prefer them all. All of them. And don't you try to pull the wool over my eyes! I'm still the one asking the questions here, not you. So, please, answer the question. And don't try to wriggle out of it! And none of that fancy talk of yours either!

I: But, for example, Leo Tolstoy contended that Chekhov's plays were even worse than Shakespeare's. And his overall opinion of Shakespeare . . .

HE: But you're no Shakespeare, are you?

I: No, of course, I'm no Shakespeare, who's saying I am?

HE: And you're no Leo Tolstoy either.

I: It goes without saying I'm no Tolstoy. But, looking at it in the abstract, in a situation like this, would you charge Tolstoy for disliking Shakespeare? Or for disliking Chekhov? Or just what?

HE (curtly): I'll tell you just what! You and I aren't here to settle abstract problems, Andrei Donatovich, but to deal with the entirely concrete political sabotage which you engaged in throughout your ten years of underground activity. . . . And we'll get to Shakespeare too, don't you worry. And Leo Tolstoy won't give us the slip either. Neither will Gogol. We'll deal with everything. Step by step, one thing at a time . . . And so, you admit that for a very long time, maybe ever since you were a student, you have hated Shakespeare and Chekhov, especially the latter's patriotic plays—*The Cherry Orchard, Uncle Vanya,* and *The Three Sisters*—which deserve all the success they enjoy in their Moscow Art Theatre productions, even those performed outside the borders of our boundless Motherland . . . Isn't that so? Even the sworn enemies of socialism acknowledge the patriotic power of those works, whereas you . . .

I: Following in the footsteps of the White Guards . . .

HE (banging the table): Don't play the fool! I'm an old Chekist! In 1918 we put people like you up against the wall! And with no discussion! (White smoke begins billowing from the Mirror, but the investigator doesn't notice as he advances toward me, his voice rising in a tone of deliberate irritation.) Where do you think you are, at a health resort? We're giving you tea, pastry, and jam, aren't we? During the war my children never saw a stick of butter! (Tears at his collar as if fighting for air.) Don't you see, I went to war for Chekhov! I smoked the enemy out of dugouts and bunkers! (The smoke grows thicker. An arc of voltage flashes in the Mirror and muffled cries are heard: "You've got it wrong again! You've screwed up again, Pashka! It's Pushkin! Do you hear me, Pushkin!" Now the investigator's face is blank with perplexity. At that very instant the phone rings shrilly. He picks up the receiver.) Hello. Who? . . . (Straightens his back.) Speaking . . . Everything's under control. . . . Fine. It's going fine. . . . What? . . . My fault. I'll correct it! Consider it done! It will be! . . . I assure you—it'll be corrected. What are you saying? It's purely educational. Preventive measures . . . No, we're not there yet. . . . I understand. Yes. Right this minute . . . It's clear. My pleasure. Yes, yes! (Hangs up. The light in the Mirror dims. The investigator moves to center stage, lights a cigarette. His hands tremble. Says to me:) Well, and so?

I: So what?

HE: You're a hard man to deal with, Andrei Donatovich! You're a difficult person. Where does your wife get her patience? You don't have any sensitivity at all. You lack even the most elementary sense of friendship, cooperation, trust. You're always trying to be the center of attention. You should be more modest, more modest . . . simpler. You almost gave me a heart attack there. . . .

I: I almost gave you a heart attack?

HE (walks over to the medicine cabinet, sniffs something, chews something): Yes indeed. I could feel myself gagging. (Mimicking:) "Chekhov! Chekhov!" Who cares about that Chekhov of yours, if you'll pardon the expression. You've been gnawing on that bone long enough.

I: But you! You were just about to put me up against the wall for Chekhov!

HE: I was? Up against the wall? For Chekhov? Either you're up to your usual tricks or I don't know how you ever got a doctorate in literature. What are you, a little boy? Don't you understand? You think Chekhov is what matters here? Nooo! Take a deeper look. A broader look. Chekhov's not the point. . . .

I: Then what is? What?

HE: You don't see? You haven't understood yet? No? Well, if you want, but just as a personal favor to you, I'll give you a hand, a little hint. . . . All right, then. It starts with "p"!

I: What does that mean, it starts with "p"? . . .

HE: What are you, a child? Have you no shame? The corpus delicti begins with "p"! I can even go further than that for you and tell you, without quite transgressing the bounds of the state secret entrusted in me, it begins with the sound "pu." And it has seven letters. One word. You still haven't guessed? The poor man! He's afraid to say the word! The poor baby! All right, let's do it together. Pu-u-u . . . ?

I (blurting it out): Purgine?!

HE: What did you say, "purgine"? Is that one of the planets? Neptune, Pluto—I don't seem to remember. . . .

I: No, no. It's more medical. A sort of laxative. . . .

HE: So, you have connections in the medical world, do you, Andrei Donatovich? Now, that's a new wrinkle. In-ter-est-ing! And what have you been up to with that purgine?

I: Nothing. The name just came into my head. A medicine. Seven letters. Purgine.

HE: Aha, I see. . . . To tell you the truth, I was already thinking . . . I was already thinking that our own Andrei Donatovich was up to even more mischief than we had so modestly assumed. Don't be offended. After all, the history of science is full of such aberrations. Poisoned wells, reservoirs. The elimination of high-ranking people by toxic means under the guise of medical treatment. Just between you and me, oh, what a sharp eye you have to keep on doctors these days! (Switching to a whisper) You know, they have every poison there is in those cabinets of theirs! Every poison there is! Disguised as medicine. And so you think—I know, I know everything you think before you say it—you think that there was never any such thing as the "Doctors' Plot." A fabrication, you think, an empty charge. And you're right to think that. For the time being, in this political climate, that's what you should think. But *we, we know!* You don't know because you're not supposed to. But we, we know! There was a Doctors' Plot! Of course, not all those doctors were involved, but some were. Judge for yourself—who would know if not us?

I: But you don't, you don't suspect me of poisoning anyone, Citizen Investigator Nikolai Ivanovich? Who would I poison? With what? Purgine? . . .

HE: You never know. . . . And, then, each of us has his own romantic dream, Andrei Donatovich. . . . "But let's get back to our sheep," as the ancients used to say. "Let's start from the beginning." "Practice makes perfect." I'll remind you again. It begins with the sound "pu," seven letters. Pu-u-u . . . ?

I: Poodle!

HE (pausing to think): The dog?

I: Yes, the dog. Poodle is a breed of dog.

HE: Have you no conscience? I'm embarrassed for you, Andrei Do-natovich. You're a man! A man! I wouldn't like to be in your shoes, but if I were—and I give you my word of honor on this—I wouldn't try to wriggle out of it, I wouldn't play smart, I wouldn't think up anything like "poodle." I wouldn't laugh. Because, Andrei Donatovich, "he who laughs last laughs best." I'd look the truth in the eye, and to the same sort of straightforward guardian of law and duty you'd be in my place I'd say: Yes, here I am, guilty, very, very guilty; I'm sorry, but, as far as the Chekhov business goes, I'm not involved in that. And then, for that one moment of perfect honesty and manly straightforwardness, you would have released me on my own recognizance, saying: All right, brother, all right, Nikolai Ivanovich, go home to your family and your child who's already missing you, and no more nonsense out of you! But to degrade myself, the way you're degrading yourself here with all this "poodle" business—that I would never do. Better to accept and endure any punishment . . . I can see, I've got eyes, I can see that you're still hoping that it'll all blow over, that it's some kind of a dream, a mirage—poodle, prattle, pudding, pimple? But this is reality, Andrei Donatovich. I'm telling you this because I genuinely care about you. Re-al-i-ty! And so, to relieve your conscience and improve your situation, I'm asking you for the third time to try to remember. "Pu," the word begins "pu"! I can give you a little more information, if you want. Here's a clue. . . . A writer! There's nowhere you can hide now. You're looking for a writer whose name begins with the sound "pu." And you can believe me when I say that this has nothing to do with purgine or poodles. Think about it, collect your thoughts, exert yourself! It's your last chance to tell the truth. I'll say it again: a writer, a classic, a Russian classic whose name has seven letters. . . .

I: Pushkin!

HE (settling back in his chair): Finally! That's right—Pushkin! . . . The very same Pushkin who—and now I'm quoting you—where is that? (rummages through his paper and quotes)—"who came prancing into poetic greatness on slender erotic feet and caused an uproar. . . ." (Chuckles.) How did you dream that one up, Pushkin with little erotic feet? . . . It's all right, it's all right! Everything in its own time . . . You should realize, Andrei Donatovich, that this little seven-letter word may just have saved your life at the last moment. Years will pass, decades, but you'll remember this day with gratitude, and you'll thank me for forcing you—no, convincing you—to tell the truth. Your straightforward answer, "Pushkin," will be taken into account both in the investigation's conclusions and when your sentence is determined. The "poodle" and the "purgine" won't go into the record. But "Pushkin" will forever stand as a sign that you mitigated your guilt by confessing sincerely! I congratulate you! I congratulate you from the bottom of my heart! . . .

I (worriedly): But what about Chekhov? Is that still being held against me?

HE: That's totally over with now! Put Chekhov out of your mind! He's a trifle, a typo. It means nothing. It's just that you used Chekhov as a cover for your more ambitious plans for Pushkin. Pushkin is what it's all about! Pushkin is an entire continent! Pushkin is a broad horizon, Pushkin is a breath of freedom! As an artist yourself, with a subtle feeling for sound, you should know that "Chekhov" has no ring to it. Chekhov, just some guy's name. Bah! A comedian, a whiner—who remembers him today? A sort of Zoshchenko type. But Pushkin! Pushkin! The name summons up epics and epochs! . . . (Pauses.) And we're not going to let you insult Pushkin. We love Pushkin. Everyone can agree about Pushkin. Pushkin belongs to the people, and he is dear to everyone's heart. And now, with your permission, my good man, we're going to rap your paws! And your claws! Stay out of our garden! And don't go strolling arm in arm with any Svengalis from any foreign embassies around our monument to Pushkin, which, as the poet said himself, was not built by human hands. (Laughs, switches to an abrupt, angry tone.) The days of the tsars are over, you know!

I: Wait a minute! (Bright with sudden insight.) You just said the same thing about Chekhov. Let's go back to Chekhov. . . .

HE: But you've already confessed—it's Pushkin.

I: No, it's Chekhov. Chekhov was the start of it all.

HE: Enough of your objections! Why did you ascribe slender little feet to Pushkin? How do you know what his feet look like? Did you ever take a steam bath with him? After what you've said, you're no better than d'Anthes! Whose interests are served by your demeaning Pushkin's immortal significance?!

I (digging in my heels): I always exaggerated Chekhov's significance.

HE (not listening, bombastically): At a time when De Gaulle is making a grab for power, at a time when the world's reactionaries are on the rampage in New Guinea, your malicious attacks on Pushkin, carried out on orders from the Pentagon, play right into the hands of the cold-warriors. You're playing with marked cards that are grist for the enemy's mill in their effort to combat our policy of easing international tensions! Racial discrimination! Class stabilization! Nazism, Maoism, abstract art! How can the earth still support a person like you?! . . .

I: On the contrary, Chekhov's feelings about abstract art were . . .

HE: Who cares what he felt? But there is such a thing as logic, Andrei Donatovich. The logic of history. The logic of the international struggle. And the facts show that logic is a stubborn thing. Learn how to think! All that the imperialists dream of is pulling Pushkin's rich heritage out from under us and replacing it with some decadent cocktail doily or Conan Doyle. . . .

I (not listening to him): Chekhov and I are an obstacle to the cold war; we're escalating it to a hot war. *The Three Sisters* are calling upon the fraternal peoples of New Guinea—to Moscow! to Moscow! . . . Lobbing a grenade, Vanka Zhukov shouts to the imperialists, "Epikhidov broke his cue," is for you, but "House with a Mezzanine" and "The Diamond Sky" are ours! . . .

HE: Two can play that game! Pushkin's *The Captain's Daughter* is like a machine gun on wheels.

I: Chekhov's "Kashtanka" is the cavalry. Forward, Kashtanka, hurrah!

HE: The heavy guns never miss: *Boris Godunov, Boris Godunov* . . .

I: Did you forget *The Seagull?* The air force!

HE: Intelligence and counterintelligence—"Mtsyri," "Mtsyri" . . .

I: That's not fair! Lermontov wrote "Mtsyri"!

HE: What do you mean, Lermontov? Suppose he did? But you forgot the main thing. You forgot *Eugene Onegin. Eugene Onegin* is an intercontinental missile aimed at America's heart! There'll be nothing but junk left of their skyscrapers after *Eugene Onegin* hits them.

I: But, still, Chekhov . . .

HE: Not Chekhov, Chushkin!

I: Not Chushkin, Pekhov!

HE: No, Chushkin!

I: No, Pekhov! . . .

(Our voices are drowned out by an even hum of background noise. Speech becomes gesture, argument—pantomime. We get up, chase each other around the stage, each desperately arguing his point, pulling at our hair and jackets, clutching at our hearts, our mouths working furiously as we articulate soundlessly. At this point the interrogation is reminiscent of the sword duel in *The Captain's Daughter.* He, however, is attacking, and I'm on the defensive, parrying his blows, dodging, retreating. . . . A distant and very pure female voice, a contralto, singing Glinka's romance written to Pushkin's poem, begins to rise over the steady, low background noise and that of our dance steps.)

> VOICE: I remember that wonderful moment
>   When you appeared before me!
>   Like a fleeting vision,
>   Like the spirit of pure beauty,
>   Like the spirit of pure beauty. . . .

(As the angelic music progresses, I anxiously begin to listen more closely and look around as if some vague message were reaching me, even though the voice is far from us, somewhere behind and above us. The duel continues, perhaps having dragged on for several hours, days, or even years. As a result of my looking back and my opponent's obvious advantage, I stumble and fall, wounded by his silent, irrefutable gesture-argument. He picks me up, helps me to a chair, and brings over a bottle of ammonia from the medicine chest on the wall. The twilit curtain falls musically, and once again we return to the sober light of interrogation. I start coming around.)

HE: Wonderful, wonderful! How do you feel? Dizzy? Would you like to lie down? We can call a doctor for you, Andrei Donatovich. . . .

I: There's no need to. . . . Thank you. . . . It's over now. . . . It's just that I thought I heard something. . . . My head was spinning. . . . Was someone singing? Didn't you hear it?

HE: When?

I: Just a minute ago, somewhere close by. Wasn't there someone singing?

HE: Are you crazy! Who would sing in a place like this? This isn't Symphony Hall. . . . You're too impressionable. There's nothing to worry about. Everything's right on track. And even though you and I had to work and argue a lot today, the worst of it's behind us now.

I: It's all over?

HE: Well, not all over. But almost. You've testified to the fact that you made, how should I put it, insufficiently correct statements concerning Pushkin.

I: The idea of sufficient correctness can't be applied to statements about Pushkin. . . .

HE: Fine. (Makes a note.) Oll-rait, as the English say . . . And then you agreed that—from a strictly logical point of view, unintentionally and not even suspecting that you were doing so—you played right into the hands of those who wish us ill and who wish you ill too, Andrei Donatovich!

I: How can a person know in advance whose hands he's playing into? Probably even Pushkin himself wasn't aware . . .

HE: Splendidly put! (Makes a note.) I don't know about you, but, as a result of our substantive conversation, despite certain differences, even some of principle, I still have the feeling that we made genuine contact here. Mutual understanding, mutual assistance. I will make every effort to be of help to you, and I expect you to reciprocate with the same sort of support. Isn't that the way people are supposed to act? Am I right? What do you think?

I: I didn't quite catch what you were saying. I'm mixed up. Confused . . .

HE: "All was confusion in the Oblomovs' home." (Laughs.) These things do happen, they do. (Confidingly) It would be undesirable, extremely undesirable, if you took your own confession as some sort of burden forcibly imposed by us. Each and every person should arrive independently at the decisions that are of vital importance to him. And that includes an understanding of his own guilt. . . .

I (shuddering): But I haven't admitted that I was guilty.

HE: What do you mean? Regardless of the facts?

I: Regardless of the facts.

HE: In the face of logic, the logic of history?

I: Even in the face of logic. I have not pled guilty.

HE: There, do you see! . . . But it's up to you. If you want to indulge yourself, be my guest. It'll only make it all the harder on you. And in the end it's not for you to determine the degree of your own guilt. Other bodies exist for that. . . . You won't be needed any more today.

I: I'm free, then?

HE: Free for today.

I: (rising): I can go?

HE: Go where?!

I: I don't know, home?

HE: You've got to be joking! We've only just begun talking. All we've had is a taste. And you want to go home!

I: So, then, what happens . . . to me now?

HE: How can you ask? We'll put you on trial.

I: But when? How soon?

HE: What's your big hurry? Today was just the first session, preliminary questioning, that's all, Andrei Donatovich.

I: And will there be many more sessions?

HE: That's up to you. No one but you.

I: No, what I want to know is, approximately how many times do you question someone like me before the trial?

HE: It varies. A hundred sessions. Two hundred sessions. It all depends on the person. . . .

I: A hundred sessions?!

HE: Yes. And today was the first. (Picks up the phone.) Duty officer? Come get the prisoner! (To me) Don't get upset. We look into absolutely everything. Everything. Do you have any complaints? Additions? Clarifications? (Rises.)

I: No, I don't.

(Enter three operatives from the group seen before, now in military uniform.)

HE: Conduct a search of the prisoner. No need for him to undress now. Later. (To me) A record will be made of all your belongings. You can rest assured, not a single thread ever gets lost here!

(They take my briefcase from me and extract the books and notebooks, remove my watch, frisk me, turn my pockets inside out, and place everything in front of the investigator, at the edge of the desk. At the end they remove my belt.)

I: Why the belt? I need the belt!

FIRST OPERATIVE: That's the rules.

SECOND: It's so you won't hang yourself, buddy.

THIRD (checking my pockets one more time, in a half-whisper): Don't make such a fuss! They might let you go yet. . . .

HE (with two fingers fastidiously picking up my handkerchief from the pile on his desk): And what's this?

I: My handkerchief.

HE (even more fastidiously): You can have it back. (The handkerchief is handed back to me by an assistant. They toss all my belongings together into the briefcase and take it away.) See you tomorrow, Andrei Donatovich! I'm sure you'll be given something to eat. And so I wish you a good night and pleasant dreams.

FIRST OPERATIVE (hissing): Your hands!

I: What about them?

FIRST OPERATIVE: Hands behind your back! (They lead me away.)

HE (stands motionless for several seconds, rubs his face with the palm of his hand as if deeply weary): What a day! (Dials a number on the other telephone.) Comrade General? Sorry to disturb you. Code 686. Request permission to report. We've finished for today. What?

. . . With great pleasure. He's breaking, where can he hide? He's already caving in. . . . Yes, yes, he admitted a lot. . . . And we've only just begun, Comrade General! It's just the start. . . . (Hangs up, walks over to the little table I used, and drinks the tea, which has not been touched and is cold now.) "We'll rest, Uncle Vanya, we'll rest!" (Picks up the other phone.) Duty officer? Bring in the next one. The next, you know, witness. Has he been waiting long? An hour and a half? Doesn't matter— it's good for him! (Hangs up. Paces.) "We'll rest. . . ."

(Curtain)

Daniel and I were confined in separate cells to await sentencing. The Supreme Court, however, was in no hurry to make its ominous pronouncement. This pause was extended out of all proportion, since the sentence had, of course, been determined in advance. All that was needed now was a prolonged interim to create the majestic impression that the sentence was being carefully weighed during that tense intermezzo. I don't know how other prisoners react at those points, but, after a futile struggle and my obvious defeat, I was overcome with the serenity of the doomed, who shift the burden of care onto other people's shoulders. The seven years in a camp plus five in exile that the prosecutor demanded stretched out before me like a plain so boundless that it was simply better not to think about it at all, not to sit and wait impatiently for the coup de grâce from the court.

I'm not the first, nor am I the last. People sentenced to capital punishment do not, as a rule, seriously believe they'll be executed. There are cases of people breaking into laughter on hearing their sentence, thinking a joke was being played on them. They say that the anguish starts when they're on death row. . . . Those who had been given sentences of twenty or twenty-five years—and who were still alive when we entered the camps—had only snorted ironically when slapped with their sentences. They sooner expected to see the end of the world than the end of their sentences. Now old men, winding up their sentences, they laugh at the wild young men they once were, unable to believe the day would ever come. We all have our own ways of denying truths that exceed our reason.

While waiting to be welcomed back into the courtroom, I kept trying, from a lack of experience and from foolishness, to win my rights from the warden, saying that either Daniel should be transferred to my cell at once, or me to his. I had heard that this was the standard practice when the ordeal of the trial was over. At the very end the codefendants are placed in the same cell, a waste product of no further use to the court. Until then Yuli and I had been brought in from Lefortovo and taken back for the night in different Black Marias so that we couldn't shout anything to each other. Now that would appear no longer necessary, and there could be no harm in reuniting us. But, naturally, the more I pressed to see Daniel, the more I cut off any chance of having that happen. Jailers love to do the opposite of what a prisoner desires, to frustrate him all the more. Had Daniel and I quarreled and gone for each other's throats, as often occurs with panic-stricken codefendants, they would have kept us locked up together now: Let them fight it out! I had yet to understand fully how we were viewed by those cold and furious eyes. My alliance with Daniel was seen as a hostile attack, bourgeois propaganda. . . . They would all nod in agreement: "Yes, yes, of course Daniel will be transferred to your cell. . . . That's the rule. The law. Don't worry. Just a little more patience. . . ." Then, later: "You see, the problem was, they couldn't find a guard to escort him. We gave specific instructions. But the warden either forgot or got mixed up. I am the assistant warden, and I can assure you that you will definitely be together in the isolation section at Lefortovo. It'll happen. You'll be spending plenty of time together. You'll be sick of each other. What's the hurry?!" The reality was that we would be kept apart until our camp terms were up. . . . To this day I cannot understand what they were so apprehensive about.

All I wanted was to give Daniel a hug at our funeral feast, to ask him about his health, congratulate him on his baptism in the trial's icy water, clear up some final details—discuss the mechanics

of how they had picked up our trail, bugged our conversations—
and, finally, to hear about his interrogation, during which, even
when at the end of his strength, he had still sought to protect me.
I knew that inwardly, having sensed it with my flesh and essence,
and from the course my own interrogation had taken. My love,
my pride, Daniel was a king. But that was not what I wanted to
say first, not what I was dying to tell him.

I had had a bad dream back at the beginning, just after we'd
been arrested. I dreamed that Yuli was nearby in a cell that, in
real terms, was thirty or fifty cells from mine, behind stone and
steel, most likely on another floor. He was sitting cross-legged and
hunched over on a cot exactly like the one on which I was sleeping.
He was leaning against the wall, pale, exhausted, his shirt torn.
But what struck me most about Yuli at that moment was the cross
on a short black cord around his neck. What's he doing with that?
I wondered. He was never especially religious, he never flirted with
Christianity. . . . Of course, after some reflection you realize that
the cross signifies the end of everything; it transforms this corrupt
life of ours and begins it anew, from point zero. Before that point
you can be whatever you like. But you have only to conceive a
burning desire for that cross to bring your life to an abrupt end,
an absolute crossing of the ways. It's not that a person has to die.
He has to be transformed. He can go on living, be fruitful and
multiply. But at least once in life, each of us is brought before the
cross, that reminder of what is real, that bridge to be crossed.
Don't be frightened—this need not necessarily take the form of
torture or some burden that will make you groan to high heaven.
No. Just bear witness, acknowledge, dig through your memory:
this is the cross you have to bear. Perhaps it wasn't your own cross
at all, but someone else's. Still, sooner or later, no matter how
well you hide, your own cross will appear before you. And when
it does, bring it straight to your lips. . . .

Naturally I didn't go into all these details in the dream. One
thing was certain: Daniel was there somewhere, behind walls, not

looking like his usual self. Sick maybe, or, worse, losing the battle for life in a prison or a camp, with the eternal cross around his neck. It's a sin, a grave sin on my soul. I ruined my friend Daniel. Like a junkie, I got him hooked on literature, that wasteland, that sinkhole from which no one emerges alive. Calm down—he crawled in on his own. I even tried to talk him out of it, saying, You'll get caught. But maybe the chance of getting caught made it more tempting. Writers, you see, sometimes have a certain urge to peep over the edge. A certain urge . . .

Not long before our arrest, at a party at Daniel's, he and I were sitting half drunk on the floor with our arms around each other. I had already come close to mourning aloud for him while stroking the rough, mitten-warm Astrakhan fur of his Negroid hair, his big hangdog, deeply creased, sagacious face, which six months later I would see with a new and nearly imperceptible twist of bitterness at the corners of his mouth; then he was under armed guard, seated at a distance from me calculated to prevent us from exchanging a word. We could only exchange glances out of the corner of an eye, grin in mutual understanding, and, our hands on our laps, give each other the Rot-Front salute. Rot-Front, Yulka! The writer is locked up inside us. And we may well ask if all writers don't have one foot in the grave. Aren't they always trying to get a little mileage from their own premature death in life? I warned him. Locked up. But, still, to see a friend as a prisoner sentenced to death? . . . Literature is kaput. No, only Yulka can speak for himself. . . .

But what more useful way to occupy yourself in the void of waiting, while the judges dine and dawdle on high, assiduously prolonging their secret session as if they had something to decide and were wrangling over our fate, already determined by others? Fortunately, they had left me with a file containing some paper, and an officially approved pencil. Pens were forbidden, as potential instruments of suicide, but prisoners were allowed a pencil by law, especially if they were in for a "literary" crime. There might be a chance I'd write an indictment of myself to forestall the sentence. Or perhaps I'd dash off an appeal. This time the law was on my side.

I began scribbling some nonsense, whatever came to mind, nothing that bore any relation to the case—it was mostly about the book I intended to write someday. I couldn't think of any other way to be of help to myself. It's not that my mind was teeming with ideas. And I was not moved by the passion to write or by a literary impulse, but by the instinct for self-preservation, prompting me to hold on for dear life to my pathetic profession just as it was being taken from me for all the world to see. It was important to me to retain the memory of myself as a writer; this was the only reason to stick it out. If I had lost the game of life, my card beaten, then I would move to a sheet of paper, that miniature desert island where you can try to make a new start.

The book would be about its own writing. A book about a book . . . You don't know where it's heading when you start. But you keep on writing and writing. With your eyes closed . . . The language should give you a ride on its own waves. That's what language is for. And it is full of deep yet intelligible surprises. . . . All things are worthy of respect, as are the words used to name them. Words are more respectful than things. And you're no longer living amid things but amid words. Seriously . . . And you immerse yourself in the sweet, peaceful, moving world of prose. . . . In the extreme, if need be, to invent a language accessible to none . . . and, dying, to know that all the words were in their proper place . . .

Strictly speaking, I had no theme, no subject crying out to be embodied. I had neither heroes nor images apart from that dream of a book whose purpose and beginning were unclear, and, were it begun, I would still have no idea how I was going to write it, and when, or where the next pencil would come from. The point is, this was a book that would never be written, but, self-enclosed, like a spore pod, it would abide within like hope, at a distance from the author.

I have not written that book, and there's little chance I ever will. But to make mental contact with it always buoys me up in my darkest hours: when all seems lost, that book suddenly reappears and saunters about as if slowly ripening, growing, even if its entire meaning lies in its own sweet evanescence. Yes, yes, all you do is think about it, but you cannot bring yourself to approach it and you show no signs of ever sitting down with it in the future. Pure possibility, unclear, unsatisfied, it has the right both to be itself and to be completely different from and unlike itself, itself unaware where its own outline is taking it, how the subject will develop and the sentences fall; it is free to exist without coherence or constraint, brimming with dreams and images that shimmer before your eyes, but still it remains a mystery, a freedom unused, like that of a person released from prison yesterday, the gates opening up an entire world to him. As long as he travels by train to points unknown (and until it's our turn to take his place, convicts under transport), until the book appears and approaches, you say, in a slow voice choked with high emotion:

"Not now. Later. Stay up ahead awhile, in that mysterious consciousness created by the constant attraction you exert, that anticipation of bliss and terror that come from obeying you, when every day is measured by the number of pages produced during the night. Stay the way you are, expand beyond these walls, forget about me, wait until I get used to the idea, catch my breath, and I am free of effort and the intrusive habit of writing, take pity on me, you can see how weak I am, how unable to grasp what you want, why you stare reproachfully at me, like an ancient prophet, asking decisions and sacrifice of me, tomorrow I go to the camps, I must dry crusts of bread, rent a room, ask for rolling tobacco, get myself eyeglasses, make coffee before I can sit by your cradle for years and years, let me live a little, give me an unpaid leave, let's go our separate ways, let's wander around the city and not do anything, not think about denouements or translating streets into pages, let's go see a movie, look, the ink's run out, I'm out of paper and there's not enough paper in all creation for our joint adventures. Go, you can go, we'll meet again in seven years, in the same place, if you want, let me live without you for a while, even if it's in prison, shadeless and in ignorance, even if it's for a year, even a month. A day. Wait, where are you going, you heard me, let's run away. You're all that I have in this world, in this cell. Without your protection where can I bend my knee, lay myself down, sink into oblivion—save me, take me with you, carry me away, O my book! . . ."

. . . About three weeks later, on the night before I was to be transported, I was pulled out to see my investigator, Pakhomov. We greeted each other like old friends. By then we had spent so much time together that I had somehow taken a shine to him; he was a real person to me, having, I would say, become the most acceptable, the best of the masks, especially when compared with those spectral judges and with what I thought awaited me in prison. For all his manipulation, he saw me as a living human being, more or less, and I tried to reciprocate by discerning the same in him. But not to win his favor. A well-mannered official, he was the one who had placed me under the ax of the indictment and everything that followed from that. But, if only because of our constant contact, Investigator Pakhomov, unlike the other inquisitors, acquired a real face in my eyes, as well as those little details that generally allow us, for better or worse, to judge a person's character. In any case, in the spectral world of prison, he seemed substantial to me, tangible if elusive. And after the trial it was a pleasure to see Pakhomov.

This time, our last evening together, he seemed distressed, an expression of both satisfaction and depression on his face. He felt sorry for me in a fatherly sort of way. Like many others, he had known the sentence in advance but, in the line of duty, he expressed his sympathy and sadly washed his hands of the whole thing, swearing up and down that neither he, Pakhomov, nor any State Security agency were involved in my ultimate fate.

"I give you my word, no one here thought they'd slap you with so much! . . . It's not what we wanted! . . . But what can you do—it's the law! Outside our jurisdiction! Seven years, that's a lot! And strict regime on top of it! You brought it on yourself! You shouldn't have acted so stupidly in court. . . . I warned you, and now you see the results. And the final speech you made at the trial! Personally, I don't know exactly what you said there, but everyone agrees it was scandalous, outrageous . . . out of line . . . just simply out of line! . . . Why did you do it to yourself? . . ."

He was shifting the blame for my stiff sentence onto me. That's understandable. With rare exception, no one likes to be an executioner. How many times, before this and after, did the people who were destroying me confide in me to explain that I was to blame for it all. And they would say that they were my friends. . . . Why had Pakhomov joined the ranks of evil? He was just distancing himself from me, as from a sinking iceberg. He was the good, ordinary person he claimed to be. Not one iota worse than me.

Recently, in Paris, I dreamed of Pakhomov's round and childish face with its plump little wart near the mouth, where they sometimes grow. And he spattered saliva all over what I'm writing here.

"I'll never crack! Don't think I will. It was them who cracked, the old guard! But me—I don't crack!"

What was he driving at? We never used words like "crack" or "old guard"—where did they come from? Dream and reality rarely coincide.

Of course, there was a great deal that bound the two of us. And if we happen to meet again, I will still try to take Pakhomov at his word, as he took me at mine—to draw me out. Interrogations cut both ways, and there is no end to interrogation. Meanwhile, what can you say? Well, he was somewhere in the middle—a good investigator, a decent person. Even his name, Pakhomov, spoke well of him, with its peaceable ring. And his first name and patronymic, Victor Aleksandrovich, were also plain, a touch homey, though not overly so. No need to be afraid of him.

Then, as we were saying goodbye, he seemed downcast for some reason. Later, much later, it became clear just what was weighing on Pakhomov at the time. The trial had miscarried, and you had a hand in that, you writer. Don't flatter yourself: you weren't what mattered. But the case had been given a good start, blessings, publicity, it was moving right along, wildly successful, but then, because it did not culminate in a confession and repentance, it fell apart. Imagine that happening in a novel. All of a sudden the hero goes out of whack, slips out of the plot, out of bed, literally out of the Beautiful Lady's embrace. And the hero says: I'm going out for a walk. . . . And that, after all our hard-won achievements in public trials. When anyone can see what a just country this is. And not to plead guilty in front of the Supreme Court, to try to wriggle out of it in front of the Supreme Court, to try to wriggle out of it there—that's sabotage. Like blowing up a long-awaited new building. Like sabotaging public transportation. Or a factory. And just when everything was going so well. Fireworks. The Forum. Oh, don't you believe that your seven-year sentence had wounded Pakhomov's shaggy heart. Otherwise he wouldn't have been a Lieutenant Colonel for Cases of Special Importance. You're the screw-up! You're to blame for it all! Meanwhile, those people were working on your case, without taking a day off or even time to shave, when they would have liked to be running to the store. And while people were rotting away in cells and camps, they were hammering away, toiling indefatigably, hatching a golden egg. An Easter egg. And now it's broken. A mouse ran by, hit the egg with its tail, and smashed it. It's the same as that fairy tale! All this has to be seen at its true value. Our trial was supposed to be a present to the party from the KGB on the occasion of the 23rd Congress. A model trial served up with an eye to the West on a crisp snow-white napkin . . . But could people in the West ever understand? And where's the sequel, the retribution? What's to be done? I ask you: how are such things even to be expressed? With miracle plays, Central Committee troikas jingling with little bells, pulling Lenin in a sleigh into the Kremlin, with executions, with the rehabilitation of Stalin, with order, with psalms and salvos beneath Semichastny's star, his bitter star, his lofty rolling tear . . .

"You have only yourself to blame," mumbled Pakhomov, thinking some thought of his own. "You have only yourself to blame, Andrei Donatovich. . . ."

I am able to reflect on Comrade Semichastny solely in abstract terms, on the shape and sound of his name, which has left me with a purely graphic impression, a signature descending the spider's web of the indictment. A surprisingly long name, and one that does not seem to befit the high office he holds. Even General Volkov seemed a more serious name, not to mention Pakhomov. Judge for yourself:

Chairman of the Committee on State Security of the U.S.S.R. Council of Ministers, Colonel General

Chief of the U.S.S.R. Bureau of Investigation, Lieutenant General

Investigator on Cases of Special Importance, Lieutenant Colonel

Lower and lower, line by line. Probably because Semichastny signed above the two others and with more of a flourish, he assumed a long, articulated, Quixote-like shape in my mind. And were that shape to enter a room, special openings and apertures would have to be made in the ceiling, precisely marked off and measured, so that there'd be a place for his narrow-chested torso and underdeveloped shoulders, somewhere for them to disappear, his upper body housed above and forever inexplicably absent. From below all I could see were his unsteady, sickly, stiltlike legs, descending in a signature. Who could have foreseen that this vague feeling, stemming solely from the extended outline of the minister's name, would soon prove true, and that Semichastny, the Komsomolets, the lanky boxer who took the Olympic gold in his match with Pasternak, would disappear from the horizon, like a skater yielding to the record-breaking Andropov? . . .

"Now you've really done it!" said Pakhomov with gentle reproach. "It would all have blown over if you had acted smarter."

Retaining my composure, I told him about the way I had been examined in court, which he pretended to be hearing for the first time, feigning surprise; that, after all, was another department entirely, one further down the line of links and concepts, one independent of the investigation—though I don't see how—a different department, one in which he was prevented by law from intervening, to avoid conflicts of interests and other such irregularities, and so that the proper conclusions could be drawn, to none of which I had any objection, and, on the basis of those apparent differences among various stretches of the conveyor belt, he berated the higher-ups as not knowing their ass from their elbow. He seemed to have compassion for me and to be taking an involuntary delight in the vileness of his judicial colleagues until, after a few chuckles, he caught himself and said:

"But do you know what kind of letters we've been getting ever since they started writing you up? Not that this is what we wanted, you can take my word on that. Hundreds of letters! Demanding the death sentence for you. It's no joke. . . . Here's one from a poor cleaning woman whose son was slapped with eight years for petty larceny. And you! After what you've done, you get seven? . . . Why did you attack Smirnov and the prosecutors Kedrin and Vasilev? . . . You should be grateful to them, and bless their names! . . . The whole country thinks you got off easy. . . . Suppose we let you walk out scot free right now—you'd be torn limb from limb. . . ."

His tone was one of bitterness mixed with open threat. How was I to know that Pakhomov was spouting the Don Cossack

Sholokhov's speech at the 23rd Congress? "Prepare for battle! To horse! This is a holy war! Glory to the party!" Trick riding. A heavy-artillery polemic was on with the West. Naturally the letters, the press, and the entire nation were against me. And it was only he, Pakhomov, with the help of his punitive machine, who was still protecting us from the fury of the people. But even they were not all-powerful, he hinted, spreading his hands. If, by request of the working people, the court reviewed the case, then . . . That I believed.

My cellmate, a good guy, not a political, sighed and said: "Just hope they keep you in Lefortovo a while longer. Until it blows over. You don't know what the real criminals are like. For them political prisoners are the same as Nazis. And you're even worse than that. They might mutilate you because of what they read in the papers. . . ."

I had already seen a few of the papers. Next to nothing. Nevertheless, the general climate indicated that the nation would not tolerate turncoats in its midst, and prison was the safest place for them. My cellmate dried some bread for me on the radiator to help get me ready for the transport, and he kept praying to God that we wouldn't be shipped off right away—that the memory of Daniel and me would fade first.

"Want me to give you some good advice as a goodbye?" asked Pakhomov, his face brightening as if he had just recalled something. "Not as a KGB investigator, just as a person with some experience of life . . ."

I was glad to listen. Since my interrogation had ended, I had even taken a liking to him, or, to be more precise, was interested in him from a strictly psychological point of view, interested as to the form human nature took in that special and, for me, strange variety of beings who make it their profession to catch and crush their fellow men. It's always interesting to learn exactly what crocodiles eat. I thought that through him I would in time grasp the mystery of power and the enigma of modern history, and of a society whose life work is the destruction of life, personality, art in general, and me in particular. . . . As a person, as the individual I always suspected him of being, Pakhomov roused no antipathy in me, and I harbored no ill will toward him. It's just that our views differed on a few points.

Pakhomov broke out laughing. "On your guard already? Andrei Donatovich, you shouldn't always think people are trying to deceive you. Here's some simple, friendly advice: shave off your beard. Shave off your beard before you're shipped to a camp. That's what I recommend. . . ."

"And when's the transport?"

"I really don't know. That's outside my jurisdiction, you see. . . ."

He made his usual fastidious grimace, which I knew inside and out by then, and which this time indicated that he had no connection with the prison system. The very mention of prison jarred him oddly. At one point when we were still getting to know each other, he had asked, "They're probably feeding you badly *in there,* Andrei Donatovich, aren't they?" He said this with sympathy, lowering his voice, while at the same time expressing his extreme regret that, for all his wish to, he had no power to help me in any way. I remember asking him irritably, "What do you mean, *in there?*" He hemmed and hawed grandly to avoid that unpleasant term: "Well, in there, where the supervisory personnel . . ." However, all I had to do was express an ironic doubt—that he, an Investigator on Cases of Special Importance, who had worked closely with prisons his whole life in that office, did not know how prisoners were treated or what they were given to eat in *his* prison—and he took sincere offense. And, I assure you, this was not a part of the usual daily chameleon tactics required by his job, to which I was quite accustomed by then. No—it was an outburst of genuine indignation. Why? What's the connection? Prison is one thing, an investigator's another. Two different things! They were even under different ministries—the MVD and the KGB. The MVD wore crimson caps, the KGB light blue. But the main thing was that their functions couldn't be compared. Did I really think that it was he, Pakhomov, who was holding me there, guarding me, feeding me poorly? That it was he who had arrested me? That he was the prosecutor, the judge, the prison, and the camp? That he was all that?! His was a very specialized field—investigation. A specific area with definite limits. From the way I talked, he, Pakhomov, might be the entire state, the press and society all rolled together! . . . He was right about that. To be frank, I did in fact think that he, Pakhomov, was all that. It was just that he did not yet know this about himself. However, he did know when the transport was. Down to the minute!

"What do you think, Victor Alexandrovich, will Daniel and I be sent out together? In the same car, going to the same camp?"

"I'll say it again—I'm not up on that. But most likely you'll be together. I hope so. . . . Cut off your beard, that's my advice. This evening. Ask the surveillance staff; they'll take care of it. You'll feel like a new man. . . ."

"And where am I being sent?"

"I don't know that either."

"To the north? The east?"

"Probably not to the north. Just between us—you may even be going south. South of Moscow . . ."

He smiled. Even an investigator will occasionally say something just to make you feel good.

"Kazakhstan?"

"There, do you see what you're like? You want to know everything. . . . No, no, I'm not saying any more. But get rid of the beard. It doesn't suit you. . . . It'll cause you trouble later on. The crooks, the criminals, they might set it on fire. They'll put a match to it and it'll go up like a haystack. . . ."

"I'll shave it off after they set it on fire. There'll be plenty of time for shaving my beard."

Pakhomov glowered. Was he concerned about me, or was he trying to intimidate me, to take me down a peg? My cellmate was also alarmed by my beard. Why call any unnecessary attention to yourself? They could maim you. . . . But, ridiculous as it may sound, at that moment to shave off my beard would have been a sign of surrender.

I don't attach any significance to my appearance, my image. I don't give a damn about beards! But they kept at it, kept insisting. . . . Repentence? Self-betrayal? Loss of face? And why was that Pakhomov, Investigator on Cases of Special Importance, making a fuss over a beard? No, you bastards! I'm not giving in. In short, little by little, I was becoming a criminal, as they call us, a mean and distrustful zek, calculating every step, taking nothing at face value.

It stayed in their minds. A year later, a long camp year later, a Chekist who was passing through went to see Daniel, who was operating a machine in the industrial zone of Camp 11.

"Greetings from Sinyavsky!" he said, watching intently as Daniel turned out some crap to meet his quota. "I was just in Sosnovka, Camp Section One. Sinyavsky asked me to give you his regards."

"Thank you," said Daniel without turning his head. "And how's Sinyavsky?"

"Fine. All right. Healthy. He shaved off his beard recently. . . ."

"What do you mean?" asked Daniel, still without turning his head.

"Just that. He has no beard now. I saw him myself. We talked. He sends you his regards. . . ."

Needless to say, I had never set eyes on that person. And I had not shaved off my beard. They were obsessed with my beard! And I had sent Daniel no greeting with any Chekist. . . .

When parting with me, Pakhomov advised me one last time: "The thugs will set it on fire! And it doesn't suit you at all. Mark my words!"

The transport was in fact the next morning. All the way it was supposed to be, just what we'd read—German shepherds, guards with submachine guns. "Left, right, left. I'll shoot without warning." I was wobbly on my feet. It was the month of March. The fresh air made my head reel. Would they really shoot you if you slipped and fell? In the distance, the rear of a train station. The Kazan station, I think—you couldn't tell. Small, dark figures swarmed around the sleeping cars. It was light out. And slippery. I was boarded from what seemed a very private platform. Not a soul in sight. An empty car. Bare metal. Down a long, barred corridor covered by grillwork, then on to the front compartment. Stop. A compartment for three. For me. A Stolypin car. A half-hour hadn't passed when I heard footsteps, swearing, clanking, a crowd; they were cramming the prisoners into their cages, compartments, without putting any in mine. Of course, I'm a political, I'm dangerous! On the other side of the partition, cage after cage was being packed with petty criminals, pros, nonpoliticals, all jumbled together. The poor devils! And there I was, lording it up all by myself, in a compartment for three, no doubt to prevent any disturbances. I could catch names, voices. Loud laughter, curses, fights.

"Lyuba, Vera, want to suck me off?"

I was used to that by then. . . .

"Go fuck yourself!" snapped Lyuba or Vera. Flirting. Trying to keep her spirits up so as not to burst into tears. She shouted "Go fuck yourself!" merrily enough, but there were angry tears in her voice. How many years had she been given—eight or ten? I felt somehow ashamed at being alone in a compartment for three. . . .

Then we seemed to be pulling away. But where to? I didn't believe Pakhomov. South or north, what difference did it make? We were on our way. Or seemed to be. I'd never been in a windowless compartment before, where there is only the clack of the wheels to soothe you with the knowledge that you're on your way!

Boiled water, bread, herring were passed out. A stretch of corridor could be seen through the diamond-pattern grillwork on the door. A guard ran by, snarling: Who needs the latrine? Me, me! They took me out. A soldier ahead of me, a soldier in back of me. "Hands behind you! Don't turn around!" Squinting to the left as

I walked, I saw a wall of people, a zoo of eyes, fingers, noses. "Move it! Faster!" And then suddenly I was struck from behind by the sound of my name being shouted.

"Sinyavsky! Sinyavsky!"

No stopping! I had a wild idea: could it be Daniel? Yulka? Here? In this transport? Who else knew me? But that wasn't his voice. . . . On the way back I squinted to the right. Zeks, zeks, and more zeks, packed like herring in a barrel. Once again, from behind me, a shout: "Sinyavsky!"

And then—laughter. No, it wasn't Daniel! But who? It weighed on me. I suspected that the guards were spreading the word, or else it was a setup. They wanted to teach me a lesson, intimidate me. Pakhomov had warned me more than once: They'll set your beard on fire. Now those warnings seemed about to prove true. . . .

The head of the convoy walked over to me. Young. Poised. Chiseled. A breech bolt of a man. He regarded me calmly and coldly in my cage.

"How is it," I asked, "that everyone in this car knows my name? You have everyone's papers. And there was nobody here when I was brought in. None of those people has ever seen me before. Why are they shouting at me? Did you tell them who I was?"

Rocking slightly on his heels, he stared at me long and somberly through the grillwork. He was thinking. Then, as if I were Pugachev, he enunciated with malice, "Everyone knows you now!"

A marblelike face, handsome as marble can be; the veins were red with restrained hatred of me, veins that, let's hope, would not flush with darker blood and burst; the face was still statue-white. A face like his could serve as a model for monuments to the legionnaires of the convoy service, a soldier who has you in his sights, the hatred in his blood roaring and tearing at the leash, but who uses his will power to restrain it and, his face as blank as a drunk's, maintains military discipline, taking a proud and scornful satisfaction in not killing you, in only taking your measure and,

finding you unworthy of his attention, clicking his heels and continuing down the car.

"Everybody knows you now!"

I was in a bad spot. It was clear that the guards had spread the
word on who I was and what I was in for. What wasn't clear was
where I was going and how long it would take. . . .

They unloaded us from the train that evening, or that night—
between the darkness and the searchlights, you couldn't tell what
time it was. Everyone together this time, regardless of classification.
Crammed into an enclosure like a large flock of sheep, we turned,
jostling each other on the snow, the searchlights aimed right at
our formless mass.

"Where are we?" I asked out loud.

"Potma! Republic of Mordovia!" replied the man beside me,
who must have been a nonpolitical. "Don't you recognize it?
Haven't you been here before? Pardon me for asking, but what
prison were you in?"

"Lefortovo."

My voice was firm. Lefortovo was a trademark for me. My
father before me had been imprisoned in Lefortovo, and I used to
bring him money there, two hundred rubles in the old currency,
nearly every month. I still didn't know if Lefortovo had any special
ring or meaning to them. But I had been in Lefortovo. . . .

"Lefortovo?" several voices chimed in at once. "Look, this one
was in Lefortovo. Where was he, Lefortovo? . . ."

Now, when I say that proud banner of a word "Lefortovo," I
know what I'm saying. And I would like to see Lefortovo take its
place right alongside Lubyanka, Butyrka, Taganka. . . . Lefortovo
has a special standing among connoisseurs. Legends and mysterious stories have grown up around Lefortovo; I'll tell some if
there's time. But, meanwhile:

"I was in Lefortovo."

Then I saw three prisoners shoving their way toward me. They
looked like serious people, independent, their eyes parting the
crowd, which opened like a fan despite the lack of space.

"You were in Lefortovo?"

"Yes, I was."

"You didn't happen to see Daniel or what's-his-name, Sinyav-sky, when you were there in Lefortovo?"

"I did. I'm Sinyavsky."

I stood there bracing my legs, waiting for the first blow to fall. Then the unexpected happened. Instead of hitting me, they hugged me and shook my hand. Someone yelled, "Let's carry Sinyavsky on our shoulders!" But he was cut off: "Shut up, shithead. Not now."

It was in the large, communal cell—I had never seen any that large or that communal before—a cell that could accommodate half a transport, where we were to sleep in rows, strictly ordered to lie on our right side so that we'd all fit on the plank beds and not breathe in one another's faces—it was there that everything came clear. Those were knowledgeable, intelligent people. Repeat offenders. One had four previous convictions. Another had five. I was the only intellectual, the only "political." They told me that the day after tomorrow we'd be distributed along the branchline to the various camp sections, of which, judging by their numbers, there were nineteen. We wouldn't see one another again; our paths wouldn't cross. After a time the politicals are separated from the regulars, obviously so that the natural flow of the people would not be polluted by any hostile propaganda. Were they afraid of ideas? Infection? Still, as they say, the people on top know best. They had the experience of the revolution behind them. But who could have been more ideological and active than my good friends the criminals? And I didn't understand who the really dangerous agitator was—I, or they. Each of them hurried to express his respect for me, to put it mildly. They had read about it in the papers! An important person in the criminal world! A boss! . . .

"They were talking about you on the radio, Andrei Donatovich! . . . I heard it with my own ears! . . . On the radio! . . ."

Fame is valued in the criminal world. But there was one other thing that I grasped then: that all this was also done in defiance of the newspapers, prisons, and government, and in defiance of meaning. Because, to them, the abuse heaped on me by the radio, at meetings, and in the press was an honor—I'd been honored! And the fact that I had smuggled my manuscripts out to the West, had not confessed, and had remained unbowed at the trial conferred me with exaggerated stature. Not a person, not a writer, but some kind of Thief with a decorative capital "T," as in the old incunabula. And, to tell the truth, I liked it. It was flattering, as if it were just what I'd been waiting for. I had never experienced fame in such fullness before, and I never will again. And I will never deserve and never hear any better criticism of my work, alas. . . .

"You really let them have it good!"

"I just thought about it, you wrote it!"

"Seven years is child's play! You won't even notice, it flies by so fast. . . ."

"I'd have faced a firing squad to be in a brawl like that!"

"Hey, Pop, I've got a question for you; I'll believe whatever you say!" butted in a young man convicted of hooliganism. "Will communism come soon? Just give me the word on that. . . ."

There was nowhere to turn. In principle, there could be stool pigeons among them. Even before the trial, Pakhomov had given me some parting counsel: Watch out; if you start up again in the camp, verbally or in written form . . . But the little crowd around me, unaware of the reefs contained in cunning Article 70, was now standing in silent fascination. They were all waiting for my answer.

An experienced teacher, I answered evasively: "The thing is, I've already gotten seven years for trying to answer that interesting question. . . ."

The convicts were exultant, apparently rejoicing that communism was not just around the corner. For there was no justice in this world, and there never would be. . . .

Then, just before sleep, a man stood up on a plank bed on the other side of the room, a joker with a tubercular face. I recognized his voice: he'd be the one fooling around with the girls on the train, striking up acquaintances. He was all skin and bones. You could just about see his ribs through his leather jacket, which was worn all the way to the lining. He had the air of someone playing to a receptive audience.

"Listen, Sinyavsky, it was me who shouted your name when they were taking you to the latrine!"

I threw up my hands in amazement. "How did you guess? Did someone tell you who I was?"

"No, no. I just saw a funny-looking guy with a beard, and so I shouted 'Sinyavsky.' Just for a joke, that's all . . . I'm sorry. We didn't think it was you. . . ."

Yes, Pakhomov, you're not having any luck with my beard. You were taken in by the newspapers. And tricked by the criminals. It never occurred to you that your efforts would result in my being honored and fussed over, me, the writer. And by whom? Whom?! Thieves, hoodlums, bandits, who'd cut any man's throat, no matter what his rank. And who used to cut the throats of people like me when you put them up to it. But times have changed, haven't they? Have they stopped taking you at your word? Not me, but the people, your people, Pakhomov, the people you come from and are proud of and bow down to and are always saluting; not me, but the people you warned me of, saying: They'll maim you, set you on fire, tear you limb from limb! . . . Is it your turn to be afraid of them now? My time has come. My people won't kill me. And, I'm afraid, they wouldn't kill you either. I don't think they'd set your beard on fire, even if you had one. You've lost the argument with me—you've lost, Pakhomov!

In the camp, people you had ground under come to me, not to you, to make confession, for consolation. Maybe he'll write something again someday, who knows. It is I who will be asked by a hardened criminal who has slits for eyes, and who had done so much time that he is ready to lose his life, which of the stool pigeons or administrators he should take with him for the good of the cause. What's the difference, you only die once, so give me some advice, writer, but be specific, tell me who. It will be me and not you who will have to talk him out of killing anyone in a passing moment of rage. And the informer sent by you will come crawling over to me and, looking me in the eye, will betray you, lay his cards on the table, telling me that you want information on me and that he'll lie through his teeth to you about me. The man assigning jobs, determining which prisoner goes where, will summon me and, after locking his door behind us, will admit that he could not come up with any easier job for me, because your hand had reached there from Moscow, from the KGB, appending instructions: "Use only for heavy manual labor," signed Pakhomov.

To what do I owe all this good fortune, in your opinion, Victor Aleksandrovich? My easy disposition? My beautiful eyes, as you were fond of saying? Not at all, it's due solely to my notoriety as a writer who disagreed with you, turned a few somersaults, and landed on his feet, on an equal footing with the thieves. It's because of my books, which you charged with being horrible, slanderous, lying, filthy, my criminal books, which no one here apart from you has ever read or ever will read, books that are published in foreign countries, to which no one here has traveled or ever will, books that are not understood or needed there. But none of this is essential or important. I was taken off the packed train ahead of everyone, all by myself, at the first little stop in the camp— Sosnovka. "Goodbye, Andrei Donatovich! Goodbye, Andrei Donatovich!" chanted the people in my car. They were being sent farther on down the branchline, but there was already a guard with a submachine gun and a German shepherd waiting for me down below, to bring me on foot into the zone. "Right, left, right. I'll shoot without warning."

"Goodbye, you guys!"

As I went, I was pursued by cries from the jam-packed train cars:

"Goodbye, Andrei Donatovich . . ."

"Turn around one more time and I'll shoot," said the guard without any malice.

"Goodbye, Andrei Donatovich . . ."

After all, Pakhomov, those men suffocating in those windowless cages had nothing to gain by chanting my first name and patronymic, new to them, in such perfect unison. And the fond, happy goodbye they wished me was out of keeping with the situation, Victor Aleksandrovich, and with their leprous lips. And it wasn't just done for show. How would you continue the interrogation now? I only know one thing:

The sea has accepted me! The sea has accepted me, Pakhomov! . . .

II

. . .

The Public House

Dear reader, did you ever happen to spend any time in a public house? If not, then allow me to make the telling of this story easier by beginning it with a description of the modest, barrackslike hotel adjacent to the guard shack and the checkpoint gate at the border of the camp zone and the through road that runs past it. The public house could be called a neutral prezone area, even though it is in fact situated within the grounds of the zone, jutting into it like an unattractive oblong promontory, a peninsula surrounded on three sides—not counting the fence—by the plowed forbidden zone and barbed wire. The fourth side of this isthmus was the guard shack, where the supervisory staff lived—the entrance to and exit from the public house. *Basta.*

Here, on prison grounds, once a year—for three full days at best, or twenty-four hours, or one short night—a prisoner and his lost family do everything they can to restore their lawful rights and duties in a welter of kisses, a wealth of tears. And that is why these establishments are called "public houses," as they were in the old days, and, dear reader, all the shades of meaning apply—brothel, inn, orphanage, the last goodbye. Prison, you see, lends everything a perverse, sarcastic meaning. But there is no more beautiful and sacred place on earth than a public house, and, at the same time, no higher and more distant mountain from which to contemplate the hamlets and dales, the rivers and ravines scattered over the world. Here, once a year, by permission of the administration, demons congregate with angels, husbands with wives, children with fathers, and the living with the dead. The only question is who it's tougher on. And who are the dead? . . .

Cubicles along a corridor, windows that face out on the fence—neither quite the world, nor quite prison. Except that every once in a while a guard stomps by on the well-worn path, and the cry "Who goes there?" rings out, echoing as if in the mountains. The changing of the guard . . .

A little room to yourself, everything quite human. Two chairs. A night table. A table. A bed. White shades on the window. Cover the bars and you feel right at home. . . . And now, since you have been allowed a little personal happiness, there's everything your heart could desire on the table. Every last delicacy. White bread. Lard. "I don't feel like eating." "Gorge yourself!" Canned goods—cod liver. Real butter. Lump sugar. Jam . . . The visitors stuff the emaciated prisoner's belly—for the year just past and for the year to come. You have three days, maximum, to eat it all. It's a real responsibility. That's the main thing, the reason why the peasant women have come with their bundles and bags, why they changed trains three times, stood in lines at train stations for tickets, slept at those stations. Will they be allowed in soon? Will they be allowed in at all? If not let in at once, they go to the free settlement and rent a mattress for three times what the price should be from a prison screw's tight-fisted wife. Meanwhile, at home, at the other end of the world, no one's milking the cow, the children are sick, and her unpaid leave from the Machine and Tractor Station is already up. . . . And who, we might ask, is running the house in her absence? They do everything themselves, everything, the good women. But who, if not they, would feed and honor the prisoner? Nothing but skin and bones, he can barely put one foot in front of the other. God forbid, he . . . And he's got five years of his sentence to go, seven, fifteen. . . .

Oh, Russian women, draft horses of the nation! And not just

Russian women. Lithuanian, Ukrainian, Armenian, Jewish, Kir-
ghizian, and Lapp women, they all come to the public house from
every corner of the land. What a word—"public"! There was
something girlish about the way they came to feed their men. Some
of them don't even know the word "mother" in Russian. They
mumble their own language. But the world is cold, and the authorities are strict. They keep you hanging. They say: If your
husband doesn't start thinking differently, doesn't change his behavior, doesn't fulfill his quota at work, I won't allow the meeting.
I won't, and that's that! Then he laughs, the snake. They can do
whatever they want, those enemies of the people. . . .

For once in his life the prisoner can stuff himself. Relay greetings
to his children. His wife could sit there forever, sadly enjoying the
sight of him chewing his food. But he's feeling too good, he doesn't
want to eat. He pushes his plate away: it's too much. . . . Home
burns like a fire in his eyes. . . .

Having dealt with the ham and the cabbage pie (which she baked
herself), let's not forget the second entry in our accounts—the bed.
They eat at the table, and on the bed they . . . Why hide it? Pardon
my indiscretion, but what would you have him do on the bed if—
think of it—it's only once a year that he gets to leap onto his
woman? They go into the room, lock the door so no supervisor
comes barging in, and then it's—let's have some fun! . . .

There was a story about one bull of a man who, because of that
very temptation, was dragged handcuffed straight from the general
meeting area to the SDB, the "strict-discipline barracks." He had
gone right for his wife like a tank, and before the guards knew
what was happening, he had thrown her down on the floor. He
managed to come before they tore him off of her. She, of course,
had opened her legs for him. Fiery soul that he was, he slashed
his wrists in the SDB. . . .

Another lady-killer had the good fortune to strike up an acquaintance with a group of women zeks while they were under
transport. The guards were dumbfounded when they noticed that
the women had made an alcove for the lovers. Facing the guards,

they had arranged themselves into a semicircle, screening the couple from view. He was beaten for that afterward, beaten good—alcoves, the very idea! Real carnival theatre, my dear women readers, commedia dell'arte, skirts, fans, and all . . .

You might say they're "thex-crathy," as one of the free camp workers, who lisped, used to say. I doubt that, though. It's all more serious and more basic than that. It's a matter of restoring honor, of keeping a family alive. . . . And a woman who's changed trains three times is not in the mood for just fooling around. Of course, she wants it too; she hasn't had that itch scratched for a long time either. But mostly she wants to give her man pleasure. And support. For the year to come, and for the year just past. So he will remember her and pity her, and also so that the machine doesn't get rusty after so many years idle. By the time he's free, it won't be working. And then he'll turn to drink! . . .

And so, my fine young ladies, there's almost never any sleeping done on the beds in a public house. We can catch up on our sleep back home in the zone—there's plenty of time for that there. They lie in bed, aware of every sound. The woman is grateful to be able to feed her man, to hold her man. The men start turning into such savages there. Sometimes the lusty young guards would make wisecracks, but usually in a friendly way, in a good mood themselves: "So, Sinyavsky, did you knock off a good one?" But in the zone I never heard any prisoner say: So, Sinyavsky, did you get your rocks off? Sometimes they'd walk with you as if to a wedding. "Quick, to the checkpoint, the guard shack! Your wife's here, get it? Does yours wear glasses? Then it's her. By the entryway. She's got a knapsack and a suitcase!"

But when you come back, it's like coming back from a funeral. "I know, it just gets you all stirred up. There's nothing worse than those meetings! It's been eight years now since mine's come. And I'm glad of it. It's easier on me, and on her. . . ."

By way of a joke, someone will ask: "What's new in the free world? When are they going to declare an amnesty?" And they laugh and curse at each other—to console me. They understand:

I'm just back from the public house. . . . The sooner lights-out comes, the better! . . .

But let's take a deep breath and once again cross the mysterious threshold of that *pension,* which, like a factory, operates around the clock, never stopping, never resting. Only the guests change, in one room today and another tomorrow. The guard rattles the bolts, checking to make sure everyone is where he should be, or to see if anyone needs escorting to the production zone. . . . I won't trouble you, or myself, with stories of how they search you before and after a meeting. Had you hidden something where it wouldn't show? A ten-ruble bill, a note, a pack of tea? . . . How, to be extra safe, they make you change into special public house rags. All the same, it's: Spread your cheeks, open your mouth! . . . I wouldn't allow myself to wonder beforehand how many days they would allot me, or whether I'd have to go to work or not. Just let them leave me alone with my wife as quickly as possible. She and I paid no attention to each other, like strangers—somehow that seemed the proper thing to do. In the room, we locked the chain and threw our arms around each other. We were together, in each other's sight!

"Masha! Mashenka! . . . Let me see you, how are you? How's Egor? Is he healthy? . . . Thank God. So, then, let me have a good look at you." To swim in a face as in a river, like the one we finally reached when we were traveling in the North—remember? Suddenly there it was, its gleaming length menacingly close, and so we cried out, thinking we were at the edge of a cliff, until we got our bearings and realized that this was the river, the Dvina, or the Pinega, that we had been looking for, and we sat down right there, dangling our feet, watching the water move slowly past. . . . These meetings convince you that the face is not a portrait but a landscape, which the eyes devour abstractly all the way to the horizon and back, but still it's ungraspable, beyond the reach of perception. Vainly you grope to focus on that face, to see it. Its soft, dissolving outline blurs, becoming an image of barely tangible space; it overflows its own contours, extending like a river that runs right through your fingers. The face is not a flower, as many people suppose it to be, but the way into the public house and the way out. We don't know where that leads. And the shape of the cheek . . . You cast one glance, and circles spread along the water as from a tossed stone, receding from the center toward the forest and the sky. . . . All you can hear is: Dusya! Lyuba! Valya! Tatyana! And do you realize that you appeared in a dream? It was a dream, do you understand, a dream. . . .

But she doesn't understand that at all. At a loss what to say, she tries anyway: "Eat the sausage. I brought it for you. They're hard to get. . . ."

But it's beyond human power to resist the magnetism of something which has come true! If this isn't madness, then what is it? . . . The face.

I begin with the face because it's the most important. I don't know if we do this with men too, but we love a woman for her face, choose her by her face. It's cruel. "Choose" is not the word, however—we fall under the spell of a face, we go over the waterfall, we fly through the air and are smashed on the rocks and we barely notice. A beauty strolls down the avenue, and if she makes the right little move with hand or toe, it's all over. Maybe it's unjust, maybe it's wrong. Where's the mind in all this? They say that, if Cleopatra's lips or nose had been even just one millimeter shorter or longer, all human history would have taken a different course. And she was a queen. What about us? . . . It's all up to us! One look and the woman is a beauty, a great lady! What a lovely nose she has! Her airs, her eyes! The shape of her cheek . . . By then your unimaginable fate is hurtling like an artillery shell toward its target—*baboom*—and all because of a chance impression. For the rest of your life, to the end of your days . . . A millimeter? A queen . . .

Now I'm lost myself. It's a riddle. A mystery. And I begin with it—the face! . . .

The nose, the mouth, and the profile as a whole were beyond reproach. Not because they were perfect, but because they were mine! I perceive my own features in the face of a woman I'm seeing for the first time. How can I put it? The features of my soul. Pay attention to women's names. Men use them to call out to their lost souls: "Dusya! Vera! Tatyana! Nadya!" And there is no response.

Meanwhile, there goes the finest version of your soul walking through the Language and Literature Department in full sight of everyone. "But you're mine!" you exclaim, still not knowing her name. "At last! And now you won't live another day, another night without me. You're locked in my heart. . . ."

She doesn't look at you. And she walks past in such proud profile, as if she hadn't heard a goddamn thing. "I've found you!" I cry without making a sound. "You're mine! At last!" "Who goes there?!" comes the cry at the meeting house, bounding like an echo in the mountains. . . . By then your fate is the high road that runs from that first cry to that last.

Whenever I thought about Mariya in the camp, I'd always end up at an impasse trying to recall the way our acquaintance began. To be more precise, not our acquaintance but our first encounter, which, naturally, she failed even to notice, hurrying to an examination, her heels clattering through the Literature Department. Although at the time I did say to myself, "Look, there's the woman you're going to marry," there was so much yet to come! When you see a face whose features—beautiful or ugly, it doesn't matter—suit your soul, you don't debate or struggle, you just go after it. And it doesn't matter whether she reciprocates the feeling (she'll reciprocate the feeling later). It doesn't matter if she likes you or not (she'll like you later!), or what she thinks of you the first time (what difference does that make?). And let's imagine she actually turns you down (the fool! the dope! she doesn't even know who she is!). You go after her anyway. You buy that pig in a poke (we'll take a closer look later). You go after her the first time you see her, for the beauty of her face, the likes of which you'll never find again. It's stupid! This isn't a matter for the mind. We're a millimeter from death here. . . .

When you look back on it, you wonder what else she could have done. Does she have any idea how serious that all was, that we would have gone our separate ways if my soul hadn't cried out? Now she says, "Oh, Sinyavsky, take off your shoes and come sit quietly with me for a while. . . ." What I stand for is the face that first attracted us and then, as a result, followed us like a dog. I stand for art. Because there too everything hinges on one tap of the chisel, two or three brush-strokes, even if it's only the artist who delights in it. No one else can see what you see: "What do you find so special about her? Where'd you dig that one up?" But the one thing I know is that she was meant for me!

The camp revealed how well conceived the whole thing is. A wife should feed you. A wife should write you letters and be able to read between the lines of yours. She should raise your son, guard the hearth, and run the household as if nothing had happened. And if you don't survive, she should keep on with everything that you were called upon to do—your place, your work, the snapped thread—and stay with it until the end, to her own grave. "Do you understand?"

"I understand."

She looked at me as if her eyes were going to pop out of her head—exactly, I'm sure, the way I was looking at her. So that nothing would go unseen.

"You understand?"

"I understand."

There's a reason women are always saying:

"And so Boris says . . ."

"But Kostya told me . . ."

"Vasya and I . . ."

"Andrei thinks . . ."

As if a spell had been cast on them . . . And it doesn't matter what in fact her Andrei said. This is an incantation of memory, a sign that they're "always together," whether his name be Borya or Volodya. Listen to how women always work in their husband's names whenever they're chatting. Living or dead. He may be missing in action, but she'll work him in. By the way . . .

"Yesterday, mine . . ."

"And mine, may he rest in peace . . ."

She builds a nest against her fear. "You and me, us together." No one else. We'll work as a couple. You cling all the closer to your wife when you're at the edge of the abyss. You cry out in your sleep, at the edge of the universe: "Mariya! Hold on! Stick it out! You're all I have left—remember!" And her answer reaches you: "I'll do it! I'll do it all! But just don't you forget about me, there in that prison paradise of yours. . . ."

And so here we are in rack and ruin. Outside, a locomotive blows its whistle, alerting the camp of its arrival. Get up, guys, the coal's been delivered. . . . The whistle sounds again. The flash of electric welding, like northern lights against a heavy, starless sky that knows neither sleep nor rest . . .

Everyone has his own itch to scratch. My wife and I have a life that, if you will, is like an "industrial novel." Have you heard about those novels of the working class, novels like *The Hydroelectric Power Station, The Stalingrad Tractor Factory*? Have you read the Richardsons and Rousseaus of our century? The Abelard who lost his flaxen curls so early? The production line. The conveyor belt. Marriages of convenience. The cadres, it was said, decide everything: We'll step up the schedule. We'll reduce the cost of living. And so it follows that the old Soviet writers, Fadeev, Avdeenko, were not lying all that much either. . . . What's a family in this country? A production unit. Keep your eye on the cement— you're working on the Five-Year Plan! . . . I see Mariya take the checked notebook safe and sound from her knapsack and begin writing furiously in it. She's a real master, for at the same time she's writing, she's going on and on about how nice and cozy it is here, like some provincial hotel. Somewhere in Kirillov . . . in the North . . . Remember: it was in Pereslavl-Zalesski! . . .

But it was Vologda that came back to mind. A seemingly well-bred young man ran ahead of me into the post office and wouldn't get off the phone, his voice a hysterical treble. "This is the prosecutor speaking! You hear me? There's been a murder—on the corner of Chapaev and Furmanov! . . . You hear me? . . . A murder! . . ."

We went straight there. A crowd had already formed. A young woman of rare beauty was keening beside the prostrate body. That stopped me in my tracks. Ritual lamentation! . . . The ancient rite was, however, punctuated by the onlookers' quiet, good-humored remarks: "What are you wailing about? Your sweetheart's not going to die. He'll come to. . . ." Apparently out of youthful inexperience, the prosecutor had gotten overexcited. Murder had been averted by a blow with a brick to the back of the head. They had put the brawler out of commission. Someone had already pocketed the knife, which had fallen to the ground, so it wouldn't be entered in the police report. The girl was still overflowing like a river, saying that mean, envious people had taken her man's life, so kind, brave as a falcon. She was rudely upbraided for that. "You whore, why did you slip the knife in his hand when he stumbled out here drunk to fight? The guys just knocked him out, that's all. They saved him from going to prison. . . ."

Infuriated, amazed, she broke off her lamentation and surveyed the crowd with a clear-eyed, utterly tearless gaze. Her eyes slashed me along with everyone else.

"Yes, good people, I slipped him the knife—me, I did it. Yes, that's how much I love him!"

She didn't say the words, she sang them. Listening to some inner melody, she reproduced it in speech, held back by no shame: "Yes, I love him, the bandit!" The word "love" clearly brought her pleasure. And then she went back to her traditional keening. . . .

My wife pulled out the notebook. "Read this!"

" ....

..........A stenographer's record of the trial ....

.............................which I sent to the West...............................
...................................."

I was used to this little game with the notebook which was only
for the two of us. I strained my mind to grasp it—news from the
life after death. A papyrus. "To be continued," I thought in passing. Trying to keep the scissors from clicking, Mariya cut the paper
into strips like herbs and tossed pinches of paper macaroni into
the saucepan: Aragon, Tvardovsky . . . A soup of celebrities. Eh-
renburg . . . Don't make noise with your pencil! . . . Shalamov.
Acting like an old friend. Ginzburg . . . Solzhenitsyn—he didn't
have to get involved. He had other things to worry about. But
what had prompted him to speak out was the belief that a writer
should seek to win fame in his own country! . . . A petition . . .
Vigorelli . . . Who's this Meniker? Vika Shveitser was fired on
account of you. . . . Golomshtok's pay is being docked because
he wouldn't testify. . . . Tell Daniel . . . Duvakin . . ."

The white strips streamed through the public house. Like tele-
type. Or like hearts tapping to each other in code. But why those
god-awful turns of phrase, then? Win? Fame? I don't owe him
anything. . . . You can stop worrying about Pavlovsky. He demanded that you repent. He threatened to expose you. And then
a second sentence would be added to the first. . . . They're searching
apartments! Searching apartments! There's a wolf hunt on. Vy-
sotsky . . . But we'll try again. That's true, isn't it, that we'll try
once again? . . .

I could see her face brighten, infusing me with a sense of right-
ness, both about my arrest and my being in the labor camp. Wolves.
Family. Production. Then we added some boiled water to the pan
and poured the soured noodles down the toilet, laughing to cover
the sound. Up to mischief again. Outside, the locomotive was
calling out to be unloaded. Blowing its whistle again and again,
the goddamn thing was asking to be searched before being let into
the production zone. Coal had been delivered again. And the guys
had to get out of bed. Emergency work. And then all through the

night, like the northern lights, the flash of electric welding . . .

How they hunted me, never letting me out of their sight! . . . Late one evening we were walking down Vorovsky Street, on the way back from Arbat, having forgotten a letter at home. Mariya said, "Look, in that archway!" And, in fact, ten paces from us, a little light was rolling errantly along the sidewalk. Someone had tossed a cigarette away. But there wasn't a soul in sight! A raw chill under the archway. No sign of life. But the cigarette was still glowing. . . . She nudged me with her elbow. "Let's take a peek!" But courage isn't my strong suit. "Who cares? Let them follow me like phantoms. Then again, it might have just been some robber at work. We shouldn't disturb him. . . ."

Mariya is daring, bellicose. The complete opposite of me. Our friends joke, "You two have the usual symbiosis of a sea anemone and a hermit crab." I agree. An "industrial novel." She knew I'd end up in prison when she married me. She just didn't like it when I started going on and on about it, more all the time. "Don't bring it down on yourself!" she'd say. "Please. Words have a way of coming true. . . ." But I wasn't calling it down on myself. What mattered to me was to understand the situation, to do the ground-work. . . . And the upshot was that we had not worked out a sensible plan about how she was to live when I was gone or what to do during the investigation. It was left up in the air. . . .

One day we were strolling through Vagankovsky Cemetery and, as usual, I was complaining about the West, that we hadn't received a word from our poor author. It had been three years since we'd sent Tertz abroad. Just wait till they arrest me. . . . She listened and listened, then said: "Don't be blasphemous. If I'm still alive, I'll do what you asked. I'll bury you alongside your mother. But I'll put your name and Tertz's on the stone. I'll carve in the names. Or put his name on a bronze plaque. Next to yours . . ."

Needless to say, I approved. That would be some joke. The pernicious author resting in peace in full sight of everyone, but out of reach. And, like birds of passage, his manuscripts would have migrated to foreign lands. She and I never returned to the subject. A long time would pass before I was hunted down. . . .

The first news I had about Abram Tertz in the West came in the most banal of circumstances. The Soviet literature section, consisting of fifteen people, was having one of its usual endless meetings at the Gorky Institute of World Literature. The speaker, a dark-haired, plumpish woman who had been invited from another section of the Academy of Sciences, was reading the annual report on the perfidious foreign press's response to socialist realism and Soviet achievements. The use of such surveys had been established during the previous spring, that of 1959, with the obvious aim of increasing the Academy's militancy by furnishing it with material from the secret archives. Heaping this secret information on top of the usual demagogy, the speakers demanded aggressive action from us along a broad ideological front. Everyone was yawning wearily. All of a sudden this woman, who translated from English and French, mentioned my shameful pseudonym distinctly, her metallic tone of voice devoid of any vanity or personal involvement. "At last" was what flashed through my mind. "Oh, will Mashka be surprised and delighted! . . ." But the well-trained speaker did not bat an eyelash. Could she have been so accustomed to the secret archives, to plucking living molecules from the sea of bourgeois publications and setting those names down on shore? I, however, would, rather, have thought that Tertz's exotic name, with its touch of sepulchral superiority, would be somewhat to her taste as a woman without university degrees but enjoying trust from above, or perhaps as a Jew who knew several languages and had a slight sense of the insider's superiority. Wake up, you Ph.D.'s, you doctoral candidates, senior and junior scholars, she said, a mysterious impostor has appeared in the West, his breed, identity, and origin unknown, a spider that allegedly spins its web of manuscripts here in the Soviet Union. It spins them here and publishes them there. They might be forgeries. The foreign press has offered a variety of versions on that point. And she provided some quotations, poorly translated back into Russian. Still, he can be found, recognized . . . by the gleam in his eye. . . .

Everyone seemed to cringe. These hostile incursions had brought the electricity of a detective novel into our scholarly ruminations. All I recall is that my ears were on fire instantly. Shamelessly on fire, like a boy's. My face was blank. I sat straight in my chair, legs crossed, as if nothing were the matter. But those ears of mine, those ears were possessed, growing larger and larger. Liquefying. What could I do about them? How could I hide them? Ears aren't manuscripts. If I could just run out of the room! With each new reference to Tertz, my ears, like a vampire, distended with new, claret-colored flesh. I did not feel anything, I was not aware of anything except my ears. My goddamned blood-drinking ears. All my colleagues had to do was turn their heads and take one casual glance—and they could nab the horrible, big-eared Abram Tertz right there in their own midst. Grab him with your bare hands! No proof needed . . .

However, everyone was gazing lustily at the plumpish speaker and not at me. She fired off the names of magazines: *Encounter, Kultura, Esprit.* Quote after quote. Devastating evidence. People, be on your guard! . . .

Mexmat came running over to me at the end of the report. The graduate students had made up that nickname from his first name and patronymic, both common among workers, and bestowed it on that chatterbox most likely because of his cultivated knack for spouting nonsense that sounded right and his automatic party-activist manner combined with roosterlike cacklings of noble rhetoric. Mexmat—always on the firing line, at the cutting edge.

"I've got it, Andrei! I figured it out from the style. In reality there's no such person as Tertz. He's a fiction! A forgery! Fabricated by some clever Western journalist. The quotes gave him away. Who could imagine a writer living in the Soviet Union, who knows our country, history, and psychology, all of a sudden portraying Stalin with a "mystical mustache"? The mentality is all wrong! Exactly the kind of lapse a foreigner would make! Something like that would never enter your mind. . . . What Soviet would ever make a blunder like that? Mysticism in our life? The 'celestial Kremlin'? An anachronism! A mistake! A forgery! . . ."

Then Mexmat was off on his way. There was a strained smile on my face as I mumbled, "Yes, yes . . . in all likelihood . . . Mikhail Matveevich . . . It's hard to imagine. . . . A forgery . . ."

My ears were burning like a pair of lanterns.

I set off on the trudge home with another of my colleagues. The air was fresh; a snowstorm was brewing. My cap covered my ears. The streetlights were on. A breathing spell. My colleague and I were neighbors and were friendly outside the Institute; usually once a week, after the meeting of the Soviet literature section, we would take some air together, chatting as we strolled the side streets near Nikitsky Gate, walking home together, one of us occasionally dropping by the other's. We were friendly but we kept a certain distance; as the older man, he looked out for my welfare, taught me about life, initiated me into the intrigues that went on behind the scenes, and he gave me a spaniel from his litter as a present, a marvelous dog. Not a party member, he was on good terms with the authorities and people in general, a benevolent man of letters. Even though he is no longer among the living, let him remain nameless here—just an honest, inoffensive colleague on a snow-white street. . . .

"Mexmat doesn't know what he's talking about. He's a chatterbox. A scatterbrain. Blah-blah-blah. He's always jumping the gun, trying to figure out what the line will be. . . . Don't believe him, Andrei: it's no forgery. Tertz is clearly from here. They wouldn't be making all that fuss if he weren't. They're sending out a signal. And, don't worry, he'll be arrested soon enough. Maybe they've already discovered who he is and are keeping him in their sights while they check out the evidence. And there we are at the Institute racking our brains. . . ."

I objected, but not strenuously. There was no reason to go into details or to display any interest or anxiety. But I had the rest of the day off, it was a holiday for me, and my ears were safely under my cap. There was no one at home. Mariya had left that morning to lead a group of Chinese tourists—high-school seniors, pensioners, military people—around by the nose in Ostankino. There'd still be time for me to surprise her with the news. Snow was whirling in the air. Finding a needle in a haystack wasn't easy, even for the KGB. What coordinates did they have? Anonymous, one of two hundred million! They had no address! I was in bliss, immersed in a snowfall that concealed us from the entire world. How could they ever identify him? I agreed that there was no question, no doubt that, if he continued his smuggling, sooner or later over the years they'd uncover him. Let's assume they seize a manuscript at customs from some touring artist. Or some faithless friend shoots off his mouth when drunk with a bunch of people. But if he is alone, alone in the world? Like the snow in the sky . . .

A foreign film with the breathtaking title *The Invisible Man* played at one time in Moscow. Based on H. G. Wells, of course, but I thought it would be more interesting than the book. Unfortunately, as a child I was too poor to go to the movies, and so I never saw it. Later it disappeared from the screen and I did not find it revived, no matter how much I scoured the listings. As if he had never existed, that invisible man . . . However, after the war, a film captured from the Germans with a different title, *The Invisible Man Walks the City,* was distributed, and I rushed to see it like a little boy. And you know what? It was clearly some other film. Trash, it paled by comparison. . . . But the real film, unique, irreplaceable, was lodged in my mind, imprinted there with redoubled intensity, retold to me so avidly by the fortunate few who had seen it with their own eyes that it was as if I had not missed it at all.

The invisible man is in a hotel room undoing his bandages, unwrapping his head. He throws off his coat, his glasses, his gloves, and there is absolutely nothing left of him—transparent and elusive as an angel, his true life form. Except for the things juggled madly in his invisible, convulsive hands. He robs a bank. Bonds, valuable documents, and money fly down the street, over houses and trolley cars. He derails a train. Running from the police, he leaves a trail of wet, shoeless footprints in the virgin snow. They open fire, determining his location by the trail. In the hospital he gradually comes back to life, but he is at death's door. Dimly at first, a skull appears on the pillow. As rigor mortis sets in, facial muscles and what had once been tissue are superimposed on the skull. The final shot is of a young man's face shot through with light. And a wonderful girl bends over him like a sprig of lilac—the eternal bride of the invisible man, now lost and gone forever. But what if he hadn't run across the snow?! . . .

However, my partner in that conversation took a gloomier view, judiciously muttering about computers. "Andrei, these days it's no big deal to calculate who a person is by his style and the language he uses. The frequency with which certain types of expressions are used, certain indices, the theory of probability. They can feed samples of his literary work to the computer and it'll come up with the answer. The person being sought, the X in the equation, is not just anyone off the street. He's one of us. Educated. With a modernistic streak. What are the variables here? He's either from Moscow or from Leningrad, with an outside chance of Kiev. You can be sure it's not anyone from Berdichev. And so that means the computers are narrowing the field. Do you really think that no one knows who this writer is?" I do, I really do, but mum's the word on that. That's a secret. Snow is falling. A curtain of snow. How nice it is when it's snowing. And style, thank God, is not the same as a person's fingerprints. Or his character. Or his way of life. Sometimes the person and the writer are completely incompatible. Different handwriting. This is not calculable. And why make all those calculations just to wipe someone out. . . .

This leads to a dispute, the old dispute on the freedom of speech. I make reference to Pasternak. That's safer. Poetry is more innocent. Lyric poetry. Why don't they publish him? Or Akhmatova? "Are you looking for trouble?" And those endless cries: "Say you're sorry!" "Say you're sorry!" Mexmat had run to our basement apartment to try to convince Mariya to exert some influence on me. But there's a certain boyishness and adolescent stamina about her. A steadfast tin soldier . . . "It was pointless for you not to have repented. Pointless! You're not up-to-date! At a closed party meeting, Ovcharenko tried to seal your fate: Expel him! Alien bacteria have penetrated our Institute. Rotten liberalism! . . . And that great thinker pounded his feeble worker-peasant chest with his fist. Like Suslov. An anemic Stalinist. A spirochete . . . Don't think I'm making this all up. Someone in the party acted out the whole thing for me. Shchebrina seconded it from the pulpit. As you know, when he's at the Institute he doesn't say a word. But there he let go and turned into a regular preacher. And he delivered an anathema, a real anathema: 'Finyashky'—he meant you—'has an anti-Thoviet beard.' It doesn't matter how he said it. His teeth get in the way of his tongue, or maybe it's all the saliva and froth. No, this, I'm sorry to say, is a serious political charge. In the old days . . . Then he declared that Babadzhiev—who's also one of the younger staff people—has a Soviet beard. But Sinyavsky's is anti-Soviet. . . ."

"What do you care what Shchebrina says? He's no authority. Everyone knows about him. He screws all the female graduate students; the poor girls wouldn't have been admitted to the Institute of World Literature if they'd refused. That's his idea of an entry exam. It's the old man's hot Cossack blood. Do you remember, he almost got caught with Alexandrov in the scandal with the actresses. . . ."

"But Khrapchenko also demanded you be dismissed! He was on the old Committee for Artistic Affairs, it's no joke. He's a minister! . . . By the way, Andrei Donatovich, it was Dement and Mexmat who saved you. No matter how little I personally think of Mexmat, he put up a little fuss for you, by going against Ovcharenko. He said: Let's re-educate Sinyavsky. Leninist principles. A talented guy. A budding critic. The group can deal with its own problems. And Dikushina, Dikushina backed him up! . . . And now you're standing up for the past again, for Pasternak? . . ."

A snowy pollen swirled on the asphalt, creeping along in little streaks and whirls. Snow and ground wind. Like in the country. As soon as the wind starts whirling and howling, the peasants will say that the devils and witches are celebrating a wedding, playing pranks, dancing. And so there was a column of dust on an icy road. There's an old belief that, if you slip a knife just right into the side of a snowy whirlwind, there'll be blood on the blade when you pull it back out. And blood is proof. Proof that there's something alive inside that whirling snow . . . Did you really expect that? It's just a white spider scurrying along the asphalt, ensnaring Moscow's side streets in its web.

"Come on! Come on! Those are meaningless fears! Pasternak is no danger to anyone. Publishing a dozen books won't make the state collapse. Oh, what beautiful books there could be in Russia! In the store windows."

"And how about Poland?"

"What does Poland have to do with it?"

"There's a direct connection! If we publish Pasternak, Poland would celebrate by allowing independent journals. It's not like East Germany there, you know. The Poles turn up their noses at us as it is. Allow artistic freedom in Russia, and Poland will secede."

"Why keep Poland? It's costing us plenty as it is."

"Poland will be followed by Hungary, Czechoslovakia. . . ."

"The vassals . . . The satellites . . . With one wave of my hand I set them all free. Fly away, little birds!"

"You're balmy. The Baltic States will follow on the heels of Eastern Europe!"

"Fine and dandy! We won't force them to love us. . . ."

"The Ukraine! . . . And the Caucasus, which is not so far away either. . . . No, you are not going to squander an empire because of some Pasternak, are you? Is that what you want? For the first time, do you hear me, for the first time in history, Russia has access to the Indian Ocean! Africa! Central America! And you want to give all that up?"

"Let's not exaggerate things, we're killing ourselves. . . . I'm not arguing. It's just words in the wind. Ostankino . . . Hold on. . . . He deserved it . . . And China! We forgot the Chinese! . . . Want to bet on it?"

"A few more months, a year tops, and you can rest assured they'll catch that invisible man. And that's a good thing too. It can't be allowed. If the crack isn't plugged, manuscripts will start leaking out. A whole other literature. Bad examples are infectious. Think of it like this—if they decided to let a little information filter down to us here in the mud, can you imagine what must be going on at the top right now?

"Secret agents. Counterintelligence. International espionage . . ."

In fact, the snow was not falling but landing. Go count the snowflakes! The state, interests of state . . . Excuse me, but what does politics have to do with it? . . . Oh, if the blizzard would only hit us harder! We'd never be found. . . . Cybernetic machines. Lists. Typewritten pages. Indices. Diction. With what frequency does the word "notion" occur? "Breakthrough"? "Unique"? . . . I hate it. China. America. Snow. A whole other literature . . . "From the Nile to the Neva, from the Ganges to the Danube!" Pasternak could never have written anything like that! . . . Snow has a cybernetics of its own. . . . Even I can still remember when there were Chinese in Moscow. They used to sell magical colored fans. If you opened them one way, they revealed an image of a phoenix, and if you opened them the other way—a dragon. I only saw them; Mama had no money. But even I could buy the balls packed tightly with sawdust, and attached to long elastic bands. Five kopecks apiece. The Chinese were always smiling. No one laid a finger on them. Where did they all go? In what year did they disappear? Was it after Lake Khasan? . . . Snowflakes . . . Every last one taken. Not one left. What business did snow have with human beings? Was cosmic communism being built in heaven? What did we need America for, the Danube, the Baltic States? What good was an empire if there wouldn't be any art? . . . The end and the means . . .

"Stop it, Andrei Donatovich! You're almost starting to sound like Abram Tertz! . . ."

Strange that all that talk from years and years ago should wend its way to the public house. Just as if this were the denouement of a detective story, a model for a board game of cops-and-robbers, a game that had started God only knows when, a clue from a secret-police dossier in your pocket. No, the fugitive cannot know the full extent of the manhunt spread out through the ravines and gullies, closing in on him from every side. Originating somewhere in the uncharted regions beyond human ken, all that reaches him are danger signals that flicker in fantasylike specks before his eyes.

Mariya was shredding the strips and placing them neatly into a pot while I, bent over the notebook, attempted to reconstruct events after the fact from their shadows, which were galloping like horses, as if I were doing a collage for which I had neither the glue nor the patience. A tear here, a pattern there, raving nonsense somewhere else . . . To tell the truth, we did not seek to puzzle out the labyrinth of our indefatigable persecutors, satisfying ourselves with the chance, unconnected bits and pieces that occasionally precipitate out from our supersaturated life. What's the point of sitting in prison and trying to figure out where, how, and through whom they picked up your trail? You don't cry for your hair after you've lost your head. And, besides, I'm not a fan of detective stories. Flight is necessarily more absorbing than pursuit. We used to lie in ambush in the burdocks in summer. . . . In the country, as children, our liveliest group game was Cossacks-and-bandits. We'd break into two groups and go running through the woods and ravines. I never wanted to be a "Cossack," always a "bandit." . . . There were, however, always those who would invariably volunteer to be Cossacks. . . .

Once, when signing the record after an interrogation, Daniel noticed a familiar-looking page on the investigator's desk. He had typed out a single copy of his novella a few years before, using the one-finger method. I do not have the right to remain silent here: it was I who had passed that novella on to the West. What he saw on the desk was a photocopy of his novella *Redemption*. With the help of God, the original had reached other shores and appeared in book form, but an offprint of the typescript had somehow made the return trip, to end up in a mouse-gray folder. And Yulka had recognized that sole existing copy. . . .

But, more to the point, the manuscript was not part of the case against him and was displayed on the investigator's desk as a trophy. Perhaps they wanted to dazzle Daniel with the extent of their reach, their scientific thoroughness and completeness in tracking down those errant pages. Yes, you writer, you can sweat to find ways of hiding and concealing your manuscript and yourself, you can flush your sinful handiwork down the toilet, but there's a photocopy in Lefortovo! . . .

Indeed, I was astounded by the tidbits Mariya brought me at our meeting. What sweep! What scope! But what the hell was going on here?! Didn't they have anything else to do with their money, didn't they know how to expend state funds? And could they have begun their long search with an unsigned typescript? Without even knowing the author's name? It was not the person who wrote it that had to be determined but the one who delivered it, the channel of communication. The rest was simple: whom did the foreigner meet with, whose homes did he visit? Install bugs, dispatch someone to spend time with the people under suspicion and keep an eye on them. And that, in all probability, was how we were found out. . . . So, then, why increase expenses by having people hang around foreign publishing houses and rifle through their files, pay bribes, why risk valuable agents—all for the sake of stealing an entirely ordinary typescript with some corrections made by hand, perhaps in ink? . . .

In a fit of temper, a gloomy lieutenant general had reproached me with the amount of scarce foreign currency that had been paid out to track me down: "We paid eleven thousand dollars in gold for the pleasure." That's not all that much, I thought, unimpressed. Not expensive at all. And will a KGB man ever really tell you the truth? He might have just taken a figure off the top of his head in the hope of rousing my last, feeble remnants of conscience: Look what a pretty penny you've cost your own country! Or was he simply calculating in hard-currency terms the cost of keeping us under surveillance, which I estimated to have begun about seven months before they sprang? But did the figure include the salaries of the officials, high and low, dispatched to keep an eye on developments in art and on the comings and goings of foreigners? Personally, I would have increased the figure, taking the entire operation into account. Eleven thousand dollars over a period of ten years? Insulting.

On the other hand, however, let's not rack our brains over the costs involved. It wasn't so long ago that they were shooting people for this sort of thing. And, if you can imagine, in Paris a well-informed individual swore up and down that, when he was in the U.S.A., he had heard with his own ears a senator say that the KGB had been informed of Tertz's real identity by American intelligence—in exchange for data on a new Soviet submarine. Mariya and I were immediately enraged by this. Cut the price! A little humility, please! Even the KGB wouldn't go in for that sort of cultural exchange. Eleven thousand dollars and not one cent more, do you hear me? And that was probably an atomic sub with two warheads. No, even I don't put myself on the same level as a submarine, even I don't think that highly of myself. . . . But, if my memory does not betray me, there was an incident, one that was talked about. . . .

Vinogradov, the then Soviet ambassador to France, held a large reception to celebrate Russo-French friendship. Whenever he had a free moment, he would circulate among his guests, playing the pleasant, chatty host; he would also do a little fishing, casting his line with virtuosity at the person who was my impresario at the time, the hook delicately baited with kindly laughter, little jokes, and champagne with its nose-tickling bubbles. "Of course, of course, I've read it. But, to be honest, I doubt whether authorship can be attributed to anyone back home. The style, you see, the style is wrong. . . . Did someone bring it to you from Moscow? From Leningrad? What guarantees do you have? Did it just come to you out of the blue? Let's discuss this in the abstract. Purely out of curiosity. Cultural bonds. Paris Opéra. The Bolshoi Theatre. The Impressionists. Debussy. But who brought you the manuscript? Where's it from?"

The publisher, an old hand who knew who the connection was, was at no loss for words. "No one brought it to me. It came all by itself. In an envelope. From the Soviet Union. By mail."

"By mail?! . . ."

"Yes, by mail!"

The ambassador bit his tongue.

Circuitously and with delays, sometimes of several years, and with a certain margin for distortion, news of the search for that fugitive author would reach our shop. We had covered our trail well. That had worked in the past. The only question was, how long could it work? God only knows. . . .

Four years later, after another meeting of the Soviet literature section, I was, as usual, out strolling with my colleague who, as I have said, shall remain nameless. Once again it was snowing, and once again the speakers had been harping about that invisible spider, that black magician who was lurking somewhere close by, just around the next corner.

"He's had it now," muttered my colleague. "He's gone too far."

"Amen."

"He won't last another month. I'll bet you on that. The foreigners themselves will hand the go-between over, signed, sealed, and delivered. . . ."

Amen, I seconded. Still, how come there hasn't been any talk, or any gossip about it?

My friend told me that he had recently been paid a professional call by a Slavist whom he had not met before. "Well, we ate, we drank, then my foreign guest began bragging about smuggling, and his contacts with influential newspaper people. Fine, we were all alone, but what if there had been somebody else at the table?

It makes you sick to even think about it! But then the Slavist said with a smile, 'I have at my disposal all the secret information about that frivolous writer whom your secret police have been tracking with so little success. I have great admiration for the man. Of course I know his real name,' he said with a look at his notebook, 'and his place of perm-a-nent res-i-dence. . . .' He jots down Russian words that are new to him in that notebook, so he was also practicing his Russian pronunciation on me, the swine. But he doesn't make mistakes in speaking. Then he said, 'I've heard that this Count of Monte Cristo'—he looked at his notebook again and laughed—'is all the rage in Moscow, a big hit. And I've got him right here, in my pocket! I'm a capitalist!' And then the idiot whacks his starched shirt. His suspenders. I tried to distract him: Let's have some vodka, let's drink some whiskey. I changed the subject, trying to put it on a more professional footing. I said that in Alexei Tolstoy's novel, *Peter the Great* . . . He wouldn't have any of it, didn't want to hear about it. All he cares about is Tertz's true identity. He just asked that I didn't tell anyone where the information came from. Otherwise his confidential sources would be greatly distressed. And he was also very concerned about what would happen to his protégé if the police were suddenly to uncover him: Though you understand, of course, that he has it coming . . . Yes, I understand. But how does that Tartar know that I won't run and inform? And that I hadn't invited him to my apartment as part of a special assignment? How does he know that he wasn't speaking to an undercover agent? The parasite goes running to bare his heart to the first Soviet he meets. 'I believe in your honesty.' . . ."

I looked around stealthily. Dusk. The people in the distance were moving their legs soundlessly, like sleepy flies. Had Mariya been there at the time, she would have launched a squadron, a hailstorm of sarcasm and insult to disavow and destroy the scandalous, transparent silence built up around us. She would have rent the air while tearing that provocateur to shreds! . . . But Mariya was taking an art-history course at the Abramtsevo Institute of Jewelry, and I was the farthest thing from her mind. My wits always fail me at the critical moment. I have never been terribly quick on my feet or definite in my gestures and reactions. "Sinyavsky," Mariya says, "you're always behind and bogged down, it's your nature, and you cultivate all those faults." I don't do anything of the sort. I'm simply unable to improvise and make the right remark on the spot. And snow was piling up as in a winter's tale from the beginning of the last century. And, lying in wait, my heart shook like our dog Motka's tail. . . .

Then I began carefully extracting the detonator from the German bomb. Neutrally, casually, as if it were a matter of no concern and the whole drama were being played out somewhere at the other end of the world, "And so?" I asked. "So, who did he turn out to be, that . . . person? . . . Residence? Profession? Sex? Age? . . ." As I spoke those words, I seemed to withdraw through the air, leaving a formless snowman in my place. I dragged in "sex" as a sort of forced grimace of feigned misunderstanding, a way out, a way to mitigate circumstances, the sort of gesture we sometimes make to protect ourselves from relentless fate, like a girl raising a brightly colored sleeve to ward off some danger. First establish the sex (am I a man or a woman), the age, the city, and only then the person. I didn't even raise the issue of Tertz's real name, fearing that my friend would answer me the way Porfiry Petrovich had answered Raskolnikov: It's you, sir, you, sir, who killed her! . . .

No, the foreigner had been too embarrassed to point the finger. And so, did he know the name of his intended victim or not? He was probably just a Slavist flaunting his erudition about our internal affairs. On the other hand, he was glad to confirm all the hints, all the intersections that in fact diverged in various directions from the truth. . . .

For an instant my colleague seemed to hesitate about telling me the secrets in which—far, far away, as in a sniper's scope—my little body twisted and turned. He mumbled, then made a dismissive gesture with his gloved hand: the hell with him, that Slavist was shouting it from the rooftops anyway!

X the unknown lives in Leningrad. A bachelor. A loner. An engineer by training. He'd been in prison before. In his sunset years. Retired. Periodically sends his manuscripts out through Poland. Where he has relatives. His features include being bald as a cue ball. . . .

I almost fell over. . . . Poland, now, was a stroke! And so was Leningrad! The rest was just rumor. I took off my hat, shook off the snow, and smoothed my hair. It had passed. . . .

Our life is like the little story that asks, How can you cross the Soviet border? It's best at night, New Year's Eve. For the road, take an empty sack, a walking stick, and a lantern with a candle stub in it. Catch a cat at evening time in a border village, and hide it well in the sack. Light the lantern at the shore of a river that is frozen solid, and hold that lantern openly in front of you on your walking stick, letting it show against the snow. Let yourself be spotted from a distance: "Someone's trying to make a crossing!" When you're somewhere around the middle of the river, a border guard will call out to you from his cover, a quarter of a mile from you: "Stop! Stop or I'll shoot!" Freeze in your tracks. Obey the command to the letter and drive the walking stick with the lantern in the snow. From a distance it'll look as if you've stopped. But you keep going with your sack. Meanwhile, the border guard skis to the lantern, discovers the trick, and sees your footprints heading west on the snow. He sets his dog after you. Just when you are halfway across, you let your cat out of the sack. The cat runs back toward its village in Soviet territory. And, naturally, the dog goes after the cat. By then you've crossed the border. . . .

But where's our walking stick? . . .

"Happy New Year, Masha! New happiness!" The two of us always celebrated New Year's together. Just the two of us. A tree, shimmering with bulbs. A candle. Like two old pirates, we'd drink to good fortune. To having survived the year just past. To having as much good luck in the new year as we'd had in the old. To hang on for at least another year! At least another year! . . . We'd work to keep our trail covered abroad. We'd play hide-and-seek. We'd hoist false flags. Send the cat—to Poland! The lantern—to Leningrad! We'd elude the roundup. . . .

One evening, the janitor's wife, who had come from the better classes, beckoned Mariya over in the front doorway and whispered: "Mariya Vasilevna, two men were here, asking who comes to see you, if any foreigners come by. I said, How should I know whether they're foreigners or regular people?" For years now, since the business with my father, the janitor's wife has been keeping an eye out for us. Her son, a criminal, a young man in the prime of life, had committed suicide in a camp, having first managed to dash her off a note: "Mama! It's like a fairy tale here!" I cannot help pondering that remark: if it was like a fairy tale, why did he commit suicide?

A knock at the basement door. A messenger from the Institute. Shchebrina wants to see me in the office. Me? In the office? There Shchebrina is very amiable to me. Amiable? To me? He has never once said hello to me, and now all of a sudden he has a smile for me. A smile? For me? An urgent Academy of Sciences assignment for me to Kishinev and Kiev. To arrange scholarly contacts. Me? Arrange scholarly contacts? Me, on assignment? That was a first. I'm not the type. There are always those who'll jump at the chance of a free lunch in any of the Union's republics, though they do prefer the Caucasus. Someone apparently needed me out of Moscow on those specific dates. Why? Was this a precaution against my meeting with delegates from an enemy country, even though I had no such intention? Or was it to make a secret search of our apartment while I was off in the middle of nowhere and Mariya was stuck at the All-Union State Cinematography Institute, immersing glossy actors in a flood of the Gothic and the Baroque? Or to connect some fucking listening device through one of our neighbors' walls? Daniel's neighbor had alluded to that, saying, "Yuli Markovich, it's a mistake not to lock your apartment door when you're going to be out for a while. To keep strangers from entering the premises." "Who'd go into my place? There's nothing there that would interest a burglar. Nothing but books." His neighbor, a pensioner and always at home, could not help keeping watch over the empty apartment. And he cast a gloomy sidelong glance as if some unsavory type was already in Daniel's apartment. "Bah, Yuli Markovich, what do burglars have to do with it? Don't be an idiot!"

Flustered, I ran to buy the tickets. Mariya invented hellish punishments for the directors of my Institute, who were becoming more illiterate and untalented all the time. It didn't matter that those were doctors and academicians who had risen from the ranks of the workers: Shchebrina, Khrapchenko, Ovcharenko, and the director himself, Ivan Ivanovich, whose nickname was Vanka-Cain. . . . Even though they say Cain had been at receptions given by the Queen of England and the Queen of Belgium, his conversation with lesser mortals was restricted to cursing. Was our patriarch imitating the customs of the Central Committee, or someone even higher? . . . But now, in Mariya's version, instead of going to Kiev and Kishinev, I had been magically transformed into the director, which resulted in my being able to select the staff. No, I have no desire to administrate, though I would do my duty. But I can't forget Ivan Ivanovich saying angrily, "I don't want anyone getting any original ideas here! I'll make you pay for it if you do, I'm warning you!"

An exam would be announced for all the administrators just mentioned. They would each in turn be locked in the director's office for a period of up to five days, and each of them given a subject all his own on which to write a composition, as is done in high school. No dirty tricks, the simplest subjects—Griboedov's "Woe from Wit," *The Inspector General, Fathers and Sons . . .*" If you want Kafka, you can have Kafka. Even Romain Rolland . . . You can have the text open at your desk, in folio. But I do request that you work without any aid from the criticism industry. They already had all that information at hand when they were

busy plagiarizing it before. The telephone would also be disconnected, to avoid any prompting from postgrads or seminar leaders.
You will be so kind as to spend the night on the director's comfortable couch. All by yourself. With no girls whispering their
undergraduate dreams in your ear. As for food, you can order
whatever you like from the Prague restaurant. Cognac is not forbidden. You'll sit there and be able to fabricate any research you
want. The sadistic twist to this competition is that, if there's even
one original idea, one fresh expression . . . One other point—the
handwriting should not fall beneath a fifth-grade level. . . . When
everyone is through and the results have been checked, we guarantee that at the end of every composition I will write the following
conclusion in red pencil: "To be dismissed for professional incom-
petence." . . .

"Of course, we heard what plots you were hatching there in the
Institute," the doleful head of the camp would say to his new
prisoners in Mariya's fantasy. "You wanted to hang us all by the
balls on Red Square. All the leaders . . ."

However, while we were making jokes, they were excavating.
Sifting through the sand, straining water through a sieve . . . What's
going on and how is it being done, beyond our ken, outside our
field of vision? . . . Only the echoes reach us. And with a time lag.
But less and less of one. Someone takes off at a run and disappears
down the sidewalk. But his cigarette is still smoldering. . . . A
small glowing ash, one not left by a human being . . . And then,
all of a sudden, the entire horizon around you is buzzing with
unfamiliar guttural voices. And what is being said? Nothing at
all. Take a step, you bump up against a detective. Turn around,
and there's no one there. Were you seeing things again? No, here
they are! By the door! Outside the window! In the air! You're
not the only wily one. There's a whole world of invisible beings
around you. . . .

Blushing the color of a tea rose, the rosy-cheeked girl at the
Lenin Library counter speaks allegorically and without censure as
she reveals that on Monday the record of my borrowings was

taken for inspection. A list of the books I'd taken out over the last two years. I bowed deeply to that flower girl with the modestly downcast eyes. They're using old coordinates to form a profile. What does he read? Do you recall Diderot's remark: "Tell me what you read and I'll tell you who you are"? My mother often complained to me about her job at the library. Some Man in a Gray Suit would appear in the young people's reading room and look busily through the shelves and the card catalogue. He would note down which works of fiction one suspicious youngster or another had checked out. It went against all the aims of education! These were children, the future of our country! And the books themselves had been through all the filters twenty times. . . .

Still, I was not really frightened because my records had been taken. I was, after all, a researcher. And I remembered my mother's telling me that everyone's lending records were kept for exactly two years, no more, then sent out to be pulped. The Lenin Library could not provide the KGB with anything more solid than that. Physically, the library didn't have enough room to keep all those records. And if they were counting on catching me by the quotes I used in *On Socialist Realism*, well, that book had not been written two years ago but . . . God give me memory . . . My mother was still alive then and . . .

That wasn't irritating, but being tailed was. They had us staked out. Although they had not picked up any direct scent, they were dogging our heels. To complicate matters, I had always intended to check out a mass of books that had nothing to do with me. To use them as furniture. Or barricade myself with them but not read them—Turgenev, Sholokhov, Alexei Tolstoy. . . . Let's say I was suspected of being sympathetic to the Decadents. I'd use Abelard and Fadeev as an alibi. They'd be looking for Pasternak, and I'd be reading Herodotus. Then they'd be looking for Herodotus, and I'd check out Darwin. Then they'd . . . and I'd . . . Dizzying. There are thousands of books there; no one could keep track of them all. A barricade! Don't bother me. I'm doing my research. In the end, either I am a researcher or I'm not! I read what I want. I've read that sometimes criminals have plastic surgery done on their faces, skin grafts. I should have altered my identity too—by fictitious readings I should have feigned being a good, loyal citizen on my lending records. Taking the plunge. Disappearing for a few years. Evaporating into books. And then, surfacing at the other end, boldly demanding "The Library of Adventure" for respectability's sake. Sherlock Holmes. Nat Pinkerton. I'm no minor. I have the right. If I knew English, I'd ask for Agatha Christie! "Murder on the Rue Morgue"! In the original! Or the Count of Monte Cristo—what better literary patron for a convict on the lam?

That would have cleared me in the KGB's eyes: "Leave the man alone. You can see what's on his mind by what he reads—Dumas, English detective novels—no harm in that. The man likes to read, he's interested in literature. . . ." But we're always too busy, we never find the time. It'll work out somehow. We let things slide. Then one day it all comes back to haunt you. But by then you're already on the hook. . . .

We were drinking at a banquet, teachers and researchers. An Uzbek girl who had lost her virginity to Shchebrina had just defended her dissertation. It was a Shakespearean feast. Boisterous. The girl's Buddha-like father, the head of a provincial committee, had rented a floor in the Prague restaurant to celebrate his daughter's success. Toast after toast! "Yes, we are Scythians! Yes, we are Asiatics! . . ." I said when my turn came, quoting Blok's poem in an effort to pay the girl a compliment, but she missed the point. . . . An old academic, a woman with a mustache and an international reputation, nudged me with her knee under the table: "Andrusha! If you only knew how fed up I am with being a prostitute!" "What do you mean, Tamara Lazarevna? Did you say that for effect? Or just as a turn of phrase?" So many papers. Real scholarship, not autopsies. The woman was Shakespeare incarnate. In female form, of course. Ugly, as befits a professor, and with a mustache, but why go on about that? Ninety years old. Her husband was an academician. And he had an international reputation too, in comparative linguistics! . . . "I'm tired of prostituting myself. . . ." The old witch was laying it on. "I'm telling you, like you were my son. To sit at the same table with Khrapchenko, Ovcharenko . . . I'm tired of yessing people. . . ." So that's it! But who's forcing her? She could have written in peace, written just for herself and posterity, and published abroad. They wouldn't have thrown her in prison, not a woman like her. . . . Her body was turned toward me. Her face was nothing but wrinkles. Her mustache could not be seen. Her mustache was lost in the noble, dark-green, etched bronze of her face that seemed tattooed for battle. "Don't forget, Andrusha, what cruel times we live in! Be careful. I'll cast a spell—there's a bit of the gypsy in me. . . ." As if I were born yesterday! I know what kind of times I'm living in! What did she mean? Let her say it, I won't tell anyone! . . . She wouldn't make it clear. "Though Birnam wood be come to Dunsinane."

But the haughty tsarina Tamara had already turned away, proud to have been of help to me. Then, in a loud voice that reached the length of the table to Khrapchenko, she said, raising her glass and her breasts like Lady Macbeth: "Mikhail Borisovich! Let's drink to the thirties!" The 1920s, the teens, the first decade, all right. Was that a slip of the tongue? I whispered, "Did I hear you right?" She nudged me with her stout leg. "To the thirties!" Khrapchenko nodded wearily: "To your health . . ."

Then, after her prophesying, I thought of the three witches in *Macbeth*. While fanning the flames of Macbeth's ambition, those swamp spirits did not lie in the least when saying that the king and his children would not inherit the throne, but they did lead him into deception and utter exhaustion with their sarcastic remarks about unprecedented consequences. That they did. Both by what they said about the forest going mad and about Macduff being avenged by a man not born of woman. There was no double dealing there. The power of their dark prophecies lay in their incredible literalness. The same is true of Oleg the Wise. The mystery is concealed in the skull of Oleg's horse—a poisonous snake that was not foreseeable. Meanwhile, the prediction: "Death will come to you from your horse" has a convincing ring to it. Even though it was a bit off the mark. Enticing. What does that mean—from his horse? That was avoidable. If he hadn't taken fear of his horse, Oleg the Wise could have continued living in clover. And how "wise" was he anyway? It was the sorcerer who was wise. No, Oleg brought his own death down on himself—because of his foreknowledge of it. He came to disaster by seeking the best way to avoid it. But if you look closely you'll see that the sorcerer left something unsaid. He didn't say straight out, specifically, "From your horse's skull." The witches were wily too. They did not say, "By cesarean section." Or that the soldiers would cut branches off trees and use them as green camouflage like modern-day paratroopers. Mustaches hanging over their lips, they make their prophecies. A phantom child wearing a crown. Birnam Wood! Who'd believe it? Fortunetelling leads us deeper and deeper into temptation, absorbs us, then hurls us mercilessly together with the brute facts, which are in their own way impartial. The unthinkable comes true, now frighteningly obvious. The fog of the rough draft is suddenly dispelled by a gust of wind, and you're left face to face with the built-in ending promised by the tale, more direct and simpler than we had ever thought or imagined. We are overwhelmed. The clarity and precision of this reason-defying *fait accompli* tells us, through Shakespeare's lips, that peering into the future will only make the calamity worse. It is not a deception that deceives us but the truth that has grown up around us and overtakes us precisely because of the precautions we took to avoid it, having once spotted it at a distance. Isn't that why our fate is always vague at first, ambiguous, allegorical? And don't the witches make use of this? Until everything is played out. I beseech you—don't make predictions! What's the point of hints? Where is there a man not born of woman? Where's the cesarean section? What kind of forest comes down from its place on a mountain and moves like a wall toward Macbeth? . . .

We encountered a forest like that in the Swiss Alps. It was a forest on the offensive, one that left us with no memory of landscape apart from an image of black spruces assaulting the mountains, one after another. The higher and steeper the mountains, the sparser the trees became, raked by a counterfire of stone, wind, and ice, like machine-gun bursts point-blank from the bare upper slopes and the cloud-capped peaks. All the same, fresh coniferous troops kept clambering up to aid and reinforce them, unaware of the last fatal charge. The forest could not conquer the mountain—that was beyond its powers—and it fell in battle, sacrificing itself to maintain the charge it had attempted, one to which the mountain seemed to have assented, since it needed it for its own light, feathery ascent to the heavenly heights where it suddenly turns, snarls, and hurls the forest back with cold outrage, no longer needing it, a feeble literature no match for those heights. In that peaceful valley, gazing at the tragedy being played out by the high mountain range and the decrepit, smoke-befouled spruces that rushed almost hourly to storm strongholds known to be impregnable, I was inwardly on the side of the trees. I cheered them on. What persistence! Everything that we had ever striven for seemed to be achieving its culmination here. As they had once before in the public house, the paths of our innumerable accomplices and comrades merged and came to an end here. One after another, they drag themselves to the top of their tomb. Some crawl. Some are bent. And look, that one is already turning somersaults, roots in the air, reaching the ice. What an impulse for the impossible, that same readiness to risk everything for flight and ascent. There was something religious about their severe, subversive labor. . . . But there and then I was shown, to my sorrow, the daring and the inconclusiveness of language which every writer's intention hinges on, clings to, and falters on. What, from a lack of experience, we take for style and artistic idiosyncrasies, is only the latest doomed effort to exceed the bounds of the language and the space allotted us and, in a frontal attack or a flanking maneuver, finally to speak of things that cannot be spoken of. Language is about what's beyond its own grasp . . .

Wasn't that what haunted Pushkin in his fruitless attempt to create an escape through poetry? And isn't the same thing to be found in Lermontov's "Mtsyri" ("The Novice")?

> Long, long ago I dreamed
> of seeing distant lands,
> to learn if earth was beautiful,
> to learn if we were born to this world
> for freedom or for prison. . . .

It turns out that we are born for prison. And yet all we think of is freedom, escape. . . . Escape, even if it fails, is a component part of any poem. And if we take a larger view, it is part of any human creation. Escape is our crowning glory. Oh, yes, we are all kings! Unseen. Unheard. It's not we who flee. The soul's the fugitive. . . . How many prison legends, intricate as carpet patterns, instruct us in the technology and poetics of escape! . . .

"Don't argue with me. You haven't been in prison as long as me. You couldn't come close. No guts . . . But I knew a thief who was sick of this life. And do you know what this guy dreamed up? He swiped a saw from the kitchen, and as soon as the sun went down, he and a couple of other guys started using the saw he'd swiped to cut a timber pine, or—I don't remember exactly—maybe it was a big spruce, a hundred years old, which was about thirty yards from the forbidden zone and which the guard staff had overlooked. They rubbed soap and sprinkled dirt on the saw marks. . . . On the third night, they climbed up the tree and sat there, swaying on the mast. Down below, their friends cut the last anchor line. That guy had everything figured out—the angle of the incline, the length of the fall—and at four o'clock on the dot the goddamned tree starts crashing down like a bomb. It smashed down the fence and all those fucking tricks, traps, and wires. The trunk stayed in the zone, but the top of the tree was on the other side. . . . And not a scratch on them! They just sailed through the air and

landed. Then they hopped away like mice. The branches had pro-
vided the spring action. By the time the screw had woken up, put
the whole garrison's ass on military alert, shot up two flares from
a launcher, making it bright as day, they had already put three
hundred yards between them and the camp. The guard shot the
other guys down with his rifle, but Khadzhi-Murat—that was his
nickname, Khadzhi-Murat, though his real name was Vanka
Muratov—had already taken to his heels and was gone like the
wind. . . . That tricky son of a bitch had rubbed puppy fat on the
soles of his boots, and the German shepherds wouldn't go after
him. You could do whatever you liked to those dogs—shoot at
them, beat them, they'd just whine, crawl on their bellies, but they
wouldn't go after him. The smell of the puppy fat was stronger
than their training, and they would not follow that trail. They
were no fools.

"Something pretty interesting once happened to me too. I
crawled on my belly across the forbidden zone, cut a square hole
in a plank in the fence, and had just stuck my head through into
freedom when all of a sudden I was face to face with a dog. The
dog was on one side, and I was on the other, on my hands and
knees, with a knife in my teeth. We stared at each other; neither
of us made a sound or a move; we must have looked at each other
for a whole minute. Then the dog walked away, with its tail be-
tween its legs. It didn't start barking. . . . But after that other
escape I told you about, instructions came from the Kremlin: all
trees in the forbidden zone, as far as the eye could see, were to be
cut down, roots and all, the bastards. Since then you can't find
any decent wood in the zones. They're too worried about escapes.
. . . Who? Khadzhi-Murat? How did it all end? . . . They picked
him up near Kotlas. Still, he did make it as far as Kotlas that time.
I know that for a fact. All the way to Kotlas . . ."

"Thank you very much, Jasnowielmożny Pan, Mr. Russian
Writer! But as a Westerner and a veteran in these matters, my
personal advice to you is, don't believe that vagabond. The valiant
Murat did not jump from a tree. He went through the sewers to

escape the tyranny of the local Gestapo, who, after his first un-
derground escape from the infirmary, were not allowing him to
serve out his last ten years in peace. You're in for seven? Ah, so
you still weren't here then? But I was! Picture this. You know the
woodwork shop. And the stream that just flows by, oblivious to
it all. Murat's job was to bring the chemical waste out from the
furniture factory. But what do you think he was actually up to?
He was making himself a one-man sub out of plastic. With ballast,
everything you need, a supply of air and food. It had a paddle he
made from tin cans. He lay down inside and gave the paddles a
turn. The sub went up and down like a sweetheart of a girl who
does what she's told. . . . Now we make couches out of that one-
ply plastic for the other socialist countries to import—Mongolia,
Iran, how should I know? . . . And no sooner had the red sun
gone down than our Vanka loaded himself in that deep-sea bomb
of his and shoved off with the paddles turning. He might have
sailed away down the Mother Volga, if it weren't for one insidious
circumstance. An X-shaped barrier! The fucking thing was like a
filter there at the bottom of the reservoir. It was made of thick
Russian logs. It let water into the reservoir without letting any
foreign bodies through. If he had known that in advance, he would
have attached a bowsprit out in front or some gizmo that would
have cleared the way. But after this episode instructions came from
the Kremlin to replace all wooden underwater blocks with ones
made of welded steel. No one would be sailing out of there any
more. No! It made me cry. . . . Did he drown? No, they resuscitated
him. He'd broken two ribs, chipped a few teeth—and now they
say he's free again, strolling around like the Count of Monte Cristo!

Shots, and a shout: "Man in the forbidden zone! Man in the
forbidden zone!" Abandoning my half-finished letter to Mariya, I
dashed from the barracks. It was a holiday, the day after May
Day, no one was working, and we all raced toward the watch-
tower, where the shots were coming from. Through cracks in the
first fence we caught a distorted glimpse of a zek on the plowed

earth in the narrow enclosure between the barriers. He was a madman; everyone knew him, the camp madman. Wearing a robe, long johns, and slippers on his bare feet, he had made a dash for the barbed wire from the infirmary in broad daylight. Where did he think he was going? He didn't have the physical strength to climb over the second fence, not to mention the other obstacles. He could never have gotten very far in those long johns and slippers. And nothing would have been easier than to lead him by the hand like a child back from the plowed-earth zone, but they had opened fire on him.

They used exploding bullets. I hadn't fought in the war, so I hadn't known there was so much blood in a person. And the beef of us! Have you ever seen a side of beef in a butcher shop? Ours has exactly the same color and composition. That was the first time I had seen it live, and in human form. . . . Riddled by bullets, he had fallen to his knees, that madman in a hospital gown, and raised his hands, seeming finally to have understood what was happening to him. But they kept firing round after round until he stopped twitching. The meat continued moving up and down for a few more seconds, though not of its own volition, but because of the exploding bullets that had struck him and the plowed earth around him. . . .

Everyone from the dormitory zone had crowded around the forbidden zone. It was the 2nd of May, a proletarian holiday, and now look what had happened!

"Fascists!" yelled those who were in for being communists.

"Communists!" They were outshouted by those who had already been burned by communism.

And the guys with no interest in politics hurled the oldest and worst camp insult: "Faggots!"

At the time, all those words sounded like synonyms to me.

The submachine gunners walked across the plowed earth to our zone and quietly warned us: "Disperse to your barracks! If you don't, we'll open fire!"

When picking up that side of beef, those boys, who hadn't even started shaving yet, were trembling in fear, their lips pale, as they repeated their sentry call: "We'll open fire!" It's a good thing that no one was foolish enough to throw a rock over the barbed wire. The crowd withdrew, growling a scroll of meaningless, equivalent curses: "Faggots! Communists! Fascists! . . ." I went back to my letter.

Dear Masha,

You will never receive this letter. No matter how much code and how many circumlocutions I use, it'll never get past the censor. . . .

With my own eyes I have just seen poor Klaus killed in the forbidden zone in an "escape" attempt. He was not quite right in the head, but he was a quiet and sensible zek, an ethnic German from the Volga. He only had six months to go on his sentence—of ten years (for another escape). I didn't know him well, but recently we had been brought closer by a strange situation: the false report of my untimely death.

You remember, when we saw each other six months ago, you told me that a rumor I was dead had suddenly started circulating in certain circles in Moscow. No one knew how the rumor had started or who'd launched it. Later people said that it resulted from a mixup on the part of some Western journalist. Just another rumor. You did tell me that our friends now became doubly attentive to you, sighing softly in your presence, and that Super, good guy that he is, could not restrain himself and said: "Mariya Vasilevna! No matter what, you have to know the truth. A rumor keeps going around that Andrei Donatovich passed away recently in the camp. Do you have anything to drink?" And then he burst into tears. . . . I can imagine what that night was like for you! The next morning there was one call after another to the KGB, who denied the false and foolish rumor with a laugh: "We would have been the first to know if anything had happened. . . ." And, really, none of this did the KGB any good. At the time they even moved up our meeting so that you could see for yourself that I was alive and well. . . . Later you wrote that the whole thing had nearly given you a stroke. But it too passed. . . .

And now picture this: I left the meeting where I first heard that absurd story. I told no one in the zone about it. It was just then that Klaus came back to the zone from the SDB, the strict-discipline barracks. As you know, when someone comes back from in there, we build him back up with plenty of tea. That evening, sitting with friends and passing a black mug around in a circle, Klaus felt a little more like himself and said with a laugh:

"They thought they could trick a fool like me! For three nights in a row, they kept shouting about you, Andrei Donatovich, that you died, you died, you died in the zone! . . . But I'm on to those tricks by now! They wanted me to beg their pardon, so I could be released from the SDB ahead of time and pay my last respects to you! But I'm no fool! I saw right through them! I didn't lower myself. . . ."

I tried to determine the date—when had he heard those shouts? It more or less coincided with that business in Moscow. I asked who was shouting: I wanted to know. The others paid no attention. "Forget it, Donatych," the other zeks said to me. "You know Klaus has a screw loose. . . ." But it was eating away at me. Once again I realized that the KGB was mixed up in it, even though—I repeat—I was aware that at the time they had no interest in my death or in rumors about it. Who else would call out like night owls in the SDB, saying the same thing that was being said in Moscow. Klaus kept telling his story and laughing. "But I didn't believe them, Andrei! I'm no fool! I knew you weren't dead. I knew it was just a setup. . . ."

Our little stove lit his sunken cheeks. They know how to starve people in the SDB. After the tea I took Klaus outside our barracks and, in the dark, with no witnesses, I asked him: "But who was yelling, Klaus? The guards? The supervisors?"

The question amazed him. The supervisors? Not at all . . . So who was it? The zeks? No, there weren't ten zeks in the isolation section with him, and they were all good people. None of them had anything to do with those shouts, nor could they have. It was a trick! A cheap trick! "Listen, Klaus, try to think. Who shouted to you that I was dead?" I said, pressing the madman for an answer. "It's extremely important that I know, do you understand?"

And then he calmly told me that two secret KGB agents had been assigned to him for his entire camp sentence of ten years. And it was they who did the shouting. Did you ever happen to notice them? No, you couldn't. They were secret agents. . . . But they went with him everywhere—in the zones, the SDB, the hospitals—one on each side. They were always trying to confuse and deceive him. But Klaus never believed a word they said. He was on to their tricks. Oh, Klaus was no fool! . . .

Masha, now do you understand who was shouting? It was demons, the demons who accompanied poor Klaus. In a strict-discipline barracks, who else but a demon would know the Moscow gossip of the moment? It may even have been the demons who launched that rumor. What a coincidence. And who knows how far the shadow of evil extends over us? . . . As you see, I am alive and well. And six months have already passed since that ridiculous business. It all blew over. But today, May 2, Klaus was killed in the forbidden zone. He only had half a year to go until his release. Could those two demons have convinced him to dash into the forbidden zone? . . . See you soon. Love and kisses. Only six months . . ."

"What time is it?" you ask.

"Half past one."

"Oh, no, half past one already?!"

All meetings fuse into a single illuminated night. But what would be the point of living if it weren't for the meetings that had already taken place and those that were yet to be? "Don't go! Stay another minute!" we say each time, secretly afraid that one of us will go and never return. Even in ordinary life we prolong the fateful hour with conversation or coffee, a game of dice, a restaurant; or you might say, "Read something aloud; I suddenly feel like hearing something read aloud. . . ." It's just to prolong the moment, to delay parting, and to be close to each other until they come to take you away.

But all the same you two don't see eye to eye, and when, moving closer on the bed, she says, "Come sit here a minute . . . here, on the bed," you reply offhandedly, "Why should I sit there? There'll be time for that later. I should run to the store right now, for some beer and bread. . . ."

One sense in which women are better than us is that they usually ask us to sit beside them with no special purpose or reason in mind, just because they want us there with them. A woman will say, "Sit a minute! Stay with me!" "Why?" you ask. Why drag it out? It's almost time for us to go to work. Or to war. To conquer or be killed. But she doesn't change her tune: "What's the big deal? Sit with me a little while. Stay a minute. . . ." Or "Give me a little love." Or—even better—"Marry me." . . . That's the limit!

Have you ever seen a waterfall? It falls without a care in the world and smashes to pieces on the rocks. And we feel sorry for it. Isn't that because we recognize ourselves in it? Falling, falling from its precipitous height like a demon devoid of any faith, it finds every obstacle only an occasion to hurl downward all the more swiftly and relentlessly. Aren't the pauses we devote to explanation in fact attempts to restrain the waterfall? The woman who at that moment offers you her hand to keep you from stumbling, so that you spin furiously in place for a moment, before falling with even greater fury, but now to swim downriver with the current—she's the one who becomes your wife. . . .

"Mariya, where are you?"

"I'm here."

"Where? I can't see you!"

"In the garden. In the street."

I run to her voice. But she isn't there.

"Where are you?"

"In the attic . . ."

I climb up to the attic: nothing but cobwebs.

"Where are you?"

"In the basement."

"Which basement?"

Images from folklore will carry us further and prompt you with phrases like: "And I'm a sapling," "and I'm a duckling," "and I'm your cap." I clutch my head in despair—it's all senseless. You'll never understand anyone. Because your home's long empty, because you never had a home.

Then suddenly they're yelling: "Donatych! Get up! Listen, your wife's here. Does she wear glasses? Then it's her. Go run to the guard shack!"

It had come true. . . .

The man in the barracks most knowledgeable on the subject of women was the sort of bitter clown drunks can sometimes be. He was in for terrorism but was guilty of the most ordinary and believable sort of murder. His mother had taken ill and, as will happen, the chairman of the kolkhoz would not let him have a horse: To take her to the hospital? It's twenty miles. Either she'll come around or she won't, doctor or no doctor. He was drunk; a fight started. The chairman cursed him out and hit him with a whip. But the man was no fool and ran to get his rifle. And there's your act of terrorism. He hadn't shot just anybody but a kolkhoz chairman, a deputy candidate. . . .

In the course of his twenty-year sentence, this terrorist had studied women from books. He had a thorough knowledge of both *Anna Karenina* and *Carmen*. I won't mention his name so he doesn't get slapped with another political sentence. He was a wise man and a bit of a poet, the kind who amuses other zeks with his colorful way of speaking.

"Karl Marx declared that the essence of woman was womanliness. My ass. What the fuck kind of prophet was he? The essence of horse is horsiness, and the essence of sheep is sheepishness. Et cetera, et cetera . . . But what is it we like about a woman if we like her? Karl Marx, a woman is like a shot of booze with a good kick to it. Or, to take something more refined in the style of the 18 Brumaire—Muscat or Uzbek red wine. Each to his own. The best thing about women, Marl Kax, is their gaiety. What we look for in a woman is that she's full of bubbles and fun, and not have anything put on about her. We can do without the put-on stuff, Mars Kal. The happiness doesn't come from the advertisement. There are women collective farmers with a face only a mother could love who can get you hotter than some sophisticated temptress. Even if they look as unfeeling as a marble sculpture on the outside. But they've got that liquor inside, Friedrich Engels. There should be laughter and play inside of a woman. And that's when you find the highest proof, Feuerbach. And a woman without that gaiety is better off being run over by a tractor. . . ."

I agree. Isn't it written that she was from Adam's rib? Flesh of our flesh, bone of our bone. But from a rib: from the side, to the side! A deviation from the rule. One tending toward laughter, gaiety, tears, fire, air, water, and clay. I will form you. Look, the breasts are already appearing! Weaker and hardier. More shameless, and kinder. Noisier and quieter. Drawn more toward the animals and trees. The fish and snakes. Laughs more often, cries easier. Sings like a bird. Sneezes like a cat. Dresses—like a tulip. A divergence from man. Not an individual but a nation. Not a stone but a landscape. Grass. A bonfire. A lake. A road . . .

. . . But what's happening in the public house's other rooms? The same thing. Lullabies. Chitchat. Mischief. The main thing is that no one is sleeping.

"I didn't want to go, Mama. The consul tricked me into it. He says to me, 'What are you afraid of, Vasilev? The statute of limitations has expired. There's no legal action hanging over you. You want to go as a tourist to Minsk? Go if you like. Spend some time with your family. If you like it, stay. If you don't, go back. No one will force you to stay. What's it to us? Your old mother is exhausted. Go visit her,' he says, 'while there's still time. Your father went to the city committee and said, Find my son! my only son!' . . ."

"You're talking crazy, Stepan! We buried your father in '62. . . ."

"How was I to know? The consul swore . . ."

"And he took you in. . . ."

"No, he didn't! That wasn't it! . . . At the same time I also got a letter from you in Minsk. The assistant consul . . ."

"I don't know a thing about that. I never sent you any letter."

"What do you mean? Mama, you said: 'Come visit us, Stepan, there's no danger. Nothing will happen. The statute of limitations has expired. It was confirmed in Moscow, by the Presidium. . . .' You got a confirmation, and I got a ten-year stretch! They took me right off the train, in Brest. . . . And the other letter that came in the mail from you . . ."

"I didn't write you any letters, do you hear me! I had a bad feeling about the whole thing. They kept coming to the house and pressuring me—'Write to Stepan, write to him, he misses you. . . .' "

"So they pressured you into it. . . ."

"And I told them I wouldn't. I didn't have your address. Was he still in Belgium? Where? I haven't heard from him. And they were all polite—'Don't worry, citizen, set your mind at rest, we'll get his address. . . .' But I stood my ground and told them I didn't need the address—I can barely read!"

"But it was your handwriting! I recognized your handwriting!"

"Handwriting, handwriting! I only write Dashka in Sverdlovsk twice a year. It looks like chicken scratches. . . ."

"So what do you think, then? Was the letter fake, forged? . . . And who's Dashka?"

"Your sister, Dashka. Did you forget her? She's married now, with a daughter—in Sverdlovsk."

"Sverdlovsk? . . . Maybe they forged your handwriting. Maybe they touched up your letter to Dashka and sent it on to me. But why was it postmarked Minsk? . . . The envelope was postmarked . . . postmarked!"

"I'll be dying soon, Stepochka. I haven't got ten years to live . . ."

The nights in the public house are very quiet. You can hear the floorboards creak. Or a mouse rustling by. But that's not a mouse, it's a tape recorder ordered installed by KGB Major Postnikov, the head man in Yavas. You'll never see him in the zone—he always lies low, the viper. Still, everyone knows that Postnikov is in charge, an *éminence grise,* and that he installed the machine on instructions from Lubyanka. It was Postnikov who introduced taping in our camp—to listen in on conversations, to learn about connections, channels. . . . The only thing that's not known precisely is where the tapes are sent and how they're made. Valka Sokolov, a first-rate poet, a genius, after a cup of coffee or tea would improvise poems aloud when he was in the public house. Here are two lines of one of them:

> To the soul you're pure ozone,
> Greetings, O zone!

While reciting it, he added, "Record that, Postnikov!"

Later, when he farted, emitting the gas with a terrific noise, he shouted again: "Record that, Postnikov!"

And what do you think happened? They canceled his meeting. Kept him from seeing his wife. What conclusion can we draw from all this? Only one—they're recording us! Valka proved that. You might say: That's impossible. . . . Of course, from a logical point of view, they can't listen in on everyone. Taping is pointless. Ridiculous. Record people getting it on? It would take tremendous effort, and you'd need freight trains to ship all those tapes. Still, new prisoners are always warned: "Watch your mouth in the public house! They're listening to every word you say in there. They have a secret machine under the floor! . . ."

And, if the truth be told, ours is not an ordinary camp: ours is for spies. To be blunt, it's a camp for artists and other wise asses. For especially dangerous state saboteurs. People like you and me!

Why wouldn't they consider taping necessary? Them?! Don't be an idealist. The state's got all the shit it needs for that. It's the first order of business. Questions of war and peace are hanging in the balance. Chekists can get anything for money. From the ends of the earth. America. Japan. And, as a last resort, they'll steal. Did you ever hear of "The Spy Plum"? Do you remember the photograph in the magazine *Science and Life?* A Japanese invention! A plum, an ordinary plum in a cocktail glass. You blow through your straw. There's a transistor inside, an ultra-high-frequency transmitter in the pit. You think our people would let something like that slip past them? They live and breathe for things like that. . . . They have whole institutes for that sort of thing! Whole industries! The Academy of Sciences . . . And so, good people, don't you think that they would install everything conceivable and inconceivable in our meeting house, the latest word in technology? That they wouldn't put the opportunity and the device to good use? Not to do so would be unforgivably naïve on their part. . . . Don't sleep, Postnikov! Turn on your machine! Record, Postnikov, record! . . .

We'll record a conversation too: a father and a son who haven't seen each other for about eighteen years. It seems just yesterday they parted. The boy doesn't remember him: he was raised by an aunt. Fine. But they say you can't hide from the Soviets, even in a root cellar. They found the father. He had worked for the Germans, was sentenced to death, with the usual commutation to twenty-five years, firm. He cooperated with the Chekists. Within limits and without any loss of dignity, he played it both ways. Still wet behind the ears, just starting out as a lieutenant in a small border-guard unit, his son was respectful, well mannered. The father was hard as nails, the son was still a kid. . . .

"This is an order, Alexander—don't come visit me any more. There's no need to. And don't write me any letters—I can live without them. I know our system as well as you do. I served in the army, I went to school too. . . . Don't stand out in the crowd! Do your job. Do an honest job, as befits an officer. I can see my past causing you trouble down the line. If it hasn't so far, it's just an oversight—but it still can. It still can! Beat them to it—renounce me. There's nothing shameful about that. You have my blessing as your father to do it. Inform your commanding officer. Stand up at attention at a meeting and announce, 'They hid it from me before, and I thought he was dead, but now that I know the truth, I don't want to call that foul traitor my father any more!' Say that—'vile,' 'contemptible'! You have my blessing for it. Join the party. Live a quiet life, like everyone else. Don't send me any packages, just renounce me; your aunt can send the packages. Remember, you're carrying on the family name. And no emotion when I die. Work your way up. Carefully. Take it slow. Don't push it. You're already a border guard, that's one! An officer is two! Join the party, that's three! . . ."

Record that, Postnikov!

But Major Postnikov has no need of such trash. He knows it anyway. The father works for him. He wears the armband, he sings in the choir. If the son follows his father's orders and makes a career for himself, he'll be another Major Postnikov. Is that worth taping, though? The father could not help bragging to both sides, ours and theirs, that he had advised his son the lieutenant (a lieutenant, mind you!) to join the party. . . .

What's wrong with that? The father is right in wanting to inscribe and immortalize himself in posterity, after what he suffered because of the Germans: Let the boy do well, even though my life has been ruined. That's intelligent. Legitimate. A concern that the family not die out. Everyone wants to live. The authorities can understand that. The son is not responsible for the father. He has made his way in the world. Good boy! . . . As one of my cellmates said to me about the harmfulness of literature: "I recommend that when the time comes you try to get your son into the military. Put him in military school. At a very young age! Or have your wife do it when he's a teenager. The book's closed on you. You'll never live this down. But it's your duty as a father to be concerned about your son, so that he turns out to be a decent person. He might even reach the top, become an important officer. The warden of a prison . . ."

"What, my son?! Better that he . . ."

"What's so bad about that?" he said, bristling. "Look at Trayan. He's a smart guy. Educated. In charge of all of Lefortovo. And I bet the women go for him! I'm telling you, being a warden is a respectable job. Trayan's a colonel!"

As I listened closely, I began to understand what makes the world go round. What do you think it is—bayonets? fear? deceit? Not at all. Nothing of the sort. It's our country's great and unique class unity, one that is stitched together with living thread and an iron needle, making an unbroken and untarnished bond between KGB people, party members, industrialists, generals, lieutenants, and the lowest World War II collaborator rotting in a camp. . . .

Even Postnikov would agree with me on that. He had a new prisoner yanked one night as a preventive measure and blew his top at him. "I don't understand young people today," said Postnikov in distress, sadly clasping his hands. His hands were pale, his eyes vacant. In all those years I've never actually seen Postnikov myself, but people tell me he's a snake. "You kick up a fuss with all those 'ideas' of yours, samizdat, Czechoslovakia. You run around cackling like a chicken about to lay a rotten egg, if you'll pardon the expression. The foreign radio stations make up stories about you—'dissidents,' they call you, 'human-rights activists,' 'heroes.' . . . But what kind of heroes are you? That's nothing but talk. Harmful talk. Your brains are out of whack. You don't know life. You don't even know what you want. And you've been to school. You graduated from the Institute. You could have become an engineer. A factory technician. Shop foreman. You'd have a co-op apartment. A young wife. A beautiful home. Leningrad. Architecture . . . But I advise you to behave yourself in the future. . . . We've got all sorts of lowlife here! There's even some 'writers' here. Yes, yes, I know, you've already met one of them. Beware of contact with him. He's a terrible person. A total anti-Soviet. Stick close to the working class. Yes, of course, there are even some of them here—a black sheep in every family. What can you do? This isn't a health resort. Some of them were up to their elbows in it—mass executions, gas chambers, Buchenwald. And they're suffering the punishment they deserve. But they're people too. Like anybody else. They work. They fill their quota. They're reforming. You can even understand their side. They were trying to save their own skins at a critical moment in history. They adapted to reality as it was. Of course, they didn't understand everything, they made mistakes. And now they're paying for them. But still, you can see how it might happen. It's natural. Human. But what's your excuse? People like you—'ideologicals,' 'politicals,' 'writers'—I give up. I don't understand. . . ."

"I don't understand," says Postnikov with a sigh, somewhere far away, on the other side of the barbed wire, at the other end of the tape. And all this spreads in circles through the meeting house and the zone, like a slow leak from an immense tape recorder. . . .

"Did you hear that? It's a mouse again!" says my wife with a smile, pretending that the tape was a mouse.

"Yes," I say, "probably a mouse . . ." For some reason mice breed in our meeting house. It's the food, of course. All you could want. And so they squeak, and poke around. Mice are mice. There's nothing special about that. . . .

Something really did run past squeaking. . . . The reel must be jammed, or the tape ran out, or it's not winding right, or it squeaks on the turn. That sound makes you feel ill-at-ease. The machine is dying, secondhand, written off, good enough for the likes of us. Maybe they could use it in a camp? Still, you can never be entirely sure—maybe it was a mouse. How can you ever know? Maybe— by some mistake—it actually was a mouse! . . .

We will not, however, give in to illusions, my friend. Or let ourselves be charmed. A mouse makes you diffuse and scattered. You stop paying attention. Here you have to maintain control over yourself. No matter what, we won't say anything risky in the public house. We'll talk all sorts of nonsense and, as the saying goes, write on water with pitchforks, and not say anything real. We'll cry, but we won't say anything real. We'll grit our teeth, we'll despair, triumph in our fantasies, love, die, and be buried, but we won't say anything real there. . . . In this situation, all that we'll say, my friend, are things that will stand us in good stead when they're tape-recorded. And, to be cynical, I'd even say that we'd be better off if those weren't mice but tapes, KGB Major Postnikov's snakes of tape. . . . Listen, Major, imagine that when we're in each other's arms our minds stop functioning, that we don't hear your rustlings when we're discussing mice. No, you take the snake of misinformation we give out for an inoffensive mouse caught in a trap. Grab it, swallow it. Swallow it live! . . .

Something snakelike does indeed crawl into your soul. I speak sadly and seriously as if I were revealing a state secret. And to her frightened eyes I make a gesture, saying: Don't panic! Don't! It's a trick!

"I'll tell you a secret," I say, "but not a peep to anyone. Lately there's been something I can't understand about Major Postnikov. He's supposed to be a major, an educated man. With many years of service. Rumored to be intelligent. He knows people. A psychologist. But for some reason people like him consider a writer the worst of all criminals. Nothing could be worse. Many prisoners can't even bring themselves to walk over to me because of what they've heard about me from the officers and guards. To say the least! "A total anti-Soviet!" I'm treated like a leper. . . . There's one cannibal here. Don't laugh, he's a real cannibal: he ate his friend after they made their escape. . . . But in the KGB's eyes he's a babe compared with me. No, I got the story wrong. They didn't eat the third guy, they just drank some of his blood. That was somewhere in southern Siberia. They were dying of thirst. And they quenched that thirst—on his jugular vein. They didn't go another two hundred yards before they came on a stream.

I feel filled to bursting with camp stories. And I tell them to divert attention from the truth. Sometimes I break off. But the

task at hand is something else—to anticipate Pakhomov and out-
wit him.

Or, just recently, there was this guy, a real worker. In for actual
military espionage. What kind of espionage? A pitiful attempt.
Not done out of conviction—he just wanted to make a few dollars.
He'd read enough of Sheinin, Ardamatsky, the Soviet press. And
he'd barely arrived when they warned him, in headquarters: Don't
associate with Sinyavsky. I might infect him with syphilis, bourgeois ideology. . . . In other words, writers are now worse than
spies! . . . That prisoner, of course, did not come anywhere near
me. And I heard about all this indirectly. . . . Meanwhile, that's
fine with me. You can live a more peaceful life in relative isolation.
It's time to do some thinking of my own, about abstract, intellectual things. About the future. Pushkin. The theory of art . . . To
be frank, I'm not much concerned with people and the camp. They
don't interest me at all. I'm tired. . . .

Just to be on the safe side—so that Mariya will not get the
wrong idea and so that no pencil will move in response to something we say—I gesture in the air, using our signal system, drawing
hieroglyphs that tell her the opposite of what I say. Their tape
recorders have still not been equipped with television cameras. As
one of the tougher, criminal zeks summed up the situation, "They
spend eight hours a day on the job, thinking of ways to screw us.
But we're thinking about ways to screw them twenty-four hours
a day."

And so I don't write, I do drafts. I dissect myself. Don't believe
what I say, don't believe my words, believe me: I have plenty
of friends here—no one is afraid here—they punished this pig
by locking him in a clover patch—my head is bursting with
new impressions—it's like a fairy tale—I won't have time to tell
everything—just to remember it all, to contain it: that is why I
speak. . . .

You might well ask: How do you do that—write without paper?
But, with your permission, I will not answer the question. It's a

secret. That's my secret! It could still come in handy. If not to me, then to someone else . . . Our entire face and body are essentially composed of written characters. The nose, for example. Or the eyes. And if words are lacking, there are always the fingers. There are ten of them, after all. Twenty, counting the toes. An alphabet in themselves. A person is nothing but an interjection. All the punctuation marks, all the letters, are within us. We don't write with words or with ink, we write by miming. Like deaf mutes. Ultimately, we can write with spit on the palm of our hand. With fruit juice on our forehead. With a small bird in our mind. With a crane flying across the sky. Just write. It'll reach somebody. . . .

Meanwhile, along with the Easter cake, the night stands watch on the table casting radiant shadows, signals, on all those cups of black coffee, jars, bottles of condensed milk. A wedding loaf . . . It's still night, may the Creator be praised. Day moves, but night, like a sentry, stays in one place. The coming of evening, dawn, sunset defines the progress of the day, but the night has no such image. You, O night, contain the public house and all it contains. And all at once! In your boundless expanse. Night, like a cornerstone in the disorder and vulgarity of the day.

I continue thinking out loud, peering up at the ceiling, figuring on getting Postnikov's goat at some point. No, no tricks this time—openly, the truth, from the heart. Let him edit anything from the tape that might impede his further advancement. But is it even possible to impede Postnikov in any way? He can take what he needs from the tape, all the juiciest plums. But before they part us, separate us, there's still a chance to fix in Mariya's mind and memory all the silver mines and veins of gold I have contemplated so that our wealth does not, without some attempt at opposition and struggle, disappear to no purpose on a tape that may squeak but still does the job. Record, machine; turn, machine! And if worse comes to worst and it actually is a mouse—the mouse will do us no harm! . . .

I will tell the story of the "Buchenwald Tocsin," the anthem our camp authorities forced certain cadaverous prisoners to sing on a stage during the holidays. You'll never hear this anywhere else. A choir composed of people who collaborated with the German military police, Beria's accomplices, war criminals (what better group?), performed a camp requiem for the souls they sent to perdition and for their own. The two shades are close. Those ex-hangmen sing loudly and with gusto, savoring the anathema. Knowing of what they sing, they sing on behalf of the victims who are anonymous but who still demand public lamentation; they sing to reform by atoning for old sins, and as a meager martyrdom of their own. A double, a triple blasphemy, rolling with a passion through the dimly lit, stinking mess hall that is also used for amateur concerts. There's a bitter, perverse pleasure in hearing the undying strains of the "Buchenwald Tocsin" in a Mordovian jail. How fervently those fascists sing! Their faces so gaunt and burned out! . . .

The songs "Lenin Is With Us!" and "The Party Is Our Helmsman!" sound even more menacing when howled from those old men's lips, wide open with fear and greed. What wouldn't you sing for the right to get a parcel or a ruble to spend at the canteen? Back in the barracks after the concert, tormented by ridicule, a member of the choir vainly attempts to justify himself: "Listen, you guys, I was just opening my mouth, I didn't sing a single one of those lousy words. . . ." But then someone else will intone with sepulchral delight, "Lenin is with us." . . .

Mariya signaled with her fingers as if she were playing a scale on an invisible harpsichord.

"Did you hear the mouse squeaking? . . . Still, it's so quiet here. . . ."

What she's saying is: Don't let yourself get too carried away! Calm down! Or she's just tired of this compulsory game played on two or three levels of consciousness, where mouse and snake alternate, change places, and the zone with its phantoms no longer figures as a locale in my as-yet-unwritten books but has become, if you will, their style and incentive. I catch myself feeling that, for the most part, I'm at ease in my skin here. Not just as a person who has grown used to the life around him, but as a writer who has at last found himself in his work. There's a voluptuous pleasure in slipping into this torture garden full of marvelous creations that, in some strange way, are a continuation of my own capricious ideas, my own long, slippery snake-mask. Who could have foreseen it? I could! And my place is—here! This is an extension of what I had contemplated earlier, on lower levels. I am happy to be in a camp.

I realize that, when speaking of the "Buchenwald Tocsin" or Postnikov and his mysterious tape, which I keep trying to locate— or anything else, for that matter—everything, absolutely everything, assumes an irritating, double image in my telling of it. As if this perverse double life that sets words and deeds at cross purposes like the crisscross pattern of a thatched roof, or a woven basket, bore some relation to a form that can at once be identified with me and with the secrets of this house of ill repute. With all its pipes, corners, partitions, at which the all-hearing mice nibble constantly. A shelter tightly covered by a thick gutta-percha skin that includes both the situation and the crushed will of the artist, the life story of the adventurer who, without meaning to, steals as a spy into paradise, a spy who is at one with that paradise. Does it matter how its physical image is designated, described? Taking delicate steps, he surveys his domain with a sharp-eyed gaze like some sort of Casanova. Twisting and turning, the plots casually follow his wind-tossed cloak. He has not arrived and has built nothing. But a long-sought point has been reached from which things become more interesting and cheerful. Why do you think I am writing all this? To share what I've seen? To relate my experience? No, when your soul ceases to be limited to you alone, you lose your modesty and your arrogance, and you slip like a snake into Eden, not for purposes of temptation or knowledge, but to be a part of the body of the human race, to lend beauty and final form to the idea you have found—and that is when all your inventiveness, your writing ability, whatever you want to call it, is involuntarily transformed into the plot of a novel that has all the power of life, love, journeys to distant lands; the villain is already behind bars, though not a line has been written. Simply to reflect on what has happened to us charges both the style and the subject. You light up a cigarette with a keen sense of your own sinfulness. That feeling runs alongside your thoughts, your actions, and your passionate, unnatural impulse to write. . . .

A TREATISE ON MICE AND OUR INCOMPREHENSIBLE FEAR OF MICE

We have mice in our house in France. The situation's gotten out of hand, but what can you do? If there were two or three, we could have lived with it. It would have been our pleasure. Somehow they belong in houses, and they're nice little creatures. Their ears pricked up like a bear cub's; minuscule eyes; a cone-shaped, nosy little face forever in search of something; a long pink tail. I always ask people why mice have tails. Nobody can explain it to me. . . .

Mostly I like mice, and don't have anything against them. It is, however, their nature to hop wherever it occurs to them to hop. They will sit on the dinner table in broad daylight, on the sugar bowl, even though it would seem there are plenty of packages of barley and flour for them. Recently my wife, Mariya, caught sight of a young little mouse on the sideboard. Fixed by her hypnotic gaze, the little idiot kept running back and forth, with no idea where to go or how to get off the sideboard. It slipped off one end and fell all the way to the floor, squeaking in terror. It must have gotten hurt and had the daylights scared out of it, the poor thing. And why shouldn't it be scared! Just imagine being stared at by a colossus wearing eyeglasses and, to compound the horror, moving two of its fingers like tongs and saying, "Tss, tss, mouse!"

My wife is not afraid of mice, and that's the reason we've got them walking over our heads here. Look, there goes one! Look! I'm here writing, and it's running down the shelves of an eighteenth-century bookcase. Can you imagine? Eighteenth-century! Following it out of the corner of my eye, I wonder how soon it will start gnawing through the book jackets, and then what? In the kitchen we leave open packages of flour and sugar, various spices, crackers. Otherwise they'll start on the books! the manuscripts! . . . And as a writer I find that offensive. Why do they have to go straight for the books? Where's their patience, their sense of loyalty? . . .

I've been afraid of mice since childhood. But my wife, Katerina, isn't afraid of mice. "Darling," she says, "they're so little." I don't need to be told they're little. But the smaller they are, the—how to put it? . . . Look, there goes one! . . .

I was not afraid in the camp. Not even of the rats! The rats in our camp existed at the border of the visible and the invisible. There was nothing but scrap iron in the camp, and so what they ate is a good question. But you felt happy every time you saw a rat. They lived more or less on the same level we did. Big, heavy rats. With thick tails. And no problem! I remember clearly how they would begin stirring and darting about before a transport of prisoners arrived. And we would use the rats to figure and judge by: If the transport doesn't arrive tomorrow, it'll be here the day after! Wonderful! But how did they know? Why did they become uneasy? And yet really there was nothing to eat there but iron.

Now I'm a free man and I live in France—Tatyana and I have our own house in Grenoble—but all it takes is one miserable mouse to plunge me into gloom. Not because, like all Europeans, I am afraid of epidemics. It's just unpleasant, that's all. Why here, I think? . . . My wife, Linda, a Jew, trained as a doctor, is always telling me, "Murochka, there are more bacteria in your mouth than you'll find in those mice. Generally speaking, there's nothing dirtier and more infectious than the human mouth. I'm a bacteriologist. Eat some garlic. You're too civilized, you make entirely too much of a few rodents. If you still loved me the way you used to, you wouldn't even think about them. You'd say: Yulya! Yulenka! My darling! Come over close to me! And it would all pass."

My response: "Pussycat! Mouse! Come close to me! . . ." On the other hand, who's this Linda? And where did that Yulenka come from? Your name's Gertrude! You're from Holland, aren't you? That's right, that's right, I always suspected it was Gertrude! But look, my love, they have taken our stove apart. In our own home in Brittany. They have dragged out all the asbestos, polyethylene, and parts a gas stove is made of and are gnawing away at them. You see that, Linda! . . .

"But they're so quiet," objects Barbara. "Like me, just like me! Why are you being so coarse, so tactless?! . . ."

And she bursts into tears.

I agree. I agree with everything. But still I shudder when a little silent gray ball glides along the shelves or speeds along the table or past the bread basket. You don't shudder, Paulina, but I do when I see one. I have no idea why. I'm not a woman, after all. Near Volokolamsk, I was invaded by mice, inundated with them. And I set traps for them regularly, every night. In the morning I would take out three or four dead mice and feed them to our magpie, which had an injured wing and which turned out to eat carrion exclusively—it would not accept bread, potatoes, oatmeal. It lived in a shed with everything its heart could desire until one day it took off. I had a good harvest of mice that year. Judging by the mousetraps, there must have been more than a hundred of them that winter; then the number rose to two hundred, three, four hundred, and I stopped counting. But the magpie had a use and a passion for them! . . .

And now a woman who has more feeling for mice than I do, a dazzling woman with the brilliant fingers of a born pianist, wearing a bright-red robe, her fingernails blood-red, her face pale as paper, is screeching in fear and grabbing the mouse with her painted hawklike talons, not knowing where to run with that warm little ball, dashing about the room, out of her mind, furious that I'm not coming to her aid. Then she finds the solution in the bathroom and flushes the mouse down the toilet. The mouse swims back up to the surface, still alive, soaking wet, hanging on to the edge of the marble toilet with its little paws. . . .

Forgive me, reader. Don't be too hard on me. And don't be scared. I made it all up. There was no such woman with the fingernails. None of it happened. . . . It's just that I don't know what to do about them.

They squeak. They jump. If caught, they'll scratch and fight. They rush about, they sing and dance. O mice, O mice, why am I so afraid of life? . . .

I don't have to go back very far to see myself as a child, locked in my room with the lights on. Oppressed by waiting for my mother to come home. She's always late from her job at the Gogol Library on Presna Street, and I'm always afraid she's been run over by a trolley car. I hold my breath as I sit trying to read, to draw, not to think about anything, but a mouse is constantly scratching, scratching under the shelf. I shout at it, I stamp my feet, I throw a book at the shelf. It falls silent for a moment; then it starts gnawing away again, driving me out of my mind. Or, to my uncontrollable horror, it comes rolling silently out in a little ball from under the shelf into the bright, bright middle of the room. There is something mystical about its ability to disappear and suddenly reappear—silent when you see it and invisible when you hear it. Mice would seem to exist beyond the reach of mind and meaning, messengers from another world we cannot bear—the world of darkness. It's shameful to be afraid, I know. But you can't suppress it, there's no escape. One ran by and then hid. And you can never be sure if it was really there or not. It just preys on your mind—any second now it'll be back! . . . It's scratching. It hasn't even disappeared yet, and it's scratching again. . . .

. . . I can hear that our neighbors to the right, on the other side of the partition, are restless too. Their voices don't reach here but, judging by the creaking floorboards, he's pacing back and forth as if it were a job he'd been hired to do, an old prisoner habit. Who was there and what was going on? I'll find that out later in the zone. My good neighbor, a Jehovah's Witness, will weep for his brother from Kishinev—not his brother in religion, his brother by blood. The brother had shown up once in four years and stayed less than a full day, and even that seemed long to them both. The sad part is not that they failed to come to terms with each other though they were at it all night, but that the next morning one of them is taken back to his power-saw bench while the other pops back to Bessarabia, where he teaches political economy in a higher party school. The problem is that this brother sees the prisoner not as someone suffering for God and religion, bearing unyielding witness, but as a stubborn moron, a sadist who wants to stay in prison, if only to cause his family pain. The brother had done wrong in coming to the meeting carrying only a briefcase, and an empty one at that. He sat at the table as if at a session of the Presidium, drank water from the pitcher, rubbing his forehead to keep awake while trying to talk some sense into his brother and convince him to rejoin the human race. Apparently the zek could have signed a declaration right then and there, one which his brother had prepared in advance, stating that he had broken with the Jehovah's Witnesses—one stroke of the pen and he'd be out the door, freedom! . . . But no, he kept pacing back and forth like a caged animal; his face, disfigured by pockmarks, was darker than the night.

"You should have at least brought a pound of sugar," he says.

"What, they don't give you sugar here? What's the point of lugging sugar around?"

"Other people do. Other people bring things. You must have seen them when you were being let in. Children, old people, all carrying something . . ."

"So what? Those are probably their own provisions—for the three days and the trip back. What do I need that for? I had dinner in the settlement. And tomorrow you'll get a good hot breakfast when you go back to work. By the way, the food situation here is pretty decent. For example, I had a chop and vermicelli for dinner. Not bad at all, quite edible. I even asked for seconds. Compote . . ."

"That's how it is in the settlement. On this side of the barbed wire . . ."

"Are you too lazy to run over to the settlement?"

"And how am I supposed to get there, fly? Over the forbidden zone? . . ."

"I can't believe it. Are you saying they don't let you? The canteen there is just a hop, skip, and a jump away. And I'll tell you, the food there's almost as good as in Kishinev. . . ."

"The canteen's for the free camp workers! The free ones! . . ."

"You know, brother, you're a hard man to please. You don't like the service here? No waitresses? The wrong sort of tablecloths? . . . I'm sorry, but it all comes from your fanaticism . . . your unwholesome state of mind . . . your belonging to that sect. . . ."

And once again he starts nagging his brother about all the harm that comes from those underground meetings, the superstition, the magazine *The Watch Tower,* which had been addling his brain ever since he was a child. That's when he had earned his first sentence—by refusing to serve in the army, making himself the laughingstock of the entire village. His father was so enraged that he came close to chopping his son's head off with his ax. He dragged him out to the courtyard—"Put your head on the well! We've never had a monster like you before in the family." And he put his head on the well and said, "Chop it off!" His mother saved him. . . . Now he has two children of his own and he's serving his third term.

A comrade who holds a position of authority in Yavas, a major with a law degree, literally wept: "It's beyond our powers! Your brother won't submit to moral re-education. Remember that he has only himself to blame. We're not bashful about these things. We'll slap on a fourth term, and a fifth. . . . He abandoned his children. He doesn't live with his wife. The marriage wasn't registered. His passport is blank where it says 'married.' She came here once. But put yourself in our position. Can we encourage immorality in a labor colony, a public house? And so she left empty-handed. . . . She's no better herself, always with the Jehovahs! The Jehovahs! She's always witnessing back home! . . . She should have gotten married to someone else in the meantime. Or started up with some man . . . Is there something you could do through party channels? Say a word to someone? You can see what'll happen. The children will be taken away and put

in a boarding school. Don't you have any pity for them? The
children! . . ."

The head supervisor in the public house is a man with nerves
of steel, but this situation caused even him to shudder: "Citizen,
you're a member of the party, you're an experienced teacher, and
you hold a high education post in the government. You instruct
people in Marxism and Leninism. And you allowed your own
brother to sink to such depths of savagery?! . . . . It's heartbreaking.
The man has no pity for his own children—he's doing his third
term. Still, you should have tried to have a little influence on your
own brother. He's your own flesh and blood, not some piece of
garbage! . . ."

What does "brother" mean? It's just a word. An eternal reproach, a blot on your record. You should try to influence him!
You Cain, don't you see him walking around as if in a cage and
hammering away at the same point again and again:

"You could have at least brought me a half-kilo of sugar. A loaf
of white bread as a present . . ."

"What do you mean—now there's no white bread here?! I'll
never believe that. . . ."

All through the night, a long, futile night, the brothers wrangled
about bread and sugar. They did not raise their voices, but they
would keep at it until Judgment Day and the last Armageddon. . . .

Meanwhile, in our room, Mariya was spinning a yarn, telling
me the story of the chicken. And, I'll tell you, a wonderful chicken
it was, one that must have been sent us as our recompense. For
Yuri Krasny, Mikhail Buras. For the person who did not dare
deliver my final paycheck from the Institute; cursed though it might
have been, it was still owing to me: "I'm not the Don Quixote
type, you know! . . ." And for my childhood friend and schoolmate,
my neighbor on Skatertny Street, a wealthy merchant who was
close to being an anti-Soviet and who crossed the street when
spotting the wife of a man under arrest . . . A war hero, a disabled
veteran who had fought in a penal battalion, said straight to my
widow's face after the trial: "A shame they didn't shoot him! I'll

always be sorry about that!" It is terrible how people immediately change under the influence of fear.

Yes, I know. Not everyone was like that. The braver souls. The altruists. The list of martyrs continues to grow to this day. . . . But at the time, at the beginning, the chicken outweighed everything else. Returning from her latest interrogation, my wife discovered it wrapped in a piece of blue paper on the floor in front of our door, which was locked. A chicken! Who could have brought it? No note, no name. If Egor's friends had brought it for him, they wouldn't have left it like that, unattended, at the mercy of fate, in the corridor of our escheated apartment—in a bright-blue wrapper. It must have come from the military food store on Vozdvizhenka Street. It was like a flash of lightning on a stuffy, oppressive afternoon. I can see it from here, from the public house, clear as day. A fresh chicken! Manna . . .

This mysterious present caused a rift between the generations. One softhearted old woman, a distant relative, an ex-Bolshevik whose prejudices and fear of purges were boundless, insisted: "Throw it out! Throw it out! It's from the KGB! It has to be poisoned! They want to get even! . . ."

Mariya, representing the younger generation, maintained that, on the basis of what she knew from the interrogations, they could eradicate us by perfectly legal means. Nothing could be simpler. They had plenty of evidence. What did they need some chicken for? Those days were gone. . . . The quarrel—and here's the rub—was really about the specific nature of the current historical situation, the two sides seeking balance like the pans of an unadjusted scale. One side said it was "blood lust," and the other that the "tigers were full." To make a long story short, the question of the century—as I saw it from behind the scenes—came down to whether to cook or to throw out the magic chicken that had been deposited on our doorstep in charadelike fashion. . . . In the end the question was, had there been a 20th Party Congress or not?! . . .

The younger generation, as always, was victorious. They went blindly ahead and cooked the chicken. The day after eating the chicken soup, Egor woke up alive and well, without even the slightest upset stomach. Trembling, glancing back, the country had entered a new dimension. And, meanwhile, there was a new sort of stranger in the land, one who came to the house of a person under arrest bearing in his hand not a stone but a chicken wrapped in crinkly paper!

I can feel myself fall instantly into ecstasy whenever I hear about that fragrant chicken, carried straight from a deep freezer to our door in some enchanted briefcase. It's Dickens, it's a Hans Christian Andersen story. "The Cricket on the Hearth." Perhaps that's the reason Catherine the Great wrote to Diderot about the chicken floating in every Russian *paysan*'s soup every Sunday. The chicken, Catherine the Great, the store on Vozdvizhenka Street, and Diderot all came together in my mind—in one bowl of chicken soup. That soup evaporated up to the clouds like nectar forming the Russian empress's initials in gold, while down below, our mouths gaping, we gazed at the light-blue plafonds swirling with muses and cupids which bear her upward, along with baskets of fruit, censers, and celestial buttocks, all of which, by the laws of perspective, rise higher and higher. And, in the form of my own initials, I too am drawn up behind them, the angels and the clouds, to the blue heights, and, intoxicated by the aroma of the soup given to my boy as a present, I no longer notice the mask of Voltaire, a grinning old man, that hangs from the ceiling, arguing with Diderot. "The chicken, the chicken turned out not to be poisoned! . . ."

Needless to say, the stranger who brought it disappeared without a trace. He came, he set the chicken down by the door as if laying his own head on the line, and then he left. Was that the end of it? But it had to be resolved. . . . Ever since that time, the worn-out newspaper cliché "dissident" has meant an aromatic gift to me. Yes, ladies and gentlemen, something has changed in Russia. And perhaps the first "dissident" was that unknown person who brought us the chicken. Say what you will, I measure from where I stand, from my own front door. You can die, and no one will hear you cry out. There was never any goodness in the world, and there is none now. God is all that is left, but God is far away. You have to take a sober view of things. And to accept fully everything as it is: both Yuri Krasny and Mikhail Buras. But someone came and placed a chicken at our doorstep, in shiny blue paper. . . .

"The ice is breaking up! It's starting to thaw!" I proclaim at this crossroads, in this secluded little inn where we are spending the night as if on our honeymoon. To tell the truth, I had my doubts about the thaw back then, and I have them to this day. Still, a stranger did come, bearing a gift. . . .

"Let in some air," requested Mariya. "There's so much smoke in here, you can't breathe. Air out the room. . . ."

I took the hook off, carefully opened the door halfway, and then was taken aback by the sight of Lieutenant Kishka, the head of the guard, on his hands and knees at the far end of the corridor. His chest dangling with medals like a pregnant bitch's nipples, he had taken a bead on our neighbors to the left. How long had he already been sunk in contemplation there—a half-hour, or more? Had he crawled over without his boots on, in just his woolen socks? We hadn't heard him. His eye pressed to the keyhole, Kishka seemed unable to disengage from the sight of copulation, which he reproduced in solitude with his own body like a dog seized by lust. Catching the sound of my breath, the huge spermatosaur tore himself part way from the keyhole without turning his head, which was now red as a torch. Then he dashed back to the guardroom from which he had apparently crawled for a little vicarious pleasure during the dreary hours of his night watch. It was both as if he had never been there at all and as if he had disappeared into the bushes, behind an iron curtain, before I could guess what had brought him here. There was a young couple next door to us that night. I no longer recall why they had been sentenced to a separation of five years, or perhaps it was seven. Their bed was a gold mine for Kishka. . . .

After waiting until he dashed back to the guardroom and bolted the door behind him, I shut the door more firmly than usual, just for insurance, then spat out a stream of the most vicious curses.

"What's the matter?" said Mariya, surprised by my sudden return.

"Nothing. I just thought of something. . . . By the way . . ."

I admit that I did not wish to inform her of what was happening. Why should I? To make a scene? Sound the alarm? Ruin the night? The latter was a possibility both for us and for them. . . . I didn't feel like doing that.

"Everything's all right," I said. "It's nothing. One minute . . ."

Fortunately, the useless keyhole in our door had been stuffed with cotton batting, no doubt by the family that had been there before us. A wise precaution. Cotton batting . . . What a shame, I thought, that it wasn't a used tampon. . . . And that snake . . .

But the question was what to do. Wake the young woman? Embarrass her young, inexperienced lover with unwelcome worries: "Turn off the light, stuff the keyhole, so that tomorrow, if you're going be here tomorrow, he won't be able to watch you"? Tear the veil of purity from the marriage bed, telling them that they're being watched and that everything they were up to in bed was no more than a movie, a sideshow for them?! . . . What's the difference? I'm no oracle. Am I to transform their shell into a punishment cell to which Kishka had private access, like a paying customer enjoying the sight of a pecker pecking away, climbing to improbable, savage, futile spasms (but let the man get a little something while the getting's good). Unfortunately, I'm no moralist. Is it my job to educate that couple, to plunge them into shame and desperation? They're not children. I'd had enough. I let loose another savage old-time Russian curse that rocked the walls but indicated nothing besides our general helplessness. Later on I opened the door a second time, to air out the room. . . .

In fact, the air was so thick you could cut it with a knife. The curses mixed with the stale cigarette butts in the saucer gave off a stench that darkened the air, not to mention the various discharges, digestive and otherwise. Those latter, as if created expressly for these walls, introduced a moral tone into the proceedings. It made me ill-at-ease: *Romeo and Juliet!* . . .

I seemed to feel some residue, like the powder used to exterminate bugs, sprinkled on my hands, my cheeks, all over my skin. Absurd. I felt like washing. Wiping my face with a towel. Even though at moments something spiritual seemed to precipitate out of the air, it was even viler than the smell itself, some dense original sin that was not localized in one point in space but was evenly distributed throughout the galaxy, taking the form of little pox, the kind children come down with; you thrash, as in a dream, trying to wipe it away along with your whole face, but something keeps preventing you. . . .

Once again I think of the poet Valentin Sokolov, who, when the authorities were playing games with him—whether you get to have a meeting or not depends on the way you behave—said, "I better tell my wife to watch out—they're using her cunt to bargain with! . . ."

And that's true. This is a house of commerce. Debauchery. How dare they steal from the mouths of paupers? I wouldn't object if they'd been spying on free women, even in the bathhouse. It's always pleasant to lay eyes on a naked woman, I agree—it's soothing. But here? At death's door? Once a century? Whatever defies reason unhinges you. . . .

Lieutenant Kishka, his medals dangling, had loomed up before me. The guard at the gates of paradise, on official assignment, wearing a short sword, and down on all fours. As if, like some monstrous cephalopod god, he had become envious of Adam and swelled out of his orbit to cut into that session. To look through a keyhole. At a perineum. But why?! I cry. What did you create him for if you planned to have him assume the posture of a lumbering animal, an apple in his pocket, the mark of shame? We got along fine without you when we were free people and lived carefree as animals. But here you have locked us up and you come stealing up on us. You rise to your full height here. Every night you inhale the sperm that we release, once a year, our hearts smoldering like censers. Marvel at the sight, feast your eyes! Take it all in! You still haven't seen anything. Not a thing. You have missed it all, Kishka! . . .

Sometimes you drag yourself over to say goodnight to your wife and she's already falling asleep. "You're funny," you say, tucking her in like a child. "Why am I funny?" she asks from her sleep, but without waiting for the answer. And I think: Because I love you. A love that has a sadness to it. Who will tuck you in, my love, when I'm not there? That's all there is to it. Done thinking, I walk away. . . .

But dawn is always watchful. It's not dawn yet; it's still a long, long way to dawn. We hide in the depths of the night as in a cocoon or as we do in our coats when it's windy; or, when it's darker, darker still, we hide in the tingling darkness of electricity. But dawn is approaching, and it is already afoot, invisible, a ghost in a house collecting tribute from those who live there, for living there as all people do. There were still five, no, six, no, eight hours left. And all the while there's the feeling that someone has died. And that was probably true. There is someone dying in our midst every minute of our lives. Dying in prisons. In hospitals. Or just on the highway. Except that we don't notice. We don't think about it. It happens in secret. All during our life, someone is being led away into extinction. Not wanting to, you look back: Could that have been me? Did it come for me? . . . Here you don't speak of the rope. The rope dangles above us. Here you just smile and ask:

"So, you're still alive?"

"I am. And you?"

"Alive! . . ."

I pace the room with a pendulum's motion, in refutation of the popular belief that animals walk monotonously back and forth in their cages with no idea of their situation, naïvely thinking they'll find a way out—if not on one side, then another. The animals rush from one locked door to another in a manner of which little is known. They take a sniff, then run back. . . . I too would have preserved that bias, if I had not mastered through practice that wisest of laws—the slow, shuffling pace from one wall to another, which gradually affords us greater breadth of vision, the serenity and spiritual balance that permit clearer reflection on all the clashes and their developmental logic, which could ever occur within those walls and outside of them. Your apparently pointless amblings from one end of the room to the other assume the task of extracting and elucidating meaning, or, to be more precise, this action coincides with the growth of meaning, which happens quite independently of you. It's like tuning in to a call signal. You walk back and forth, focusing your mind, which, distant and detached, accompanies you in all your wanderings. I am convinced this is what the animals are doing. Captured, all hope lost, they do not seek a way out but, to keep from dying, they use pacing as a way to begin resonating with the other levels of consciousness that are always pulsating everywhere, and then they begin living by the laws of literary existence, which does not butt up against the wall but quite simply bypasses it, and when we speak about ourselves, we also listen intently to the beat of universal life, which carries like a recitative and to which our lives and thoughts are synchronized without our even knowing it. Do you really believe that all your thoughts just sprang to life by themselves in your head like worms? A head is such a little thing, and thoughts are so very big. Thoughts come mainly from the air, or, if you prefer, outer space, which flickers in the summer lightning of words you can't yet catch, and so all you can do is turn toward them in time, listen closely to them while lumbering back and forth, back and forth, within the confines of a cage, a cell, a book.

A guitar sounds in the mind, a string quivers in the fog, the source of our troubles, disturber of the prisoner's peace.

Impatiently I ask Mariya, "Do you remember the song I think it was Shibankov sang to us? By the way, they don't sing that song here, for some reason, and what better place for it than here?! . . ."

In fact, I can't sing a note. I have no voice. I use my fingers in an effort to show her what I have in mind, the tune I'm trying to recall. How did the song begin? . . .

"Do you mean 'When I Met You'?' " she asks, reading my mind. "Of course, I remember it. . . ."

"Yes, that's it!"

I kept that mute music going, and, walking in a circle, I recalled the rest of the nice song, so lacking in my tuneless rendition. It's a good thing Mariya had reminded me how it started:

> When I met you, the bird cherries were in flower,
> And music was playing in the park.
> I was all of seventeen then,
> But had already seen more than my share. . . .

There are melodies—not even melodies, snatches of melodies—heard long ago, as if in another life, forgotten melodies, ones perhaps never even known, but which still mysteriously bring back memories, a single faint note causing them to surface. In solitude, prison, foreign lands, those worn or imaginary entries in our early and seemingly lost memory are especially dear to us. It's as if you are walking down the street, in the comfort of a noisy crowd, talking to yourself, delirious with a song, and you become a man on his way to see his girl, the man who murders her out of jealousy and who now awaits the firing squad. So go sing, to the accompaniment of life, your own unique and universal life, and don't worry about how or why that murder happened and whether it was real or not. The criminals have their own repertoire of songs. One of those cruel ballads that, ever since I was a child, have made my mouth go dry and my chest constrict with a passionate, pernicious anguish at my inability to sing along with everyone else. Why do I like this song, then—is there some affinity of souls at work here? Or does the irony hidden in that magic music reach deeper into the heart of a modern man than the old standards? After all, there was no park, no noisy crowds, no music. Nothing of the sort. Still, you go along as if all that had happened just yesterday, and was the only thing that mattered in your life! . . .

"How does it go from there, Masha?"

" 'Afterward, all I could remember' . . ."

"Yes, that's right!"

> Afterward, all I could remember was the flashing lights
> And the cops blowing their whistles. . . .
> I roamed the waterfront till dawn,
> Feeling your eyes burning behind me. . . .

Aha, that means he has already killed her! So, do you think the murdered woman is staring at his back, accompanying him with a vengeful gaze, like Nemesis? That he is tormented by a phantom of conscience which he fears and flees, jumping fence after fence? Wrong! Is that really what you thought? She follows him with an extended gaze, flashing suddenly like a searchlight, a gaze of gratitude and compassion. Poor guy! How much longer will he have to run around in circles until he comes to the promised meeting with her, their rendezvous in the park?

> I heard from the guys that when they buried you
> Everyone cried, cursing the killer. . . .

Which was right, because those were children who were buried. But this time the killer was me, the author. And I was the only one who didn't cry.

> At home I locked the door and looked at a photo of you.
> You were smiling, you looked so alive!

Everyone wept and grieved. But I rejoiced: she was coming back to life! I felt a touch of presentiment: she had been saved! That she had betrayed him, why, with whom—that was secondary and, by the way, the weakest part of the song. But the poetry reigns supreme as soon as he picks up the knife, and hope enters the picture when I catch him and stab him with the words: "She's back from the dead!" His elbows on the table, his face streaming with tears, he asks: "Why did you go and do it, girl? How could that ever be set right? How could you have gone on living, what would you have done with yourself, if I hadn't killed you?" He's not just a thief, he's a murderer! And she's no angel either. But she wanted some beauty out of life. Her heart's desire was to return after death to her initial innocence, to a children's holiday in the park, like *Romeo and Juliet*. Curse all you want now, the deed is done! Go back! Throw yourself in his arms! It wasn't you, it was himself he sacrificed to an unquenched love toward which he now runs, without looking back, its rays illuminating his face with the joy of reunion. . . .

Tomorrow they'll read me my sentence of death,
Tomorrow my eyes will be closed,
Tomorrow they'll take me out to the prison yard . . .
And that is when you and I shall meet!

When you and I met, the bird cherry was in flower. . . .

Then the same thing all over, from the start. As if a scratchy old record were spinning in your brain, starting the same life cycle each time, if not for me then for someone else—what's the difference? The only thing is, you and I didn't meet in the park, a fashionable resort, or a restaurant by the sea. . . . You don't see, you don't know where we are. . . .

"Excuse me, please," says Mariya, interrupting my thoughts. "What would you do if they allowed us a meeting in a morgue? I don't mean that figuratively, I mean in a real morgue. For three full days. Or one hour. Would you refuse it?"

"Of course not! Anyplace is good. . . ."

"Now I see. . . . Not another word. We are in a morgue. Do you understand? In a morgue. And we're putting it to good use. . . ."

Night is longer than day in the meeting house. But even though it is multiplied by all the sleepless nights ever spent here, the night finally begins to pale and cease to be. It's time! No joke. The hours are numbered and the doors are locked. There's nothing left to be said. Dawn at last begins stealing in through the window, an unwelcome guest expected since yesterday. It joins with the silence, making drinks bitter and embraces tighter, more passionate, whipping you on not to lose this last chance at farewell. It's as if you were offered the opportunity to drain the "cup of life" in one gulp when you were given this shame-stained, panic-stricken room for the night. Then you begin to realize that the flesh, or, how to put it, the animal principle that, under normal conditions, instills shame in you, or, if you're lucky, pride and good cheer, is not the plaything of the idle rich and sensualists, but while you're alive is a way of finishing what words could not fully say to your sole confederate and deputy on this earth in the time God has allotted her.

"The language of the eyes," the novels say, "can be more eloquent than that of the lips!" And it can. Anything can happen. Lips. Eyes. . . . But now I will venture a generic definition. All the eloquence concentrated in you must be shifted, for want of a better analogy, to a language of gestures, which, moreover, are expressed mainly by the lower half of the torso, which can neither see nor speak. This would be an unlikely thing, were it not for the instantaneous instinct of self-preservation, which abandons us to grasp at straws at moments of extreme danger. Like blind kittens, like earthworms, we squirm and grope at each other, seeking the clearest way to send coded signals about ourselves and the sufferings we endure. Without diminishing love's enchantment, this makes it more meaningful and kinder. And if, as they say, death results from sin, then here, where death is close at hand, the balance suddenly shifts in sin's favor, as if this sin brings aid and salvation and is a prayer for help, a confession, and an incantation all at the same time. From a hearty frolic it can turn into a dialogue initiated by a single touch, a dialogue that can, in principle, even find expression in words, that most approximate and oversimplified means. Words something like:

"Know who I am and forgive me. There's no one else in the world. Nowhere, never. You are the only one who understands. Think of me before the end. Until the end. Think of me. Think of me. Understand me, think of me. . . ."

No, I have no intention of doing a literal rendition of that ancient pantomime. I know that everything would get lost in my version. Intellectual shadings automatically lend the tale an irrelevant technical aspect, almost an invitation to look past the words to the cadences and spasms of the genitals. Meanwhile, in the circumstances at hand, it is not part of my task to do engravings of sensations, no matter how pleasant, but, rather, to render the logic of what transpires within these wailing walls. People do not take delight in life here; here they part company with life, bid it farewell. Here people carefully bury their hope: but what if that hope should suddenly begin to sprout?! . . .

This logic is not, however, translatable into any intelligible and articulate language that would make sense to anyone except for those who take part in the rites, because, delirium incarnate, that logic is inarticulate and violates the limits of our nature, our mind. Still, you might ask: What did he say? And what was her answer? . . . Here there are no divisions into "he" and "she," no questions and answers. The question is an answer. And here sex is on an equal footing with death. At last! . . . Just what I've always been waiting for. Here they coincide. It is not laughter but death that frees my lips to speak of the forbidden. And to fall silent. To disappear. To dissolve in the brilliance of approaching day. That illumination of mind lasts only an instant.

"Think of me," you say. "We're parting now! We won't see each other again. You have to understand that! . . ."

But once again you do not say anything real, you just drone on and on, waving stumps for want of hands, and the meeting is nearly over, and you, you nitwit, you slept through it all without managing to get anything said. You start telling it all over again, from the beginning, from the end, you beat your head against the wall, you hunt for words, you invite it back, you complain, and you console. . . . For the most part, that exacting ceremony is well known to all and what is curious about this kind of poker is that two-of-a-kind is as good as a full house. A little boldness goes a long way. . . . This is not done out of conceit, but because you haven't got anything else left to your name. You have no tact. You're as nervy as a cardsharper caught in the act, and what you figure is that she's a cardsharper too. Two cardsharpers, and no one else in the game. Two of a kind, we understand each other. . . . And this final argument makes what you say convincing, because it moves to root you in life by vaguely illicit means, despite there being every indication that you do not exist. Your shamelessness is the sole self-evident proof that you do exist. And it is a sign of the trust between the two of you.

"Here! Take me as I am. This is what I'm like!"

And, as if in response, an age-old tremor comes from the walls. Cries and psalms. How can this be translated into intelligible language?

"I'm so grateful to have been able to live my life with you, the rough and the smooth . . ."

"Will you always remember me? . . ."

"Will you come here again? . . ."

"Do you remember the trip we took to the North? . . ."

"Will you remember me when I'm here dying alone without you? . . ."

The rest—the rest she can think of herself. And she can do as she sees fit. It's all over for me! Crushed, slandered . . . Furious that it's all over, you are no longer manifest as a person, a member of society, but as an appendage of yourself, an intellect that is possessed and which continues its harangue with those same thunderous verbs: "Believe! Understand! Remember! Stay!" A high-flown, almost tragic tone, though one, I assure you, entirely without foundation. Still, in the end it has become clearer to me how children are actually born, and what conception is, in and of itself. Your wife has surrounded you. Committed you to her memory. Entrusted you. Understood you. And conceived. It's not so much a matter of genes. Or molecules. But of understanding and memory . . .

They say there are species of fish, and of insects as well, that dutifully die in the act of impregnation, the ultimate goal, for which they strive and prepare. . . . Do you think we are so very far removed from them? Or that they don't care about living? Oh, they want to live, all right! But apparently for them death and conception intersect as the dual purpose of existence, the condition for the continuation of their breed and species. Is that true of us as well? I don't know. In any case, I did observe something of the sort in me and about me in the public house, in the camp.

III

∎ ∙ ∙

My Father

I think of my father whenever I'm going up the stairs. It's a tough climb. Wheezing, once again I count the stairs, like the pages of a dog-eared book. I figure the distance. How many landings to go, three or four? We couldn't do any more than that. For me, the hard part's not going upstairs, but going down. You can fall at any moment, lose consciousness. . . . My father wasn't that way. Later in life he would clamber up three or four floors and suffer from shortness of breath, heartburn afterward. He'd take sodium carbonate and say, "Old age is no pleasure, and who'll put you out of your misery." He loved to joke.

I am a repetition of all that as I climb the stairs. It has all happened before—the shortness of breath, the heartburn. Not to me, to my father. He took those steps ahead of me and bequeathed me this wheezing and panting reminiscent of old age. "You're so much like your father!" my mother would say in horror. When I cough, blow my nose, when I turn my anvil-heavy head or twist one shoulder up, I'm him all over. My father did it exactly the same way. When I open a newspaper, frown, belch—him to a T.

We don't think about our fathers when we're children. We're afraid of our fathers; we try to please them when they're home from work. Thinking of our fathers, beginning to feel for them, that comes with age. When you've become a father yourself.

161

It's true, though: I started aging early, when I was around thirty, or maybe twenty-five. Childhood, adolescence, then a long-drawn-out leap and there I was, old. That's why I was able to communicate with my father. But it's only now that I'm beginning to think about him. Now, in France? What's the difference whether you remember your father in Russia or in France! Nothing cuts you quite like that. I'd like to have enough time, to live long enough, to wheeze, spit, and snore him back to life.

Sometimes I become afraid—because there is so little of me. He's ousting me, taking my place—he's in the twist of my back, my neck, the way I climb the stairs. I have no control over any of it. I'm getting lost in the process, vanishing. But then I get hold of myself a little, regain my senses, and think: God be praised—does this mean you're alive, Father? Are you alive?! . . .

Naturally it all began in my childhood, with the semolina of which I was not particularly fond. That's when it all started: a spoonful for Mama, a spoonful for Papa. I was faithful about keeping my promises. It was a ritual, almost a prayer. A ritual performed only when I was eating, never before a meal, and never after. I didn't dare be fussy when I was a little older. We were poor as church mice, and my mother ran herself ragged filling a bottomless hole. But in the bloom of infancy, I saw no limit to my powers and fancied myself of vital importance. Everything depended on whether or not I cleaned my plate. It would loom before me like a volcano, which had to be subdued before its crust congealed and the whole ritual was ruined. Appeals to my nobler feelings and higher nature quelled my disgust, all part of my struggle to redeem mankind's sins. Spoon in hand, I seemed to be liberating mankind from hell—mankind, which through my endless fault had lapsed into childishness, fallen into disgrace, and hung heavy in a whitish mass, stalactites in a cave, a mass I cannot swallow and which clogs in my throat at my first attempt to blaze a new trail for it. No, that was not mere caprice. To do my duty without some reward would have been beyond my powers. But I had it firmly in mind that there was something more serious about all this than a dessert spoon dangling from my hand instead of the ark of the covenant, and right behind it, me, smeared, sticky, and still behind in the battle.

Then Mama would speak edifyingly about the family, responsibility: "For Papa! . . ."

How could I refuse? Now, counting the occasions on my fingers, I can say with assurance that never since have I prayed with such fervor or so sacrificed myself as I did with those spoonfuls of semolina that had to be swallowed every day just to stay even. As if this were the payment due from me for the right to be in the world pursuing my own ends. Like everyone else, I had to earn that right by pulling my weight. But I must not overstate the case. At the end I had the most pleasant of ordeals awaiting me as my reward, and that is the real reason I'm recounting the slippery tale of the semolina here. To foreshadow events would, however, be indelicate of me, to say the least. Again that fear of thinking about the future. There are phases that we do not have the right to alter, and so let us proceed in order: "One for Mama, one for Papa" . . .

I was a little boy, and I did my best. In the belief system I had at the time, I thought I was providing some urgently needed help. I was inspired by the idea that I was of use at home, a home that meanwhile was slowly coming apart at the seams. "One for Grandma, one for Grandpa, lick the spoon. . . ."

Then came other relatives, and friends (fortunately few in number), and my revolutionary zeal to give my all would begin to flag. It was so tedious, so pointless to swallow a spoonful for Aunt Liza, Uncle Fedya, even one for Alik Liberman, a little boy who lived near us in Moscow, on Khlebny Street, and who went away every summer to sunbathe on the beach in Alushta. Seeing things taking a turn for the worse and my strength waning, Mama would use her ace in the hole—Grandfather's dog and cat. It would have been treason not to mention them.

"One for Bulka, and one for Muska!"

We were in the final stretch, the finish line in sight. I would look forward with excitement to the moment when the most sacred names would be invoked to urge me on, the names of those most in need of my help, names she would pronounce as if making a toast.

"One for the Bicycle! And one for the Rifle!"

For them I would have eaten a double helping without the slightest twinge. But they both came at the end of my epic lunch, and that cost them dearly. Sometimes they would not be mentioned by name, for some reason omitted, and the ritual was for naught. Maybe they were held in reserve, like a battalion, for the final assault—I don't know. Or perhaps Mama, who maintained her peasant customs and ways, could not bring herself to make those idols full-fledged members of the family. My mother suspected my father's influence there, and that caused her misgivings. In any case, I too would have felt ashamed if custom were violated and their names used out of order. And to come out with any sort of counterproposal was somehow considered impermissible. The upshot was that my idols suffered from neglect, but my consolation lay in knowing that tomorrow we would have our revenge. True, we would have to start from the beginning: One for Mama, one for Papa. . . . The form was rigid. . . .

Even after I had grown up a little, the Bicycle and the Rifle remained icons to me for quite some time. More precisely, there were no greater treasures in our family. My father's Bicycle and Rifle were held in high esteem by the people we knew, and visiting hunters would smack their lips in respect. The Bicycle had gears that shifted twice as fast as other bikes' and a rear drive chain that had been made by a Belgian company. The Rifle was also a rarity, manufactured by the Western firm of Piper Baillard. Remnants of bygone luxury . . . In my early childhood, I most enjoyed being with my father in Rameno, during his summer vacation, when he would appear riding his bicycle down the country road, dusty and sweaty, his rifle slung across the seat. His bicycle would be locked up for the winter in Syzran with friends of his, the Kurochkins, but the rifle traveled back and forth with my father to Moscow.

I just can't picture him in those days without his rifle. No sooner would he appear than out would come the ammunition belt, small shot from a copper tube, an extractor, power, wadding. I was not allowed to touch the powder but could handle the shot as much as I liked, which is why I remember it so well. How the brass and cardboard cartridges were loaded. How they fiddled with the percussion caps. Bogdanov, a graying electrical engineer from Syzran, would ride over on his bicycle. Dressed in khaki, a silver watch chain in his vest pocket, wearing steel-rimmed glasses that were also suspended on a chain, he was a severe, intelligent-looking confirmed bachelor who smelled of tobacco and dogs. Sometimes I'd also catch a whiff of gunpowder about him, and his eyeglasses seemed to gleam with gunfire.

My father respected Bogdanov for being a man of few words and for his old-fashioned manners, those of an ascetic engineer consumed by a passion for the hunt, which in his opinion was no subject for idle chat. When going to bed, he would simply ask my father, "What time should I wake you, Donat Evgenevich? Three or four?" At midday we'd see him coming back with a red-feathered gray hen and a brace of partridges hanging from his game bag. When eating the game, we'd spit the shot out onto the tablecloth to keep from breaking any teeth. Later my father revealed to me that in the forest Bogdanov would unfailingly limit himself to a single statement: "Shall we break for a smoke?" They'd sit down and take a rest.

My father didn't smoke, didn't drink, and by that time was a worse shot than Bogdanov. And for that reason he was jealous of him, but he did not let it show. His right eye, damaged by the beam of a searchlight, had been failing him for quite some time, a white blotch spreading on the light-blue of his pupil. He couldn't see anything at all when shooting from his right shoulder and had taught himself to switch the butt to his left shoulder, but that wasn't comfortable for him, and he missed quite often. In short, my father was definitely overshadowed by Bogdanov. But they say that, when my father was a young man, he would drag himself home from hunting, covered with woodcocks like bunches of grapes—to the indescribable horror of my mother. Woodcocks, of course, take to the air suddenly; they're small and fly in zigzags. And he'd bring them down!

My father would set himself the most improbable tasks. There was a bit of the failed inventor about him. During World War I, while waiting to be called up, he practiced writing with his left hand in case he lost his right hand at the front. That makes no sense to us here in this diaspora of ours, and strikes us as some lordly air, some eccentricity. First we lose a hand; then we start practicing. We're pragmatists. But he was drawn to things that required strenuous effort. After reading a few books on modern power engineering, he worked out a scheme in which nothing was lost but everything went into outer space as a cloud of will power. An atheist, he screwed himself into heaven like a light bulb, and naturally that fell through. Everything he did fell through. . . .

He liked to discourse on the peculiarities of science during the years right after the revolution, when he himself had worked for a while studying hypotheses that had originated with the people. At that time most of them were trying to invent perpetual-motion machines. The academicians would sigh and throw up their hands: "But my dear man!" They knew *a priori* that such things were impossible, but they weren't quick-witted enough to prove it, since the whole thing worked out quite well on paper. Then another budding scientific genius discovered the secret of extinguishing volcanoes. His idea was dismissed, since volcanoes aren't exactly a pressing problem in Russia. In despair, the self-taught scientist began a correspondence with Mussolini, offering to tranquilize Vesuvius. That connection with fascism cost him his life. My father's guess was that we had let a discovery of world importance slip by us. . . .

But let's leave the ridicule to the professors' conscience. Once a year Uncle Lenya and Aunt Vera, from Sukhumi, would visit us in Moscow. Back then that splendid city still bore its old name of

"Sukhum," and I had heard that many Russians were living there. A chemist whose head was nut-brown from the Sukhumi air, Uncle Lenya ran an important laboratory from which once a year he would visit Moscow to scout around in hopes that my father would put in a good word about his experiments at the Ministry of Defense. Wearing a shapeless white top and white linen pants that for the same reason did not quite strike me as appropriate on him, he was as striking as a Negro with the black leather glove he wore to replace his left hand, which had been blown off by something that far exceeded dynamite in power. One time he and Aunt Vera gave me a set of blocks as a present. All the same, I tried not to look at Uncle Lenya any more than I had to. He was also missing two fingers on his right hand. I'm not exactly sure what came of his work, but later on my father would say that our Katyusha rockets may have been Uncle Lenya's doing. Very possible.

Meanwhile, I too was in tune with the times and trying to invent something useful. To this day I have not given up on my first invention. I wanted to invent a thick gas that could form a perfect copy of a cloud around an airplane. It could float quietly along, high above the earth, sprayed out of an atomizer, and no one would suspect that the cloud contained an airplane! With a cloud like that, we could fly to Berlin and bomb it by surprise.

Another, longer way to Berlin was to dig an underground passage under Poland, take the Germans from behind, foment an uprising. Back then we all dreamed of a world revolution and sought the solution that would work the quickest. . . .

Ideas probably do have to be paid for, and when my father was arrested in 1951, the neighbors' gossip had it that at night he and I were digging a passage under the Norwegian embassy, across Vorovsky Street from our cellar on Khlebny. We intended to use that underground route to ship some espionage intelligence to the West. As a matter of fact, the cellar was sealed after my father's arrest. I was not to be arrested until fourteen years later, and by then my father was no longer among the living. But he left that underground route behind him. What persistence! How long ago all that was—the underground passage to Berlin, one spoonful for Mama, one for Papa. . . .

My father wanted to make a man of me. He was forever the revolutionary, but he did not join the party, and that might have been what saved him. He was in the Left Socialist Revolutionary Party when the revolution broke out, and from then on that hung over him like an indictment, creating an atmosphere of frustrated heroism and long years of hopeless poverty. As I recall, my father was always being purged from one position or another because of his Socialist Revolutionary past. Fortunately, he didn't hold any high position, had no friends, never allowed himself to make any risky remarks in conversation, and he bore with pride his dedication to a cause that had long since excommunicated him. When first questioned, he said to his investigator, "I give you my word as a revolutionary!" The investigator roared with laughter: A wooly mammoth! A mastodon! He would have been better off giving his word as a nobleman.

One day my father and I had come out of the baths and were waiting in the cold for our streetcar. I was whining because I couldn't spot a number 15: "Not ours either!" "It's not fifteen again!" My father remained patient, holding me firmly by the hand. Suddenly an idea struck him. "Because you can't control yourself," he said in an authoritative tone, "here comes a number fifteen and we're going to let it go by on purpose. And if you start moaning and groaning again, we'll let the next one go by too. It's time you started developing some will power." Indeed, we let our streetcar pass us by. I didn't make a peep, and we stood there waiting forever, even though it was late, and cold, and Mama would be worried. The experience did not result in my nerves' becoming any less weak, but we're not talking about me now. My father was always the revolutionary. Preparing for the worst, he instructed me in will power and self-control. And worse did indeed come to worst for him.

My father slept without a pillow, using instead a small headrest thick as felt. He placed the unused pillow over his head, so he did not have to worry about noise. When I grew up, I tried to talk him out of it several times, but always in vain: "In prison," he would reply, "they might not give you a pillow. You can't get too used to the soft life!"

I didn't agree, and I still argue the point with him in my mind. But this isn't about me, it's about my father.

Apparently he was an excellent speaker and knew how to set a crowd on fire. Somewhere in the Urals, in 1917, 1918, in Petersburg, in Syzran. Amazing notes would be passed to him during political rallies. "We'll stretch your Red hides and use them for drums!"—they were expecting a restoration. Compliments from girls: "You look like Kalyaev." He used to quote those notes with a smile: though a failure, he was vain. He had to flee nooses and bullets several times. He was surrounded when the Czechs attacked; he saved his bicycle. Or the Reds would throw him in jail by mistake. He'd fall asleep while waiting to be taken out and shot. They always let him go. . . .

From his gentry background my father had retained the enviable habit of not worrying about food or clothing, and not doing his dishes or making his bed—it would only have to be done again later—thus displaying his cold disdain for bourgeois vulgarity. A revolutionary nobleman knows how to live the simple life. By the 1930s the new men, former shepherds, were wearing gabardine suits, trying on hats, purchasing credenzas. My father considered it beneath his dignity to give any thought to such petty matters, and my mother battled with him over this burning with shame because of our poverty, our lack of rights, our fear, our oppressive neighbors. I trembled along with my mother, but I understood my father's view better.

One time in 1933 Mama, who worked at a library, managed to wangle a discount ticket to a health resort in Novy Afon, on the Black Sea. My father, as it happened, had to stay in Moscow and had no vacation that summer. There was hunger in Rameno, the drive for collectivization was on, and we made rusks out of black bread for Grandfather. My mother and I were crazy about the Caucasus then. I would go out hunting for wild boar with my bow and arrow, dismissing the wisecracks made by one of the resort's managers who had a shaved head that wild boar should be hunted with horseradish and salt. He was simply not a hunter and had no idea what went on in the Africa-like palm and bamboo thickets in the surrounding area. Needless to say, I did not dream of encountering either tigers or snow leopards, which, to judge by Lermontov's "Mtsyri," once roamed those parts. But wild boar rushing from the thickets with their tusks bared were a natural part of those mountains and that health resort, which had formerly been an old monastery.

By the sea, we made the acquaintance of a girl whose name was Medzhi, an aristocratic Georgian from the city of Tbilisi. Apparently I fell in love with her, without realizing that she was older than I and had finished second grade that spring. Now, I would say that she had a certain womanly languor about her, and a faint mustache was already making its appearance on her swarthy and enchanting little face, as will happen with dark-haired girls from the South, who become young ladies much earlier than we can imagine. While our mothers were chatting, Medzhi and I lay on the sand and engaged in a sharp exchange of opinions, a little struggle for a place in the sun. She somewhat flauntingly allowed that they had a four-room apartment in Tbilisi and that her father earned so much money that he had given her a piano for her birthday, which she had already learned to play. But I didn't believe her, probably because I liked her. Unaware of the shame she was bringing down on herself, Medzhi kept upping the ante. I started doing a little bragging myself, so that my beauty would not be alone in talking nonsense. I said loudly, and with pride: "In Moscow we live in one tiny room—in a basement. And it doesn't have a bathroom or a sink. It doesn't have anything. There's just a big iron bed in the middle of the room and a desk covered with my papa's papers. There are two bookshelves, and a rifle hanging on its sling in the corner."

And, indeed, at that instant I could picture with perfect clarity my father's dark little den, dense with cobwebs because he allowed no one to tidy his room, for fear that his papers might be disturbed. But that wasn't the whole truth. I hid a good half of the truth from Medzhi—that on the first floor in that same building, accessible by the same front door, we had additional living space in a communal apartment where my mother and I would hide from the neighbors in the evening and read the newspaper, and where my father would sit and drink tea with us. I seem to have let that second room slip my mind for a minute in order to appear in my full glory before Medzhi. I wasn't lying. I was just idealizing reality a little.

A look of fright shot across her eyes, her lips curled with contempt, but then, catching herself in time, she burst out laughing, as intelligent women do when they detect humor, as if to say that I, a boy from a respectable family, which is how she saw me, had for some reason just made an unsuccessful attempt at a joke.

All of a sudden, my mother suddenly began anxiously preparing to leave and, saying it was time for us to go, took me from the beach. Her face was covered with red splotches, which happened rarely with her. As she lectured me all the way back to the resort for my militancy, I now learned that she had overheard part of my conversation and had been burning with mortification as I put on a show for that little bourgeois girl.

"Why did you lie to Medzhi about us living in the basement?"

But I hadn't been lying. I had just mentally transferred the whole family into Papa's fabled basement so that we could all live together and be away from the neighbors.

"You really found something to brag about! You lowered us in the eyes of strangers! You disgraced us! . . ."

Disgrace? But that sounded better to me: a rusty old bed, the revolution, the rifle. . . . And all the rest of it had basically been in keeping with those proud furnishings and said to all the world that we were poor and we were superior and not some kind of capitalists.

Twenty years later my neighbor, a barmaid, snapped at me in the hall: "Your father's been arrested? Long overdue! He's an American spy! A manufacturer! But you can see his bosses overseas didn't pay him well: your father wore shabby pants all his life. . . ."

And Mama kept saying: "Yes, it's true, we're poor! But it's nothing to crow about. Weren't you embarrassed because Medzhi lives in a four-room apartment? And she's already learning to play the piano! . . . And your father . . ."

She burst into tears.

It was beyond me. The shadow of class hostility had passed between me and Medzhi. We never saw each other again. Mama started taking me swimming at another beach. But I didn't understand my mother. On the other hand, would my father have understood and approved of what I'd done?! . . .

Now, when I chuckle over that misunderstanding—as all we adults laugh at our childhood, as if to say we were idiots then, whereas later on we became intelligent and powerful—I feel like saying that nothing's been lost yet and it still isn't clear who was right in that argument about being poor. It's just that I had come to firmly believe that being rich was bad. Why else did we make the revolution?! . . .

That same summer, while Mama and I were swimming in the Caucasus, my father was involved in an incident that would reverberate for years and leave a scar on him, and on me in some way too. He had left work late one evening and, by Nikitsky Gate, behind a stand where Caucasians with flashing teeth shined shoes and sold shoelaces, he glimpsed a thin, bare leg and a sneaker; he grabbed the leg and pulled out a boy my size and age.

"What are you doing here?"

"Nothing. Spending the night," said the boy soberly, not in the least afraid. "What's wrong with that? . . ."

He was an ordinary homeless Moscow boy, one of many who at that time flocked like sparrows on the city's squares and avenues and by the train stations. By then they were almost an integral part of the ancient capital's color and flavor. But my father was struck both by how terribly thin the boy was and by the sober dignity with which he explained how he had suddenly come to take up residence in a place where he had no family or friends, and where he lived a solitary life by begging, which, for a scrawny little kid like him, and a Ukrainian to boot, was an act of heroism. My father was especially struck by the reason the boy had had his hair clipped short—Efim Bobko (that was his name), solid as a muzhik, told my father that, with the first money he had acquired by begging, he had gone dutifully to a barber shop, to avoid getting lice. It must have been the boy's peasant conscientiousness in performing that last act before going to meet his fate that made my father's heart bleed. The old populist brought the boy back to our place on Khlebny Street. So as not to leave him alone in the empty apartment, he would drag him along to work until he could contact friends and use his old revolutionary connections to get the boy placed in a good Moscow orphanage. We had neither the money nor the room to adopt Efim. Later on, out of jealousy, my mother would say that my father came to love the boy because she, desperate for rest, had taken me away from my father to the Caucasus, but that wasn't true. My father did not lose hope of someday locating one of Efim's relatives and returning the boy to the Ukraine, where he had two grown sisters, Natalka and Dunyashka, though his mother and father were dead. During the famine, his older brother had dragged him along to earn a little money. But his brother had come down with typhus on the way and been taken off the train. . . .

In the end Efim became my stepbrother, even though he lived at the orphanage and visited us on his free days. Skipping ahead, I'll say that, no matter how many inquiries my father sent to Kiev, Poltava, Zaporozhye, and other provinces, and no matter how much he scoured Moscow's hospitals in search of the brother with typhus, he never succeeded in discovering any of Efim's family. Perhaps his sisters had died too or had enlisted in a work brigade and gone to the Far East, where Efim's older brother had supposed

he would find them after a while if he hadn't come down with
typhus. Efim didn't remember the name of the district, the province, or the town where he came from. How would a peasant boy
know things like that? "Strain your memory!" my father would
badger him. "What big city did you go to from your village—to
market, let's say, or to a fair? . . ." Efim would think and think
but could never remember anything definite. Of all the Ukraine,
he knew only Kiev, though he had never been there, had never
seen it. In those years the Ukraine seemed to have been swept
clean. Later on I found out that famine was the janitor's broom
sweeping people into the kolkhozes there. All I remember of those
jolly days is Mama weeping for Grandfather, who had stayed on
in Rameno, near the Volga, where the famine wasn't all that bad.
But she'd become terribly upset when fine ladies in nightgowns
would throw bread and butter from trains to half-wild dogs:
"Throwing bread to dogs when children are dying!" Once again
I failed to understand her motherly intolerance, for she loved dogs.

When I came back to Moscow (I started school that year), Efim
Bobko and I did not become good friends. I wished that he'd hurry
up and find his grown-up sisters and brother. What interested me
was learning to recite Lermontov's "Prisoner of the Caucasus" in
the grand classic style of the Russian poets. I thought there was
something missing in Efim. A quiet boy, his hair cropped like a
soldier's, he had an ugly, prominent birthmark on his forehead.
"A Lilliputian!" I thought, engrossed in *Gulliver's Travels* at the
time. There was a sort of impenetrable wall between him and
everyone else.

He liked it in the orphanage, where he studied with a will, going
from one grade to the next with commendations, a model Young
Pioneer, as he was expected to be. Efim outstripped me in political
development. But for some reason he didn't read the books that
in my naïveté I pressed on him. To do something nice for him, I
copied out some passages from Gogol's *Evenings on a Farm near
Dikanka*. But Efim's colorless and somehow boiled-looking eyes
were not even drawn to Gogol, as if all those Ukrainian cottages,

and those Ukrainian boys and girls dancing the Gopak had nothing to do with him. It was only the poetic epigraphs to *Evenings on a Farm near Dikanka* that caught his attention, but the songs and humorous sayings he copied in his notebook did not strike me as very witty.

> Poplar, poplar, don't be sad
> That you are so green.
> Cossack, Cossack, don't be mad
> That you are so young.

He would copy everything painstakingly, unsmilingly, as if he were discharging a duty toward his native land, alien and distant, to which he had no intention of returning. I was jarred by his coldness to Ukrainians. But he was doglike in his attachment to my father, and even though that too went unexpressed, you could feel it there somewhere in that boy, silent and still as a stone.

After a boring day together, after dinner, our duty done, we would see Efim off on his way back to the orphanage. He seemed relieved to be free of us. When saying goodbye, we would give him twenty kopecks for the streetcar—ten for the trip back and ten for when he came to visit us in a week, on his next free day. At one point Efim revealed that he had been covering that fairly short distance on foot and putting the money away for some more opportune time. That was unpleasant, because he would invariably refuse any other money, no matter how modest the amount, but this money, earned by honest labor, he accepted. In effect, that meant he was coming to see us once a week for those twenty kopecks. "Let him do as he sees fit!" was my father's judgment, but I could see that Efim's plodding, peasant thrift was not to my father's liking.

After saving up for about three years, Efim suddenly went out and bought a camera, which he seemed to want not for childish amusement but for some unclear, long-range purposes, maybe for the trade that he should have been learning since childhood, or to earn a little side money. I simply don't know. It was a mystery: the orphan lived by some plan of his own devising, one that was inaccessible to me.

Over the years he came to see us less often, but before the war he came to say goodbye, after graduating from eighth grade: he was enlisting, leaving to study at an army music school in Klin. "An army music school?!" It turned out that Efim played the trumpet. "The trumpet?! If you'd just go to a technical school. We'd support you. . . ." Didn't help. Efim mentioned other children from the orphanage who were also enlisting: they'd be given uniforms, food. . . . It was too much to understand; we were going our separate ways. Once again, restraining his irritation, my father made a gesture of dismissal, saying, "Let him do what he wants! . . ."

. . . Efim reappeared on the horizon at the very end of the war. I was serving in an army air-force unit at the time, stationed outside Moscow, taking correspondence courses in literature; he had come back after being discharged, and our paths crossed. He had dropped by Khlebny Street to see my father. Discharged after suffering a severe concussion at the front, Efim wore a hideously tattered army topcoat that was too short and yet hung on him like a sack. A girl he was friendly with from the orphanage had somehow made her way to Klin, and he was hurrying back there, but we had a few minutes of real talk, our first. We found common ground in cursing the army and the officers. He puffed greedily at his hand-rolled cigarettes, coughing horribly, and, as if apologizing, explained that he had learned to smoke at the front because cigarettes killed your hunger. I had never before noticed any such malice in him, open and pained, lively and distilled. As if the war had plowed him up again, bringing his bones to the surface, where they now jutted out in all directions, like broken spears. Efim disappeared again. A few months later my father received very upsetting news from him, and now I am coming to the point of this detailed account. Unfortunately, the letter was not saved: my father was quick to destroy that document, which could have endangered Bobko. I won't attempt to re-create its style, but will retell it in my own words.

In this letter, Efim asked to be forgiven for having deceived my father ever since that day when my father had dragged him out from under the shoeshine stand. This was the reason he had visited us less and less often as he grew up, even though he considered Uncle Donat a second father to him. Efim couldn't look him in the eye. And later on he didn't have the courage to confess his deceit: he was too afraid of offending a straightforward, honest person, a "true revolutionary," by revealing his ingrained lack of trust in him. Efim wrote that he was the son of a kulak. They had been dispossessed as kulaks in 1933 and exiled to Siberia. He had no grown sisters in the Ukraine. He had no one there. He had lied about not knowing the name of his village, to keep his trail from being picked up. He had pretended to be too young to remember the district, the city, the province. And, who knows, we might have learned that there was no such village in that place and never had been. Moreover, his last name wasn't Bobko. And he didn't have any older brother who'd come down with typhus. . . .

What happened was that he had been deported by train to Siberia along with his brothers, sisters, mother, and father, who had been dispossessed as kulaks, and some other old people. They were being taken there to die of hunger; on the way, Efim had escaped and hidden under trains. His parents had given their oldest boy their blessing—"Run; maybe you'll survive. . . ." And then he went over it all again—Uncle Donat, the lies, the shoeshine stand by Nikitsy Gate, the seven-year-old boy hiding the secret of his strange genealogy from the whole world. . . .

"Did you write him?" I asked my father when he had finished reading the letter with a short chuckle.

"Of course I did. He didn't answer. I'll write again and try to track him down. He may have moved somewhere from Klin by now. . . ."

But Efim hadn't moved. From an old friend of his we knew at the orphanage we learned that Efim Bobko had died in the hospital in Klin from the aftereffects of his severe concussion and from the emaciation caused by hunger. . . .

How good it was to go hunting with my father in woods I'd known as a child. He'd walk up ahead with his rifle, I'd follow behind with no rifle, playing the role of pupil, and I'd carry the game if there happened to be any. But we practically never came back with anything: as a rule Papa would miss, accompanying each shot with a hunter's quip: "In the air, in the bag!" All the same I'd be shaking when I asked him, "Papa, are we going hunting today? Will you take me with you? Let's go."

My father was able to roam the woods for days, or weeks on end, saying that somehow he breathed freer with a rifle in his hand and could think more clearly about everything that needed serious thought. No doubt that was his tribute to tradition—his youth, his gentry ways, his enthusiasm for the "people" and revolution. . . . In old Russia, hunting by and large was considered the privilege of landowners or visiting shootists. Of the other estates, it was only eccentrics, dissolute philosophical types, who took up hunting as a pastime. . . .

But all I had to do was launch into some wordy discourse and my father would cut me off: "You don't talk in the forest!" It was true: an animal could be hiding behind a bush, or a person. It's better not to run into strangers in the forest. You don't know what they're doing there, or who they might be waiting for. You keep your rifle ready. Anything can happen.

My father had any number of instructive tales about not fooling around with guns. One night someone knocks at the door of an underground print shop but, out of drunkenness, he does not use the signal knock, instead kicking the door with his boot. The man inside is frightened. "Who's there?" "Police! Open up!" The man inside shoots at the door with his Browning automatic pistol. Then he opens the door—it's his comrade!

Before it was confiscated, I once shot the Browning—in the woods, at oak trees. My father issued orders: "Hold your arm

higher! Aim! Aim it!" My arm would jump, recoil from the roar.
I was six years old. Mama wouldn't have allowed it. But my father
had had the Browning since the Civil War; it was legal. Then they
came to his basement room: "Hand in your weapon!" "Look for
it yourself!" But they didn't have to. They just lifted up the pillow—
and there it was. He was lucky not to have been arrested that time.

Once someone had tried to put a scare into a forester by coming
out from a bush and saying, "Hands up!" Without a moment's
hesitation the forester let him have it with both barrels. His gun
was already cocked. It made a mess of the man's stomach. Buck-
shot. But point-blank, both barrels . . . "What have you done?"
wailed the dying man. "I was just kidding."

"Did they put him on trial?"

"For what? You don't kid around in the forest. . . ."

My father came to a sudden stop. He couldn't get Efim off his
mind. "Can you imagine that—a seven-year-old boy and already
living the underground life! . . ."

I tried to imagine it. I was drawn to the terrifying mystery of
life. But my father was thinking of the time that first summer when
my mother and I were keeping cool in the Caucasus and he had
taken Efim to the Moscow River for a swim. Efim must never have
set eyes on a river before; he wouldn't go in the water, and he
wouldn't let my father swim away from him. He ran along the
shore shouting, "Uncle Donat, don't drown! Don't drown! Don't,
Uncle Donat!"

"His whole life was a conspiracy! . . . Can you imagine! . . ."

It was harder on my father than on me, of course. In his view,
the country was going to pieces because it was failing its own
ideals. Efim Bobko's letter and its touching revelation were a knife
in his back. So much suffering came with that scrawny slip of
a boy!

"Don't drown, Uncle Donat, don't!"

A kulak? Nonsense. Then my grandfather in Rameno would
have been dispossessed as a kulak too; he had an orchard, a cow,
a house with a terrace. . . . If Mama hadn't insisted: Hand the

cow over, join the kolkhoz. The orchard went to seed after that. But as a student I found it easy to criticize: Stalin, collectivization. . . . My father had taken a different reading; he took his reading from the angle of 1909. The angle is extremely important in our fate. That's where the dance begins. When still a student, my father plunged into underground work. The first arrest, the break with his parents. His gentry mother fell at his feet: Don't go, you're my only son. She lay down in his way. He stepped over her. Petersburg. Exile, a lark at first. Ozerki. Syzran.

"You read *Crime and Punishment* when you were a little boy. Your grandfather—the monarchist, the conservative—he adored Dostoevsky. But he used to tell me: You're still too young for that!"

Sometimes, under the spell of memories, my father would break his own commandment: "You don't talk in the forest." I would never interrupt. I liked the way he had read Dostoesvky in high school—he'd lie on his bed, read a little, then fling the hateful book into the far corner of the room; he'd get up, walk over to the corner, pick up the book, lie down, and a page later fling it away again. A perfect response to Dostoevsky, the way a person ought to read him. Walking around a room, lolling about on his bed, getting up, going from corner to corner, my father struggled and labored to overcome the aristocrat within him. I'm afraid it wasn't Raskolnikov who drew him to revolution but Sonya Marmeladova. A provincial in Petersburg, a student, an aristocrat by birth, my father had been horrified by the prostitutes.

"You can't imagine it: three rubles. One ruble for the older ones. The same price as two pounds of bread!"

He was bowled over when he read in the newspaper that the tsar had fallen. He hadn't expected it. It was joy. He was in Ozerki. He'd been on Nevsky Prospekt the day before and had seen it with his own eyes: banners reading "Bread!"; crowds of women. He hadn't understood. And the next day he opened the paper and there it was—the February revolution.

I chanced to reread *Crime and Punishment* later on, in Lefortovo

Prison. Strangely enough, it brought me relief; while reading it I filled my lungs with the "special summer stink," plunging into that irritable, nightmare world, like a fish into water, unable to get enough of it. My cellmate grumbled: "You're off your head! Reading Dostoevsky in prison? You should have chosen something to distract you—Turgenev, Bunin. *The Childhood of Bagrov . . .*"

But the stench of Dostoevsky stayed me well. It was not *Crime and Punishment*'s radiant ideas or the goodness it preached that helped me in my despair but its noxious, arrogance-preventing atmosphere, an ax handle over the head. Like cures like. How very appropriate that this was the book that made a revolutionary of my father. I couldn't put it down. . . .

We'd roam through the forest, then enter a birch grove. The air would immediately become fresher and more innocent near the birches, and the trees themselves seemed like clearings in a dream. Open sesame! And they opened. You could see through a birch trunk as if it were a window. Let's get out of here! Officials at the Visa and Registration Department try to intimidate people by saying, "You'll see, you'll come back for the birches! You'll miss them!" They bait their hooks with birch trees. "All right," you think, "if I miss the snow, I'll fly to Greenland. All right!" I never suspected that there are more birches in Norway than in Nesterov. Shall we take a little break and go to Norway? . . .

And just what are those Russian birch trees in the woods? White crows, white bears of trees. Up on their hind legs, snouts to the wind—there's a breath of spring in the air. In fall, winter, early spring.

A birch grove is like a zoo. There are rhinos, there are condors, and there are birches. All exceptions to the rule. God created birches to refute our ideas about the color and purpose of trees. They're rare as white bears. . . .

No, I didn't think about trying to change my father. He was the product of 1909 just as I was the product of 1948. Everyone takes his own reading. But, oh, how my father banged his fist on the table that day as he told Evgeny Nikolaevich to "shut up"! He understood, my father, that this was no laughing matter, not to be talked about: Enough! And he never said a word on the subject again. "And what was Evgeny Nikolaevich's report on you supposed to mean? . . ." He understood, without having to ask any questions. He understood everything.

Evgeny Nikolaevich was married to Aunt Natasha, my father's cousin. A professor of electrical engineering, he was afraid of death, which is natural enough. Happily joking in his chair, he would constantly be grabbing his wrist and checking his pulse. He had a heart condition. I used to walk over to see them on Sobachy Square, where they owned a cozy little house which was declared uninhabitable and demolished when Novy Arbat was being built. The house was permeated with the smell of wood mold, pots, medicine, kerosene stoves, and Aunt Natasha's cats. She was charitable to cats. She would keep three or four of them in the house, afraid to let them out into the yard, where the little boys might do them harm. And that was why all their windows were kept closed. Evgeny Nikolaevich strung netting over the windows, but still the house did not get enough air, which affected the professor's blood pressure and irregular pulse. They were a couple of old, unfortunate, helpless, landowner types who had survived the revolution because of his scientific achievements and his peaceable disposition. Evgeny Nikolaevich would pay the most dangerous hooligans in the courtyard three rubles, five rubles, as a sort of salary. The local police inspector also extracted tribute, and frightening Evgeny Nikolaevich with tales of robbery, brazenly sold him his own police whistle for fifty rubles—as protection against thieves. Princess Urusov came to wash the floors in the building. And the Countess de Salias, who now worked as a nurse in the polyclinic, would come to the house to take Evgeny Nikolaevich's urine in for analysis. And he, an intellectual and a commoner, would revel in the ironies of the Bolshevik revolution as he shouted to the courtyard after her, "Countess! Come back! You forgot my urine!" "Stop it, Evgeny!" Aunt Natasha would react angrily at such moments. "Remember who you are and who I am!"

Her maiden name was Vsevolozhskaya, and she was of the best family, while he was an unknown, a Soviet professor named Matveev. Their home served as a counterweight to my revolutionary past and my father, who was as red as the flag. Aunt Natasha did not visit my mother, who was of peasant stock, even though she had taken the special Bestuzhev higher-education courses for women. Aunt Natasha regarded her with pursed lips when my mother visited her. But, in accordance with the gentry code, my father and I were forgiven everything. We were welcome guests there.

I visited them more frequently after my father was arrested.

They fed me and lent me money, the way relatives do, to be sent on to him in Lefortovo Prison. As a form of barter, I, a graduate student at the time, would write Evgeny Nikolaevich's reports on dialectical materialism for him. He could not make heads or tails of that false doctrine. At one of his seminars he was once asked the fourth law of dialectics. "What did you say?" said his professor in delight. " 'Diaelectrical'? . . ." With the help of my crib notes, he became known as a great Marxist in his department at the Rybny Institute. They even tried to talk him into joining the party in his old age.

But death, as they say, sneaked up on him (though he did die after my father). Cackling with good humor, Evgeny Nikolaevich would say, "No, no," and give our debate a painful twist, as he was fond of doing. "My dear Andrusha, whether you like it or not, science has determined that we die, we die, and that's it. Marx wrote on the subject too." And then Evgeny Nikolaevich would feel his pulse, looking around, blinking nervously in his sarcasm. He couldn't wait to hear my comeback to his irony, anything that was more consoling than Marxism. I didn't keep him waiting. Using arguments—if not very scientific, then at least a bit more hopeful—I rushed to dispel his ghastly fears, so understandable in an old man. He made a pretense of arguing, then cheered up, letting himself be convinced and sighing with relief. Again and again, like a boy first learning of death, he longed to believe: Maybe, who knows, in the end, why not, it might be true, it could be, let's assume it is, O Lord, that would be good, we'll see, but maybe not, how could it be, oh, if it were, if it only were! . . .

It went on like that for several years until my father returned— after the amnesty. During the celebration, welcoming my father with refreshments, Evgeny Nikolaevich began by saying: "You know what I have to report to you, Donat Evgenevich—it turns out that your son's religious. . . . Ask him yourself. Andrusha, is there a God in heaven or not? . . . Is there a God in heav——"

"Shut up!" roared my father furiously, banging his fist on the table. And Evgeny fell silent. Then, as if nothing had happened, the conversation took a more peaceable turn—to exile, prison, rehabilitation. . . . The atheist had killed the fun—with heaven, which he did not acknowledge; with his son, who wasn't the way he should be. The professor was intimidated by him. My father was abrupt, remote, just, magnanimous, and bold.

"Shut up. You don't talk in the forest."

He simply disliked idle talk.

But it was in the forest that he spoke most openly with me. No one could overhear him there in the forest. And if he had a dog with him, so much the better. You just shouldn't make noise. And on we'd go, deeper and deeper. As always, he'd go ahead with the rifle. And I'd bring up the rear, rifleless. Or else we'd walk side by side or sit down for a while. He'd reminisce about his own father's funeral, the trip from Petersburg to Syzran, the requiem mass. The fat priest in the church, angry at the freethinker, nearly brushed my father's face with his censer in order to make him, the atheist, flinch. But, his father's son, he stood by the coffin, holding his head proudly, maintaining his silence. The only son, the heir to wealth . . . the black sheep.

"Just imagine—I had come into my inheritance, and I noticed that my mother, my own mother, had begun speaking differently to me. With a sort of respectful tone. Only because I had become wealthier. Money! It can buy anything! Think of it—money! . . ."

My father spent his inheritance on revolution. After his mother's death, that is. The town house, the diamonds. All of it, thrown to the wind, to revolution . . . To the wind? No. Before his death, my father regained consciousness and asked, barely able to speak, as I bent over him, "Well, how's your *Picasso?*"

He knew that the edition had been confiscated upon review by the Central Committee. They had decided to kill the book on Picasso that Golomshtok and I had written. What did my father care about Picasso and painting? He didn't know much about art. He just sensed and trusted that it was somehow important. My father wanted us to live a life with a "higher meaning," as he used to say, whether that meant Picasso, who was alien to him, or "socialism," "revolution," which had been so generous in settling accounts with him. He thought that what was "higher," the "spirit," did not disappear after death but entered the nebulous sphere of the Will, the vast mind of history. . . .

Perhaps the essence of that "socialism" was that a person rejected his mother and father, his high school, the world of flirtations and dinner parties, and, in defiance of the obvious, began to live a higher life. Which way were you Christians looking when humanity was abducted by atheism right from under your noses? . . . The revolutionaries were drawn to the heights. What match were all those petty officers, who thought only about themselves and their estates? In the short run, the socialists proved the more spiritual. They wanted to feed others, worse off than themselves, and live the life of the spirit, a life of higher meaning—the egotists. Who could have known back then at the beginning how it would all turn out?

A person's last words before dying are not necessarily his crowning glory; *but,* on the contrary, they often distort and overshadow who he really is. His character, his experience, and his dignity are left behind like a useless pod. We have no right to judge the roots of a once-tall tree by those pitiful, wrinkled little leaves trembling in the wind. And yet . . . just as my father asked about the Picasso book, my mother, when she was dying, asked, "You didn't forget to eat the cottage cheese?"

Oh, it's so painful. How are we going to die? . . .

It doesn't matter, it doesn't matter at all, if we say stupid things. Those things are innocent in the face of death. They are touching; they reveal us as unfortunate and lovable creatures, little children who understand more than adults do.

We did not know that Evgeny Nikolaevich was dying the last time I was allowed to visit him in the hospital. The doctors were vague, evasive. He was lying on his back in a private room, and, left alone with me, he sang his usual tune, wondering if there really was nothing at all after death. He writhed as if being tortured and paid little attention to my inconsistent exhortations, so paltry in the face of his fear. All of a sudden he asked me to hand him the bedpan, which was beside his bed. He didn't want to call a nurse. I had trouble controlling my hands as I helped him relieve himself. He suffered from a severe heart condition and was forbidden to move in the slightest. Without changing position, his hand on his pillow, Evgeny Nikolaevich suddenly squinted oddly at the slowly filling bedpan.

"Look how little it is! . . ."

He burst into tears. . . .

I didn't know what to think. A terrible mystery was revealed: evidently he was dying and saying farewell to life in his own way. It wasn't that the old professor placed any particular value on that decrepit part of his body or was much concerned with it. No, he was mourning for himself, so little now, and stretched out helplessly on his back. And what was there I could console him with at that moment? . . .

And then we were past the oak clearing and among the nut trees. Soon we'd see the pines, and the larches, which for some reason had been my favorite since I was a child. The larches! . . . The wonderful thing about oaks is that their bark, twigs, and leaves

all have a carved, uneven look. They say that oak is hard. It is.
And its leaves are like oilcloth, leathery, tough; expose the wood
pulp and it'll rust like iron by winter. But an oak—after it's been
cut, torn apart, with the large irregular serrations on its leaves—
resembles its own bark, which in turn—rough, mighty, dark—is
reminiscent of roots and soil and the earth's perishable surface.
As if the leaves retained the memory of the whole tree, and the
tree that of the earth.

It must be because I grew up with those oaks that I imagine
them as the first trees on earth; right across the road from the
house in Rameno was a forest of oak, nothing but oak. . . .

I had gone to see my father as soon as he was exiled to Rameno
after his release from Syzran Prison. After a quick exchange of
kisses, he gave me a dry account of his time in prison, then nodded
at the road.

"Shall we go for a walk?"

"Let's go. . . ."

We didn't have the rifle with us. The rifle had been confiscated
during the search, along with a gold pocket watch my father had
inherited and an issue of the magazine *Amerika*. Still, we knew
why we were retreating to the woods. Thinking we were off hunting, the neighbor's dog trailed after us. And that was good: a scout
dog might come in handy in the woods that day.

To tell the truth, I was exultant, overflowing with questions to
ask my father and stories to tell him. That's putting it mildly. He'd
been held nine months for investigation, and we hadn't known
where. I'd been afraid that he'd been executed, and then, suddenly,
a gift: "Five years of exile to place of birth." To Rameno, his own
home, though by then we had only the summer house left, Grandfather having long since died. Given what was happening in the
country, my father's sentence seemed a humanitarian act. He, however, took a dimmer view: he had expected to be acquitted after
a thorough investigation, which would show he had committed
no crime. Two weeks before this, when I was visiting him in Butyrki
Prison, he managed to shout out that we shouldn't worry, he'd be

home soon. I didn't believe it. But he did in fact succeed in presenting documentary proof that he had not been an American spy in 1922. In 1922, as a true revolutionary, he had been running a district branch of the national education department. During the famine he had distributed American gifts to the schools and kindergartens. Thirty years later he was called to account for his connections with the ARA, the American famine-relief society.

Since the charges of espionage were finally dropped, my father assumed he would be released. But, to his surprise, he was slapped with Article 58(10)—anti-Soviet agitation, of which there had not been even the slightest hint in the preliminary investigation. But it was clear: at that time, the last Mohicans of the revolution—former Mensheviks, anarchists, SR's who by some miracle had survived the 1920s and 1930s—were being purged in Russia along with Jews. For some reason, they didn't try to stick him with a more interesting charge; they gave him the minimum—exile, five years, for agitation and propaganda. My father had been rounded up with the SR's. . . .

Incidentally, there was a sequel to his successful struggle against the famine in the Volga district in 1922. He encountered that sequel in person in 1952, when, just out of a transfer prison, in shaky condition, a sack on his back, he dragged himself through dusty Syzran, which he knew so well, wondering how to cover the ten miles to Rameno. The bike was gone. It had gotten broken, and, besides, my father couldn't have ridden a bike. He was stopped at an intersection by an old woman, a former schoolteacher; though he didn't recognize her, she remembered him from better days, when he worked in the district office of national education (they had arrested him then too but released him quickly). Later on she'd heard vague reports that he had moved to Moscow, which was why she decided to rush over to him for help:

"You live in Moscow but you don't know anything. Here in Syzran there hasn't been any sugar the last few months. It's outrageous! It's sabotage! And you, Donat Evgenevich, should be concerned that proper supplies are delivered to the town where you were born, grew up, and, as I recall, did a wonderful job of organizing food relief for the children and the teachers, even under very difficult historical conditions. . . . I urge you, as a personal favor to an old schoolteacher, to call whoever has to be called in the Kremlin and tell them straight out that there's been no sugar in Syzran. . . ."

From the old days, she still considered my father a higher-up, almost in government. But he could barely stand on his feet after the prison air and was busy calculating whether he had the strength to drag himself on foot to Rameno, his place of exile. . . .

In the forest my father kept silent even though we were a respectable distance from the village and in no danger of being overheard. Unable to remain silent any longer, and seeing no point in it, I asked, "Did they use that issue of *Amerika* as material evidence?"

I had bought that issue at a Moscow newsstand, literally on the day before the search. I'd been lured by the high-quality color picture of a work by Picasso, one I hadn't seen before. But when the four of them made a rush for that ill-starred magazine—"Hey, look, *Amerika!*"—I could tell which way the wind was blowing. Moreover, the plainclothesman, a specialist in such matters, examined my bookcase and spent an especially long time thumbing through a collection of stories by Maxim Gorky published by Parus, a Petrograd house. Suddenly his curiosity was piqued: "Tell me, does Parus happen to be in America?" "No, it doesn't happen to be in America," I hastened to assure him, more certain now that they would try to pin something "American" on him. But what? There was nothing American in our house apart from that copy of *Amerika* magazine, which my father didn't even know was there. Later on, after the search, I made a statement to the MGB that the issue seized belonged to me. By the way, *Amerika* was completely legal and sold at all newsstands. . . .

"No, they never mentioned your magazine. As I said, there was nothing after '23 in the charges. But you know"—I could hear an inappropriate, forced carefreeness in my father's voice—"you know what, let's be quiet for a while and just breathe the smell of the pines. Just look at that forest!"

And it truly was an unusual forest. From the low hill where we stood and across a fissure in the ground, as far as the eye could see, the forest stretched to the north, the northwest, and the east of Rameno, for dozens of miles, and seemed to reach Moscow itself. You could stroll in peace there, skirting the towns and villages, and never see a soul. My father was being cagey with me, avoiding the subject as if dodging pursuit, the inscrutable load on his shoulders his alone to bear. Stoop-shouldered, shuffling, he kept looking to the side—I suddenly felt terribly sorry for him. For a moment, it seemed to me that, at twenty-six years of age, with my great fund of knowledge gained at no little cost, I was more experienced and hardier than he, who had been exiled to live out his old age in the place where he had been born in the now remote nineteenth century.

Not long before this, when I visited him in Butyrki Prison, he had seemed haler and heartier than I had expected, despite his deathly pallor and the shouts of the guard who stood like a monument between us in the corridor formed by two rows of barbed wire that reached the ceiling. Monkeys and small vermin, polecats, porcupines, are kept in fenced-in areas like that at the zoo. Except that here the spectator himself is also locked in a cage for his hour-long visit with a relative, who is in a parallel cage. Along with the happiness I felt at seeing my father alive, I also remember leaving there with a deep sense of satisfaction at having been behind bars, if only for a short time. I was in a phase where prison fascinated me like a whirlpool.

But our conversation never went anywhere, for nearly every sentence was interrupted by the monotonous exclamations of the overzealous clod of a guard whose bulk almost obscured my father, and who had turned his impassive, medallionlike profile to us both.

"How are you feeling? What are they giving you to eat?"

"You're not allowed to talk about that. I'm warning you."

"What are the charges against you?"

"You're not allowed to talk about that. I forbid it."

"How's your mother? Is she feeling well? Is she . . . working?"

"That's not allowed, I'm warning you."

"Is the weather all I can ask about?"

"If you don't stop this, I'll cancel the visit."

"Will you be sentenced soon?"

"It's strictly forbidden to talk about that."

"Well, what's been happening at home?"

"I'm warning you for the last time. . . ."

All the same, my father behaved normally and, while observing the regulations, seemed calmly oblivious of the barrier erected between us, as if the guard were an inanimate object or some meaningless idol. One thing surprised me: even though I kept nodding that everything was all right at home, he wouldn't stop asking about Mama's health and my graduate work, which was coming to a successful conclusion. Later on we found out that, all during the investigation, they had tried to make him believe that I too had been arrested and that Mama had lost her mind.

That day, through that prison barrier—a double row of cells screened with fine iron mesh and separated by a ditch—he was visible only from the waist up, wearing an undershirt that blended with the paleness of his face into a single, vague blur against the background of the dimly lit stall. That wasn't my father but what seemed a faded photograph of him, an embryo of his familiar face, preserved in alcohol in a jar, a bloodless premature child. . . .

Now, in the sun, in the forest, he had come back to me, come back to earth from a spectral world, with all his beloved features; even if he was pinched and hunched, he still had his usual presence of mind, a calm, seasoned old man who'd seen a thing or two and was smart enough to take his time.

Casting sidelong glances at him, I thought how infinitely much each of us contains, even if all we count is personal memories, leaving aside a person's soul and its source. Leaving character and personality aside, memory alone bestows us with a unique design, a means of ensuring the species' survival and, if you will, that of world history as well, which we bear in our wake, regardless of our knowledge or experience, but simply by dint of having mastered the land around us. The long, long memory of everything in the world trails behind each of us, whether it be of what we have heard, seen, read, or experienced, or of strangers' faces, books and newspapers, prison, or a road we once drove down.

Maybe because this time I too had taken a bit of an unusual way to Rameno, and my father was the only person I could tell about it, that human life struck me as a long-distance train in which we are all seated in our cars and, leaning out the windows, we see both the history of the world (even though no one invited us to), and our own past, so precarious. In a train you always think about that which you've left behind but which still trails you, like the cars behind you. And those cars are full of people, each looking out the window, in a train that beats time with the rails, a grid of books and events that are beyond us in every sense. History is not something we make or study. History is something we pass through. We remember it, and we pass it on without even noticing. Where, I ask, would Homer and Shakespeare have disappeared to, what would Julius Caesar be and all the breeds of animals, from the extinct ichthyosaurs on, if we didn't keep them in some corner of memory and drag them along behind us, like rolling stock? What are we? What am I as a person? We don't have any meaning. But those who will come after us, who will change to another train and go farther than us . . . !

At first I wasn't much bothered by my father's silence or his confining himself to brief replies that conveyed nothing and sounded absurd there in the woods. Ultimately, he was the best judge of how a man should act when leaving prison for exile. Before releasing my father, could they have made him sign a strict oath not to divulge anything, as I had heard was sometimes the practice? Or had he been beaten during the investigation, and did he now find it awkward to tell his own son about that? But he would have been straightforward about telling me that, he was straightforward about everything. Most likely, he would have scorned any prohibition, since he trusted me and spoke with me, man to man, without any sentimentality. Thank God he was a man with experience.

But I was impatient, if not to hear all his stories, then at least to pour out everything that had built up in me. Starting with the night-time search of our basement room, where I, having grown up a little, had taken my father's place; as he got older he moved in with Mama on the first floor. The evening before, he had left on a business trip to a tire factory in Yaroslavl. He had been taken off the train, and we only learned that he had been arrested from the search warrant. For the first time it wasn't hearsay—I feasted my eyes on that document, that state secret of human destruction. The way they walked, their boots crunching softly over the broken glass—the bureau drawers yanked out to reveal well-washed, emaciated linen, little bottles, various miserable belongings, and the tumbling junk that, for some reason, made you feel ashamed in front of the people carrying out the search—stepping over a layer of the books, rags, and photographs they'd looked through and discarded as unnecessary. The way they leafed through the books, each one individually, in search of hidden notes and remarks penciled years before in the margins. How they held my little packets of prophylactics up to the light for a closer look, grimacing with distaste, as if that were the first time in their lives they'd seen such an abomination. On the other hand, all four of them roared with childlike laughter as they sat on the wide bed at whose edge my mother perched, clenched into a small fist—they'd been amused by the pictures in a book on midwifery they'd chanced upon. People are always human. They needed a vacation too.

"Hey, take a look at this one!"

They were looking for evidence of a crime.

They overturned the garbage can in our kitchen and left it like that, a pile of potato peels and bits of meat they'd poked at. They hadn't touched our neighbors' garbage cans, having taken our word they weren't ours. Our neighbors had not gone to work that morning and were sitting hushed in their rooms. A soldier with a rifle was frozen in position at the apartment door and did not allow anyone in. A peasant lad, he had an expression that seemed to say that he too was a prisoner and no party to what was happening. He made an effort to remain aloof. He just stood there with his rifle and didn't bother anyone. I never saw any like him again.

The search lasted from 2:00 A.M. until 11:00 the following night, twenty-one hours. We were taken to the bathroom under guard and not allowed to close the door, so as not to be out of their sight. But toward the end, late in the day, they were good and tired themselves, and I succeeded in palming a few of the diaries I had kept as a child and some of my timid first attempts at literature, and stuffing them into my pockets. I had taken my father's advice and not kept any journals as a youth. "Watch out, they put people in jail for diaries these days. Don't be an idiot," he had warned me at the end of the war. Now I see that he was just trying to protect me. . . .

The books they unearthed, and their failure to find any serious evidence, irritated the searchers, and they went after me on any pretext.

"Tell me why your library, if I may call it that, has so many prerevolutionary books in it? And why it's so skimpy when it comes to prize-winning Soviet authors. Yes. Skimpy. Why?"

Now they were charging us for what wasn't there. Their icy contempt, mingled with a keen, covert mockery of my fate, took my breath away. In an effort to say something that would be both as precise and as distracting as possible, I replied that my specialty, which they could check, was late-nineteenth- and early-twentieth-century Russian literature. By that time I was doing a dissertation on Klim Samgin, which provided me with something of an alibi. And that was the reason, of course, that I had so few Soviet writers and so many prerevolutionary editions. . . .

"I can see that! I can see that! You've got nothing but Andrei Bely. . . ."

Like Mucius Scaevola, he extended his hand toward the steel

bookcase where my Russian Decadents, collected over the years as a sort of antidote, moldered in fireproof safety.

"What do you need Bely for?"

"To the best of my knowledge," I said in an attempt at parrying, "Andrei Bely is not included on the list of forbidden authors. You can buy Andrei Bely's works at secondhand-book stores. Or take them out at the library . . ."

"Yes, I know. But do I have to remind you that in Russian *bely* means 'white'?"

A finger was raised. An ember of hatred glowed in the pupil of his eye. . . .

But at one point I lost my head and couldn't find the right objection. Having looked through my old student notes, the KGB man called my attention to a sentence that began with the words: "The official definition of socialist realism states . . ." This was followed by a faultless quote from our university text-book.

"What's wrong with that? I don't see anything so terrible there."

"You doooon't?!" He raised his voice. "The o-ffi-cial def-i-ni-tion?!" He was nearly shouting at me. Then, having made a sacramental pause that befitted the full seriousness of the words he had quoted, he fell on me with a fury, his voice becoming a whisper, rapid and rabid:

"So that means, in your opinion, there is also an unofficial definition of socialist realism? . . . Well?! . . ."

It was as if he had the power to shape the future. I'll say here that this incident, along with the overall tone of the search, undoubtedly served as the seed of Abram Tertz's scandalous essay that would be cooked up some five years later. Later on, I did in fact desire to voice an unofficial definition of socialist realism. But back then I had nothing to hide.

"What is this, an interrogation?" I said, trying to avoid the subject.

"Yes. We want to know what you really meant by the word 'official'!"

"So far all you've shown me is a search warrant. Show me an arrest warrant and then you can question me."

This looked like explicit capitulation on my part. . . .

He whistled meaningfully, then spoke, addressing no one in particular; while his colleagues, rummaging in other corners of our home, did not turn their heads toward him: "Look at that, will you just look at that. The son's worse than the father. We'll be taking that into account. And we'll get to the bottom of all this!"

The threat did not materialize. But, like many another Soviet citizen, I could not fall asleep before three in the morning for six months or more after the search. After three o'clock, fine; you could stop expecting them to appear at three.

There were other reasons for that too. But everything in good order . . .

I rushed to communicate all this news in one breath to my father, the only person who would know what I meant. I would have kept only a single detail from him, one I had also, as far as possible, kept from myself. But now it's time to mention it.

I had not opened the door to the basement room when they began pounding on it at two o'clock in the morning. The banging made the plaster fall. You could sense that this was a hand with the right to break down the door, smash it in. As I pulled on my pants, I was still hoping that it was the police, tipped off by the neighbors, come to check my papers. Suddenly the door was opened and I saw my mother, key in hand; she entered the room first, a coat over her nightgown: they had gotten her out of bed and forced her to open up the basement. She was followed by the four men of whom I have already spoken. Two voices closed in on me:

"Hands up!"

For some reason my mother spoke very distinctly, the way teachers enunciate in school:

"They're here with a search warrant—in connection with . . . your father's arrest."

And while they frisked me for weapons and turned my pockets inside out, I thought about the intonation my mother had used, with its barely audible stress on the words "your father's arrest." I realized that what she meant was: They're not here for you; don't be afraid; your father's been arrested. . . .

To tell the truth, they should have arrested me, not him. Without knowing anything, my mother still suspected this was so and, like a she-wolf who has just whelped a cub, she used my father to shield me. She simply loved me more. . . .

"Papa, there's one important thing I should tell you. It's a secret. A week before I came to see you . . ."

I hadn't seen my father in such a fury for a long time. He even shouted for me to be quiet at once, saying that he was in no mood to listen to my nonsense. Why was it nonsense? And what did moods have to do with it? He wasn't a man of moods. The vague gesture toward the distant forest accompanying his angry outburst explained nothing at all. It was just a forest. There wasn't a soul to be heard for at least half a mile. I even felt somewhat bitter, after all the anxiety and vicissitudes I'd experienced in racing full-speed to Rameno. Why should I be quiet? And be reprimanded?

In fact, my father was a hard man to get along with—the result of all his tribulations, his ruined life. "He's a tyrant!" my mother would say, meaning that he was unyielding. "He doesn't want to settle down like everyone else, and, look, he's out of a job again." Or else, "He's writing a novel with no hope of getting it published." Or, "As a matter of principle, he won't make his bed in the morning, and he forbids me to dust his desk." Or . . . Isn't that enough? My father was capable of telling an unwelcome guest to clear out. He would suddenly flare up at someone, then after mulling it over would consider himself the offended party. But only once in twenty-six years did he ever really take me to task, shouting so loud I can never forget it. Which was exactly why he was doing it.

Despite my parents' precept—money is not a present for children—I spent the money Aunt Natasha gave me on the first book

I had ever acquired on my own. Assuming the entire risk, asking no one's permission, I bought the book in a used-book store. A book all the kids in the courtyard were forever buzzing about. But that marvelous book was an unattainable rarity back then. I envied the other kids for a long time, imagining what the illustrations looked like, until one day, not believing my own eyes, I spotted a copy on the counter of a bookstore. Pleasantly shabby, the copy had a yellowish cover and was mysterious, like a girl you've fallen in love with but still know nothing about. Now Aunt Natasha's five rubles in my pocket seemed there for a purpose.

I had not even finished devouring the first chapter when Papa came home earlier than usual and seemed to sense something fishy was going on.

The cleverest ploy I could come up with was to pretend that I was studying, with an open book in front of me.

"What are you reading?"

". . . I'm reading a book."

"I can see it's a book, not a newspaper. What book?"

"Mayne Read's *The Headless Horseman*."

"Whaaat?! . . . Where'd you get it?"

I had to confess my sin. In the first place, I had allowed myself to spend five rubles on my own pleasure, knowing full well that we didn't have a kopeck to our name. To justify myself by saying that the money was mine, a present, that Aunt Natasha had said, "Buy yourself whatever you like, child!" would have meant sinking even more shamefully into the abyss that had suddenly gaped in front of me. What did "my money" mean if my mother and father were taking food out of their own mouths to feed me? What was I—a bourgeois, a shopkeeper, a thief?! Didn't I see that sometimes Papa wouldn't eat with us so there'd be food left for tomorrow? And what about the rent? And the light bill for the last three months? And the holes in Papa's shoe? . . .

In the second place, my guilt was blown out of proportion by the fact that I had bought and was reading *The Headless Horseman!* By Mayne Read! That's the limit! An empty, stupid book;

the garbage can was the only place for it. Not only was it empty—
it was harmful. And not only harmful—reactionary. And not just
reactionary—it was ridiculous cock and bull, utter nonsense, without a word of truth in it, and, most important, was that there was
not a single idea to be found in all that fantasy, all those idiotic
adventures. Take "Shagreen Leather": it was a fantasy, but what
meaning it contained! What style! And this one? *The Headless
Horseman?* A person who reads such trash inevitably ends up a
drunkard. As my reactionary grandfather used to say to my father,
"A glass of vodka is the first step, and a broken life the last. . . ."

Had I used the money to buy, say, some watercolor paints, a
compass, or even a book but a useful book, one that could help
me in life, there wouldn't have been any uproar. My father himself
had given me James Jeans as a present and the Flammarion book
on the origin of the planets. A finer point should be put on this.
My father was a truly encyclopedic man. With the exception of
aesthetics, he knew absolutely everything: geology, chemistry,
mathematics, philosophy. . . . He read Avenarius and Hegel, whom
I realize he preferred to Marx. He knew astronomy, biology. . . .
For the most part he had a selective knowledge of literature, although there too he displayed an uncommonly perceptive mind
and was astonishingly knowledgeable. . . . Economics, geography
. . . Later on I was to outdo him in one area—the reading of books
like *The Headless Horseman*. The end result was that I substituted
my father's encyclopedic knowledge, his will power, his moral
strength, with the sublimations of reading. But can comparisons
really be made? . . . Ichthyology . . .

In short, the books my parents gave me for my edification
stemmed from the broad, rationalist tradition of the sixties and
seventies of the last century. They never forbade me to read anything. You want to read Boccaccio, read him; you want to read
Jules Verne, go right ahead! Maupassant was even better: "I'm
serious when I say that." Though there my mother did raise some
faint objections: "For a child?! . . ." "Doesn't matter, doesn't
matter, let him read it! He'll make his own sense of it. . . ." But

for all his breadth, my father so ridiculed Mayne Read and other such frauds that it made my heart sink. And it was shameful to realize that *The Headless Horseman* or *Baron Münchhausen*, for which I was still too young and had not come across either, were what I was dreaming of.

Unexpectedly, my mother displayed solidarity with my father on this one point. She disliked Mayne Read on educational grounds, and for some reason she thought my imagination feverish enough as it was. She considered it her sacred duty to use all her powers to protect me against the bad influence of fantasy, mysticism, immorality, and decadence. . . .

Needless to say, soon enough all those precautions proved useless. But, owing to my rationalistic upbringing, I acquired a certain—let's be blunt—flaw. I always have the feeling that I let all that was most important and most beautiful in life slip by me, that I had lost it somewhere back in my childhood, and that the unread *Headless Horseman* was galloping on ahead without me. And perhaps that's why in the end I became a writer, out of a sense that something was missing: to make up for lost reading! . . .

"What should I do with it now?" I said, completely crushed by my father's comments and everything that had befallen me.

"Do whatever you want. . . . If you want to read that crap, read it! I won't stand in your way. . . ."

It was evening by the time I went out to the courtyard, pressing the slender book to my heart. The courtyard was deserted. It was dark out. I stood for a moment wondering whether to give *The Headless Horseman* to Alik Liberman, my best friend, who read everything without obstacles and who had even managed to read *Captain Grant's Children*. . . . But what kind of a person knowingly gives a harmful book as a present? And what if word about it got out?!

When I came back, downcast, my hands empty, my father's mood improved.

"So, what did you do with it?"

Even more crestfallen, I replied, "I threw it in the trash!"

"A wise choice. The right thing . . . And don't be down in the dumps about it either! Think of it—Mayne Read! Five rubles! . . . Take me, for example—I had to overcome worse problems than that. . . ."

And then he told me a funny story about how his relatives, and even his mother, thought for a long time that he was color-blind, unable to tell the colors apart. In fact, he could tell them apart— with his eyes, but he always got the names mixed up. . . . The whole problem came from his idiotic gentry upbringing, and it was difficult to rid himself of it. When he was a child, instead of teaching him clear and simple concepts like "yellow," "green," "blue," etc., all his governesses, aunts, and grandmothers filled his head with recherché nonsense like "aquamarine," "canary," "turquoise," "beige," and so on. As a result, they all got so mixed up in his mind, and he became so sick of it all, that he was no longer able to call the colors by their right name. Even though he could see them all . . .

I smiled as a sign that we had understood each other and were reconciled. But something was eating away at me. Not only because I had been forced to forsake an old and cherished desire but also because, in so doing, I had committed two new crimes. I had lied to my father about throwing the book in the trash. I had not thrown Mayne Read in a trash can. In reality, not knowing where to put or hide my *Headless Horseman,* I had cut through the courtyard to Vorovsky Street and, under cover of dark, I had placed the book cover-up on the sidewalk. Like a poisonous plant. A terrible, beckoning trap: Let some boy I don't know find it.

All the same, in my quarrel with my father, which continues to this day, it was he who proved right, as far as *The Headless Horseman* was concerned, not I, who nursed a grievance. Out of some superstitious fear (and because my desire faded), I avoided Mayne Read for many years, just as we all avoid our old sins, and I made no effort to find the lost book. I must have been around seventeen when, in a bad mood and wanting some diversion, I picked up a copy in the library. And none of it was the way I had imagined. A dead body, a corpse, its head already cut off, was tied to a horse that was then let go to gallop through the pampas. Crude, banal, and boring. Totally jerry-rigged. And I had thought that *The Headless Horseman* was about a headless horseman! Not a phantom but a horseman galloping along even though he had no head. Such things can't happen in real life. But in a book, a real book, a horseman can always gallop along, even without a head. . . .

Well, here are your precious larches. You asked for them, didn't you? We'd reached them now. The farthest ones. In Rameno we always divided the larches into the close ones and the faraway ones. Mama would ask, "Well, what do you say, should we go to the close ones today, or the faraway ones?" "The faraway ones, the faraway ones!" The faraway ones were taller.

You practically never see larches in the forested plain of European Russia. They seem to grow specially well in small, shy stands, so that, when coming to them, you run your eyes slowly over them—their minuscule open cones, their cautious needles gathered into tufts, brushes, their long parallel branches emerging at every level from a trunk as straight and serene as a palm tree.

Of course, if you look closely, every tree is fantastic, as is every creature, every human being. But what is fantastic about the larches is their gentle, understated allusion to how utterly interesting the whole world is and to how there is nothing to fear in savagery and evil. Intelligent flora, they may well shed their needles so that they won't be suspected of being coniferous and malicious. . . .

The larch is not an inviting tree and does not call out to be visited; svelte prophetess of the forest, it keeps its distance. If its picture could be drawn in words, I would have drawn it. There is nothing random or preconceived about the intricacy of the larch. Everything about it is so spiritual that you see that the dark fantasies that overpowered you were only a faint shadow falling from its top, part of a fairy tale in which Papa and I, or Mama and I, ascend—to the sun, or the stars, as we wish. . . .

Still, I did not think that my father was afraid of something and so was shielding me from trouble like a child, and shutting me up like one too. That wasn't his way. He wasn't afraid of anything, although he could not abide people's bewailing the obvious, like the government's anti-Semitic policy or Stalin's megalomania. Nothing worse, he used to say, than going to jail for shooting off your mouth.

He was not even afraid of death. He had learned how to face down fear at a tender age. In the evenings, when his aristocratic parents were off visiting, having left him alone in the big empty house, he would come down into the dark hall with a large stick in his hand, shouting, "There's three hundred of us here! Three hundred! . . ." And the phantoms would scatter.

Unlike my father, I was afraid of everything. When I was a little boy, an old woman would visit me in my dreams. I could never explain who she was and, waking with a heavy heart the next morning, I would timidly complain to my mother that the "old woman" had come to me again. As usual, my mother suspected that someone was having a bad influence on me and demanded that I confess which of the older children or nannies in the court-yard was filling my head with ridiculous superstitions about ghosts and witches. But I swear that no one was instilling any such thoughts in me at the time; it was all the work of my own imag-ination. It was not a hallucination but a reality, as real as could be, that came to me in the night, always in one and the same guise, with the sole purpose of frightening and oppressing me with its cold, concentrated malice until my heart was worn ragged and ready to leap out of orbit because of that gaze, fixed glassily and unwaveringly upon me. It felt as if she were slowly hypnotizing me, allowing me neither to flee nor to regain my wits.

I don't know; maybe Avdotya, who lived in our communal apartment, had cast a little spell on me, to destroy our family because we were of the intelligentsia, which, in her view, ranked us with the manufacturers and landowners who had been liquidated as a class. In any case, some time later Mama discovered a photograph of me as a child under our kerosene stove in the kitchen, a photograph that one of us must have dropped in the hallway and which had now been returned to its owner, the eyes having been first poked out with a needle. Mama was outraged by Avdotya's vandalism, and she blamed my father, the revolutionary, for being unable to curb an ignorant woman who had lost all restraint. But no one in our family believed in witchcraft. Besides, the old woman who tormented me at regular intervals was not in the least reminiscent of Avdotya. There was nothing human about her; an eternal, primordial hatred was stamped on her lifeless, seemingly icy brow.

Had I been seriously ill at the time, I might have taken her for Death or a decrepit Fate who had decided to cut a useless thread while it was still short. But I was healthy, cheerful, carefree, and, moreover, still too young for her to have been sent down on me for my sins or for reading books that were seductive, fantastical.

Things reached the point where I was afraid to fall asleep and would lie in bed with my eyes open, to delay her sudden appearance for as long as possible. The old woman came to me in my sleep but she came quite regularly and always looked the same, and so, trembling, I would recognize her at once and in my sleep would connect each of my previous dreams of her into a single chain of agonizing visitations. All this compelled me to assume that she had a real existence in some other dimension and, hating me for something, me specifically, had set herself the task of edging me out of life. I had no idea what my good parents thought about the constancy of her appearances and mission. But one time, on my father's advice, when she next stole up to the head of my bed and, her eyes fixed on me, was already reaching out with her crooked fingers, I marshaled my forces and brandished a ruler at her. She recoiled. The old woman never came back after that. . . .

* * *

We lingered a while in a sparse aspen wood. "Let's take a breather!" suggested my father, and from his friendly tone of voice and his suddenly cheerful and smiling eyes I guessed that it was here that he intended to tell me, calmly and matter-of-factly, about everything, once and for all. Like an experienced hunter, he had chosen a place that was remote yet quite bare, with a clear view in all directions: no one could steal up on us unseen. Besides, our dog would have started barking. I felt relieved.

"Now, listen carefully and don't interrupt without a good reason," began my father with that gentle, drawn-out intonation he had used in the distant past when telling me stories that were never frightening, a touch edifying, and too close to real life, and which he made up as he went along. "And please don't worry that your father's lost his mind. I don't rule that out as one possible explanation, one working hypothesis. But, incidentally, it's precisely my ability to analyze my own mind critically that indicates there's most likely something else, something entirely different at work here . . . some new technology, some invention. . . ."

He laughed out loud and, crinkling up his eyes, scratched himself behind the ear with his middle finger, as he always did when his mood turned humorous and he was ready to make jokes at his own expense.

"Who the hell knows! Maybe I really did go off my head. It's funny. But, mind you, I'm not insisting on any of it, the way a madman is supposed to. It's not an obsession. Or a phobia. I'm fully aware of everything. If this in fact is some psychological disorder or shock, I hope it passes: I'm not feeling too bad at the moment. But if it's something else, and I think it is, I should warn you about it. . . . Even when I was in there, I informed them that I would tell you everything, only you—so that there would be no misunderstandings. You have to keep a sharp lookout with them. You never know what the hell they're up to. . . ."

"What do you mean—in there? And who did you inform?"

"In Lefortovo Prison, toward the end of the investigation . . . Don't be afraid, it's nothing all that terrible. It'll take a little time, but you'll understand. Are you wondering why I'm dragging it out, acting like a fool and telling you to be quiet? Forgive an old man his little strategies. I delayed it because I was waiting for a quiet moment when there was nobody around. Especially since this'll be the first time. I had to wait until you'd settled down after the train ride and your mind was clear. It'll all look much simpler later on. I'll fill in the picture, and we can discuss things in detail. But remember—I can't be sure of anything. It's possible I was seeing things, I admit that. But what if I wasn't? And it was all real? . . ."

I listened to my father, never taking my eyes off him and not supposing for a single second that there was anything wrong with his mind, as he kept sadly hinting there might be. No sooner had we broken the ice, than his perennial brilliance returned to him, his rare critical ability to weigh and analyze everything, his own mind included. His usual self-possession and cool foresight had come back as well; for me to have any fears about him would have been as ridiculous as doubting the purity and value of that summer afternoon that seemed purposely created for a complete and serious talk, the two of us out walking, just as we used to, in the Rameno woods. The one thing I couldn't fathom was why he couldn't be sure of anything and what he was warning me about, if he himself was going to speak plainly and openly about Lefortovo and the sufferings that prison had made him imagine. And what did he mean by saying that he had waited for the most opportune moment to warn me? . . .

"You mean you still don't get it?" he said, genuinely surprised by my puzzlement. "It's just that right now they've disconnected from me. For a while. They're taking a break. But they listen in at other times. I can feel it. It's something like radar, but it's a two-way connection. Just more subtle . . . It picks up brain waves. Do you understand now?"

A slight chill went up my spine, as if a breeze had stirred the air. Perhaps one had. The sparse aspens rustled faintly overhead. . . . I should admit that I never believed that aspens tremble from fear even when no other leaf in the forest has stirred, as has been believed since time immemorial by the common people who for some reason were never overly fond of that trembling, sensitive tree. I also don't believe that Judas hanged himself from an aspen and that aspens have lived in fear-ever since. I find that disrespectful to trees. This is just how the leaves are on aspens, innumerable silver vanes on longish stems. There was a stillness there in the grass, not the slightest breeze was stirring, but perhaps a storm was already brewing up where the tops of the aspens reached the sky. And they were warning us: There'll be rain soon, soon the entire forest will raise the cry—then you'll understand! . . .

"Did they beat you, Papa?" The question had been at the tip of my tongue since that morning, though I hadn't had the courage to ask it. . . . But now it was too late to put it off for some easier time. I questioned my father about everything as coolly and frankly as he answered.

It turned out that he had not been beaten. When threatening him, the investigator had brandished his fist often but never allowed himself to use it. He did spit at my father a few times, not saliva but most likely a stream of air shot through a short tube specially concealed in his mouth. At times, trembling with nervous tension, the investigator himself would become so wrought up that he would need a drink of water, and you could hear his teeth chattering in fear against the glass. . . . He used the worst curse words in the book, and he stamped his foot, of course—a stupid habit of theirs. In his regular cell at the transit prison (he'd been in solitary until then), a fine-looking little old man had waltzed over to my father and ceremoniously introduced himself: "I am Nikolai Iohannovich Fokht, Doctor of Physics and Mathematics, an honorary member of the British Royal Academy, a Gonzales Prize laureate, vice-president of the International Electronics Society, with honorary doctorates from the universities of Milan, Brussels, and Paris, or—as my investigator calls me—a hairless cunt!"

I was struck both by my father's precision with detail and by his sober and malice-free tone when recounting these none-too-pleasant facts, which had been so deeply imprinted on his monitored mind. He also seemed to be using me to check his mind's clarity and objectivity. He had nothing to hide, either from me or from those whom he might by then have convinced of his complete innocence. It may have been that absence of any political transgression, past or present, in thought or deed, that induced him to allow himself to be mercilessly abused.

An innocent man was defenseless against the X-rays used by the investigators, who persisted in suspecting him of something. Why should he try tricks and evasions? What was there to deceive them about? Why should he throw up safety barriers around himself the way we all do? He had nothing to repent, no reason to implore. Fearing nothing, he inwardly addressed his torturers with all his self-possession and will: "Please, take a look and see what kind of 'enemy of the people' I am! What kind of 'American spy' I am! It's ridiculous! . . ." But that's just what they wanted. Soviet society's inability to offer any resistance to all the historical outrages committed against it, stem primarily from the absence of any real corpus delicti. That gave the rulers a skeleton key to open people's souls which were defenseless and in psychological disarray. . . .

Moreover, all the accusations against my father concerned him alone, and so no betrayals were demanded of him, no violations of integrity. Those accusations also went back thirty years, more than half his adult life. Most likely it was the length of time involved, and the fact that he did not try to hide anything that induced the experimenters at Lefortovo to perform a surgical puncture on the tissues of his unconscious.

My father's hunch was that at that time experiments on the brain were being performed in Lefortovo, using a machine shipped back as war booty from Germany, one that Hitler had not had time to implement fully. What it was exactly my father, of course, did not know. Once, when being questioned, he lost consciousness from an electrical current applied to the back of his head just as the investigator's attacks were increasing to a fever pitch. Prior to this, he had been placed in front of a new metal device that he had not noticed in the office before, and he had also been ordered not to look behind him. Lying on his back on the floor when he came to, my father saw the investigator's eyes white with fear as he worked at resuscitating him. . . . Later on doctors were called in during the interrogations; in civilian clothes, they would stride importantly about the office, observing or commenting casually, at a distance, since for several months after the experiment the prisoner's face had assumed a masklike quality.

Perhaps they were afraid that they had succeeded all too well and were now unhappy about being unable to disconnect entirely from that strange, two-way connection with the subject of their experiment. . . . I do not rule out the possibility that, when breaking the rules by telling me all these details, my father was keeping, or trying to keep, those who were monitoring him at bay. After all, everything he said was heard in Lefortovo, if not immediately, then later on. And the references to Nazi Germany, from which the entire procedure had been borrowed, did not speak well of the people involved in this experiment. My father was not denouncing them or taking revenge for what they had done to him. He was simply warning "those fools," drunk on world domination, that they'd gone too far. Standing alone in the forest, the old, crippled revolutionary was still trying to make the ignoramuses see reason, and to keep them from ever again inflicting the terrible, fatal blow that had already been inflicted on him. . . .

I automatically looked to the north, where, behind the wall of forest, Moscow lay in wait, crouching down on its paws.

"Listen, it's six hundred miles from there to us here in Rameno! Or maybe a little less as the crow flies. Do you really think that at that distance they . . . ?"

"What about telegraph and radio?" was my father's reasonable objection. "What are the limits on knowledge? You know about taking bearings from the army. It's the same principle. . . . And we still have no idea of the brain's hidden powers. Its ability to receive and emit resonances, to send signals—they're studying it."

Taking our time, stopping for breathers, we climbed a hill, then halted and turned; the small, damp aspen wood was now below us, the treetops choppy as a sea. Looking at those gray disheveled plantings marring that bare region, you had to wonder if it too was going mad bombarded by signals from every side. As if a swarm of demons were raging in the leaves amid the silence of the forest, as if cats were leaping along the aspens' frail trunks, squirrels, deer, all alarmed by a furious Morse code, microscopic dots and dashes still imperceptible to us, but already splashing and raging beneath a sky that was as serene and clear as glass.

"Tell me, are you hearing any kind of voices? Are they taking photographs? Are they trying to make you believe something? Do they want anything from you?! . . ."

No, they weren't trying to make him believe anything. And, no, they didn't want anything from him. It was just that he sometimes spoke about one thing or another—spoke mentally, of course, only mentally—with . . . With whom? With a few different people. Usually with the person conducting the experiment at Lefortovo and who was still there, kept, my father suspected, in strict isolation. This man, Lev Subotsky, a close acquaintance of my father in the past—they used to get together, talk—was now simultaneously a prisoner and his control, someone to talk to and a spy. . . . Subotsky had probably been selected as the most suitable candidate for the job because of the way he thought and spoke. My father did not hold it against him—Subotsky still wasn't entirely on "their" side, and the man had some interesting ideas. But it's possible this was someone else passing himself off as Subotsky; my father had not seen Subotsky in prison with his own eyes. Sometimes other people, Chekist physicians, joined in the conversation out of scientific curiosity. They too behaved decently, intelligently. They were quite correct. No threats, no attempts at intimidation. I detected no persecution complex in my father.

I was ashamed because, while listening to him and asking him questions, I was also looking for signs of a mental disorder that could explain what had happened to him. Detecting none, I found myself in a blind alley, and seem to have become enraged by the simple scientific hypothesis that his brain had in fact been tapped and was now under surveillance. And that was me—me!—who accepted every last fantasy, fable, and faith! Who believed in devils, in magic, in a God in heaven, whatever you like! In bad omens. In everything and everyone only a person who has lost faith in himself can believe in . . . And suddenly his madness seemed to have a sound and perfectly plausible basis. It was easier, and made more sense, than that silence broken only by the song of birds and my father's gentle voice as he gave me a dispassionate and detailed explanation of his misadventures in prison. He didn't complain or make accusations, he was fearless. . . .

But how could their wireless telephone operate across that silence, that tranquillity of nature, across the six hundred miles from Moscow to Rameno, to the forest where my father and I stood in a thicket talking? How could they eavesdrop on us? . . . They could.

A cell. Crisscrossed rays. Ordinary rays of electric light, wide, like those of a searchlight. At night, on the wall, apart from the rays, the imprint of a face with its eyes gouged out. You could tell it was a photograph. An enlargement—the touch-ups and scratches visible in the neon light. The same photograph someone dropped in the hallway? No, a different one. I'm older, around nine. You could tell the image was being projected. No fancy tricks. He used to show slides himself. In Syzran.

"We know! We know! . . ."

A familiar voice. Subotsky's? No, not Subotsky's. A recording. An attempt to intimidate him, he figured.

"And your son's worse than his father! . . ."

They were trying to intimidate him. . . . White doves were flying along the two crisscrossed diagonals of the rays. Doves in a cell? White doves?! . . . A hallucination, nothing more than a hallucination . . . No, that wasn't quite it either! Then he strained his will to remember what it was: stereoscopes, movies. . . .

And then—music. Damn them! Singing the "Varshavyanka."

"Hostile storms are brewing. . . ." The bastards! A song from the revolution! The singing became louder. Grew closer. Then it was there. Was it coming from under the table? Louder. From all four walls. Overwhelming . . . Cover your ears, now, to keep from going deaf! . . . The peephole. In the tomblike silence, the supervisor's voice: "What are you doing? No sleeping allowed . . . Out of your cell!"

Interrogation. The cell. Interrogation. The cell. Interrogation. The cell. Doves flying . . . Interrogation . . .

"A psycho! Ho-ho-ho!"

An echo. Faster. The brain was starting to go. The main thing was not to fall to pieces! The brain!

"You shit-eating SR White Guard!"

Doves flying . . . Another photo? A family photo? On the wall? . . . Two people behind bars, a third, the lady of the house!—hee-hee-hee!—a champignon spy. Yes, a champignon spy! America. Ara-ara-ara-ara! . . .

"You motherfumotherfumotherfumother!"

Nonesense! The important thing was not to forget words. "Transcendental." "Empiricism." "Pyroxylin." "Trinitrotoluene." "Ichthyosaur."

"Ara! Ara! Motherfu . . ."

Transcendental! Pyroxylin! "A and B were sitting on a pipe"— small problems were also useful. . . . "Explanation." "Crystallohydrates" . . .

"Hostile storms are brewing. . . ."

There's three hundred of us here! Three hundred of us!

"Paaapaaa!"

I didn't get it right. One for Mama, one for Papa, one for the Bicycle, and one for the Rifle. Didn't I get it right? Stay there, you degenerate. I won't let you by! Let's take a break for a smoke. More powerful than dynamite. Ozerki.

"Psycho! Ho-ho-ho! Your word as a revolutionary! You look like Kalyaev. An SR? A leftist? On top of all that, a leftist?! Amer-

ican? Mayne Read? *Jour fixe?* There's only one place for you—
on the garbage dump. Shall we go hunting?"

"Don't, Pa-paa. . . ."

Ozerki. Avenarius. Kok-sagyz. Rubber. The tire factory in Yaroslavl. Sonya Marmeladova. Narkompros. Syzran . . .

By an effort of will, he fought his way back to the surface, and
we were standing in a clearing—silence, wilderness, the birds chirping. . . . "And that's how," he said, "they smashed me to smith-
ereens . . . how they tuned in. . . ."

"But if . . ." I said, feverishly seeking an explanation while we
were alone with no one to disturb us. "But what if all that's
happening to you right now is . . . self-induced? The final aftereffects of recordings you heard at Lefortovo?! . . ."

I no longer doubted that it all had really happened. The photographs on the prison wall, projected in enlarged form and ripped,
the very ones he had described, were family photographs that had
disappeared when our home was searched. While straightening up
after the pogrom, gathering up the photos from our album that
were strewn over the floor, my mother and I had been unable to
find those very photographs. . . .

"Well, it's possible," he replied, and I could see that he had no
desire to explain it all to me again. "Entirely possible. One half
of the brain speaking to the other half—it's not out of the question.
. . . But where's the guarantee? In the meantime, don't say any
more than you have to to me. Not one word more than you have
to! . . . I shouldn't know about those things, I shouldn't know
about them! Is that clear?"

Yes, it was clear. He was referring to everything that I was
bursting with and could barely contain. Everything I had dreamed
of telling him in private as I raced to Rameno, everything I had
to say about the prison stay bestowed on him and from which he
had now finally emerged. But no. My father was afraid. It was the
first time I had ever seen my father afraid. Afraid that I might let
something slip to him and that I'd be thrown in jail for it. He was

suppressing the very thought. His thoughts were being monitored. . . .

He raised one hand and gave me a signal with his fingers, a soundless snap. They'd tuned back in! Watch it—they've tuned back in! . . . A generator had started up somewhere in Lefortovo. Strange—he and I were still alone in the vast, deserted woods, but guests were hovering unseen above us. . . .

But in principle that made no difference now, for I had been warned. Neither my father's features, voice, nor mannerisms changed. With his usual verve, he peppered me with questions about Mama, my dissertation which needed to be finished quickly, Aunt Natasha and Evgeny Nikolaevich. . . . And I answered the questions as if nothing had happened, except that now I wanted to remain silent. . . .

To skip ahead, I will say that all this lasted for another two years, while father was in exile. Mama and I weren't able to visit him often. He had to find work and earn some money. After the amnesty and later, after he was rehabilitated, those brain phenomena began to taper off. Finally they disappeared entirely. Mama never found out about them. She died a short time later. And my father died too. The reality of what happened to him remains a mystery to me. Perhaps with the death of Stalin and the shake-up that followed, the scientists finally relinquished their hold on him. And it's also possible that, over time, my father simply started feeling better, the terrible wounds inflicted on his brain scarred over, and the hallucinations stopped coming back. Like him, I accept both variations.

But back then, when we first saw each other in Rameno and had that long conversation in the woods, my happiness at being with my father was mixed with an unquenchable longing, as if, being together with him again now, I had lost something forever. We could loll about on the grass, joke, play with the dog. We reveled in the sight and smell of each other. And we were more cut off from each other than we'd ever been.

I had to hurry back to Moscow, leaving my father alone and

helpless with those prophetic voices, in terrible desolation. He was also powerless to help me in my solitude. He was never to learn what I thought or where I was headed. I did not have the right to burden him with that. But this does not make me any the less guilty toward him. . . .

We returned home through that same aspen wood. A wind had sprung up, and now it was frightening to look at those seething trees. Spirits were at work, and I could not break free of them, for I too was raised into the air by a feeling of what could be called reverential terror. It was as if, while looking at those trees, I lost myself in that swarm of muttering, dancing leaves. It may just have been caused by the wind; still, the hair on my head stood on end. And, as happens at moments of great intensity, that terror both opposed and verged on the ecstasy I felt at what I saw and experienced.

My father's state must have communicated itself to me. I both understood and took upon myself his rumbling remoteness from the entire world and his rigorous concentration on thoughts and images to which he alone had access. But that was not the most important thing. A way out suddenly seemed to have been found—not for him, for me. A way was open, signals could be heard, and nothing and no one would stop me. . . . The mark of damnation and happiness was on my brow.

My father stood beside me, and he too silently watched this spellbound, localized whirlwind, circling in one spot like an animal. He probably had his own ideas about what it was. The sun was starting to set, but still there was not a single cloud in the sky. . . . Inwardly I said to my father, or to future opponents yet to be, or to myself: Look, see for yourself. This is the reality that you ignore, disdainfully calling it "fantasy." Here it is! There's no need to fantasize, it's enough to see it, and it doesn't matter in the least what you call it. You can call it a tree, or a human being. Whatever you like! The tree is me in an imagined dream. The tree is my father. It swirls; you look closer; it seethes, as you and I do, like the universe in an abyss of hypotheses and hyperboles. Our encounters, clashes, losses—it all seethes together in words too exalted for us to utter. All reality seethes. . . .

Yet that was not the most important thing at the time either. I don't know why but, ever since the image dawned on me, I've always thought that a writer withdrawing to work and do some real writing retreats to the forest, so that no one will see him or hear him. With a single idea in mind: "Time to put me on paper," says the forest, becoming a text.

God, what a fabled kingdom this is! You can't tear yourself away. You just want to keep looking. Communicate—with whom? with people? readers? I don't think so. They'll seize on any word and prove that none of it is true. I know them! The text is the sole refuge. Not too dense, not too sparse . . . But, remember, there's no way back out of a text. We're in the forest.

There's another important thing that needs to be said: You mustn't think while you're writing. You have to disconnect yourself—lose track of yourself, lose your way—but the main thing is to forget yourself and live without thinking about anything. And how beautiful that is! At last you're gone, you're dead. The forest is all there is. And we enter the forest. We enter the text.

For that reason, the most important thing in the book you're writing is its mystery. For the author, for you. That is what excites you, what draws you in and quietly does its invisible work. That is all we need. And it's not important that people will argue and say, "He made it all up, those things didn't happen." They're in the fields, and we're in the forest. What they want is scope, scale, reproduction. . . . But we are obliged to remember our refuge, our text, our secret paths. All they know is heroic epics and art's relationship to reality. . . . And meanwhile all we have in hand is stories.

. . . Need I add that I did not breathe a word of this to my father, either in the forest or when we had returned home?

IV

. . .

Dangerous Liaisons

I was in love with the actress A., who possessed mediumistic powers. At a séance, all she had to do was touch a finger to the light blue saucer she used as a pointer and it would jump up, as if recognizing her, hover just above the table for a fraction of a second, and then, with a ringing sound, dart with unflagging zeal about the board, answering people's questions with dizzying speed. In an ordinary séance, if it is not mere sleight of hand, the letters combine listlessly, almost reluctantly, a formal politeness shown the demanding gathering. Names and dates get mixed up, the spelling is botched, and the result is utter nonsense, unworthy of an otherwordly experience. Or else, idiotic as a stuck record, the pointer persists in repeating curses like "ass" or "fool" over and over, to the considerable embarrassment of the pretty young lady attending her first séance. I was told that these were not the souls of the dead descending onto the pointer, or currents flowing from our fingers but, rather, was the work of "elementals," a lower, primitive level of life that is adjacent to ours and invisible to us. We cannot communicate with them. Like worms or bacteria, they exist in a dimension beyond our reach. Aficionados sometimes refer to them as "idlers."

But no sooner would A. waltz up to the table than everything would somehow change. Nearly all the answers would be interesting. And the saucer's inert porcelain would literally come to life from her touch, suffused with warmth and blood, teaching object lessons in applied magic.

For the sake of fairness, it should be noted that A. herself, a woman well along in years and living on a pension, could not bear all that toying with the occult, and it was with the greatest reluctance that she would sit down with the saucer—once a year, and only after considerable persuasion: "Look, A., the thing is, it won't move without you." "What do you mean, it won't?!" she would reply irritably, placing a finger vertically against the cool saucer. And it would resonate immediately, as if all it had been waiting for was a single electric touch of the actress's hand. But she would also be quick to withdraw from the enchanted table, wrapping herself in a gaudy shawl. She had good reason to shun such encounters. . . .

A. had been seeing unusual things, ever since she was a child. Her governess, a pious, pedantic old maid, irreproachable and vindictive in her bearing, constantly hammered away at the child: "Don't fidget at the table! Stop showing off! Don't hunch your shoulders! Don't you dare look at yourself in the mirror! You are the daughter of a Russian nobleman, not some French tart! Even if your stepfather did die penniless because of your mother's extravagance, may he find peace in the alcoves of heaven, in the embrace of a chaste houri."

At bedtime she would have A., in just her nightshirt, kneel behind her on the cold floor; dressed for the evening but wearing only her corset and beribboned pantaloons to keep her dress from getting wrinkled, the English governess would offer the girl an example of genuine piety. One time A. stole a look at the Englishwoman—as she prayed devoutly, two imps the size of walnuts were dancing vigorously on a spot where her dyed hair was pitifully thin. Those imps were tremendously pleased to see that the girl had understood: the prim and proper governess's thoughts had strayed, and God only knew where. . . .

Nothing's more interesting than telling ghost stories with a bunch of friends. But nothing's more unpleasant than encountering a ghost in real life, as A. did when she was an adolescent growing up in Soviet society—in broad daylight, in the Arbat section of Moscow, she saw B., an actor at the Vakhtangov Theatre, an old admirer of hers. It had been more than a year since he had passed away. And there he was, as if nothing whatsoever had happened, mingling with the crowd, striding along in the general direction of Smolensk Square. More out of habit than anything, A. called out faintly to him. B. shuddered and looked back, but of course pretended not to have recognized her. He had not changed in the slightest, and was even still wearing his suit made of a speckled material. He had a solid-looking package under his arm. Taking a closer look at it, she gasped: wrapped in tattered newspaper, the shape of the object seemed to indicate that it was a small cast-iron urn of the sort that, sometimes in more sculptural form, are used as decorations on graves. She had no desire to follow B. to determine whether it was really him or someone else. . . .

Soon, however, she had further occasion to see for herself that things do not always go as smoothly in that other realm, as we might think, ladies and gentlemen. A. had a friend (we'll call her V.) whose young husband had died. Ten days had not yet passed when A. dreamed of the deceased. He complained that V. had had him buried in a new pair of boots. They pinched his feet. He went on to explain that custom required a person to be buried in light footwear, slippers, to make the journey to the hereafter easier. That's why the dead are carried out feet first. I have a journey to make, he said. And in what? Boots. My feet are numb. Bring me some slippers tomorrow. First thing . . .

"Where am I supposed to bring them?" asked A., frozen in terror. Quite calmly, the dead man gave her the name of the street and apartment number. Memorize it, he said, and tell it to my widow. . . . Bye!

The next day A. went rushing to her friend. But V. wouldn't hear a word of it: You shouldn't read so much Madame Blavatsky at night! she snorted. She had wept so much, grieved so much, and yet she wouldn't believe it! That's modern girls for you! What should I do? thought A. After all, he's waiting, he's counting on the slippers. And it'd be interesting to check it out—why would I have memorized the exact address if it's meaningless?

Assuming sole responsibility, A. took a trolley to a funeral parlor to buy a pair of paper slippers. These are inexpensive slippers, available in all sizes, and specially made from black paper glued straight onto cardboard soles. The dead don't need a lot, do they? It's all going to rot anyway. Other things may run short, but the country always has a good supply of paper slippers. However, to find a little cross, for example, or candles, or a wreath is out of the question. Not under these conditions. But not even the Soviet system could bring itself to abolish that final act of charity—paper slippers for the dead. And, for that, may its memory live forever. . . .

And so she bought the slippers. She grabbed some flowers at the market, choosing them intuitively, without haggling over the price, then took a cab to 10 Trekhprudny Lane, apartment 7. And then miraculously—Trekhprudny Lane, which she had never heard of before, turned out to exist. And there was also a number 10. . . . As soon as she entered the courtyard, she was struck by the unusual number of people shuffling up and down the staircase in the front hall. Everywhere she looked there were old women still in their house clothes, children hushed and wide-eyed, listening for something. . . .

The door to number 7 was wide open. The plinth and the latch had been removed. The chain, a gleaming ball at one end, hung useless. She went in. A crowd of women, the smell of fresh paint, and, despite the open windows, stuffy air, with an aftertaste of vanilla. Heaped with flowers, someone she had never seen before was laid out in a coffin on the dinner table in the center of the room. Cringing, hunched, Alla stole over to the body and thrust the slippers for Gennady between the corpse's feet. She was self-possessed enough to cover the slippers with tulips, so that the living would not guess what was happening. From Valya, she whispered. From Valya to Genochka.

You might well ask what sort of physical connections exist between this world and the next—I don't know. Ask A. She can explain it all. As for me, I'll counter with a question of my own. Have you ever worn boots that came off a dead man's feet? I have. A poor student at the time, I inherited them from some distant relative. He had died in those boots. Died in the street, of heart failure. And I was given those down-at-the-heel boots on the day of the funeral. Wear them in good health, I was told. They're almost like new. It would have been awkward to refuse. All the same, the boots and I got on quite well. And though I had other shoes at the time, I would slip into the dead man's boots, holding my breath. Do you know what started to happen? As I grew used to the boots, I could feel their tug for their former owner, to whom, as much as possible, they had remained faithful. No, they were not too tight. On the contrary, they were even a little too big for me. But their inner form matched neither my foot nor my step. For example, where his metatarsus had protruded in some way peculiar to him, there were lacunae and indentations vainly awaiting someone to fill them. And there was a slight cramping where my baby toe protruded because of all my calcium deposits, if you'll pardon the details. In short, the shoes gave me an exact impression of the man and brought him to mind at every step, agreeing to cohabit with me only for want of anything better. As I walked, my every toe kept re-encountering my poor predecessor. It's difficult to describe—this feeling from the inside. He was a good person, and I made no claim to take his place. I made an honest effort to pretend that I didn't exist, didn't feel anything. It was like foolishly marrying a widow who still tenderly loved her first husband. Personally, I have yet to take any such risky steps in my own life. But anything can happen. And if you were in my place, in my boots, you'd have no problem seeing what I meant. Think of it like this—a brand-new widow who, though faithful and attentive to you, nevertheless maintains her bond with her former other half, the unforgettable Benik, as is amiably demonstrated to you each time she makes a slip of the tongue. She may marry you, assure you, embrace you, but Benik will keep cropping up.

You are an intermediary, a medium who connects her with Benik. You are a series of irrelevant comparisons. No getting around that. Your round face serves her as a television screen on which her Benik nods to her and smiles sadly. You're like the saucer that runs inoffensively around a circle of handwritten letters that in themselves have no meaning. So, then, what's the point, if any? Why am I going on and on, unable to stop? The two of them are communicating through me. Whether I'm drinking my tea from his favorite mug or taking a walk with his wife in the garden, they are always together, so used to each other, the one having taken on the other's shape. Exactly what happened with those boots. They seem in cahoots. And they contort my feet. But that's not my point. Think of it like this—if the things that exist alongside us can take on the indelible impression of someone's spirit, why shouldn't there be efforts to exert physical pressure on us from the hereafter? Is there ever! . . . The dead leap at every chance. They grasp at a word. Grab at a hand . . .

A., B., C. . . . The pointer spins on its way. And what comes next? Alphabetically, D. is next. No two ways about that. As on a compass, the needle stops at the letter "D." Beyond any doubt. You can turn the board around and, as if on command, the saucer will still point to the same letter. There's no getting away from it.

"Is that you, D.?" asks A. in amazement.

And D. spells out his answer: "Yes, it's me. Yes, A. It's me."

And, to convince her, he calls her by her girlhood nicknames. No one else knew them. Any cheap tricks or charlatanism was out of the question. "Alenka," "Bunny" . . . And she was over sixty. She remembered that D. had used the same intonation when he had been alive. He was fond of German expressions and the subjunctive. Not "I want" but "I would like." A cultured person. Something out of Chekhov.

"Well, what would our guest like?" interjected one dolt who had been deranged by séances.

Then he drawled in a way that was both old-fashioned and all his own: "*Gehen Sie zum Teufel.* The soup is getting cold. I would like to speak with my stepdaughter, A. . . ."

To make a long story short, this was A.'s stepfather. He had been close to court circles before the scandal with A.'s mother. Dmitri Sergeevich, or Dima, as the five-year-old A., stubbornly imitating her mother, had been bold enough to call that lion of society . . . Where had it all disappeared to?

"I'm here, Dmitri Sergeevich," she said with resignation, placing her hand on the pointer. "But why are you here? And after so many years! . . ."

It turned out to be no more and no less than his desire to be back among us, an end he had been secretly pursuing in the realm adjacent to ours. He had long sought to make contact. He had been performing experiments in telekinesis and was certain that he had succeeded. He said that he was gradually growing a new astral body. Just a little more practice and then, if someone threw him a line, he could return to this world and enter a physical body.

"*Bitte. Sehen Sie!*" he said. "Look behind you. There's a cut-glass bowl filled with apples on the sideboard, isn't there?"

Everyone looked and, indeed, the bowl and the apples were both there. Now there was fear in the air. He could see us sitting there.

"And now, damnit, I will slowly move the bowl toward the candlestick. Note the parameters. Attention! I'm starting now! . . ."

A. said that all eyes were on the beautiful Baccarat cut-glass bowl. It wasn't budging.

"Did you see? Did you see that?!" exclaimed D. from behind the scenes, circling the parapet of the table. "It's moving! Hurray! It moved! . . ."

No one else shared that impression, and everyone felt somewhat awkward.

"Use your eyes, you lousy dogs!"

In his excitement over there, he thought he had moved something over here. We seemed to hear him panting. The pointer was literally streaming under our fingers. Everyone was breathing heavily. At this tense moment, the soles of his shoes may have skidded along the varnished surface of the sideboard and his head may have been visited by the slippery notion that he was actually moving the bowl of apples through sheer mystical force.

"No," Alla told him, "Dima, you're mistaken. It's all in your head. Your achievements haven't been reflected on our level yet. The telekinesis didn't work. . . ."

Then he cursed us all for having no manners.

"You're lying, you lowlife! I can see it, I can see it moving! All right, you bastard, move! What, are you deaf?"

He did not succeed in moving the bowl once the entire evening. We shared his struggle. Some people tried to help the old sinner by lending him mental support, others used hatha-yoga, exhaling prana. Nothing helped; the bowl hadn't budged an inch; it seemed spellbound. By now he was almost screaming.

"Time for you mystics to break it up!" he shouted. "Why don't the police know about this? I'm going to inform the proper authorities about this illegal assembly. That'll change your tune! . . ."

But the most outrageous thing of all was that, even in the life after death, D. remained the implacable atheist he had always been.

"No," he stated, "there is no life after death. No immortal soul. No tents of paradise. The priests made all that up. There is no God but Thor, and Hitler is his prophet! You're really an ass. . . ."

At that point he became utterly indecent, and then she, a veteran of the camps, let him have it: "Go back where you came from, you mangy dog. I know you inside and out. What kind of stepfather are you? When I was in Vorkuta I wasn't afraid of Stalin or death. So beat it, beat it!"

Here she placed the pointer on a cross, prudently sketched out in advance. The saucer seemed to grit its teeth. Then it stopped, lifeless, wings spread. The demon had flown off. His revenge was that her old furniture creaked all winter. And the saucepans hanging in the kitchen kept emitting a melodious ring. . . .

I was always eager to hear A.'s stories, always agape and agog. I went to her stories the way a boy running away from an orphanage runs to his mother. Without her stories, life was flat. The salt lost its savor. The earth became a bleak and empty place. I was drawn and braced by the astonishing realness of these stories. But I am not a mystic. In and of themselves, all those dead people, demons, and ghosts are of no interest to me. I have never had any penchant for those things, any special need of them or bones to pick with them. I simply had no evidence for believing in them or accepting their reality.

Judge for yourself. Fairy tales help us to see the world as truly worthy of life, great and significant. Seeming to be lost in the ancient past and the impossible, fairy tales remind us what is real, what has already happened, though we were just blind to it, and what is yet to be and will come to pass when we are gone. It mustn't be thought that fairy tales are behind us. They are ahead of us. Not suspecting that at all, we say a little prayer: Fairy tale, fairy tale, save me like a magic wand. . . . Impart a ground and order to everything. Fairy tales are never mere daydreams. Fairy tales begin in the most ordinary way, as life does, life as you and I live it day to day. Once upon a time. There was an old man and an old woman. Things are always good for the rich. And never good for the poor. The rich live in palaces. And the poor live in huts. The rich man has a wife bedecked in pearls. The poor man marries a frog. The rich man is wise. And the poor man is a stupid fool.

No, says the fairy tale, that's not true, that's wrong. It just seems that way to you. And I was just making believe. That's only the start, the buildup. We haven't gotten to the heart of the matter yet. As you shall see, it's not like that at all. . . .

"Alla," I said, imagining that I was embracing her knees, "tell me the story about Stalin. Tell me about seeing the vision of him. . . ."

Fairy tales brought us glad tidings of reality at the dawn of human history, at its very sources. As if the fairy tales already knew and swore to us at the outset that things were other than they first seem. Everything is more significant, realer. The last become the first. The poor man is rich. In reality, the fool is clever and handsome. Cinderella marries her true love, the prince. And the ogre doesn't catch Tom Thumb. What an achievement this is! What deep insight this required! And it's not the happy endings that matter here. . . .

"Please, Alla, be a love, tell me one more time about Stalin coming to you, when was it, the second or third night after his death. That was in Vorkuta, wasn't it? You were in a free settlement by then, weren't you? . . ."

It was. She was. Alla's fairy tale was based on actual events, constructed from facts whose authenticity I did not doubt in the least. And perhaps that was why her true-life stories were sometimes rather gruesome, bereft of happy endings, unlike the fairy tales of old. But they afforded me the joy of knowing life with greater fullness and breadth than we usually do, and thereby revealed more meaning than we see with our everyday eyes. With Alla doing her part, reality seemed to become rational and harmonious, the supernatural shedding some additional light on history, which is always filled with futile suffering. At times the miraculous will invest our realm with meaning, our realm, where everything is truly devoid of logic, hopeless, repulsive, and beyond all understanding. What yesterday appeared to have no right to exist, today receives the sanction of fairy tale. . . .

"But how did you know it was Stalin? Did he look like the photographs and statues of him? Didn't you tell me that Stalin came bursting in on you in the middle of the night, when it was dark and you were already in bed? . . ."

While I listened intently to Alla, what I really wanted to do was throw my arms around her knees, as if she were some Sybil whose sublime prophecies I was afraid of missing. There was, however, nothing grandiose about her tone. The reality of the event was plain enough, and she made no attempt to exaggerate or embellish. She wasn't playing any games, but I was—by pretending to remember only a part of the story incident she had once told—and, by the way, without any prompting. I was consumed by a desire to hear her retell that story, transparent as a brook, with her drawn-out vowels, her wonderful pupils dilating, as if, when looking at my face, she were peering into the bitter book of her own past, irresistibly marveling at what she read there. Her ability to be astonished by her own gift of seeing more deeply and keenly than others was also the best proof of the purity of her intention— to recount what had happened, word for word, withholding nothing. It's even possible that Stalin did visit her that night, because who else could his troubled spirit have found as worthy, sensitive, and receptive as she, a sorceress who had seen a thing or two? Still, we don't know whom else he appeared to. Stalin was inside everyone, like the hammer alongside the sickle in every mind. In her simplicity of heart, she thought that she had drawn him to that decrepit hut, that cumbersome cemetery at the gates of the camp through which she and so many other convicts had walked. In other words, A.—the first letter of the alphabet—served Stalin as the victim personified, magnetic in her purity.

All the while Stalin was dying, things kept going wrong in her house and courtyard. There was a driving blizzard. A tub of half-rotted cabbage in the hallway kept rumbling and croaking. Every section of the building roared, droned, yelped. In the stovepipe, a tender mezzo-soprano, perfectly articulate but for some reason doleful, sang:

The snowstorm sweeps down the street
and behind the snow my love comes walking.

Then, from somewhere in the attic, a men's choir responded:

Nothing can come between us on land or sea,
And we fear neither ice nor cloud. . . .

She had a feeling that the Mustache had already bitten the dust, even though the authorities were concealing that fact for some reason. The noises and voices in her hut made it unclear whether his minions were rejoicing or weeping and wailing. Apparently, in practice, they did both. . . .

Suddenly everything grew still. She was awakened by an uncanny stillness that surrounded her from every side. Even the grandfather clock had stopped ticking. Not a cricket was chirping. Not a floorboard was creaking. The wind seemed to have dropped under the eaves of the slate roof. And from the stillness, she knew that the beloved had arrived. Now she understood what the baying of the damned had meant. He stood in silence like a pillar by her trundle bed. In person. The Mustache.

He did not, however, have a mustache, a form, or an image. This I would call the positive expression of an ultimate negation. In the darkness of the room, he loomed like a weighty column whose top reached the ceiling, and which was not made of stone or bronze or any other normal material but of pure coldness, of something like methane or nitrogen reduced to absolute zero, yet it had not solidified or frozen but retained its gaseous form even after ceasing all motion.

Everything was visible through Stalin. The window white with snow. The dark walls. The modest icon lamp peacefully radiating its little light concealed in one corner. She knew intuitively that turning on the lights would not have made any difference. The apparition was void of all shape. . . . Nevertheless his presence—columnar, self-contained, totally detached—was unbearably dominating. He cast no shadow, no breathing could be heard, and the coldness did not even spread through the room, though, towering by her bed like some colossal cylinder, it was so concentrated that if you touched it, it would freeze your hand off. He seemed locked in his frozen solitude. And there was no question that he knew Alla was awake.

"What do you want from me?" she asked mentally, lacking the strength to move her tongue but still trying to choose and pronounce her words as if she were at an interrogation, perhaps with even greater firmness. "Why have you come to me here in Vorkuta? Haven't you done enough to me already?! You've already taken everything I had from me."

Then, not speaking aloud either, using not his voice but some inner, direct phone line, he said with abrupt irritation: "Forgive my debts!"

"What debts?!" she retorted like a peasant woman, failing at first to catch his drift. "I don't owe you anything! . . . It's you who owes everyone! . . ."

Then she stopped short. That wasn't the point. It was just that Stalin was clearly not disposed to beg forgiveness and, as always, was demanding the whip hand.

"Look, what will it cost you?" he said in a capricious tone, as if ashamed to display a moment's weakness. "I'm telling you in plain Russian: forgive my debts! Do you understand? I'll spell it out for you." He immediately switched to codes: "Mikoyan. Yezhov. Saratov. Ilich. Nikita. Saratov. Understand? No? All right, I'll repeat the initials. Siberia. Ibarruri (Dolores Ibarruri). Nekrasov. Siberia. Period. Stalin."

She was thinking how cold, how inhumanly cold he must be in the column forged from his own spirit. But, echolike, something was reaching her through the Morse code. The dead man was infuriated by her stubbornness in pretending not to know what was wanted of her. That cunt. Kirov. And it's all because I didn't eliminate him in time, Zinoviev. I didn't see to it, Rakovsky. I let that fish slip past me on the general list. Bukharin, tell me the truth, cross your heart, who could have foreseen that I would ever have to depend on scum like her? It's always the same for all of us—silent reproaches, pages of conscience. You don't kill someone in time and then, Pyatakov, it torments and frustrates you the rest of your life.

"Forgive me!" He forced out the words, overcoming his own resistance, amazed by this unprecedented humiliation after death. He was simultaneously appalled and pleased that he had done her injury—just between us girls—wiped out her family, hurled her to the Far North, to the back of beyond, the whole works, as if he had foreseen that shameful encounter. Alla, you'll remember what the dead have to go through. Stalin.

I won't conceal it—I'm afraid of writing about him. No sooner do I sit down with a piece of paper than a certain minor magic begins. Fear, confusion. As if I'd been stung by a diseased bee. My hand balks. My knees turn to water, as they say. I toss everything in the wastebasket. My pulse accelerates. My urine reeks of acetone. My mind turns upside down. Last night, while I was writing, a homeless cat I've seen around jumped in through the window and, looking for a warm spot to curl up, walked over to Mariya, who was sleeping. But it was sweltering out! By the way, it's summer here in France. It's a good thing I shooed the cat away. One "Scat!" and it was gone. But the Portuguese woman who comes once a year to give the house a good cleaning, had hung a little portrait of Stalin on the wall, without asking our permission. I came back home, and there it was, in an oval frame! That's all I needed! I said to myself. Now I've had it! . . . She had not recognized the face—and how was a Portuguese woman to know who he was? The mustache, the decorations, that chest full of medals. Imposing. Maybe he was some important relative? There was no point in yelling at our goodhearted housekeeper. She had just wanted to make the place prettier. But the point is that this happened on the very day I had just managed to work up the nerve to write the first sentence about him, based on my own recollections. Where had she dug up that picture of Stalin, a new souvenir item, sealed in plastic, which a kind friend had sent from the Soviet Union about a year ago to cheer us up and bring us up to date? It gave us a laugh at the time; then we forgot all about it. But the

Portuguese woman had come across it, pulled it out from the clutter and old papers, washed it off. I have no idea what trouble that's going to cause us. I am here writing, and he's in the living room menacing me. He emits hallucinations. I can't overcome him. Where's the old wood-goblin? Where's Lenin? . . .

For half a century—and more—we've been hammering away at one thing: "Lenin-Stalin," "Lenin-Stalin." Until it wedged into our head, if you'll pardon my saying so. If you said "Stalin!" to a young lady, the unfailing answer was "Lenin, Lenin!" "One step forward, two steps back." But Stalin is more important than Lenin! Ulyanov made the bed, but Dzhugashvili lay down in it! The young lady becomes hysterical. "Lenient, Lunar." You try to calm her down: "Steel-Slag," "Steel-Slag," "Lenin-Stalin." We feel as though we are committing sabotage. That's bad. But we don't have the strength to stop. We're not in control of ourselves, you see. Invisible forces are weighing on us. "Stalin-Lenin," "Lenin-Stal . . ." "Le?" "Li?" "Nina." I'm in her now. "Sta-a-a," she moans. I go wild: "Lenin! Lenin!" Lenina, Stalina, Marxina, and Engelsina. You can all go to hell. Not . . . But you, Stella! . . .

A voice from outer space (Leo Tolstoy's): Stop disgracing yourselves! People are looking are you! . . .

But this is just a question of phonetics, I object. Maybe it is. Or maybe it's something else. Our lives are spent on such arguments, hairsplitting. Gone in a flash.

"It must be admitted that with Lenin we had a sort of intellectual at the helm. Intelligent, American-like . . ."

"What about Stalin?"

"Stalin's a total mystery. . . . At heart he may have been a poet, a film director. . . ."

"And Lenin?"

"Lenin in his rationalism . . ."

"And Stalin?"

"And Stalin? . . . I'm afraid he's not all that simple, sir. . . . Stalin is dark, clouded. . . ."

"And Lenin?"

"You're obsessed with Lenin. 'Lenin! Lenin!' Lenin's a Martian. Have you been to his tomb? That's all I have to say!"

"And Stalin?"

"Stalin's behind the scenes. A magician always works behind the scenes. Even those of his own mind . . ."

"And Lenin?"

"Lenin makes you tremble a little. He may be an incarnation. And do you know of whom? Socrates. Incarnate . . ."

"And Stalin? . . ."

You can imagine the state Alla was in! Huddling under two blankets, she suddenly felt some coldness emanating from him. It was obvious that this was not part of a natural death but what high-minded writers, students of the Apocalypse, term the second and final death, from which you cannot struggle free, no matter how you thrash; this ice doesn't melt. The aficionados say that the souls of such people are on the mineral level. And there he was, as if at the Last Judgment, asking for the remission of his sins.

"No," Alla said, having struggled to regain control of her lips. "You won't get my forgiveness!"

He seemed about to crush her with his sheer mass. Perhaps he even intended to do just that, and had begun bending toward her but restrained himself.

"Comrade Alla, there's something wrong in your thinking." An unexpected grimace of dependence had crept into his tone of voice. "You're not thinking like a Soviet, from the state's point of view. You're not thinking like Lenin. Or like Stalin. We know there were some isolated excesses, some deviations here and there. Which affected you personally. Inhumanly. I agree. And it's not out of the question that your husband . . . He's still alive, isn't he? Your husband's still alive? . . ."

As he spoke, he attacked, froze, worked out mythical plans for his liberation after death. Apparently, incoherent streams of consciousness, untranslatable into ordinary language, were wandering though his mind, if, of course, such analogies are appropriately applied to the dead. Or was that to be heard not in the uninvited guest's utterances but solely in what was instilled by his menacing presence, causing her inner chords to vibrate? By the way, oddly enough, there was nothing Georgian about his accent. Just his usual turns of phrase, familiar from childhood.

"Let her speak for everyone! We'll elect her to the Soviet. Any nays? A fully authorized deputy to the All-Union Congress of People's Prisoners . . ."

Why did he leave her alive? She was lying there in bed stretched out like some grande dame. She must have been warm. It wouldn't have cost her anything to take the podium and say, "In the name of everyone deservedly tormented by you, I forgive your sins! . . ." As people say, let bygones be bygones. Even Myasnikov forgave him. And he didn't have a drop of pity in him. Worse than Ord-zhonikidze. A high-level decision was made, and Molotov person-ally went to prevail on him: "Myasnikov! What's it going to cost you? You understand. Go with the Boss on this one. Be human about it. It's curtains for you anyway. The Boss told me to tell you that. Go along with it. Admit you were a spy." And, Alla, if you can imagine, he went along with it. They gave him the death sentence, and the entire country, to a man, sighed with re-lief. . . . Go along with it. . . .

"Now I've got you!" she exclaimed, sitting up in bed like a witch, all fear gone. "And I won't let you go! . . . I won't for-give you! . . ."

Once again she sat up in bed. She recalled the time a security officer came to the strict-discipline barracks. That was back in Igarka. No, in Taishet. He had come to give the prisoners a scare—and had fallen into a trap. When they stuck their homemade knives to his ribs, he pissed his pants, pleading, farting from fear: I'll never lay a finger on you again. I have little children, have pity on my children. And then he left the barracks, having given them his word of honor as a communist and an officer. He immediately had the barracks flooded with water cannons. "I'll turn you cock-suckers into a living skating rink! . . ."

"But aren't you supposed to be a Christian?" said the son of a Georgian shoemaker, seeming to grin condescendingly. "You're bound by that law, no matter how you try to wriggle out of it. . . ."

Another good way to kill someone—by using the Gospels—one that I personally discovered only quite recently. As you beat some-one, keep telling him, "You should forgive me." Then you slap his face! Again and again! But don't forget to spice things up by saying, "Turn the other cheek, the left cheek, now the right one. . . ." Take your time. Beat him to your heart's content. And if he objects or complains, remind him of the commandment: You're not acting like a Christian. That's immoral. And you call yourself a writer. That doesn't satisfy him? The degenerate! Beat that nihilist! Use your boots on him: We'll teach you to love freedom. To love your enemies. Didn't you ever read about that? . . . And when they drag him away, spread your hands in a gesture of helplessness. Say he got what he deserved, the ignoramus, the lout, the misanthrope! He should learn how to forgive.

Alla hesitated.

"But you're Russian Orthodox, aren't you?" continued Stalin insinuatingly. "Let's be sensible and discuss this in Marxist terms. Where's your logic? It's the church's own teaching. . . . Who is without sin?"

He had of course been trained in a famous seminary, and now the monster was dredging up the basics. Another minute and he would have been roaring like a wild archimandrite, "Obey me, you sinner, prostrate yourself in the dust! Forgive Stalin and his men their sins! . . ."

She looked around the hut, which now seemed uninhabitable, useless. Dawn was a long way off. The North. But the candle flame in the corner and the micalike snow outside glittered faintly. Some-where a shot was fired, probably a flare gun. Shadows went flying, the snow turned green. It grew dark again. Then Alla decided his fate, speaking not to him, the Murderer, but to herself:

"Forgive you on behalf of all the others, all the zeks? God has not given me that right. People would never forgive me. But for all your sins against me, for everything you did to me and me alone, all right, I forgive you. . . ."

She was inspired. Sitting up in the trundle bed, she spoke like a prophetess, one marblelike finger pointed at the forest tundra:

"And now go round to everyone! One at a time, each one in turn. Everyone whose forgiveness you need. The living and the dead. And let each one of them forgive you individually. Beseech them in the name of our Lord. . . ."

He was gone in a flash. Before she even had time to say the Lord's name. Something sounded and writhed above the roof, as if some wrathful tornado had rushed over the house on its way elsewhere. A second later the cricket suddenly started chirping under the stove and the grandfather clock began peacefully ticking.

What had happened? Had the bound ghost trembled to his frozen depths because of the magnitude of the task she had set him? To go to every last person who had been injured or ruined by Stalin, that's a real job. Eternity wouldn't be long enough for that. But perhaps even the little leeway she had given him would be of some use. Where, to what wilds, had that creature born of darkness gone in quest of rehabilitation? . . .

One thing is certain—the house had been deserted in an instant. And Alla did not close her eyes for the rest of the night that preceded that memorable day March 5. She simply could not.

She lay in bed thinking, her hands behind her head. Thinking about what? I can assure you that it did not even cross her mind that she had passed a test of righteousness. She was having doubts. She had let the wolf slip from her teeth. Instead of sinking her teeth into that dead throat and being consumed in that column of cold. She had doubts about her own motives. That she had been untrue to herself when saying she had nothing left to lose in this life. Not true! We all cling to something. She, the sinner, was still hostage to her husband, for whose fate she had secretly feared. He was all she had left. They had met in the camp, were married in exile, and now, in that town at the gateway to the Vorkuta camps, were hiding together to avoid being arrested again. An engineer, he was working as a night-shift dispatcher at the time, and what guarantee could there ever be that he'd come home the next morning? And, to be honest, wasn't that why she had forgiven the sins of her principal transgressor? Not in compliance with Scripture, but out of fear for her husband, who hadn't come home from his shift yet? There's always something that can be taken from anyone. . . .

It was in that troubled and reflective state that Yosif Aronovich found her.

"Why are you still in bed?" he asked in surprise, rubbing his gnarled hands. "Don't you know what happened! While you were sleeping—they just announced it—the Mustache bit the dust! How do you like that? . . ."

She got up in her long nightshirt and yawned. "Yes, yes. I know. But it didn't happen last night, Yosif. Maybe yesterday, or the day before."

And then, without a word of explanation, she showed him the circle on the floor near the bed, a circle that must have been three feet across and seemed incised by some red-hot needle. A shape birds might have made. Or ants. A series of small dots. An even outline engraved on the plank floor—a column, a band, a pedestal, a base. On the spot where he had stood.

She combed her hair. Lit the stove. Grumbling, taking her time, she got the samovar going. Then, all of a sudden, she said, as women will, "Go run out for something to drink, will you, dear? Is the store open? You have to celebrate an occasion like this! . . ."

". . . And I was there and drank the mead, but there's many a slip twixt the cup and the lip."

Those of little faith think that a comical ending is the sign of a tale's ineptitude. A proof of trickery. Mere eloquence. All made up. A slip between cup and lip. But I think there's a different reason. The gates to the realm of fairy tales are marked: Entrance Prohibited To The Uninitiated. Who will dare proclaim that he has feasted with the gods? Button your lip. And easy does it with the business about the cup and the lip, my dear man. Entrance prohibited to the uninitiated. Don't bother trying, you won't get in.

Misleading though they can be, the fairy tales' sole concern is with reality. And fairy tales pass over into another reality—to be continued—a reality we find just as promising and elusive. Therein lies their charm and their cunning. They entice us. They elude us. They're akin to foxes? Akin to bears? Or wolves? No, no, akin only to themselves.

I am not afraid to say that fairy tales are full of love and great of soul. And because they are so real, they don't need to do anything but be themselves. They lead nowhere, achieve nothing. A perfect circle, insofar, of course, as that is possible—in the image and likeness of . . .

To snatch up the crumbs history sweeps from the fairy tale's table is the writer's concern and delight. Otherwise, what's there to write about? Why write? . . .

On the morning of that March 5, I was awakened by the sound of my mother crying. "What's happened now?" I jumped out of bed. "Tell me, tell me right now!" I pulled on my socks and pants.

"Stalin's dead. There was a bulletin on the radio."

I sat down, half dressed. At last! . . . I almost blurted out, "It's a time for rejoicing, not for crying, Mama!" But I held my tongue. No reason to hurt her feelings. I suspect that somewhere inside she too sensed that this was no great loss for us all. Not such a tragedy. My father was in exile. We were barely holding on. Still, she could spare a few tears. It was Stalin, after all . . .

Inside, my whole body, my feet, my elbows, were dancing a bolero. I got tangled in my pant legs, which said as they danced, "So, Stalin, was it? . . ." I buttoned all my buttons. I pulled my belt as tight as it would go: "Stalin's dead!" It didn't help. I got bogged down in my socks, which whispered advice: "Don't lose your head. Don't be in such a hurry. Keep a lower profile. Stalin went bye-bye. . . . Don't get too excited." My shoes caused me special difficulties. I usually had problems lacing them. "You missed a hole!" they said hoarsely. "Don't shake like that, it's disgusting! Lace me, lace me right, you nitwit! Do you always have to be told?! . . ." "Hurray!" proclaimed my shirt. "Stalin is dead! What, are you deaf? . . ." Finally I was dressed.

Meanwhile, it cannot be said that I hated Stalin. I had been indifferent to him for a long time. Seasoned. Cautious. A wall up. How else could you relate to him? View him as a wolf? A werewolf? A dragon? In fact it was not Stalin who roused my interest but his consequences. What new nightmare would he hurl the country into next? All you could expect from him was death. His own. Everyone's. Prison. Plague. War. And now all that had been postponed. . . .

The doorbell rang. Three times. For us. A close friend of mine was at the door. Without saying a word, the key in my pocket, I led him away from my neighbors' eyes and down to the basement. No one could spy on us there. I double-locked the door. We stood facing each other, our eyes radiant. We embraced silently. We smiled. Just like Herzen and Ogarev on Sparrow Hills. Secret conspirators. Exchanging happy smiles when everyone else was in tears. Was it a holiday? A masquerade? A last salute, then he left quickly, still silent. See you tonight!

Where to now? The good old Lenin Library, of course. I had reserved the five-volume *Foreign Accounts of the Time of Troubles.* A marvelous book and a rare edition, from the beginning of the last century. Karamzin would have envied me it. During all those alarming days beginning with the solemn government announcement of his serious illness, through the brief bulletins and the sad, lyrical music on the radio, I would run to the library in the early morning. No, I admit, not because of my enthusiasm for the work I was professionally obliged to produce, but to contemplate pure and distant historical prospects that had nothing in common either with my field or with the contemporary situation.

At one time or another we all feel a need for shelter, a refuge, one as far from the beaten path as possible. There, for a time, spread out hospitably before me were the tents of the age of Feodor, Godunov, and the mysterious Dmitri the Pretender. What embroidery! What play of mind interwoven with life's changing phases, allowing one to imagine that history might be an artistic tapestry, embroidered with a precious design! . . . Who wove it? Who placed the flowers where they are? . . .

. . . The suspicious Boris had ordered every last hair plucked from the beard of the Boyar Belsky, selecting for this operation Gabriel of Scotland, a skillful surgeon. . . . So many Poles have been slaughtered in Moscow that, under cover of night, pharmacists sliced the fat off the corpses to use in their medicines. . . . The Tsarina Marina escaped death by hiding inside the skirt of her lady of the bedchamber. . . . Human flesh was baked in pies; people ate grass and bark. On the arrival of the emperor's envoy from Prague in June, Godunov ordered wagonloads of grain to be dumped into a river at the border, right before the eyes of his astonished guest. . . . In preparation for his wedding, Stanislaw Mniszek hired twenty musicians and an Italian clown and took them with him to Muscovy. . . . Dogs licked up the blood of Dmitri's murderers. . . . They had dragged the tsar's body along the ground by a rope tied to his genitals. . . . Marina Mniszek's childhood was spent amid the forests of Sambor and among Bernardine monks. . . .

These incidents relaxed me. They diverted me from the news of the day. They distracted me from somber thoughts: Would Stalin die or wouldn't he? No need to think about that. Or was he actually going to last forever? If death was not to be the outcome, why oppress people with advance bulletins that boded ill? Why those endless classical melodies on the radio, music in a minor key, especially Chopin and Rachmaninov, instead of propaganda? Or were they preparing people? Shaping their minds? Sharing power?

Could he spring back to life after all those funeral marches? Anything could happen—Mao Tse-tung could fly him in some ginseng, the magic root of life, and then it'd start all over again! Or they could use a dummy in his place! A double! What does it matter who Stalin actually is?

To hell with them! I drive them from my mind. Whatever happens, happens. The *Foreign Accounts of the Time of Troubles* awaits me in the reading room, and can't wait. The dear, dear, clumsy seventeenth century. You can stay where you are, I'm off to do some reading. There's no comparison . . . For me, there's no question that a good book can displace life in all its meaninglessness. The book you're currently reading has an existence parallel to your own, and no sooner do you think of that book, than a load is taken off your mind. You've found an emergency exit. Be still, you demons! What do I care about Stalin? I have an appointment at the Lenin Library. A grasshopper from old Russia chirps in the tall, dry grass there. . . .

But it's always like that, it happens to everyone. Whether I'm cranking a machine for eight hours in a factory, spending time with women, or having a bite in the cafeteria, the memory of the book under my pillow accompanies me everywhere. It sings in my head, interrupting the machines' conversation. "Come back soon, you wanderer! We'll do a little reading." The siren is jealous. Utterly impatient. And rightly so. While I'm here joking around, chewing my food, or working like a son of a bitch, there, in the intimacy of the page, the lone detective fires his miniature machine gun at a gang of thugs, but is on the verge of being overrun. "Why don't you come to his aid, why don't you read some more?" the book reproaches me mournfully. "Do you forget a friend in need?" Oho! Now it's hand to hand. They've gone for their knives. And from the other end of the city I hear a faint burst of machine-gun fire from under my pillow: ratatatatat. . . . "Hang in there, Freddie!" I cry. "Help is on its way from the Urals! Here I come! . . ."

What I love most of all are old multivolume editions on history and geography. They're something you can get your teeth into. You can live a long life in those books and forget the shortness of your own. Vasco da Gama rounds Cape Verde. Magellan. Oh, long, long it all takes! Reading soothes. You're ready to live endlessly. Soothed, I fall asleep: Magellan circumnavigates! . . .

The sole subject of these books is the length of the journey. That length gives them both their meaning and their style. While traveling around the world, rounding Africa, New Guinea, those seafarers became part of the sovereign expanse of existence and thus prolonged their own days. The very point of the enterprise . . .

We see something similar in chronicles of the past. The slow transfusion of time. One thing issues from another. Everything interacts. Not like today. The chronicles may differ in their accounts. So what if one foreigner sees Dmitri the Pretender as a veritable Achilles and another sees quite the opposite? You can see the connections. There's a logic here; a Divine Providence can be sensed. This is History, mind you, not some wayside inn. History (as befits it) invested with Eternity, Eternity in the images of legend. History that we so sorely lack today . . .

. . . Dung flies crawled over Dmitri's lips. Scurrying, a metallic blue-yellow, they strove past his chin to the shore—to taste the tsarevich's blood, sweet and red as cherry jam. His mother, the tsarina, blew on his face but could not drive the flies away. Her hands were elsewhere. Deep down, under the pillows, the bent body still retained some warmth. The back still seemed warm. God forbid his soul flew off with the flies. She was afraid even to move a hand. . . .

Behind them, like a ringing in the ears, was the eternal grasshopper. And the nurse Vasilisa intoned in a half-whisper:

"And why have you left us, light of my life, Dmitri Ivanich? . . ."

The evil nurse made sure not to cry out for vengeance. That intriguing villain's son, the handsome lady-killer Oska Volokhov, was in league with the Bityagovskis. And History, as we know, could not have managed without Oska. We know, we know! Go wash your hands of that!

. . . So, what's there to discuss? Fedka Ogurets, the half-drunk sexton, has already clambered on his hands and knees up the bell tower. Just as he was, hatless and barefoot, Mikhailo Nagoi, uncle and brother to tsars, has already dashed out to the palace stairs to address the people with high emotion:

"Listen to me, listen! They've killed him, they've slaughtered him! . . ."

Gathering in small groups, the people grew angry. . . .

Meanwhile, an unearthly chill ran down Dmitri's back. His mother's hands had given him the last of their warmth and grown moist on Dmitri's cold and unresponding body. Then, no longer of any use, her hands slid away from him. Inwardly exhausted, she sought to warm herself away from his body. Still, she kept irrationally denying it, telling herself that it was impossible, that the Lord would not allow it. He would not give over this pure prince to be eaten by the worms, this Tsar of All Rus, whom glory, tambourines, and trumpets awaited.

"Jesus Christ! Holy Mother of God! John the Baptist! Nikolai the Wonderworker!" she prayed to them all in turn, never taking her eyes from the cold and bluish face of her son, turned up to the sky like an enamel bowl. The ubiquitous flies scurried over that face, which the tsarina did not recognize as the tsarevich's. No! Get thee behind me! Was this the heir to the throne? No, it was all a dream. . . . Why do all dead people, even children, look more like dead people than like themselves? Or was that the effect of some blessed intervention? Divine first aid? . . . An alien, haughty adolescent, his mouth open unnaturally, his eyelashes sharp, his body stretched out on a length of carpet. That wasn't him! Thank God, it was a trick, a substitute! . . .

The mother rose. Her hands free now, she flicked away the flies with her shawl. Vaguely she heard the voice of the Angel say: Don't give any sign. Let them think he's dead. As long as they think that, they won't kill him. Death is better protection than a mother. More reliable than the royal guards. The grave will hide the tsarevich for the time being. It's the right way. Be patient. . . .

Grieving (her hands over her face), the tsarina peered like an eagle through her tears and her fingers at everyone in the court. Near the door, wearing a shirt torn down to his navel, the indefatigable Mikhailo seemed possessed as he dashed back and forth.

"So, good people!" he said, brandishing his fists. "It was Boris's gang . . . Godunov's rogues . . . this sapling . . . this lamb. . . ."

He was shouting like a buffoon. Twitching. Waving his beard around. He knew that a switch had been made. Where were they hiding him? Where had they taken him?

"They've killed him! Killed him!" cried the tsaritsa, seconding her brother. She noticed a birch log by a stone bench but gave no sign of it. The nurse with the impudent face was still playing the fool: "Why did you leave us all al——" Blind with hatred, the tsarina struck her right between her wandering eyes with the birch log, and the nurse howled in pain. She had been imagining things—in truth, her son had been murdered! . . . As if in response, the bell sounded an alarm from the tower. Fedka Ogurets had reached the top. . . .

Boris's minions were caught in the gardens on the other side of the Volga. Those on this side had already met their Maker: some killed by ax, some by club, some torn to pieces by people's bare hands. Scraps of clothing flew about the city. Afonka Mecheny and his cousin locked themselves in a bathhouse, where they defended themselves with arquebuses. Slowly, cunningly, they were smoked out, their bones blackened by then.

The citizens of Uglich ran in excitement to their sovereign's court to verify what they had seen, to cross themselves, quench their thirst, and hasten on their way. By one end of the palace, Dmitri's mother beat her head madly against the hard ground. She called to Christ for judgment and to the saints to bear witness. Nearby, the departed, resembling no one at all, was laid out on rugs of velvet, in God's hands now. A narrow wound gaped like a gill on his neck. And even though the tsarevich was long since dead, the wound continued to bleed. . . .

I went out for a smoke. As usual, I walked past the gap-toothed stacks. The dictionaries. The portraits of Lomonosov, Molotov.

Reference books. The card catalogues. The *Large Soviet Encyclopedia,* the *Small Soviet Encyclopedia.* Marx-Engels-Lenin-Stalin. The *Granat Encyclopedia* . . . The real books are not up here on the surface but in the bowels of the library, in carrels, manifesting only in hints and suspicions that only in a library do we truly walk the earth.

It has been called "humus." But I'm not so sure of that. That would be fine, of course. For those who come after us. But history is not soil. It's stonier than that. Dangerous to life. But sound, and serious. An accumulation of books is like deep, heavy geological deposits. Mesozoic. You can find anything here. Shellfish. Snails. The babel of nations. The devil's finger. An impression made by that marvelous bird the archaeopteryx. Foreign accounts. The earth.

There wasn't a soul in the smoking room. The library seemed deserted. Did you have to clear out just because he was dead? I'd stay till closing. Be the last one out. I opened a pack of Belomors. What did I care? I hadn't come here for that. I was interested in Dmitri. To the exclusion of all else. Silence, Satan! Stalactite. Stability, Staple. Like Trotskyites, the foreign writers had their doubts as to whether Dmitri was genuine or not. Staggering! Closer study shows that the nun Marfa, formerly Mariya, née Nagoi, changed her testimony several times. First she'd say that he was alive, then that he was dead. What good was that? When Godunov's wife, whose name was also Mariya, threatened Marfa with a candle: "I'll burn out your eyes! Tell the truth—is he alive or dead?" Boris stopped her: "Wait a minute." But Marfa shrugged her shoulders. "I don't know," said the nun with pleasure. "How should a wretch like me know that? I won't lie, but if he is alive . . ."

I don't remember whether it was Roosevelt or Eden or some other visitor from overseas who supposedly was unable to refrain from saying to Stalin: "I wish you a long life, Mr. Generalissimo. But we are all mortal men and unfortunately are compelled to think ahead politically. So, tell me, who will take your lawful place when you depart for a better world, if that isn't a secret? . . ."

The Politburo quavered. A provocative question. And he smiled, the skinny bastard, the way only foreigners can. And what did our leader do? . . . He beamed back a friendly Georgian smile and then ran a sharp eye, gleaming like Lenin's, over the Politburo. More like an olive than an eye. "Maybe one of them?" He puffed into his mustache, slowly tamping his pipe. "I wonder who will succeed me. . . ." Once again he ran an oily eye over his cohorts, one by one. They were trembling, holding their breath while their fates hung in the balance. Gently he raised a finger: "Some unknown young man!"

A direct hit! Everyone roared with laughter. The old man had done it again! He'd outwitted the foreigner. And no one was offended. The shit had hit everyone. He had come out on top. They had forgotten the main thing, the role of humor in history, but he hadn't. He remembered everything. Not so very long ago he had been an unknown young man himself, and so he knew of what he spoke. But where were you going to find his likes again? For some reason, unknown young men were dying out in Russia. Where was a Pretender going to come from? . . .

The tsarina confirmed it in Taininki: "It's him! My son! It's truly Dmitri!" Even though this one had red hair, was not good-looking, and had a different sort of beard. The Politburo applauded. . . . Still, Marfa grew sad when they dragged the body in. After scarcely a glance, she turned away. True, this time he was mutilated, disrobed, indecent. "Is this your son or not?" the crowd pressed her. She shook her head. "No," she replied. "What sort of tsarevich could that be now? I never saw this person before. . . ."

What did she mean by "now"? That he used to be real? Everyone is real while he's alive. But don't the dead count any more? Don't they belong to anyone? Is there something wrong with them? How many times can one and the same treasure be betrayed? You'll see, an impostor will arise to confound you all. Soon? A little makeup. Summon the troops. A memorandum. Then go try to prove that this Gelovani . . .

It was as quiet as a cathedral that day in the abandoned, deserted library. But history was replenishing itself, brewing something that was invisible here. It's in the library that history draws on its sources and reserves. A renegade son and a conservative grandfather are side by side in the card catalogue. Convenient. To read everything is unthinkable—it would require the lifetimes of a great many people—it's enough to cast a glance over the even tide of the books' spines, which disappears underground, a storehouse closed to us now and where we will all be catalogued, some by name, others by subject. Where every letter of the alphabet is fraught with shocks. Where is Lenin? Where is Stalin? Where is Hitler? Where are humanity's best minds? Here, like labeled jars. This isn't a cemetery. It's an arsenal. A vast hangar. Reserves. These spirits rise up in rebellion; if there's a revolution up top, then it's right back to the shelf until there's another call for them. Famusov was right to worry: "All books should be stacked up and burned!..." The only hitch is that Famusov himself is already on file at the main library, He can easily be found in any index. Under the letter "G" ("Griboedov"). Under the letter "F" ("Famusov"). Or under the letter "B" ("Books")...

... The torturer had been worked to the limits of his strength. Between the acts, after judiciously discharging his duties, he would slip through the cotton curtains to rest a little in the cool half-light backstage. He'd drink water from a washbasin, rinse his eyes corroded by sweat and lampblack, and, trying not to make noise with his boots, lie down curled in a ball on a crate, until it was time to go back to work. The investigation was in its second full day—people were being tortured in connection with the tsarevich's death.

It was God's will and God's judgment that the tsarevich, suffering from the falling sickness, fell onto a sharp knife and gave up the ghost. And Mishka Nagoi and Grishka Nagoi raised a cry and feigned grief, flouting all justice.... As did his son Danila and Nikita Kachalov and

Osip Volokhov. . . . And his wife, who was shot and thrown into the water . . .

The cries, the smoke, the sound of shooting day and night had given him a splitting headache. The blood made his calluses smart. Easier said than done! Forty-four witnesses had already passed through his hands. And each one had to be tied up and calmed down. And that wasn't counting all those he had knouted and whipped! They should at least have offered him some cloth to replace the shirt he had ruined. Brand-new. It was his son Arsyushka's fault. Distracted by the sight of naked women, Arsyushka had raised a pair of red-hot tongs too close to his father's side. It's a good thing they didn't burn through to his flesh. I'll whip the boy good at home.

"I'll whip you at home," he threatened listlessly, his eyelids closing in exhaustion. But he kept one ear cocked for the clatter of boots in the entry hall, the scratching of quills, Kleshinin's hoarse, panting voice as he urged someone on.

"I did it! With my own hand! . . ." He'd shaken the suspect good, the way they'd taught him to, beaten him good. . . . Praise be the Lord, looks like it's all over. Maybe he could catch a few winks.

"With my own hand," an old man's melodious alto could be heard on the other side of the cotton curtain. "With my own hand, my good men . . ."

Arsyushka's legs began trembling. "Papa, Papa! Who did him in? Who killed the tsarevich? . . ."

His father only hissed at him—"Shhh, you little snake!"—and nudged him lightly with his boot.

He wouldn't take Arsyushka on important state business any more. Let him make the rounds of the monasteries with his mother, or chase after the girls in town until he grew up. His own fault. He should have forced the lad to learn the trade as a little boy. This wasn't like tending pigs or sowing seed. This took skill.

Tsar Ivan Vasilevich used to say to him, "You've got golden hands, Nikifor! You could repair watches. Stoves . . ." The tsar was a kind master. But he knew how to put his foot down! The tsarevich was just like his father. Until he grew up. A pity he grew up. There was light everywhere. Coming through the window, from his mouth, shining near the pink gums and the tongue hanging out.

There had been no fuss, no muss. And no clothespin had been needed to clamp his nose and make him open his mouth. No teeth had to be broken. He had stuck his tongue out himself. All that remained was to slice off the tongue, reddish and white on the top, like a dog's shameless penis. When seized at its base by the pincers, the tongue had tried to jerk free, but it was too late.

"Watch this, Arseni! And remember what you see!"

Here she comes!

Throw it on the floor. The cat'll eat it. It'll make her lick her lips.

The castrated mouth was replaced by the next victim, whose bearded face gaped in terror at the sight of the torturer. Another false witness's turn had come—to have his abominable lips cut off.

"Take a lesson, son! Here she comes! Throw it to the cat, she'll eat it. It'll make her lick her lips."

There must have been a good fifty of them! No sooner did you finish with one . . . Look sharp, torturer! They think they can blaspheme against the state and the kingdom will fall, the treasury will be drained, and the land will be filled with insolent thieves. Then you'll be in for it. Get up off that box and get your hands to work! . . . But that didn't disturb him. As he pulled out the tongues extended like offerings, he could hear a woman dissolving in tears:

"He fell on the knife. No one was watching over him. It's all over now. When the sickness was on him, he'd fall to the ground and pass out. He was like a madman. The nurses and governesses would come running, afraid he'd smash the back of his head. The poor dear would bite their hands and tear off their buttons. He'd open his mouth and grab them with his teeth. And he'd swallow whatever he bit off, the poor sick child. . . ."

The cat licked its lips. And now of course Arseni was off somewhere with the pincers and tongs.

Should he just grab the tongue with his bare hands? It was a question of hydraulics! Tongues are slippery. Finally he succeeded in seizing the soft, saliva-coated tongue with his fingernails. Her jaws were gaping open when all of a sudden they snapped shut like a shark's on his finger. The devil! Then all the other mouths that had not been shut in time began to mutter curses. Nikifor did not even have to move. He yanked his hand away and awoke from pain and bitter self-pity. The indefatigable Arseni was already on his feet, saying, "Papa, get up! It's time! They're calling us! . . ."

Suddenly the library was in a commotion. The librarians sped from one reading room to the next like whirlwinds: "Turn in your books! Turn in your books at once! The library's closed! . . ."

What's this nonsense? It wasn't even four-thirty yet by the clock. Didn't they usually stay open until eleven? The librarians were in a panic. "Take your things! We're closing! . . ."

I ran outside. From the top steps of the Lenin Library, I could see people running. Good Lord! Not two, not three, not five, but an entire street full of people running as one man. No vehicles. Vozdvizhenka Street was on the run. Packed from curb to curb. Was it an uprising? Some great event? . . .

I joined the runners to try to find out what was going on. But you couldn't tell anything from their faces. No high emotion, no rage. They trotted as calmly as could be, casting curious glances ahead and behind them. I went over to one man and asked, "What's happening, friend?" "Who the hell knows!" he replied. "They've all gone mad." A second man said to me, "You'll see when you get there, buddy!" The old man flicked his hand toward the Arbat. A third person, a woman, didn't answer me at all. She was having trouble enough putting one foot in front of the other. She was on her last legs, but she was still doing her best. I found someone who looked a little more important—a man in a plush topcoat, wearing glasses, with a certain bureaucratic air about him—and asked, "Where's everybody running, comrade? Where's everybody headed?"

"They're letting people in to see Stalin. In the Hall of Columns! They announced the body's on display. . . ."

Aha! Now I understood! We turned onto Malo-Nikitsky Boulevard (recently renamed Suvorovsky), making this loop because all the other routes had apparently been blocked off. The statue of Timiryazev. Along the way, on Tversky Boulevard, other crowds had come pouring out from other streets and gateways, merging as they streamed into our channel. I had never known there were so many people in Moscow. We were all borne by the current, but it was no longer possible to run. With less and less foot room, our pace kept slowing. It was like the parade on the anniversary of the revolution. Except there was no singing, no high spirits, though I did not observe any special sorrow either. Just people being allowed in to see their leader, curious people . . .

There was a jam-up on Pushkin Square. We almost came to a standstill. Gorky Street was blocked off. They're directing us across Trubnaya Square, explained those in the know. We turn at Trubnaya and it's straight on from there. We'll be there in half an hour. They yelled: We'll push our way in and be the first ones to see Stalin in the Hall of Columns.

Heavy with books, my briefcase was weighing me down. How could I carry it all that way? I couldn't even move my hand. Up ahead it was even more packed, people moving in a circle like a carousel or a whirlpool. It would be interesting to have a look. But my briefcase! . . . They might not even let me in with it. They'd think there was a bomb in it! Even as a child, I knew that no one was allowed into Lenin's tomb carrying a purse or a briefcase. And the coffin was probably guarded by soldiers, ringed by police and MVD. . . . I started to elbow my way out. No easy task. The current pushed me, the whirlpool pulled me. I turned on Pushkin Square and headed home, without having set foot in the funeral hall, or having been a witness to the great event. Irritating. If it weren't for the books, the briefcase, I'd already be on Trubnaya Square, not far from the body. . . .

I am not going to tell what happened to those who were quicker on their feet than I, more devoted or bolder. That's history now. Later that day history raced through Moscow like a special edition of the evening paper, piquing my idle and impure curiosity all the more. . . . It turned out that the dead man had not lost his bite. He had cleverly worked his death so that a fat slice of his congregation was sacrificed to him, immolated in honor of his sad departure, a fitting culmination to his reign! As the body of a saint is surrounded by miracles, so was Stalin's surrounded by murder. I could not help admiring it. History had been given a finishing touch.

At midnight on the dot, I set off with the friend who had visited me that morning to marvel at the funeral rites. We wandered the excited city until about five o'clock. Moscow was smoky. Fumes of incense seemed to issue from the black-and-red banners on the streetlights, some emanation arose from the compacted masses pressing day and night to bid their leader farewell. From time to time you could hear the faint, distant cry of people being crushed. The crowd was in the grip of a barrier made of American jeeps. Little jams, tie-ups, Khodynkas continued to erupt, here and there, like whirlpools accompanying the mostly even and harmless-looking stream. To my surprise, muffled cheers broke out now and again. They must have come from some green youths who leapt obstacles for the sheer sport of it. The most daring took a short-cut—along the rooftops. They called out to us to join them, promising to lead us over attics, fire escapes, and ledges to Stoleshnikov Street. But we were no mountain climbers. Satisfied by what we were seeing, my friend and I did not take any alleyways or make any artful maneuvers to reach the Hall of Columns. To gaze upon Caesar with our own eyes had not been our intention.

Later, a hundred years from now, people will tell the story of the Jew who by fortunate coincidence had rented a room on Neglinna Street, near where the Body was lying in state. His parents had been executed and he, according to the information he provided on questionnaires, could barely make ends meet; then, out of the blue—a stroke of good luck! A bit like winning the lottery. During those tense days, his building administration had issued him a perfectly legal pass to enter his residence zone, and so that clever Jew could use this lousy pass to pay his respects to our leader day or night without obstacle, though he did of course have to wait in line. He used his pass three times, he told me, three times, to see it for himself: "I went there and I couldn't believe my own eyes. He was laid out like any other dead man, with an armed soldier guarding him. A magnificent coffin, wreaths. I kept looking at him, and I still couldn't believe it. How could it be? Him, laid out? . . ."

I don't know. I couldn't share that feeling. Personally, I felt no urge to see the body. What's to see? Somehow I was mentally able to resist that incredibly powerful magnet whose epicenter radiated lethally throughout the city. He would have taken everyone else with him if he'd been able to. That night his presence was more palpable in the streets than in there with the wreaths and the honor guard. The dead man strode through Moscow, reaping a blind harvest, his iron boots cutting a broad swath. And wherever he passed, ribs were cracked, eyes were popped out of their sockets, and hair, scalp and all, was peeled off as easily as a sock. . . .

For some reason I kept recalling a portion of Nikolai Tikhonov's bad poem "Kirov Is with Us," which was written on the siege of Leningrad during the war. A weak imitation of Lermontov's magical "Ship of the Air":

> Over the ocean's blue waves,
> Only stars gleam in the skies,
> Kirov walks the city's streets
> In Leningrad's iron nights.

> From his grave, like an emperor now,
> Chin to his chest,
> Kirov walks the city's streets
> In Leningrad's iron nights.

> He stamps his foot angrily
> As back and forth he goes.

Kirov walks the city's streets
In Leningrad's iron nights.

What a nuisance—I couldn't get it out of my head. All sorts of things pop into your mind at night. . . . But why, I wonder, did Stalin like that poem? Why, after having Kirov killed, did he want him to go down in history almost as if he had been second in command, a favorite son, a younger brother? Second only to Stalin in the number of things named after him. Kirovgrad, Kirovokan, Kirovsk, the city Kirov, Tikhonov's poem "Kirov Is with Us," which received the Stalin Prize, Kirov Street, the Kirov Theatre in Leningrad . . . Why? To cover his trail? But he'd had others like Kirov eliminated before. And they'd left no trail or trace. No, it was out of genuine gratitude to the victim. A personal thank you. Compensation, a toast in the form of posthumous glory, of a sort the boy from Urzhum never dreamed. A royal requiem for the child whose blood he had sprinkled like holy water on the heads of enemies of the people who were to be put to death. Thank you, faithful comrade, for being killed by me. That's the way it had to be. Forgive me. I have paid for it. I have erected a monument to you. Kirovokani.

Kirov walks the city's streets
In Leningrad's iron nights. . . .

To put it mildly, I had let my imagination carry me away. I had the feeling that these events could not be confined to the funeral, itself more like an orgy, and that they demanded further elaboration, their perturbations fanning out in all directions. My mind raced with images, each more vivid, marvelous, and outrageous than the last, all seeming in keeping with the true spirit of the moment. I will attempt to relate that chain of consequences racing toward us from the future in a more harmonious and reasoned form than they had when they streamed through my mind in those blind hours of aimless, enchanted circling at the approaches to the Deceased.

Wait, look, read this! If not today, then tomorrow, a Pretender, a false Stalin, will arise in the Caucasus. An unknown young man. His secret disciples in the capital, a small group of friends and combat squads who keep watch over his grave, will have as their first duty to dispose of the evidence. They cross themselves, then substitute another body for the Boss's. And take His to their own inhouse crematorium on Dzerzhinsky Square (do they have some type of disinfectant oven in Lubyanka for those who die while inside?). Snatching the first citizen who's roughly the same size (grab one off the street!), they can stab and gut him. They'll paste on a mustache, not caring at all if it looks right. Toss on a wig. The next day there's a great commotion at the changing of the guard. Anyone can come, feast his eyes, and see for himself that this wasn't Stalin in the sarcophagus. There'll be talk, debate, conjecture. Where's the real Stalin? Be patient, we'll say, he's gone underground. But he'll be back soon. Just wait and see!

Beria, with his pince-nez, the most intellectual member of the Politburo and the organizer of this movement, flies to his friend in Georgia. That night (or could it be tonight?) faithful Stalinist-Leninists will scatter copies of a document about Moscow. Printed in *Pravda*'s typography, their contents will inflame the masses, stir them up. Marked "top secret" (to make them more attractive), they will read:

Top secret. Capitalist hirelings, the vile antiparty clique of Molotov and Malenkov, working in league with foreign intelligence agencies, have, on March 3 of this year, made a criminal attempt on the precious life of Comrade Stalin.

But the enemies of our Motherland and socialism have miscalculated. Our leader has taken to hiding in the mountains and will return to work, healthy and rejuvenated through the achievements of progressive, patriotic medicine. The forged government "report" about the untimely demise of our Leader should be considered an enemy foray and counterrevolution-ary lies. Their bark is worse than their bite. Death to usurpers!

Everyone must rally around the Leninist banner of the true Anointed Sovereign, Tsar, and Lord—Stalin!

Presidium of the Central Committee, the Council of Ministers, the General Staff, the Ministry of State Security, and the Soviet Writers' Union.

Secretary Gorkin

Yes indeed . . . that'd be a fine kettle of fish. Sucking on a tooth, I fantasize. You can imagine what one piece of paper like that could have started! Central Committee sessions, aglow with the executions to come. TASS denials. Mass arrests of the literary intelligentsia. Execution of the doctors and Jewish antifascists who, under interrogation, had shamed themselves and sickened us. The case of the corpse would be investigated. Who exhumed it? And who had looked the other way? . . . The Chekists shake Moscow like a pear tree, but their eyes, like those of a poisoned wolf, were turned to the south. To put fear into traitors, barges and cutters sail down the Volga and the Don, with members of the Provincial Committee who had dared to communicate with the Pretender of the Caucasus hanging from the yardarms. . . .

An attack on the flank: in the Caucasus, Marshal Zhukov, the illustrious national hero and the sole supporter of the throne, acting on his own, advances as his candidate for the Ruler of great and indivisible Russia the false Tsarevich Alexei, who had supposedly survived by a miracle when, sad for us all, the royal family was eliminated. In this version of events, the country would of course not be ruled by the sickly and dispirited tsarevich, who had hidden for more than thirty years in the Far East, the job of rural accountant his modest cover, but by the field marshal himself. The troops would not swear loyalty to any Ukrainian Khrushchev, but to the Russian Zhukov!

In the Kremlin, the core of the Central Committee, the Boyar Duma, which includes Malenkov and Molotov, is relentlessly exposing traitors: the American spy Beria, the White Guard general and secret Vlasovite Zhukov, the Japanese lackey Alexei. . . . The False Stalin, who is thirty years younger than he ought to be. The False Kirov, a criminal. And then something new—a False Lenin! . . . The latter, a decrepit old man past eighty, the former head of the Marxism-Leninism Department at the Herzen Teachers' Training College, a one-time Menshevik whose real name was Aron Solomonovich Katz, alias Zaitsev, alias Frank-Masonov, a case parallel to the bandit Vitka Kirov, whose nickname was "Mironich." The False Stalin gains a foothold in the citadel of revolution, Petersburg. The Kremlin's radio telegrams are answered: "Surrender! Or else we'll call you every name in the book! . . ."

Meanwhile, marching beneath a red banner with the two-headed eagle and a white cross on a field of black, Stalin has already quietly taken Stavropol without firing a shot, and is moving on Taganrog. The people welcome him with the traditional bread and salt. They bring out the icons. They weep for joy. Benefactor! Deliverer! Beria immediately calls on them all to swear allegiance to Stalin! . . . But the Mountain Eagle, the anointed of the Lord, Emperor of All Russia, is in good cheer and bears no grudges. Like Dmitri, he jauntily signs all papers in Latin: *In Perator*. Still, an experienced tactician, he recalls the temporary pact with Hitler, at one time mutually beneficial, and now makes an equally original knight's gambit. In the name of a unified and indivisible Russia, and, so that the dynastic line not be broken, he generously adopts the False Tsarevich Alexei, promising him his daughter's hand and his own personal dacha in the Crimea after Moscow is freed.

That single political stroke decides everything. Molotov and Malenkov flee to Mongolia. Nothing comes of the False Kirov and the False Lenin, who simply vanish in the night air. The idiotic Americans grant us four hundred billion dollars in credit. Zhukov the iron man falls sobbing prostrate at the feet of the forever laughing, youthful, mustachioed False Stalin. A great moment. Salute! . . .

It's not my fault if history did not take its designated course back then. Everything was in place. If Beria had been equal to his own pince-nez and proved more intelligent than he in fact did, had he even been on the same level as his portraits depicted him, we would not have escaped a Pretender. Had Zhukov been a braver and more ambitious strategist and risked taking full power, both the army and the people would have risen up like a mountain in response to his stern cry, the only cymbal and symbol in the country besides Stalin. And they would have come to amicable terms with Beria about a national monarchy, grounds already so deeply plowed and well manured by the Leader of Nations; they would have united under the eagle and the cross, but also under the red flag, and with no fear of killing, sparing no expense in tanks and airplanes. . . . And so my sketches, for all their lack of resemblance to history's actual canvas, were still not so far from the truth whose hidden meaning, God willing, will yet be revealed. Had the Generalissimo lived another five or eight years, or had some worthy successor been found, his equal in stature, we would have had a wonderful new round of executions, a great war, the resettlement of entire nations, a marvelous swelling of the tree trunk of autocracy rising from a soil enriched with new power and the Empire's new geography, territories incorporated from every corner of the world. . . .

However, my aerial companion that fateful night took a different and calmer view of things, one free of the gloomy exaltation that the electric atmosphere must have evoked in me. We were both so depressed by the bacchanalia we saw that we scarcely exchanged a word, but I am certain that our thoughts were far from agreeing— the usual case, since our lines of thought occasionally intersected but were basically different. That needs to be said for the sake of objectivity.

I will not go into great detail about the strange fate and character of my close-mouthed friend, whom I saw sporadically, always on his initiative, each of us consumed with his own ideas. Later, he disappeared from view as if he had quietly dissolved into his own unique twilit and uninsistent brilliance. He could be living a monastic life somewhere now. Or he may have taken refuge in some persecuted sect. If, of course, he hasn't gone down the drain from drink, which, sad to say, does sometimes happen with self-taught Russians, Russian diamonds in the rough, Russian truth-lovers.

At the time he and I were closest, he was deeply involved in the practice of yoga, to which he had been led by his own thinking and not by fashion, as would be the case much later on with all those tricky unmarried women, spiritual sybarites, technocrats in search of religion, all secretly doing it for practical reasons. Somehow it even came too naturally to him, which made you worry he'd go off his head one day. He did yoga modestly, for the results, and without a shade of affectation. His way was closed to me, and, to my shame, elicited only a keen literary response from me. But he didn't insist I share his views. He'd appear out of nowhere every so often to borrow a book or to share the latest discovery he had made in his recondite field, which he kept carefully camouflaged from outside view.

He told me that, even before we met, right after the war, in 1946, after far-ranging and radical thought in solitude, he had conceived the idea of carrying out a revolution in Russia and, toward that end, had taken a job as an unskilled worker in the Caspian Sea area, I think, where he conducted casual agitation among other ragged men like himself. He did it skillfully; it couldn't have been done the least bit better, using a crude Russian that ordinary people could understand, applying no pressure, so that those laborers would all by themselves discover their own class interests and the need for a united struggle for their freedom.

"And then the longed-for moment came, Andrukha!" That was his affectionate, brotherly name for me; he was duly unimpressed by my learning, so pale and paltry beside his deeds. "Once, at the end of the workday, a friend and I were sunbathing in the bushes by the sea and as usual I was pushing ideas that led to the idea of revolution, except that I wasn't using any stupid political terms directly, when all of a sudden he said:

" 'You mother . . . ! It's all so clear! Why fool around?'

" 'And what's so clear to you?' I asked.

" 'It's time to do it.'

" 'What, for example? . . .'

"It made my heart skip a beat, Andrukha. Just don't frighten him out of it, I thought. And so I used leading questions. Let him come to the answer himself!

" 'There's gotta be an organization,' he barked. 'That's what's so clear!' He said it straight out and very distinctly, an 'organization.' I had never even used any words like 'organization' in my illegal conversations with them. So Kolka had worked it all through for himself? God, I thought, finally! That means I haven't been wasting my time here, risking my neck in the process. O Lord, I prayed to myself, Lord, lead him to proletarian consciousness! And then I said casually, with a look of indifference: 'What kind of organization?'

"That surprised him. 'Pavel! What are you fucking around for?'

" 'Pavel' was my underground name. They practically never ask for your papers in those godforsaken places.

"But Kolka kept hammering away at it:

" 'An armed organization!' he said.

" 'You mother . . . !' I thought. Kolka's outdone me! Now you can start on an uprising on the battleship *Potemkin*.

" 'All right,' I answered. 'I'm with you. Let's say there's an organization, but what's it going to do?'

"Then he sketched out his plan: 'It's two miles from where we were to the fish cannery. Men and women walk this way in the evening. Unskilled laborers. We'll hide in the bushes. . . .'

" 'And do what? Rob them!'

"And you know, Andrukha, I restrained myself. Why show your cards before you need to? I laughed and I answered: 'Kolka, you mother . . . ! Rob the poor?'

"I shook with laughter, I really shook. I looked over and he was laughing too. Embarrassed.

" 'Yes,' he said, scratching his head, 'that was a mistake. . . . What can you get off the poor? . . .'

"Then I stood up and walked along the sand a ways. It wasn't more than about fifty paces to the sea. The sun was setting. The sea was green, very green. As I walked, I thought, 'Is he going to drown me now or not?'

"Like a knife, this incident severed him from all 'going to the people,' revolution, politics, all active life, and he hurled his remaining spiritual energy into educating himself. When I met him, he was already on that new level of asceticism, working as a laboratory technician at some pitiful research institute that obviously just served him only as a place to touch ground. What importance can position or the way he earns his daily bread have for a person who does not live the life of the flesh?

"Andrukha, the point is not to remake society, not to struggle against the enemy, not to go on all those wild-goose chases. We've had enough fantasies already! Do you remember what Socrates said? 'Know thyself.' Don't try to change the world! 'I know that I don't know anything.' And what does that mean? That the solution lies within each of us. Each one, Andrukha! It's been said that the kingdom of God is within you. It's important to choose the right key. The key! And then it'll open up for you. . . ."

One possibility after another would be projected, like an antique magic lantern in my damp basement room. You can fly to the moon or to Mars by means of astral projection, leaving the capsule of the flesh behind, peacefully dozing in a chair. Or, if you want, you can recall a previous happy incarnation on Atlantis and return there. . . . To the best of my knowledge, at one point a novel written by some foreign author, possibly Jack London, had made an indelible impression on my illuminated friend. The story was about a prisoner in a straitjacket who was being tortured. Losing consciousness from the pain, he was freed to seek an inward escape route and traveled from one land to another, on routes he had taken in other lives. Why beat your head against the wall trying to make a revolution no one needs? Isn't it better just to slip away via meditation? The body stays put, but the soul can roam. Did I secretly consider making a trip of my own to the moon? . . .

Unlike me, however, my companion was not a mere passive observer. Though he had broken with his revolutionary past, he had preserved a practical streak, a clarity of judgment, and a healthy, straightforward attitude about the restructuring of his mental life. When it was lunch hour at his laboratory he would order his supersensitive consciousness out to do a little reconnoitering: Which of the institute's two lunchrooms was less crowded that day? Which still had a few places left? A second later a ready answer would come to him: Go to the one on the Maslovka Street side; there's no line yet, and the menu's better— they're serving compote! And the tactiturn lab assistant would rise like a sleepwalker and obey those instructions. With never a miss . . .

In these things it's most important that reason be sidestepped and play no part in the discussion. Go where your higher mind tells you to and you'll never go wrong! . . .

The idea is that this higher mind is a part of each of us. It just hasn't been put into operation yet, has not yet assumed its rightful place. It can do anything. It will do anything you want, that second, mighty, suprarational mind. But you have to be careful. Let sleeping dogs lie. You must beware of setting it, meaning yourself, tasks beyond a normal person's powers and limits. My friend observed those limits. Kept his distance. All the same, he did once leap out of his body and go dancing through the air like a Cossack and, glancing down and back a bit, saw himself crossing Gorky Street, looking quite small as he calmly went against a red light and almost fell in front of the onrushing traffic. With a great effort of will, he instantly returned to mind and body. And was never in any hurry to leave them after that.

Or else he would take on one of his co-workers in a little game of chess, though "rook" was the only term he could even begin to remember. His first act would be to turn off his useless brain, transferring power to his supreme Double. Let it do the thinking, you just sit there and move the pawns toward the finish line. You can't lose. But for his game to collapse, all he'd have to do was start thinking about the board and moving the pieces himself. That was asking to lose. You had to beware of your own mind here. . . . And at the same time all this somehow fitted in with my ideas of literary work.

But the story of his that I liked best was the one about how he learned to guess the winning lottery number without ever once missing. My friend the yogi could see, literally see with his eyes, which, out of thousands of worthless tickets, was the one with the money. It turned out that a small flame hovered above the lucky ticket. A minute flame flickered above the winning stub. An aura around it. The ticket would jump up and down: Buy me, buy me! . . .

"So, did you buy it? Did you win? . . ."

He gave me a look of deep sympathy, a look you give the lowest of sinners. He quickly explained that these things had their consequences. A person who possessed such knowledge could not use it for his own profit. Was he some sort of wizard? An alchemist? That would have meant straying into black magic! . . .

"Remember, that's the most terrible sin in the world! And you're talking about buying tickets. It's enough that I could see which one would win. But I'd be better off cutting off my own hand than reaching out toward one of those little flames. . . ."

Later on I was to meet quite a few prophets who had been burned out, done in by the lottery. . . . And for that reason I do not consider my friend's accomplishment either impossible or delusionary. No, in his eyes, it was I who suffered from a serious lack of imagination.

"Everyone has his own karma," I would protest listlessly, using his lingo, and he'd readily agree: "And I haven't gotten around to quitting smoking either. And it impedes rhythmic breathing, you know. That's karma too! . . ."

"His karma caught up to him!" he said with a sad sigh for Stalin. "And where did he build up all that karma, on some other planet? . . ."

Then and there, on that square decked in mourning, his voice lowered, he gave me a detailed account of what had been going on in the Leader's residence the past few days. Since his death. I did not of course try to learn the source of this rumor, but it proved close to the facts, as they came to light later on. Perhaps a co-worker had blabbed the story to him over a game of chess. . . .

To make a long story short, a colonel, or, to make it even shorter, a colonel from Stalin's personal guard, a spit-and-polish old veteran, was on patrol at the dacha. He took a peek into the room adjacent to the office. As usual, he was checking to make sure that all sentries were at their places and no unauthorized persons were in the area. There wasn't a soul inside. Deserted. The doctor must be off somewhere: the autopsy was still in progress. Gone out for a smoke. Only the Monarch's body, guarded so carefully for so many years, was laid out, on an ordinary table that had been casually turned into an anatomy table. They may already have started embalming him, I'm not sure. A resection had been done. Everything had been separated out. All the collateral organs—the brain, the stomach—were lying side by side. The body had been lanced wide open and was now physically beyond repair, an impossible image. And the sight of those internal organs, split and spread, drove the colonel insane in the twinkling of an eye. He went mad. "Our enemies!" he cried. "Our enemies tore him to pieces because of my criminal negligence! . . ." Still, he knew, both intellectually and from experience, that the Leader had passed away. As head of the guard, the man must have had nerves of steel. He could fire his pistol from his pocket, and had looked death in the eye more than once. But that was not a sight for any bodyguard to see. Imagination was to blame. We imagined a god, and now we're going to remove his entrails? More karma! . . .

All true. But what concerned me at the time was not the facts but the image of Stalin that would be passed on to posterity. I had not known the flesh-and-blood Stalin, though once, about six years before, I did catch a glimpse of him at a May Day parade. And what I suddenly saw on the mausoleum was not the military leader, the man for the centuries whom we know from photographs, but a sleek cat. For an instant this made me uncomfortable. I was still in the Komsomol. We were approaching the speakers' stand. A girl in my row was writhing as if having an epileptic seizure. The sight of the Leader had sent her into hysterics. I took her by the arms. She thrashed and twisted. A chain of sullen MGB men hurried us along: "Keep moving! Keep moving!" We looked back as we walked. All I could think of was stout Vaska the Cat in Krylov's fable "The Cat and the Cook." A cat with a mustache. That's it?

I was half listening to my good companion speak about ways to end war and discord in the world. For some reason he was especially disturbed by our Civil War. Why couldn't Russians have come to terms like brothers? Wouldn't it have been simpler to ask: How many of you are Whites? And how many are Reds? We'll divide everything fair and square. And you can live however you want. . . . Or why is McCarthy persecuting the American Communist Party? Why not set one state aside for them? You can buy an island in the Pacific Ocean for a billion dollars. And they could have their own arrangement there. . . . He was an inexhaustible fund of new ideas for saving mankind. The ideas just came to him. There was one problem: I kept worrying that any moment he would fly away, abandoning me at an enchanted crossroads where I would spend the rest of my days diving and surfacing, diving and surfacing in my own gloomy, unappeasable thoughts. . . .

It was said long ago that Russia has transfixed the world. In self-satisfied grandeur, Russia dreams of a single mission—the kingdom of God on earth, established by an unwavering hand—and every so often Russia threatens to gobble the whole universe, torn by the old dilemma—either the world survives, or Russia does. One of the two.

Alas! We've forgotten this! Ever since the Leader's departure, we've been sinking deeper and deeper into a swamp of philistinism. All we want is to live. And the question arises: Why live, if Stalin is dead and Kirov is no longer with us? Live just for yourself? Communism will never get built with that kind of talk. Isn't that why the Supreme Deceased is angry with us, his sinful subjects, and is spilling buckets of blood on the streets of Moscow? "Do you dogs realize who you're burying?! Don't you forget that there will be a Second Coming—I say that, Stalin! . . ." He set right to work. Pounded his fist. He was looking into the future. To the very roots of things. He could see through stone.

Now, as I write these bitter lines in Paris, some horrid little eight-year-old girl, not born until 1973, is asking her mother in Moscow, "Was Stalner really bad?" Quite a question! That brat could use some instruction. Had she asked that question in 1948, when my youth was in its late flower, her mother would have been disemboweled—and so would she, as soon as she was old enough. "Stalner"?! Whom does she mean? What are you teaching your child? Oh, if they had only seen this little d'Anthès. But where can we find models to imitate today? Where can we direct the new generation's sights? O my youth! O my freshness! . . . Happiness was so possible, so close! . . . Push a little harder, a little extra effort, and we're there—the finish line! . . .

All is not lost, ladies and gentlemen, all is not lost, there's no need for despair, and the above-described historical incentives and possibilities may yet spring back to life, given the right turn of events. But the moment evidently slipped past on that sepulchral night, that fateful hour for the Empire. Breaking the rules, history replaced the hearty, momentous rhythm it had chanted throughout the first half of the century with one that is listless and slack, formless and worthless. Compare the dates that bring back memories to us all:

1900 (the turn of the century), 1904, 1905, 1914, 1917, and 1917 again, 1918, 1919, 1921, 1924, 1929, 1933, 1934, 1937, 1939, 1941, 1945, 1946, 1948, 1949, 1951, 1953 . . .

And what about now?! . . . Nothing's been happening—since 1954. Just look at what long, blurred periods now separate one cataclysm from another. And are those really cataclysms?! All right, let's say that they are—Czechoslovakia, Hungary, Cambodia. And—what's that country?—Angola. Ethiopia. It all slips away to the periphery. Lost in the sands. There's nothing to fix or feast your eyes on. We have definitely lost the beat.

Of course, I don't conceal the fact that, personally, this comes in fairly handy to me. You can stretch and yawn in your armchair. And there's been something of a future since 1954. Hope's intact. . . . But somehow all we did was talk and grow weaker. Philosophically speaking, as a writer connected with a definite period (the end of the forties, the beginning of the fifties), the epoch of mature, late-flowering Stalinism, I cannot help remembering those days with a certain pleasure, a son's sense of gratitude. I am not ashamed to say that I am the child of those grim years. All the petty machinations, all those bits and pieces of madness and horror that I describe with such knowledge here, all the witches and vampires that charged daily life with the electricity of an imminent end to the world and which, to this day, keep me from falling peacefully to sleep, at that time created something of a worldwide radioactive current or, more precisely, a shield to which I had been tied, like it or not. That era is also dear to me if only because it was then, and then only, that I came to conclusions antithetical to my times, and, gritting my teeth, I broke with society. I gritted my teeth, withdrew into my shell, retreated in fear in order to live and think at my own risk and peril.

I used to walk alone down Sadovaya Street at night, and mutter poems under my breath, in time with my pace and in imitation of Mayakovsky.

> Other countries have become bazaars,
> still others—goods at that bazaar,
> but you, Russia, remain a barracks,
> the most beautiful barracks of all.
>
> May emblems and monograms of gold
> flourish on your buildings
> in a raw and crude pretense
> to elegance and beauty.

> May your sons, fat-faced, snub-nosed,
> tug on their epaulets,
> and may the generalissimo's mustache
> be ubiquitous in portraiture.
>
> In every last godforsaken hole
> may our eyes be assailed
> by the barracks of streets, yards, stations,
> and concentration camps.

That's the abrupt ending of the last of the few poems I wrote as a young man, the one in which I realized once and for all that I did not have the makings of a poet and began timidly thinking about prose. All that coincided with an oppressive estrangement from the world around me, from life and current literature, which each day struck me as more hopelessly second-rate and backward, and, as is usually the case, with my attempts to do something of "my own," something "personal," and, trusting no one, to write for the desk-drawer notes on the Russian Time of Troubles, the Pretender, sketches for what would later become my novella *The Trial Begins*. For all that, I know that this was no rejection of my times, the century that I'd drawn like a winning card, and which kept devouring me in greater horror with its global jaws. However, the act of being swallowed is at least accompanied by the realization of your own rebellion's magnitude, one of countless pea-sized larvae with a slightly oblique discordant view of its own which makes this entire process doubly painful and infinitely interesting. Horror, shame, and squeamishness blended with a delight in living in "an age like this"—as few before you—one that both repels you and permeates your heart and mind like a collector's when he comes upon a lucky find. To feel that quintessential rarity, to touch it, at the same time realizing that this sort of contemplation has its price and leads to a bad end—still, no matter what you say, historically, I lucked out!

That's the trouble with aesthetics. The play of its gilded strings creates the illusion that it has all the fullness of existence, itself intolerable and essentially unworthy. You're happy as a little boy: Maestro, it's a disaster! And suddenly the smell of history becomes distinct and sweet. Aesthetics is in the mind! It is abstracted from reality and keeps a hostile distance on the very subject of its inquiry, while at the same time it is pulled back on a rubber band to its source, trembling as it looks with love on the dear and repulsive features, the source of its own existence. Aesthetics cares only for its own amusement. It loves to watch how that armored wonder moves with its tentacles! And what envious eyes that wonder has! I wonder what it thinks about—who next? Don't worry, it will devour everyone, me included. But, worm that I am, I'll put on airs as long as I'm in one piece. And instead of trying to charm the viper, I dream of painting it. Look, the monster has gobbled somebody again! And it's voracious too, the dog! And the coils and muscles that fat creature has beneath its protective scales! But the main thing is its little eyes! Just look at those little eyes! . . .

I won't argue; there could well have been something pathological about such feelings. Something corrupt and voluptuously alarming hovered in the air. Everything exceeded human measure. And though, I reiterate, the person of the general secretary, locked away behind seven seals in his fortress, was of little interest to me in his obvious, back-room mediocrity, I did take an unhealthy interest in the atmosphere—that of a black mass, a witches' sabbath, howlings from beyond the grave—that was either induced by him or sent down from above to lend him pleasure and support, and which, in my view, constituted the true essence of that unique reign. For the first time, history was revealed to me as a field and equation of supernatural forces. And the cruder and coarser the expression and palpable results of the hypnosis, the more irrational seemed the principle secretly guiding this mass manipulation. People became like instruments of witchcraft—flying birch-twig brooms, spinning tables and dishes—muttering words that were not their own but someone else's, inspired from above, repeated by rote, and which interpreters translated into the most primitive language, solely for the sake of appearances and for general accessibility. . . .

One time, in the smoking room of the Lenin Library, a Georgian with flashing white teeth and a student's high spirits confided to me the reason for his—as he put it, and you'll pardon the expression—success in fucking women. Not much to look at, forever short of funds, he had as compensation a slight Caucasian accent and a dashing mustache the color of rolling tobacco. According to him, these inborn trifles—combined with his smoke-darkened pipe, which never left his lips—were all it took to make women of various professions, ages, and nationalities fall all over him.

I don't know why that Georgian, who kept looking warily around and was risking his life, decided to enrich my less-than-modest experience of such matters. He may have needed to discharge a certain nervous tension. He also apparently had it in for Stalin and, in an oblique way, heaped all his anti-Soviet debauchery on him, never mentioning him by name, but without being excessively formal when it came to the details of his escapades as a Don Juan.

Of that entire adoring chorus, the only woman who stuck in my memory, and incompletely at that time, was a unique and delicious blonde. I listened as coolly as a doctor to his intricate analysis of her, skeptically allowing for a certain degree of bullshit, while at the same time being held by the story like a man who has grabbed onto a live wire.

He had had what is called a passing affair with a woman in middle age. Actually, catching himself, he hastened to point out that the story was not about him but about another one of her lovers. That was not the point anyway; that didn't matter. The story was about her, not him. She was famous in a small circle of male admirers in Moscow for having had the honor, back before the war, of having personally sucked off the Generalissimo in Sochi. I think this was nothing but a figment of her imagination. But try to check that! Whatever actually happened, fearing public knowledge and censure, she had everyone swear by everything holy never to breathe a word of her sexual secret. Still, she would be the first to blurt it out in confidence to her next lover, and, of course, one way or another, the story got around. She made a good living off it, but she was always on the edge of a volcano.

It is, however, remarkable that none of those in whom she confided, and who passed on that seductive blonde baton, either informed on her or betrayed her, to their honor as men. . . .

What the Georgian said immediately reminded me of the story, told me in confidence by my high-school chemistry teacher no less, though of course he too told other people the story in secret, despite the pledges he exacted as he began his tale of a brilliant dirty trick. "Not a peep about this to anyone! Anyone who knows about this or accidentally hears about it will be wiped out. Make sure it doesn't get around. You can see how serious this is! . . ."

Indeed, the story involved a new stage in the development of Marxist theory. In 1952, at the 19th Party Congress, Malenkov, standing in for the Leader, had just made a brilliant excursion into the realm of literature. He said that what is "typical" in art is not the "statistical average" but the "exceptional." Unheard of, that level of style and thought, coming from the mouth of a party leader. Everything—curriculums, the problems to be studied, aesthetics, philosophy, and literature—was subject to immediate review. New departments and new textbooks were created, new dissertations written. It was all hands on deck in the institutes and collectives; scholars produced works on the "typical as the exceptional" in Marxism. Learning had taken a leap forward. And no one, absolutely no one in the entire world, except a few renegades like me who were linked by an invisible chain, knew that Malenkov's entire theoretical contribution had been copied word for word from an old, long-forgotten edition of the *Literary Encyclopedia*. Nobody's written a word on any of this, it's not even mentioned in the works of the White émigré D. S. Mirsky, who like a fool returned to Russia and who, they say, managed to die of starvation in a labor camp as an enemy of the people. Meticulous historians can easily check this point by comparing Molotov's speech at the congress with that long-forgotten tome, under "R," in the entry on "Realism." . . .

"But, of course," said the Georgian with a precautionary wink, "there were no women in that select circle of hers, and, naturally, no women were let in on the secret. . . ." They would have exposed the poor slut, dragged her out in the open, I thought, finishing his thought for him. And by the way, that would have been foolish, to their own detriment. Any informer, privy to that fascinating secret, could have gone right down the line from the main share-holder, to this jolly Georgian big mouth, then to me, accidentally caught like a dumb bunny in that mesh of information. Horatio, my friend, in this life some things it's better not to know. . . . "Oho," I thought at once. "Is this young pimp trying to turn me on to that white-hot whore? He doesn't have a chance! I'll never fall for that!"

I was overreacting. It turned out that the Georgian had broken up with her. He couldn't bear to see her any more. His reason was the same as everyone else's. At the height of their pleasure they had all called her "Svetlana." He had been playing with fire. He was on the straight path to the inferno. He had learned this secret firsthand, so to speak. She had gone to bed with him out of love, free of charge, finding him as irresistible as chocolate candy. She even gave him a few rubles of her own. Everything would have been fine if, when kissing the mustache of my friend the Georgian, that dreamy woman had not fallen into a strange exaltation caused by the smell of tobacco, which came not from his mustache but from someone else's, and had she not fantasized herself as an adolescent girl, or some damned thing like that. Far from her own adolescence, she played a farce in which she was the young daughter, searching for someone else in him, the one and only one she had ever loved and desired, and with whom she had supposedly once been intimate. At the crucial moments of her orgasm, she would moan, "I'm Svetlana! I'm coming to you, my love! At last! Father! Father! . . ." No question, this smacked of incest. . . .

"A psychopath," I said dryly, swallowing my saliva. He frowned.

"They're all psychopaths. But what's a normal person like me supposed to do with them? Well? . . ."

I suddenly felt how ill at ease he was about all those conquests, which he had at first seemed to flaunt.

"But have you ever tried to get rid of that . . . uh, uh . . . that chance resemblance?" I said haltingly, trying both to be of help and not offend the hot-tempered mountain man. "For example, to change some secondary characteristic, switch to cigarettes. Try to start all over again. With a clean slate . . ."

"Too late," he sighed. "Like they say, it's in me now. I got too used to it. And it's too late to fix it!"

Surrounded by tobacco smoke, he made a vague gesture with his fingers that probably referred to his slight Caucasian accent, which women found so fascinating and which indeed was pleasant, though it did seem from somewhere else, some other planet. But his accent brought another specter shimmering to mind, that of a man who was even wearier of the burden of love, power, and glory. Stalin too had no right to divest himself either of his pensive pipe or of his candy mustache, which it was a sin to mock and which he could no longer shave off even if he wanted to. He was not a person, he had become a portrait. What a burden it must be to turn into your own portrait while you're still alive and have to do everything your worshippers demand of their god. Like the hapless pointer running in servile circles at a séance. You summon a Napoleon, and a Napoleon comes. And if you dream of a Stalin, it's a Stalin you get. Who's pulling the strings? Maybe we do it ourselves, without noticing, just waiting for him to kill one of us periodically, wanting him to, so he continues to resemble his own portrait. We'd have been alarmed if he tried to be kind. We would have lost faith in the reality of the image. What did we need all that for? Not him, us?! . . .

To change the subject, I asked banteringly, "And where's that interesting woman now?"

"In Sklifosovsky Hospital," he answered calmly, as if knowing in advance what the question would be. "She was run over by a car. Last night. She won't pull through."

He lowered his eyes sadly. As if reading my mind, he spread his hands in a gesture of helplessness, then, pointing to his heart, said, "Her heart gave out. She's past help. . . ."

And then he said something else, which he either mumbled, swallowed, or I may just have imagined: was it "denounced"? "avenged"? "celebrated"? . . . I didn't get it.

He was about to start gnawing on another bone from his stash of adventures, but by then I had lost interest. I hurried out of the smoking room and went back to my books. Of course, the Georgian was never seen in the Lenin Library after that day, as if he'd been washed away by a wave. Maybe his turn had come to be run over by a truck. Or perhaps he was arrested. Or maybe he simply took fear that I or some other confidant of his would denounce him, and he left to seek his fortune in the Caucasus, as far from the danger as possible. In any case, he did not inform on me after that conversation of ours, as I fear he had done with that hot-blooded blonde of his. . . .

. . . The Lord was still sitting on his light-blue throne. He was flanked by the Most Holy Mother of God holding a flower and by John the Baptist, his severed head on a tray which he held tightly in his hands as material evidence. Such was the composition. . . .

Our rendering here will have grandeur and style, as befits an illuminator. We will not, however, presume to exceed our powers and be tempted to make a natural, visible representation of that Celestial Light which, here on earth, has only been contemplated by the Holy Fathers and in our prayer books, but which our feeble intelligence can only grasp as a reflection through a dark and sooty glass, a reflection that fell purposely from heaven to this fragile world. So I suppose that the back of the reader's head, its concave interior, can serve as our mirror here. Concave? What do you want—a Mirror that reflects heaven directly? That I don't have. The rays of that light, however, bombard the eyes with the truth unendurably and pass through all the brain's tangle of vessels until they finally reach this opaque screen at the rear and vulnerable side of the problem. All right, it may be distorted, but, still, can't something be spied through our binoculars, our telescope, if we strain our eyes?

. . . Eternity flowed on. Stars streamed under God's Throne, on their way to their combat positions, their missions. Somewhere down below, the Great October Socialist Revolution had already taken place. Stalin had died. And then—Lenin. A hundred thousand times a minute, people asked why there was no intervention from above and why order wasn't being established. What were the Authorities doing? But the Lord was still sitting on His golden throne and thinking. On His either side were John the Baptist, holding his head out in front of him on a dish, and the Most Holy Mother of God, extending the question mark of a Flower toward the Throne. All was still, except that every so often the Most Pure Virgin would utter a grief-stricken sigh. This must have lasted half an hour. . . .

You pray to the Mother of God when they bring you in for questioning. Hail Mary, Mother of God, blessed art Thou, the Lord is with Thee. . . . When walking down those corridors, I often asked myself: Why does the soul unfailingly, inaudibly, and unforeseeably pour itself out in prayer to the Holy Mother of God? After all, you're not asking for anything. No, of course, you do ask for something, but it's no longer for yourself. A new calamity is at hand, and it's a hundred times harder to bear. There are two, three, four people involved with you still at liberty. Those devils will get to them too and drag them in for questioning. Two of them seem to have gone into hiding for a while. . . . Blessed art Thou among women and blessed is the fruit of Thy womb. . . . If things keep up like this, everyone, down to the last man, the entire human race, will be drawn into that hellish machine and pulped. Spare the others, O Lord! Thou who wast born as the Saviour of our souls . . . Will worse come to worst and all humankind be under their total control?! But they can't get to Her! The Mother of God will alone remain our witness and our advocate in heaven. Hail, Immaculate Virgin! Beyond enemy reach. May She alone be saved and shine forth, the Queen of Heaven! . . . That brings some relief. Which means that even we sinners here on earth do not cackle in vain. . . .

. . . Our Mother trembled and turned her hands, narrow as feet, toward the Throne. A buttercup fell from her lily-white hands. A new and even more lissome lily of the valley sprang forth in Our Lady's hand. . . .

"My son!" she said. "Take mercy on the Russian Orthodox. Send them a message from heaven. An olive branch. Why all these executions and wars, plagues, famines, and tremblings of the earth? And for how long? . . ."

Jesus Christ knit his protuberant, gorillalike brow, and less than twenty minutes later the Pantokrator said, as if cutting her off: "It's not time yet! . . ."

What exceeds our understanding more than Christ? Christ, who said: There is a hell! And: There is no hell! Who turned away from everything and accepted everyone. What limits has He set on us? Try to absorb them and live by them. To forgive the woman taken in adultery—who will cast the first stone? And to punish everyone who even once sinned in his heart? Still, peeping out from our own little corner, we do not believe in God, we do not trust in God. Losing our soul, we hope that the Lord will gather it in and give it peace. We offer Him bribes. Bribes! He really needs your trinkets! And He may well have your original and authentic soul stashed away like a diamond at a pawnbroker's. You'll get to see it when you die, see who you really would have been had you not been forever yelling, "Me! Me!" . . . We run around, raising a great hue and cry in our passion to understand. Until the Lord seizes someone by the hair and breathes in his ear and, illuminated, that person hastens to bring us tidings: The Lord is with you! With us! Look and see, people. He knows you better than you know yourself. And He loves you more than you love yourselves. . . . Do you see the scales, the clock? Five seconds. Four. Three. Two . . . "Go!" I cry as I wake. "Go!" Nothing of the sort.

"It's not time yet!" replied the Almighty from on high his purple throne. And without moving His head He addressed John. "What do you have to say on the subject?"

John's head cawed from the plate: "They have it coming! They deserve it! They're steeped in sin. They drink strong drink, smoke poison. Some of them are shamelessly contemplating shaving off their beards and going about bare-faced, like foreigners or women. Devils that they are, they do not know that Peter's reforms are only a century away.

". . . Mark it well, O Lord, two days ago they killed another innocent child. It may have been the tsar's son, we don't have precise information yet, or it may have been their own just and lawful ruler. Once again they have let their history slide into disaster. Baptize them, punish them, O Saviour, with fire and sword. And as if they were roaches . . ."

But then the Baptist glanced up at the Virgin from the corner of one eye, and the Precursor was mollified. He poked his decapitated head with an emaciated finger.

"Still, I'm not against it," he added. "As far as I'm concerned, You can take pity on them. . . ."

I don't know. Is human history more than an orgy, as it would truly be if God forgot man and left him alone with his own kind, is it more than just a human scrap heap but a work of art all its own, as intricately and ingeniously constructed as nature itself, that must be because from time to time the Lord Himself continues to take a hand in man's history on earth. We don't know how or when He takes a hand, and we have no need to know. Otherwise, having "understood" something, we'd lose everything all over again. . . .

I am convinced that history does not operate entirely on its own. Its laws and channels are not autonomous. History is always being watched over, and, alas, not always benevolently. Both from above, from heaven, and from below, from beneath the stage; from every side and quarter, searchlights flash, merging and crossing at a point of living light and heat: "Behold the man!" Some look on man with love, others with *Schadenfreude,* still others— simple, average people—just verify the fact: "Behold the man." There's nowhere to hide. You grow angry. Why have you fixed your gaze on me, O masks? Go ask the stork, the monkey, the elephant. They hold man up to shame! "Man! Man!" Nothing so special. Boring. I do not want to, I cannot, be one. No, they laugh: "Behold the man! . . ." It's the same with the plants and stones: Behold the man. Neither angel nor fish or fowl. At every step of the way—ridiculous, pitiable, sinful, last and least—man. Lamentation and loud laughter. One day you'll die. Then from the dead, rise: "I believe in the One God! I await the resurrection of the dead!" "Behold, the man." That says it all. I don't want to understand. Or to escape perdition. But, tell me, how do you bear that cross, "Behold the man," on your back? . . .

. . . One would have thought that, while John was speaking, the Lord would rise from His icon niche and proclaim: "Enough! My patience is at an end! Why do they make mockery and mischief? We shall eradicate them and create something new. We shall destroy that whole violent world. The four places where they pierced My hands and feet are acting up today. Bad weather's coming."

But the Intercessor bent Her humble head and washed the world with tears the size of pigeon eggs. A May downpour fell on the city of Putilov, the city of Moscow, and the city of Kaluga. Snow fell in Arkhangelsk. Novgorod was rattled by hail. Mist even settled over the city of London at that hour. And only in South America did a South American sun shine on and on. The Queen of Heaven could bear it no longer and in a clear voice said: "Have Mercy, O Lord! Give Your hand to the mother of the murdered boy. That woman, Mariya, beats her head on the damp earth in Uglich. She calls on You for judgment. And on Me as her witness. She believes as I have believed: my son is alive and God is not dead! Return the restless soul of the tsarevich to her, if only for a time. Let her rejoice. Show those with little faith the power of a mother's tears. . . ."

Our Lord Jesus Christ gazed on Her with affection. "Be calm," He said, almost breaking into tears Himself. "Be calm, Most Holy Mother, Eternal Intercessor for the human race. I will do as You ask. But what's the use of it? . . . Her unworthy son will rise from the dead and bring trouble down on Russia. Blood, much blood will be spilled because of that child. . . . Bad weather's coming."

They all lapsed into silence, Jesus Christ on His chair of cypress wood and, at his either hand, the Virgin and John the Baptist. They remained still for years, if not for centuries. And on the plate still held in the headless John's firm grip, one eye was now covered with a dull film, like that of a lizard falling to sleep. . . .

V
. . .

In the Belly of
the Whale

On the jagged Assyrian friezes, the lions growled with all the veracity of human speech, as they breathed their last. Doll-like people—seen in profile, inscrutable as battering rams, legs in step, muscles tensed—march division after division to the thunder of drums, frozen in stone. I would doubt that they're human—they are so elevated, their ritual so remote from our nature and mentality—except that below, in the second panel, their butchered bodies float upside down in the lacy stone of a river, the Euphrates, and voracious fish rush to feed on the hastily severed legs and heads of those archers, kings, gods, and dancers who march in the top panel and now drown in stone bas-relief, a procession that begins with the Flood and includes you and me. It is death that can balance out those passing throngs, from Noah to the lion in the disgrace of his final frenzy. And the lion's roar hung like a wall, like the culmination of history, filling that spectacle of gradually triumphant death, in various well-rendered poses of natural agony that would, of course, afford hunters the greatest of pleasure. Against our will, we are drawn into those dry renderings of convulsion, and would become entangled in an alien world of incorruptible guards and archers, a nation of professional chastisers—may that savage tribe perish and disappear forever—were it not that it is we ourselves who are floating down that river, bodies disfigured, were it not us marching in serried ranks in royal ceremony, were it not for those fire-breathing lions—breathing their last, like us, and right before our eyes. Here, looking down at that arena, one can well suspect that it is only on his deathbed that a person understands people, and lions, and all creatures that must die, because the movement of time is impartial, merciless, and seizes even you in passing as well as those who left the scene five millennia ago, and this slowly expiring beast, left for our edification, as it erupts in curses at the stone stream of history. . . .

In those Assyrian friezes my compassion was roused solely by the dying lions, their claws paralyzed by the treacherous blow of a spear, fixed in stone once and for all. One lioness especially. Felled by arrows in her back, her spine broken at the sacrum, losing blood, she let loose a blasphemy against that triumphal procession of bearded villains. Here you behold death. Death is realism, with none of the palls and canopies beneath which invulnerable kings are offered up to heaven, until they too, like the lion—rear legs paralyzed, a bloody foam of indignation issuing from its mouth—tumble into the netherworld through every level of the merciless universe. The Fiend. Damnation. Oh, the flood of History like a waterfall sending us over the stones of Mesopotamia! Burden of the ages, eternity of the stones . . .

Years later, in the British Museum, I was overjoyed to come across those friezes—it's the same ones! As if I'd run into relatives. Whom I'd known as a child. I had only known the friezes from pictures, of course. Prints. From that day on, I have never referred to London without its title of "city." May you be blessed, city of London! You harbored those regiments in your vast depths. Just think—where is Ashurbanipal? Hammurabi? In England? In a British storehouse? "Only S. could have appreciated that one! Only S.!" I mutter sorrowfully, as if I had lost someone, though it's probably not for me to mourn that friend of my youth, not for me to lay flowers on his early grave. But, for me, his connection with Assyria was as indisputable as his ties with the period in question here, with the art and the séances. With ghosts summoned to face their accuser. With prison.

No matter which friend or acquaintance I think of, all variously gifted, he is the one who always stands out as the true, born artist. Perhaps an artist of life—to my horror—but an artist. "*Ab incunabulis,*" "*ab initio,*" "*ab ovo*" ("from the cradle," "from the beginning," the very beginning, "from the egg"). He and I were in the A class together from second grade till eighth, and as adolescents we argued often about the source of skill and talent. Was it from birth, as he unwaveringly insisted, audaciously sanctioning himself? Or, as I thought, did it come with the pain of experience, and was it equally available to all who work at it with stubborn labor? He proved right. Despite my approach, based on Pisarev, whose ideas had intoxicated me in fifth grade, and on purely sociological considerations, and no matter how hard I worked on myself, he, Seryozha, was always first from birth.

In our freckle-dappled school, he looked like a piece of cornelian that required no polishing and was only waiting for the years to find a suitable setting. Devoid of any vulgar need for camaraderie, he studied independently, unlike myself. During class he drew pictures of knights in armor on horseback out of Sir Walter Scott's novels *Ivanhoe* and *Quentin Durward*. From the time he was eleven he wrote superb, refined poetry. In principle, those first attempts of his would be publishable today, in an edition like Gumilev's *Pearls* with its embossed and aromatic binding. S. took a knowledgeable pleasure in Gumilev, whom he read when he wasn't reading Bagritsky.

> Ships' sails slap lightly
> On the Arctic and South Seas. . . .

He also drew pictures of broad-chested frigates, and was well grounded in draftsmanship. But, most important, he had inherited—like a family estate—the new European painting, the Impressionists, Cézanne, Gauguin, which had not yet disappeared from Moscow's museums; not only that, he solemnly introduced me to them—me, a neophyte, brought up on nineteenth-century realistic paintings of Volga boatmen. He forced me to absorb them, taste of them, and abandon all shame when looking at those canvases that bristled like angry hedgehogs and resembled nothing else, but truly were closer to their sources in sunlight, air, and smelly paint than the old nags and dray carts to be seen in the dark Tretyakovsky Museum. And how was I to resist the temptation presented by the Shchukin collection, which had as yet to be banished from view by the government: in those empty, hospitable galleries on Prechistenka Street you could wander for hours in and among those mysterious, half-forbidden works of art, reciting like a precept, an exorcism, my valient mentor's piercing lines:

> Claude Monet and Degas,
> You live in me, never growing old.
> I wrote this song for you
> in the hush of a gallery.
> You looked from the walls
> Surprisingly ta-tum and dry,
> Gauguin the Tahitian
> and the madman who cut off his ear. . . .

Staggering! Van Gogh, I was to learn, was the madman who cut off his ear. And, I assure you, this poem was written by an adolescent, a fifth-grader, my Virgil of the galleries, who taught me to perceive that the green streaks slanting across the sky on the canvas were van Gogh's improvisation of rain, and that the burning midday sun, too intense for the eye to see, could be rendered as a clotted circle. We went to see Matisse. . . . But that's not the half of it. He led me through Egypt, Assyria, Babylon, and was the first to show me a picture of the frieze with the dying lion, which is why I bring him up with a shudder of gratitude today, when standing in front of that fiery slab. . . .

Back then no one had a finer appreciation of those rare works than S.; no one took them so much to heart. I hastened to imitate him. A nice-looking, Acmeist-type boy, a little standoffish, of course, from a well-to-do Jewish family, he might have been my idol, if I had ever dared to confide in him fully. His capricious erudition, his original outlook, his impeccable taste were automatically riveting. That was all he had. Nature had not bestowed anything else on him. He thought like a jeweler.

"Look at this!" He shoved my face up to a spoon on display in the museum's collection. The spoon was actually quite nice, competently designed. He spoke of it with a fervor that was unlike him, a Delphic look flashing across his illuminated face. "Look at that, will you! . . . Don't you see? Don't you see? . . . All I want from life, all I want, is to create a spoon like that one. . . ." A magical froth bubbled at the corners of his lips, a foam of quotations on coral reefs: "The gold is scattered from his cuffs of rose-colored Brabant lace. . . ." A single teaspoon! But one that lasts. . . .

I didn't understand. A single teaspoon? As a life's work?! . . . The rotten little wunderkind, he was crazy about perfection. Born the year before me, he was three thousand years older than I. He would have been satisfied with a single golden spoon! An aesthete . . . Wait a moment! Why am I speaking badly of him? Let's take a closer look. Where was the demarcation line? Where did the parting of the ways occur? . . .

I took giant steps, striving to make up for lost time. That can happen when we're young and still growing and don't want to stop for anything. Impressionism, Egypt—big deal! Just before the war, as a foil to his idol Gumilev, I'd carry around a volume of Vladimir Mayakovsky's poems, from his embryonic Futurist phase, or those of Khlebnikov, whom my guide had clearly rejected. Crudeness in art sickened him, a sprung verse, a torn canvas. Still, later on, at the university, S. was quite taken by Selvinsky's early work. But by then I was crazy about Picasso, not Gauguin. . . .

It was, I would say, a competition to be avant-garde, or, more precisely, we were two bright schoolboys hiding under our desktops from an armada of vengeful, edifying bullshit. We fled as fast as we could from the unbearable boasting and the boredom of the official, conservative style. S. helped me rid myself of realism, Pisarev, relevance, high-minded ideological content, and didacticism in aesthetics. And for that I am indebted to him. Later, however, our views diverged, but we had agreed on one essential point—that form was sufficient unto itself. It wasn't there that the rift opened, in Renoirs of perverted taste, in Acmeism or Futurism, was it? Or in political or social differences? All that changed and faded as we grew, receding into the background, though our friendship always had its ups and downs. . . .

When we were children, he was favorably inclined toward me, the plebeian, but with the irony of a mentally advanced snob who had been born into the industrial and intellectual elite, though he did not give a damn about that. And he seemed to make a point of not loving his parents. He was not burdened by his class privileges; he developed all on his own, free of caste and ethnic prejudice, which did not prevent him on occasion from laughing wholeheartedly at my Russian forelock and my patched pants. It was just that they were funny. My feelings weren't hurt. To be mocked by the well-born and wealthy doesn't hurt us until we begin to sense and disguise the vulnerability of our hearts. Hey, we know what's what! Moreover, after the war, and before he was fully grown, S. lost his mother and father. Somehow he became poor immediately, went into debt, and had a rough time of it, like everyone else, no longer aided by the lend-lease of his class. The pressure was on the Jews; Stalin was at his zenith. The doctors' plot flashed like summer lightning. It was then that S. used his powers of observation and his native wit to find a way out of the ambiguity. It came out in poetry, beautiful as always:

Turning off the pink light, the sage gynecologists
Tune in to the "Voice of America," absorbing it through
   their hot pajamas. . . .

And the lines, the lines that came next, with their Assyrian
regiments, generals on their way to battle!

You went the limit.
Look around at the evening snow:
A flight of heavy flakes on the concrete strings of the
   speakers' stands. . . .

Oh, if it all had stayed on paper! It isn't art that does us in but
art's connection with reality. That lofty meditation on our own
lowness. Seen from without . . . Objectively. What does "You
went the limit" mean? I know. For him that meant betrayal. Sac-
rilege. Black magic. And everyone liked the poem—that's real
writing! How courageous and categorical that sounds—to go the
limit! . . .

He also contrived to write poems in such a way that his personality seemed to divide in two: he achieved heroic feats with
artistic resolve. Truly, there was no denying he was gifted. Not at
all. He would accomplish something wherever he could find a
crack, the slightest toehold. He sweetened the pill. He translated
aesthetics into practice and it worked. Or was it the other way
around? What's the difference? The poems were valuable in and
of themselves, at one with his personality. His friends devoured
them. I was lucky enough to spit out the poison. By that time I
knew him inside and out. Others were still caught up by them,
just asking for it, to say the least. "His alliteration! . . ."

Having struck his blow, wiping his sword, he would evaluate
the situation soberly. Cheerfully. Admiringly. He appealed for pity
and compassion and, encountering none and feeling flawless, he
would exult. I'm beyond good and evil, my friend, he seemed to
say. Godlike. Above the barriers. He accomplished all this through

small steps (always the most telling), about which more later. Elegantly, with the swagger of a coward who has crossed a line. A Zarathustra. Observing all the rules of police provocation, he enticed two friends, two trusting deer from his own lousy little ghetto, to the slaughter—don't worry, they won't be coming back from there—and he found himself seized by some metaphysical ecstasy.

Night, he muttered, the whole of history is one long night. No one will ever find out, no one can see through all that snow. He had just committed a grievous sin and had no one to confide in. A pity. His soul was as cold as a whore. He was alone. Look around: "A flight of heavy flakes on the concrete strings of the speakers' stands . . ." What alliteration! Who could help falling in love with a talent gleaming—forever gleaming—at the boundary of the permissible, in the gaps between earth and heaven, undimming, beyond reach. Who could resist his image of a banner, red as a blood-filled mosquito, lit by searchlights in the iron wind over the Supreme House of the Soviets, the cupola. And you didn't know? Here, take this. Here, you nitwits, is a cornelian pampered from childhood, from birth. How many years did they get? Ten? Fifteen? And what if all of a sudden they're released from hell? "How could you, Seryozha?!" a friend lamented many years later. "No, how could you?" She always used to defend him. And now it's: What century is it outside? But all those P-skies, Ts-imanns, and L-zons denied it: "If Seryozhka had been an informer, he would have turned me in a long time ago. What would it have mattered to him! And after everything I'd revealed to him! . . ." He overcame everything. His chin, his face willful as a spear, straight out of Gumilev. A true Assyrian. The nose bronze, slightly aquiline. Another Bagritsky. Eyeglasses. Eye sockets. Round hips. Ample pelvis. Short little legs. Miniature feet (he took a child's shoe size). He combined everything required of a man and of a woman. A hermaphrodite. But, we ask ourselves, why didn't he denounce everyone? Why did he leave them alone—be fruitful and multiply? They weren't involved in the case yet. No attention had

above us, above me! But everything seemed normal enough down there. Meanwhile, this giant had grown deeper, widened, and, for want of any better yardstick, now took its measure in years by the millions; slowly forming empty spaces the size of Europe, with its side tunnels that no one walks any longer, and then running out of room, it set us back on our feet, the path heading for the exit, the air, which became an entrance, independently of it. Trembling cavemen, our hair on end like fur from the cold, we entered this sanctuary for the first time in our life. And what did we see then? . . . Waterfalls of stone, waterfalls of stone, stone waterfalls, of course. Towers of Babel spiraling upward, to the sky, six hundred feet, to a stone sky—the stone towers of Babylon. They say this is all the result of water. But we ask the water why it did it. We ask the earth. We ask God. No light is shed. A little girl whimpered in French, "Mama, is it made of snow?" No, of course it's not made of snow; these halls were forged out of stone, these churches, these avenues that don't lead anywhere, these cells and chambers that have ceased to flow and which freeze at their own sight, halting in fear and amazement that they were made all of stone and yet were able to flow. The twisting stalactites have been clamoring to heaven for years and years before you existed, crying: Open! to a sky hidden by stone, a heavy ceiling that could collapse at any second to crush you and to scatter the pavilions and towers along which we walk, looking around, huddled together under the glaciers, as if it couldn't cave in, until we remember that this ceiling is what turned our heads from those of simians to those of human beings.

The water drips like a hammer. The ground has been kneaded by brontosaur tracks. Drips on the brain. What? Everything is ruined. Through and through. "Sleep, little boy, don't worry your head. . . ." For there are no more mammoths. But we're still crawling. Look over there—it's settling. We pray under a stone sky. But that water is life-giving. Then, in the flashlight's flickering beam, I see them—fingerprints. I realize I don't have my camera with me. But taking pictures isn't allowed anyway. Fingerprints, red, white, black, the phalanges of fingers chopped in half, which appear with increasing frequency on the walls as we begin to get our bearings. It would be nice to stay here. Be buried. Be saved . . . But no—you crawl back up.

A primitive man, I crawl out of the shelter and, comfortably down on all fours, look up with astonishment at the sky. It's bombarding us. Bombarding us! I understand—it's trying to intimidate us. There is life on other planets. But everything has to pass through and be filtered by the stone rain of "stalin," "lenin," "hitler," "zhdanov." . . . Oh, how the star "Mao Tse-tung" once flared above us! And how cometlike was the race of "Fidel Castro" across the firmament! . . . And now it's gone. And all that remains are the same old names. How does a person live bombarded by that rain? You get used to it. You calm down. That's their job, the gods—to bomb and bombard. They can't live without it. And you live below them. Your wife goes to the store and you ask: What's it like out? Is it bombing? She makes a dismissive gesture. Crawl back inside, old man, crawl underground! Oh, the big ones are coming down now, like the rain before the mushrooms . . .

"Which sign were you born under?" we ask each other with curiosity by the fireplace in the shelter. "Sagittarius or Libra? Do you know your chart, *señora?* Or will you, as always, adamantly answer me 'Scorpio'?! . . ."

I can't speak for anyone else, but I still take pleasure in my own horoscope. I was born under the "Stalin-Kirov-Zhdanov-Hitler-Stalin" constellation. That's all. None of those Ursa Majors and Ursa Minors. The very sun of the millennium, "Lenin," once it had shriveled and shrunk, became an inconspicuous, mild-mannered little red star on schoolchildren's jackets. "Stalin," surrounded by his Pleiades ("Molotov," "Kaganovich"), shone across the entire horizon and grinned enigmatically. And with him, like a hoop of fire, the mystery, the mustached Mystery, extended above us on that romantic night. We experienced a great and unforgettable temptation, the temptation of miracle. The Antichrist alone promises us something of that sort in advance, something even more absorbing. What is power without mystery, without miracle? A mechanical force, that's all . . . And, I assure you, the role of State Security (always on guard) in lacing the stone sky with a silky pattern of stars and in the creation of that otherworldly historical dusk, was not the least important either. . . .

It is absurd to lodge grievances now against those who were enthusiastic and romantic about political denunciation. Against the masses. The nation. Pavlik Morozov. They had faith. They wept but they had faith. They slaughtered people, but they had faith. "Then, weeping and weeping, he chopped off the man's head," said S. with a little laugh, quoting from a medieval Japanese novel about Samurai. (Really, well put!) We knew idealists of the highest purity and caliber, people who were kind by nature and who were proud of their denunciations, made without any intent of personal gain. It all went along with defense, feats of labor. The Ready for Labor and Defense Sports Organization. Answering the call of the party, duty, and conscience were the fearless Chkalovs, who flew over the North Pole to re-establish the truth, the sailors of the Chelyuskin, the Papanists, those who took the Winter Palace, the sleepwalkers, blindly marching on the foe, the tough Alexander Matrosoves, thrusting their chests at the enemy's embrasure. (Fortunately, my hero is not of that ilk. . . .)

The blessed Pavlik Morozov walked among us, as if alive, like the incorporeal youth in Nesterov's visionary painting. Wasn't he the unfortunate brother rising at night from the bottom of a radiant forest lake and awaited by the inconsolable Alenushka at Vasnetsov's dacha? His head down, like a freshly killed chicken, he was himself like mist, transparent, watery, iconlike, scarlatina. A wanton little smile of holiness weeps, curdling on the martyr's lips. Sheikis holds up a bloodthirsty necklace; drop by drop, as from a medicine dropper, it sheds a marvelous pus, the poisonous lymph of innocence. Medicine. It smells like a clinic. Chlorine. Benzoin. Violets. Formalin. They say that before Easter they soak corpses in formalin. The lamb. Slender as a birch tree, he walks the fields, his eyes closed; they have killed the lad. Cut off so young in years. Denunciation and resurrection! The thoughtful historian will marvel to discover a nation's heroism and sense of responsibility in the incorruptible body of a young Stakhanovite, frozen, like Lenin in his tomb, for eternal life. An example to Pioneers and adults—Pavlik Morozov!

As children, we tried to follow in that phantom's footsteps, not by forming a network of stoolies, but by seeking adventure, honorably prepared to make the sacrifices incumbent on an intelligence officer in the coming war. We held our gallant Pioneer scarfs up to the light, looking for the hidden swastikas rumored to be sewn in them, searching for enemy threads. We couldn't find any. . . . We heard that the older students, from 7-B, had uncovered three swastikas and had sounded the alarm in time, but our 5-A class had no luck uncovering sabotage. We found nothing but plain ordinary red calico. . . .

Only Ludochka S. seemed to see something. "There it is, there it is," she whispered. "In the middle!" she screeched. "The Nazi symbol! I can see it! A real Nazi symbol!" And then she cried blue murder: "Ooo, the monsters! . . ."

Where is it? We ran over. Grabbed it from her. No stigmata. In patterns regular as Pioneer detachments, the weave was just as it had come from the factory, forming no symbols relevant to our mission. At most you might make out a rhombus. Or an isosceles trapezoid. A proletarian parallelogram . . . True, if you constructed an imaginary line at a right angle or added a short imaginary section to it from the side, then the lines of the weave might seem to contain the outline of a fine zigzag lost in its own web. An anagram. We hadn't studied trigonometry yet, of course, but it already had Ludka shaking. In a fit of disgust the little troublemaker was almost sick to her stomach. A lousy trick, was the kids' verdict. An optical illusion. Nothing to report to the district committee. Not to mention the NKVD. No one would believe you. Still, she argued, I can't stand it. I'm going home. I have a temperature, an allergy. Look, there's the rash. . . . Who'd want an invisible typhus louse on his neck instead of a Pioneer scarf? Oh, to be in the Komsomol and not have to wear a scarf!

A new development the next day. Apparently an enemy slogan had been infiltrated into the drawing of Lenin on the cover of the workbooks we were using that year. All you had to do was turn the picture a little and, in a stretch of that immortal beard, you would discover the following inscription traced in an ornate hand: "Lenin is Trotsky's friend." How was such a thought even conceivable? How could the two ideas be uttered in the same breath— "Lenin" and "Trotsky's friend"? No matter how much we racked our brains or how often we turned the ill-fated picture during class, or from what angle we approached it, we could not find anything anti-Soviet in those coded wrinkles, small hairs, and netted cellular tissue. But, using a magnifying glass, the Pioneers from 6-B detected two minute letters—either an "n" or an "m." Technology! But what if you wanted to delve even deeper? Even if you clamped it under a microscope, those lousy letters still scurried away. This was, of course, the winter of 1938. . . .

Only much later did I begin to guess that the spy's drawing of Lenin squinting did in fact conceal something suspicious, something that may even have been dangerous in a Trotskyite sort of way. It was simply that all those bacteria teeming through the nooks and crannies had scattered in panic, crawling over one another in search of cover, and so in the end sometimes turned up in the most unlikely places. It is not by chance that some worldly ladies will refer, and not without flirtatious and lascivious undertones, to their pubic hair as "Trotsky's goatee." But I was not informed of this until later on, by a general's wife of my acquaintance, a middle-aged woman. "Life is so complicated. My dear," she said, "life is not as neat and pretty as you'd like it to be, and politics comes in everywhere. But if we admit that the enemy could be anywhere, then why couldn't he be in a humble classroom as well? . . ."

On this occasion as well, S. stood out from the rest of the class because of his subtlety of mind. He was apolitical, and I think the regime left him cold. He disdained the crowd and believed in neither God nor the devil. I can't even remember whether or not he was a Pioneer like all the other children—such ordinary uniforms seemed beneath his dignity. It was as if he had grasped everything, right from the start, without going through the whole process, and was bearing it within him until the time was ripe, meanwhile puzzling me with the force of some of his other impulses.

That same winter I had the good fortune to lure my elegant friend to my house after school. Nudging him on from behind, I led him carefully through our stinking, scandalous hallway. You have not forgotten, of course, what having your first guest at home means, especially when he's a well-read and handsome twelve-year-old prince from another world. We launched into a serious discussion about Renoir's superiority to Shishkin, and Stendhal's to Sir Walter Scott, each of us displaying his exceptional knowledge. When my mother had gone off to the kitchen to heat up yesterday's soup for us, S. looked stealthily around, took aim, and . . .

But before describing his impious gesture I would like to look with a stranger's eyes at our old communal accommodations on Khlebny Street, with their standard poverty and pervasive mediocrity, all those saucepans, frying pans, the little bottles lining the windowsill, the small plywood coffin containing the dishes, the ruins of a wardrobe made over into a bookcase, unplaned planks for shelves, covered with paper to prevent splinters, a square dinner table covered by a flimsy oilcloth, a bare bulb dangling foolishly from the ceiling, a trunk. . . . Thanks to my mother, the wall space between the windows was adorned with a portrait of Karl Marx under glass, in the sort of oval frame that befits a nineteenth-century professor. Lenin was lower on the wall and not under glass, a faded family relic. Lenin was depicted dragging a log with pleasure, doing voluntary Saturday work. And on the bare wall to one side, a poster-size portrait of Joseph Vissarionovich had recently taken up residence, its edges bent under, pinned straight to the wallpaper, his face friendly, imperturbable.

Levitan's *Golden Autumn* had hung there until it was demoted by Mama and replaced by the fresh copy of Stalin's portrait she'd been given at work. She rolled up *Golden Autumn* and brought it down to Father's cellar room. And what was the reason behind this change? Was it a response to the espionage plots that kept being exposed in the press? Or was it to protect us against our neighbors' incursions? To guard and maintain the family hearth, so fragile it could fall apart at any moment? Or, as an old political-education worker, was she opposed to my Socialist Revolutionary father's example and did she want to stay in touch with the forward surge of the masses? Most likely she did it for all those reasons. But that's not the point.

Scarcely had my young friend and I been left alone than he sized up the situation and, feeling instantly at home and perceiving no obstacles, raised his hand to Stalin. What he specifically did was to extend his index finger like a pistol and take slow aim, his lips softly forming the "bang-bang" sound little children make to stand for gunshots. He cast me a sidelong glance of both triumph and evaluation that I took to mean: What do you say to that? Where do you stand?! . . . I remained silent, overwhelmed by his foolish blasphemy. Then he aimed his finger at the inoffensive poster a second time, delighting in my confusion. "Stop fooling around," I protested dolefully, without knowing quite what retort to make to his buffoonery or why it had thrown me for such a loop.

While enjoying our respect, Stalin was not an icon in our home. But neither were the other leaders, including Marx. I should like to mention again that I was raised in an earlier, utopian tradition. That was my father's doing; my mother made no effort to connect the snows of yesteryear with the present. Garibaldi, Giordano Bruno, Sofya Perovskaya were more my favorites. . . . The smiling Georgian appearing over the horizon at that time was, when seen through the filter of my childhood, a yellowish stain, one accepted by all and arousing no special emotion in me. It was whispered that he was a man twisted by an inflated ambition unworthy of the revolution but was doing a good job in developing the country and industry. So, let his portrait hang on the wall. . . . All the same, that glossy sheet on that desolate wall secretly irritated me and reopened a wound, just as we are sometimes shocked by feigned joie de vivre on the face of a terminally ill person. The portrait accentuated the room's poverty and unvarnished ugliness in my guest's eyes. It was the first time I'd seen its pitiful bareness in that new and shameful light. . . .

Of course, those innocent shots at that portrait, our paper shield, were done in imitation of the sabotage the papers were always writing about. Someone might pretend to shoot from behind a corner, but those who were caught were shot later with real guns. However, I did not see any audacious homicidal impulse or intent, even imaginary, against the Leader in S.'s gesture. It was just a meaningless game, two people alone, with no risk involved, a joke about something that was no joking matter. I would now term that treacherous act an aesthetic provocation, though at the time I was only aware that it was an inadmissible thing to do. "Assassin" flashed through my mind, even though I knew he was just kidding around. "A cowardly assassin . . ." I hadn't learned the word "provocateur" yet. . . ."

S. turned red. He tossed off his coat and fired shot after shot, now aiming his pistol at the shaky bookcase and at the sickly, dried-out potted palm on a little stand in the corner, a birthday present from my mother. I suppose he was overcome by a sense of impunity in firing at the defenseless space that had suddenly opened before him, our home's abominable neglect, the clearest proof of which was that easily riddleable portrait of Stalin. He was shooting at our humiliation, our blatant misfortune, which were alien to him. His shots were aimed at me. Apparently he had just sensed a sore spot and couldn't stop. . . .

As a rule, S. was not mischievous like other boys at that transitional age—inventors of malicious dirty tricks and endless cruel pranks, cynical escapades that verge on real trouble, all of which sometimes make the blind world of children so unbearable. Such wiseguys and junior gangsters, some from the most respectable of families, were even to be found in our school, whose administrators strove to reserve mainly for Moscow's crème de la crème. A fun-loving, irrepressible trickster, Yura Krasny figured out a way to daub his tongue with ink and to stick it out, all purple, at the teacher, as soon as he would begin scolding him for the ink splotches on his schoolwork. The Gobermans, twin brothers, would chew up pieces of paper in class and toss them from the back row at the teacher's pets in the front. The menacing Boba Volf, a big stocky boy who had stayed back and who looked like a fatted thoroughbred steer, had been placed in the first row along-side me to improve his behavior, and used to torment Lidiya Ger-manovna, a sweet pastry of a girl, a German who didn't know Russian well. Scowling, Boba would always make the same sullen response: "Herr, Herr, I'll show you some hair!" She didn't un-derstand what he was driving at.

"Herr?"

"Got any herr on it?"

I remember reproaching Boba (he liked me because I let him copy from me) and asking him why he used such language in front of girls. What were they going to think? He stood up, hulking in a suede jacket with zippers, a style new to Moscow then, the sole member of the class to own a Parker fountain pen, with which he used to doodle in his thick leather notebooks—all he ever drew were locomotives, furious express engines of various shapes. He cast a dim gaze about him and then, so everyone could hear, said, "You mean those are girls? Those aren't girls, those are cows!" And he sat back down. But because he had said "girls" with such assurance and such a manly rasp, we were struck dumb, realizing that Boba might just have already experienced something that counted for more than his forever low marks and for more than our entire high-ranking model school, for that matter. We "priv-ileged few" . . .

My favorite, Seryozha, was absolutely not one of those wiseguys. He was never the hooligan, never the brat. None of youth's nastiness had stuck to him. Correct, restrained, with a great need for the sublime, in his well-tailored, civilized little suit, he seemed to me a self-contained standard, as is sometimes the case with artistic natures who do not seek but find themselves in the original, along with the works they create. Small in stature but mature beyond his years, and already a respectable little gentleman, he took no part in our games and fights, steering clear of them out of squeamishness and out of aesthetic motives that, of course, were developed in him to an extreme, to a point where he was disgusted by all that was ugly, pitiful, or ridiculous. This might well explain an isolated instance that dismayed us greatly and suddenly placed S. in a disgraceful light.

We were, if I'm not mistaken, already in sixth grade when, out of the blue, he conceived the idea of tormenting an unfortunate third-grader, M., who stuttered. S. grabbed him at recess, called over a bunch of louts, and began mimicking M., mooing, bleating, making faces as if in front of a mirror, until the poor boy became hysterical and rushed howling at his tormentor. But what chance did that little kid have against a great-power tyrant who was stronger than he and twice as old, especially since S. avoided any open fighting? Shoving the little boy aside, S. continued on his way with a preoccupied air. M.'s friends sent an emissary to complain to us, and we, as a body, urged our classmate to lay off, making a point of saying that he had acted unethically and unscrupulously in letting himself be carried away. It was monstrous: a person who was mature, educated, well mannered, refined, with the mark of an unusual and perhaps great destiny upon him, had taken a slob's underhanded pleasure in teasing a meek and sickly child. To mock the handicapped?! No, that wasn't fair—that wasn't how a Komsomolets acts. "And where's your Pioneer scarf? Why aren't you wearing it? . . ." "Are you guys serious?" he protested feebly. "All I did was just joke around with the kid one time. Don't you know a friendly joke when you see one? Don't you have any sense of humor whatsoever? All right, I won't do it again. If it bothers you that much. I swear. . . ."

But all he had to do was run into the incurable stutterer on the stairs or in the schoolyard and the whole business would start up again. Until Valya Kachanov, a boxer who was in the same grade as Seryozha, announced that he would punch his face if he didn't stop . . . Then it was all gone and forgotten. The nasty outburst of boyish, irrational sadism faded away as suddenly and casually as it had arisen, a once-in-a-blue-moon thing and, I thought, one without consequences.

But I was mistaken. For all his virtues, S. was a phenomenal coward. But that was also one of his virtues, for his cowardice served as a brake on a talent that otherwise knew no limits. There was a great deal he simply could not allow himself. He was cautious. He avoided quarreling with anyone stronger. He used the weak for laughs and amusement. I'm afraid he was undone by his provident caution. They say cowards are drawn to betrayal. They are also sometimes drawn to poetry, though that is rarer. But the combination of genius and crime is truly rare, extraordinary; they're "incompatible things." But are they? No one has ever really checked on that.

You always had to keep a sharp eye on him; you had to be tough with him, to be able to defend yourself, even if it was put on, for show. Then he'd back down. God forbid you should reveal any soft spot, heartache, or weakness to him. He'd seize on it instinctively, at times to his own detriment and that of his reputation among his friends, which diminished with time. What do you expect from an artist? He'd shrug his shoulders. He couldn't resist. It was a calling.

Once, when I smelled something fishy, I told him straight out, "If you get me thrown in jail, you'll end up in there with me, remember that!" "What are you talking about?" he hastened to assure me. "What's that supposed to mean?! You know we're in the same boat. . . ." And his feelings weren't hurt—the beast wasn't even indignant. His ego loved the feeling of power. Had he known there was no danger, he would certainly have evened the score, but not out of revenge or self-interest—that I can vouch for. And, thank God, not from any noble-minded revolutionary idea which stops for nothing. No, it would be from a sense of the vulnerability of those closest to him. A purely physical reflex. A chance to strike. And he would simply sting unthinkingly. Like a tarantula. He was talented. The bastard was brilliant. . . .

Blackmail, you say? I agree. I admit it. But tell me—how else can you protect yourself from an assassin? The only salvation was his cowardice. . . . Fifteen years later, and for different reasons, my wife, Mariya, promised him, "Remember, Seryozhenka, if anything happens to Sinyavsky, I'll kill you!" Literally—she would hit the parasite with a hammer, slash him with scissors, if he so much as opened his mouth! That shook him up. . . . But, if you think about it, he could hardly have felt threatened. Anyway, I doubt that he was. Either by the hammer or by the scissors. I told myself calmly: Murder is the calling of cowards. But S. believed it! He really thought she'd go for his throat. In his imagination, his artistic mind, she could do anything, the Fury! And she had already branded him as an informer, shouting it from the rooftops. No matter where he turned . . . He lived like a leper. His reputation had finally caught up with him. "I swear!" he would say, turning pale. But what did his oaths mean? They were made to buy him time. Until the spring. Until the fall. Until next year . . .

Isn't that why he disappeared from Moscow two weeks before Daniel and I were arrested? He made himself scarce, as they say. "Why were you badgering that man?" hissed my investigator. I evinced surprise: "Which man? And who was badgering him? . . ." "Shut up! We know everything! . . ." They knew nothing. To be honest, we weren't badgering him, we were neutralizing him. And, apparently, only partially. Temporarily. Belatedly. Naturally we hadn't confided any important secrets to him earlier either—he wasn't the right sort for that—though there were some bits of evidence on the tip of his tongue. But did he ultimately succeed in stinging us? I don't know. I never laid eyes on my file.

Operational material is not shown to prisoners. Moreover, to all appearances, they took care of him after his first downfall. They tried to whitewash him. To whisk him out of sight. He disappeared. One thing is known—he disappeared. But how was it all going to end? . . .

When they bring you in for questioning, you pray to the Mother of God. . . . Later on I experienced that many times, interrupting myself to ask: Why to the Mother of God? Not to God, not even to Christ, but to the heavenly Mother? I could find no answer, and we don't need any answers. A person needn't know why he's attracted to one form of supplication rather than another. Trust. Be calm. Our souls are so much more intelligent and infinite than we are. . . . Look around. Lefortovo is so much vaster than Lubyanka. How huge everything is here, and well conceived. What volume! When you're taken from your cell, your head spins— floors upon floors! A labyrinth. Its interior is a many-stringed Babylon, a spiral of floors and turnstiles, a carousel. An instrument. With an immense central void, a stairwell, a shaft, with a mesh partition. So you can be watched through the interstices. A cathedral, that's what it is. A cathedral made over into a Colosseum. And netting everywhere, netting instead of ground and sky. We're like angels. It's like a circus. Are those safety nets? So no one will smash his head if he takes a running leap? Someone told me the reason. They strung those nets after Savinkov leapt to his death. He didn't want to serve his ten-year sentence, and he took to the air. How can you tell which one's the Icarus? Maybe they could have clipped his wings. He flew like a swallow. But the netting's been hanging there since time immemorial, and it's still there, so no one can escape his fate and leap from his body ahead of time, until every last point has been cleared up. . . .

My case would seem clear. And Daniel's too. What ease. What peace—to answer only for oneself. Or at worst for two people. Otherwise there's no way of avoiding all those games, all that hide-and-seek. It's better when there's no connection between them, and one knows nothing about the other, each person separate. I am a "locomotive"—to use prosecutor slang: I arrived at the station pulling only one car. But a train is usually made up of several cars. And when a locomotive is heading for a crack-up, it takes the other cars along with it. No one jumps off during a train wreck, a derailment. And how can you uncouple cars from the locomotive when you're falling? Where's the brake? . . . Interrogation! . . . The brake? . . . Interrogation! . . . It isn't a good thing to be a "locomotive"; it's very tough, O Mother of God. . . .

Meanwhile, I wasn't lying when I said I hadn't been involved in politics. Literature and art were enough for me. To each his own. A colleague of mine came to see us on Khlebny Street about a year before my arrest. A young, fashionable Marxist revisionist then, and a prominent Russist now, he said: "Come on, let's start a party of our own with a Marxist basis. We'll have meetings. We'll enroll members. . . ." By then I was already up to my ears with Tertz and other such things, and I honestly replied that I wasn't interested in Marxism or politics. . . . What an uproar that caused! "We're going to end up in the camps," he shouted. "And you, you, Andrei, are you going to sit it out in your ivory tower?! . . ."

I think of my successful colleague from time to time. And here it is—the tower, the ivory tower. From one interrogation to the next. Drop it. Don't think about it. Forget it. It's so deserted, a hospital. As if no one else were in prison here, or had ever been. Could it really have been designed just for the two of us, Daniel and me, this unwieldy building woven of iron, resembling a city suspended in air, a floating city of a building from the future, when the world has a single economy, like drawings of utopia from some other time, seductive blueprints, resembling planets in a solar system, its pistons and octahedrons reserved for the final rotations of a fully integrated universe? The cost of the electricity alone! And the staff? Each zek probably keeps ten thousand apparatchiks in a job. Staircases, staircases. And apartments for them all, schools for their children, and then jobs for them. And where's all the money supposed to come from? No easy task. The state's coming apart at the seams. If there were enough zeks per capita, they could save the country from poverty. But, as it is, only two flies have been snared in that entire web. They need enemies. Enemies are a must—enemies keep bread on their table. They can't exist without enemies. Otherwise who will pump up the muscles of the Atlas whose outstretched arms raise this entire hive to the skies, the entire disastrous structure, suspended by a web of bridges, rigging, compartments, like a ferris wheel in a Soviet Park of Culture and Rest, as in Austria, on the Prater, the Hanging Gardens? . . .

But you shouldn't think I have a low opinion of spiders. The state is sometimes compared to a spider, and mistakenly so. Nothing in common. If you see a spider, it means you'll be receiving a letter. But you won't see any letters or any spiders in Lefortovo. There everything's swept and scrubbed. It's not solely for its own amusement that the spider carefully spins its web under a staircase, in a storeroom, behind a stove, in a corner, where foolish flies may be caught. Not every fly gets caught, after all. The foolish flies don't always fly into the spider's turf. The flies zoom like MIGs, with no thought to the contemplator weaving away in the dead gloom far from them. What do they care about webs? They'll ram right through. Does the spider act on the spur of the moment, stretching its trembling traps at random in the darker and more modest places? I don't think so. Always reverent, where does it get the patience? And what does it live on, the hermit? In its pentagram, so far out of the way . . .

I am afraid that the spider is more like a poet or a musician. Its silence doesn't matter; or could it be that we just can't hear it? Its filaments are like the strings of a harp. (Isn't it wonderful how everything is like everything else?) It plays on its web and the spaces between the threads. Sometimes it may entice a midge: "Come over and take a rest!" I always felt bad about sweeping up a spider web in a room. What architectonics! And with a literary turn of mind, to boot. The insects sing and buzz. But the spider says, "Have a seat on the strings. Take a little nap." There's some sort of connection between a spider and what it builds and the sounds it makes. They're both airy. Head down. A right angle. What a trajectory! . . . I have never killed a spider.

It's silent here too. Not a single voice, not a single moan. Or maybe we just can't hear them. For what must have been six months, I didn't encounter a single soul who, like me, was on his way to or from questioning. Maybe there isn't anybody else here. They don't call it "isolation" for nothing. To avoid any encounters or accidental run-ins with another citizen who, like yourself, has been locked up in that pencil box, to keep secrets from being divulged and to maintain the silence, the supervisors communicate with their hands, drawing swastikas in the air. Or, when approaching intersections while escorting a prisoner, the guards communicate by clicks, clucks, croaks, snakelike hisses, birdlike chirps, and, as a last resort, by banging a key against the cast-iron railing, softly, melodically, which only increases the sum total of the silence, causing space to expand and sway. There are carpeted paths on the iron walkways, and footsteps make no sound. In back, in front: "Ts-ts-ts! . . . Fyu-pyu! . . . Hrm—hhh-rr-mm! . . . Ssss! . . ." It's strange the first time. Bizarre. You wonder why they don't communicate with each other like human beings and say: Someone's coming, wait a second, let us go past first! They use the fewest possible words when communicating with me—"Don't turn around," "Hands behind you"—always in a tense, ominous whisper whistling with fury. Apparently this is done to cut you off from life, to cast you into the laws of silence, which exist before eternity and after the grave, and is in keeping with the blueprint for these furious ceilings, the nets, the staircases, which are at best conducive to ventriloquy, or your escort's rare cries and trills in those dead iron forests.

But here too the building's excellent hierarchy triumphs. Worms can't sing. Fish can't hear. Sound and hearing are gifts of the air. The frogs have them; they've separated from the earth. But any insect, insignificant in comparison with us, is able to fly, and is already musical. Any mosquito. Beetles and bumblebees are heavy as bombers. The birds—so little, but how they sing! And they fly the way they sing. The nature of air, the nature of air claims what is its own! Everything corresponds so well here, the language, the composition. . . .

Take still-lifes. In the old masters' still-lifes, *nature* was hardly *morte*. To suit his fancy, the artist would capriciously place side by side (pairing them) eyeglasses and a clock, a lemon and a glass, a duck (or hare) hung head down, fresh from the hunt, shot by the man of the house, and a lute that has the right to reside on that domestic place the table. The objects correspond almost syllogistically in the way they develop their long, balanced, formal proof. The eye is guided from the bird—still warm, fresh from the lake, head down—to the lute (or mandolin). What's the lute doing there? It seems out of place, irrelevant to the hanging duck. What is death's relationship to life, and art's to these images of nature? But look closer: the bird has been killed, but the empty instrument beside it has begun to sound. What's at issue here is the future, things coming together, parallel and uncoordinated streams meet. From a dead animal to a live lute.

No, this clinic was not built for two prisoners; nor is it set in a wilderness. Nor is it there to justify the overabundance of guards (including layer upon layer of high government officials). Lefortovo is like prose. The country's enormous (inflated) rib cage, a framework, a ship (with decks, masts, rigging), it contrives to maintain the outward respectability of a modest housing (or construction) office, concealing a bureau of investigation, with its auxiliary barracks, various departments (graphologists, photographers, decoders, experts on the impressions made by typewriters [the letter "e" tends to drop], sound men), garages, storehouses, such that an outside observer will not even notice its walls, never mind the bolts, bars, window shields (which let nothing in through the windows [only a strip of sky can sometimes be seen—if it's snowing—and that only from a distance, standing on tiptoe back near the peephole]), which seem expressly created so that we find ourselves in the very depths of a hangar ruled into countless squares, in a thicket of cells, an ultimate interior, a cross section, amid brick,

in an image of space absorbed and opened to a new dimension—
one no less voluminous, however, than all the images of nature
and society that we remember had once surrounded us and which
we have now lost. I am sure that, from the outside, no one could
gauge the building's hidden reserves. No one could guess the size
of the cage concealed from view. Is it really possible, you ask, that
an interior could be immeasurably larger than what one sees from
outside? Lefortovo convinced me that it is.

Use your lateral vision to take a look around when you're being
taken for questioning, and you'll see that "around" has no meaning
here, does not apply. Lefortovo is pure interior: a snail. There
everything's in reverse, inside out. They're not called "inner prisons" for nothing. Wrong again, it's not inside out but development
from within, from a core, in the microscopic, cellular structure of
matter. How to explain it? Oh, if only I were a composer! . . .

People speak of reflecting life. I doubt it. Lefortovo Castle can
be compared to a spider web and to prose. To set traps. Sling
bridges like hammocks. Even build some kind of building, create
space on paper. That's enough. What else can you expect from a
prose writer? He strives to trump reality by withdrawing to one
side. . . . What for? Nobody knows. . . . Pardon my boldness for
asking, but why not depict it directly? Doesn't work. It eludes you.
When you write, whether you want to or not, you enter another
universe, that of writing, which runs parallel, perpendicular, or at
a tangent to the stream of life. That doesn't mean it's an illusion
or a fabrication. God save us from aestheticism. An artist cannot
and should not be a snob. An eternal toiler, a spider. It's just that
different laws apply. You're operating in another dimension. And
everything that happens to you, dreaming and awake, in your life-
and-death struggle remains, wriggle as you may, on the level of
the page.

The ancient scroll, the papyrus, was probably better suited for
written language than the paper we now use, foolishly cut into
separate sheets. Scrolls could progress without interruption and at

length, like the leisurely flow of a river. But, alas, we're past scrolls. We're in books now. It's time to turn the page, to separate.

Still, what part did S. play in the night that was my youth? . . . At one point later on, mutual friends who had already given their parting curses to the late lamented began to press me, saying: "What, are you crazy?! Him, a genius?! At the very most, he had some talent. And not all that much either. He matured early and he faded early—by becoming an informer. The two things don't go together. Haven't you read *Mozart and Salieri?* 'Genius and crime are two incompatible things.' But don't worry, your 'genius' will trap other simpletons yet, the bastard! . . ."

I don't agree. He rules over my childhood dreams like a Mozart. What was the source of his character traits which violated the harmony of that image through both secret and overt betrayal? Were they from birth too, we might ask? Were they an outgrowth of his brilliant talents, which tended to subject everything to art? An experimental aesthetics, albeit of a secondary sort? But does this mean that his "crimes" do not run counter to his "genius" but flow out of it and are inextricably fused with it, perfectly combined? Pushkin must have gotten it screwed up somewhere along the line. . . .

Hold on, my friends, let me think. What is it you're trying to make me believe? You know, I'm afraid he was never even a criminal, not for a minute—and that's the catch. All in all, if you take a good look at him and think a little harder—as I happened to, out of necessity, to save myself from him—you won't find anything evil, dark, insidious, or demonic about him. Just as you won't find any goodness, conscience, or honor. Those concepts simply do not apply to him. As if they had all been cut out of him in childhood, a superfluous appendix. A dead man, if you will. A visitor from the world beyond. But a genius nonetheless. An innocent genius! . . .

"But you're saying . . ."

"That's right, I am! . . ."

The specialists, the gynecologists of the occult, say that there are peculiar creatures in our midst, creatures with a different ZIP Code. Occult science refers to them as "shells," if I remember correctly, empty shells with the shape of human beings. They were born that way, lacking a soul, and are not to blame for it. What they have instead of a soul—some gas, or vapor, or perhaps the ether of some state higher than our own—I'm not up on that. But all the rest, all the machinery of the form, is available to them, and they are to be found in various walks of life, enjoying success and progress there to a superlative degree. Scientists, artists, colonels, and diplomats. And I've been told that "shells" are even to be encountered among spiritualists themselves who—what a laugh—ruminate on all aspects of this problem, examine it, affirm it, deny it, without suspecting their own transcendent affiliation.

When the problem is posed like that, who among us can vouch that he is not a "shell"? Our only hope is that shells are an exception in the human community, one in ten or a hundred thousand, like geniuses, we won't quibble over terms, who, for all their evil deeds, are still human beings, while *these*—it's so confusing you want to throw in the towel—are simulacra, talented casings in human form. We might ask how we can be certain beforehand, before we die, that we are human, truly human, with our own irreplaceable soul and original body? I pinch myself! I'm not one of those, am I, one of those, God forgive me, counterfeits perfect in their resemblance, handsome, intelligent, and also conscious of themselves not as hollow men, stuffed with all sorts of nonsense, but as human beings no worse than others, even better, more inspired, brighter? But that is not a definitive sign either; you simply might not have had the luck to be of that variety. . . . There are no criteria. They're said to be more alluring than we are. More attractive. Smarter. Or stupider than average. But freer and more gifted. Though not always. Baser. Nobler. Anything can be. Doesn't matter. There is no way, absolutely no way you can tell them from full-fledged, standard creatures like you and me. And if there isn't . . . A dangerous business.

And wasn't it you people who told me about S. biting Irina at a student party for a small group of friends who had been in tenth grade together? I wasn't in Moscow at the time, and, as I recall, was terribly envious of you, learning *post scriptum* that all my classmates had gotten together, like a family, at the end of the war, on the threshold of paradise, while I was still slogging away in the army. . . . It wasn't I who was insulted, but you, and of course Irina. And several years later she was still unable to remove the incident's unpleasant aftertaste from her memory, while I, on the other hand, found the incident more intriguing than repellent.

And it was just when the party was in full swing, when you were vying with each other in swapping stories of success and future prospects in that heady world of higher education that so fascinated you at first, each in his own domain, that S. announced publicly that he intended to kiss Irina, right there, in front of everyone. Even after the turmoil of war that had hurled them all to the ends of Russia, they couldn't find words to communicate. S. wasn't courting Irina or trying to turn her head or excite her, and had no intention of carrying things any further. Nor did his impromptu remark reflect any male bravado or those simple, nonsensical, pleasant, spirited impulses to which, we know, slightly tipsy students sometimes readily surrender. It can be said straight out that this was not his strong suit; calm, sober, usually reasonable, he did not, I believe, brag of his adventures in love, as people will. He was apparently guided by some other motives. He had some sudden urge or was carried away: "I'll kiss her! I will! You'll see! . . ."

Those empty words made no impression on anyone. The chaste young lady brushed him properly aside: "You know where you can go, don't you? Don't pester me, you idiot!" But, having bided his time for about forty minutes, he attacked Irina from behind, like a leopard, which was somewhat absurd, given his build. He fouled up, knocking a chair over backward, and did not kiss her but seized her with his teeth and bit through her tender lip, drawing blood. And then he surveyed the scene triumphantly, like a shah: dramatic!

To his surprise, no one started laughing or cried "Bravo." Knocked to the ground, the girl moaned softly in pain, helplessness, and—as she later superstitiously confided to me—the subterranean and inhuman humiliation she had experienced after covering her cut lip with her handkerchief to stop the warm flow of blood. She rose at once and left. The evening was ruined. Averting their eyes, all the other guests began heading for the door too. It had not occurred to anyone to bash the triumphant conqueror in the face, or to say so much as a word to him. Everyone was depressed, crestfallen, stunned. But it was the culprit who seemed the most disheartened. "Can't you guys take a joke?" he muttered imploringly to the intellectuals whose backs were turned to him as they moved away. In the stairwell he could restrain himself no longer and shouted after them in a tearful fury, "Imbeciles! You have no sense of humor whatsoever! . . ." There was no reply.

What will you say now, my erudite friends? Was this one mad moment on the part of a spoiled and willful boy? Nothing of the sort! If his path in life, a bitter path, was strewn with the crystals of noble poetry as a value in itself, it can also be seen as a series of such bites, more or less awful, relatively rare, but committed with the precision and necessity of the periodic table. Psychopathic? Pathological? His nervous system was healthier than any of ours. No complexes. No deviations. I'm quite sure of that. Certain. Had he had any interesting and indecent problems of that sort, he would have been unable to refrain from happily bragging about them. And I served as something of a sounding board for him, for quite a while. And so—he had no problems of that sort at all. Regular as a robot. Even too regular for my taste. And please do not place the millstones of "cruelty," "heartlessness," and a "penchant for vice" around his neck; those words have no meaning when you are dealing with an exception to morality, psychology, and even perhaps biology. Human motives don't apply to him!

My friends, at the height of the drama, why didn't your eyes go to the hero's face, beaming with courage, radiant with rapture, and turned gratefully toward his audience? Oh, you wouldn't have felt right about that? Did that nasty act make you feel too ashamed? Were your eyes cast down? And so you let the moment slip by you. You did not understand, you did not appreciate the artist, who, unlike the criminal, is always trusting, sincere, open, impulsive, and impractical. If it comes to that, what criminal would be able to show off so naïvely, with such simplicity, and without any ulterior motive or self-seeking? Do you think that he actually needed to kiss her? Not at all; by playing that practical joke, he was, if you will, attempting to perform a dazzling vaudeville for you fools, a jolly harlequinade whose theme was the turning of humdrum prose into poetry, a trivial kiss into a witty trick. Do you remember Meyerhold, who erased the boundary between the stage and the audience? And how many generations of artists, writers, and musicians have dreamed and striven to transform the world through the magic power of play? Where's the harm if one of them succeeds? Not in bloodless verse, which no one reads, but, say, on a crowded square, or at the tea table when visiting, he does something extraordinary, unpredictable, the result of his uninhibited nature, suddenly incarnated before your very eyes from an ethereal flutter languishing in nonexistence to something at last entirely specific, physical, and at the same time worthy of amazement. Perhaps his example will be followed, and even our low and tacky life will someday become a festival of creativity, overcoming all earthly law, sparkling and free? . . . Well, think about it—he caused a slight injury to the lip of a pretty walk-on. She cried a little, and then it was over. She'll get married. Bring forth children. But who will quench the poet and director's ancient longing for beauty, he who, in full sight of everyone, had just boldly stepped over the footlights, before your eyes, in the passion and glory of selfless heroism, and who, instead of meeting with applause, has suddenly found himself stranded in solitude, the darkness of a theatre abandoned by the audience, in a wilderness exposed to every wind, to the entire universe? . . .

"What a person you've slandered!" grieved Daniel's investigator Kantov, shaking his handsome silvery head. "A person like that! . . ."

I was always struck by S.'s naïve, childishly immediate need for an audience, responsive and indulgent spectators to behold those displays of his, which, far from doing him any good, caused his admirers to feel embarrassment and a painful shame for him. Outside the inner circle, his displays were considered reason enough to avoid S. and label him a real bastard. Sometimes he would be surprised at not being invited somewhere or at being given a wide berth, but this did not prevent him, if the circumstances were right, from committing some new "gaffe," if, of course, you don't prefer some even milder and more forgiving term.

His sufferings make sense to me. What author does not dream of a favorable response to his rough drafts, though the blind crowd rails and rants at him? . . . I have to say that for many years I knew no conversationalist more interesting, fascinating, or gracious, and, later on, no better reader of my first pathetic stabs at poetry and prose, and so, toward the end, our mutual abandon in sharing confidences simply became a risky business for me, and that with the one person who could appreciate and understand me. In brief, what reconciled and bound me to him for a time, though without my ceasing to be repelled by and wary of him, was his irreplaceable and unique role in my already quite helpless and slippery life, which was on its way to playing right into his hands. As in a dream, you have to stop, wake up, break off the friendship, and escape through a window. But that's not what happened.

It's now, thirty years later, that everyone has become so intelligent, reading Mandelstam's *The Egyptian Stamp*, enjoying Kandinsky and Stravinsky, cursing the Soviet system without mincing words as if they'd been doing it all their lives. But back then . . . Where the hell were you going to find a kindred spirit when Zhdanov had the heat on? Whom were you going to swap jokes with? If a funny thing happened, who could you tell? Who could you share a sigh with, even for, say, Picasso's *Girl on a Balloon*, lost but not forgotten, so that you wouldn't be found guilty of bourgeois decadence on the spot? . . . And what a fertile mind he had for scabrous invention (Daniel owes him the idea for his story "Free Murder Day" in *This Is Moscow Speaking*). Surprising associations. Historical analogies. An Orpheus! How could you keep from succumbing to him? From relying on him? . . . Impossible.

However, I reiterate, like every genius, he was—in his murderous ideas, his masterpieces of light improvisation—a child. Guileless. Neither vengeful nor touchy. And so to trick this trickster, wind him around my finger, and mislead him when the time came did not cost me any great effort. . . . I used him. Yes, I used him in his capacity of informer and, as you will see, this is what saved me. To have your own informer in your field of vision, under your control, is, in certain circumstances, a godsend. Even though our friendship was on its way downhill, we continued to meet, and I think he, in his simplicity of heart, still confided in me even as I, like a devil, had begun to deceive him. . . .

Sometimes, however, he really could be rather horrifying. Once we were on our way back from Yura Krasny's place on Skatertny Street, where the three of us had been telling one subversive joke after another. That must have been in 1949 or maybe 1950, since I remember the atmosphere as already quite heavy; the country seemed on the verge of detaching itself from the earth and flying away. And since he'd already begun, he continued developing his idea—that nothing could be more natural for us than to calculate the number of devils that could fit on the head of a pin, as had been done in the Middle Ages. And this was going to be proclaimed a new phase in Marxist-Leninist philosophy. . . . He didn't finish with his paradox, but, as if illumined from above, he breathed a damp whisper and the faint, sweetish scent of cigarettes on my face:

"Listen! How about if the two of us inform on Yura Krasny,

each on his own, like we hadn't planned it? . . . Well, what are you afraid of? You don't have to make up anything. Just fill out the form. He *did* spend the entire evening telling us anti-Soviet jokes; he never even stopped for breath. And then he laughed about the persecution of the Jews. . . ."

"And weren't you and I telling jokes too? And weren't we laughing too? . . ."

"That's right. But that can be smoothed over . . . explained. . . . And they'll believe the two of us, not a fool like him! In these things all it takes is two witnesses!"

I hadn't thought he was that far gone. The lowlife! I felt like running away from him to the ends of the earth. But I stood there beside him, in the dark, conscientiously assuming the role of an informer like him, there on Vorovsky Street, and calmly let him know in no uncertain terms that if he informed I would not conceal which one of us three had started the joke session: "Because you can't play a double game with *them,* as you yourself know, and then, my dear friend, they won't pat you on the back, and the upshot'll be that the three of us will land in a camp. And who's going to take Yura Krasny seriously? He's just a fun-loving big-mouth who likes a good laugh, and anyway, given our position, it's just ridiculous to draw attention to something so trivial as jokes. . . ." No, I didn't try to change his mind, ask him to spare Yura, or inquire why he wanted to commit such an act. I was no longer intrigued by the riddle of his unique personality. For some reason it was over Yura that he broke for me, ceased to exist, becoming a mechanism, an instrument, like a bassoon or clarinet, which, sad to say, I still had to play, studiously pressing one key or another, the key of fear or laughter, and coldly observing his immediate reaction until he tore free of me and was splashed by light, like the Arbat district that lay beneath our feet and where I had accompanied him to the metro that dancing night.

"Forget it, will you?" he said after a moment's thought. "I was only joking. . . ."

In the glow of his cigarette I could see his thick sardonic lips form an ironic grin—at himself, at me, and at the stars above us. He brought his ash-flecked lips closer to me:

"You don't understand. I'm—afraid. I'm frightened. . . ."

"You? . . . What are you frightened of? . . ."

"You don't understand. . . . The Americans will hang me when they come. . . ."

"What Americans? Hang you for what?"

"There's going to be a war with America. And they'll hang me. . . . You see, there're already two murders that can be pinned on me. Two! I'm a murderer. . . ."

"But I'm a murderer too!" I replied with some swagger. "I've got a corpse on my conscience too. And a foreigner, to boot . . . You know who I mean. . . . You helped in it. . . . Helene . . ." We stood there, two murderers on a dark street, the streetlights off, only the Arbat awash with light in the distance. We knew everything about each other. Or, to be more precise, we pretended that we did. But there was something I didn't like about the range in which he oscillated, from Yura Krasny to the Americans. . . . The rat! It was time to disengage from him gradually. I'd walk back and he'd take the metro. We didn't want to let go of each other. He was right: in these things two witnesses are all it takes. I was trying to play the role. To identify with him. A wall. To merge with his darkness. As the saying goes, another man's heart is a dark place. Enter one and you'll see. . . .

"Don't be afraid. I'm a killer too."

Then, as if disdaining my failure, he said squeamishly and sensibly, "In the first place, all you did was try, and it fell through. . . ."

"Attempted murder is still murder. Even worse. I did everything. . . . The sin's on my conscience. . . ."

The most important thing was to convince him that I was the same as him—capable of informing! So that he would report it! And not suspect me . . . But by that point he was laughing. Glad that I had failed but still had sinned: I was sullied. That was a good sign. Yet he always had an unpleasant way of laughing—no smile, the words issuing clear and distinct from his mouth:

"Ha. Ha. Ha. Ha. One foreign woman and you botched it. . . . She told me about it herself. . . . As a Soviet citizen it was simply your duty to turn her in. . . . But I did it all on my own! And to friends! Breughel and Kabo! With my own two hands! Do you understand?! . . ."

Now he seemed to be bragging, and that was a load off my mind.

"Forget all that! Just drop it. I'm a killer too. All right, so it was just once. That's enough! There can be too much of a good thing. You've done two. And I've done one. What's the difference? We've done our share! See you on Judgment Day! See you to-morrow! . . ."

Five years passed. Or six. S.'s old friends Breughel and Kabo, who'd disappeared without a trace and for no reason at all, re-turned alive from places people usually don't return from, and much the worse for wear. . . . But, meanwhile, remnants of sub-marine surveys, hunts, deep-sea exploration, had risen from the seabed to the surface—like a secret place on a map where battles had once taken place and every bush was riddled by gunfire, every knoll watered lavishly in blood. Who's going to excavate those trenches now? (Kabo and Breughel . . .) Only a surviving veteran will poke a crooked fingernail at a zodiac-meridian known to him alone. "At this insignificant point, we repelled three enemy attacks. And in a spot over there in the woods, two hundred meters from here, a mortar shell tore off my leg. . . ." It's the same with our topography too. Everything is covered over, forgotten. But some-one remembers and waits to mark the scorched and faded map with a black fingernail (Kabo and Breughel . . .).

It was while the kindly professor was making tea for his favorite student that S. rushed to the bookcase, with his usual poetic im-practicality, to list the more odious editions and then to slip that list into his pocket, but the operation was interrupted by heavy fire, a surprise counterattack by the enemy, teapot in hand. Still, S. emerged unscathed by cunningly allowing that he had had a passion for bibliography that went back to his childhood. Why was he listing the titles? Only to make it easier later on for him to have a sense of what was on those shelves if he wanted to borrow, if he were allowed to borrow, one of those many treasures. Times were bad! The censorship was everywhere! The kindhearted host did not chase the dog out of the house. . . . No fool, however, he did take the list from S. and tear it into small scraps; turning the book-loving bibliographer out on the pretext of having a headache, he locked the door, and from then on slammed the phone down on S.'s obsequious calls. . . . But he'd get his—a search! . . .

Where to now? To the East! On business. A vacation. Not on special assignment. Just what you might call a tourist . . . There, at another distant point on the globe, on the border with Asia, he spent a few days in a cozy, provincial, geranium-lined apartment belonging to the sister of one of his bosom buddies from Moscow, whom he'd sold to the devil and who'd gone up like a match six months before, for next to nothing, a pointed remark. This was both cheaper and more comfortable than renting a bug-ridden bed in a packed hotel, and it was also somehow more attractive, more poetic, closer to the original. That was really something! To approach a bleeding sore inflicted on someone else's family, to touch it with a suckerlike finger, you, the source of that bleeding sore. How can you avoid falling into a sky-blue well when you look within yourself?! He was taken for an angel. He'd been sent by her brother! He was the last one to see her brother on the night before he was arrested. Someone her brother trusted. And S. guilefully let the sister know that he might be in danger too, about to be picked up! He played the role of conspirator. "I'm Seryozha from Moscow! . . ."

The sister shudders. Weeps. Raises a piece of cambric lace to her right eye. Blows her nose. Says, "I just hope they don't arrest you!" "Anything can happen," he replies enigmatically and with a worried look. "After that sad story . . ." he says and borrows money in case he's arrested. He ensconced himself like a king in that home; he drank with an air of importance, ate interesting dishes made especially for him, fricassees, and, lighting up a cigarette, he fell into pleasant reveries, sighing deeply. What could be finer! . . .

"No, there was no bad blood between us. We parted friends. He was a brother to you and to me he was . . . like a brother too. Yura Breughel! A true friend!" he said, musing aloud, sipping his dry wine gravely, magnanimously. "He never denounced anyone, even though I personally was extremely open with him. Extremely . . ." A bit confused here, he suddenly finds the right image, which springs to mind as if on command. "I have the feeling that he's sitting right here with us at the table right this minute, his eyes looking piercingly at us through his glasses. I can see him— as if he were here in the flesh. Excuse me, madame, may I have another? . . . No, thank you, I don't drink vodka. Come closer. To his health! I wonder how he's doing in his cell right now?! . . . Here we are drinking and eating while he . . . ?!" S. was on the verge of tears. Sincerely. Have you read Evreinov's *Theatre for Its Own Sake?* "It's you, his sister, I feel sorry for! A sort of Saint Bartholomew's Eve is coming for us, for all of us! . . . But we're still human beings. And I've come to see you at this tragic hour only to lend you moral support. I don't abandon friends in need! Not like some people . . . I don't want him there in prison thinking his friend is heartless. . . ."

And it was all sincere. A little hammy. Grand. Nuanced. A mixture of gaiety and melancholy. And limpid memories. Like that young wine, heady and slightly acidic . . .

Don't pick him to pieces! He doesn't know how it happens either. He's like a medium. He becomes mesmerized; he's as innocent as can be. He's invulnerable to evil; it just bounces off him. And into your minds. Even now he addresses you from the next world with bitter reproach and a child's bewilderment at your cruelty toward him. No, he no longer swears that you have slandered him, as he, in the face of the obvious, stubbornly insisted for what must have been about fifteen years after the memorable scandal, the witnesses to his romp returning to life ahead of schedule. But now he knows who's to blame for all his troubles. And those, unsurprisingly, are the very people on whom he had informed, whom he had buried alive. You guys, he says, have besmirched my name and ruined my reputation, and for no reason. Some friends! And remember, they only had to serve five of their ten. That was a loss for me too—five years! And my whole life fell apart because of you. My career went nowhere. I couldn't show my face in good society. People whispered about me. Cold-shouldered me. Avoided being frank with me, wouldn't open up with me. Compare the two and see who has it worse, you or me. Where's the justice in this world? . . .

Well, there's something to that. No person fits the category assigned him. And just what are the limits? And, who knows, maybe yesterday's traitor will accept the cross on the barricades tomorrow. And the day after tomorrow he'll become a Buddhist monk or pull some other quirky, unpredictable stunt that eludes all definition. How am I supposed to create characters, paint portraits after that? What, am I crazy? Every character has a frighteningly vast range and can go flying off at any second. *Bon voyage!* Forgive me if I have dwelled on my young friend; my interest in him was not artistic but pragmatic. My life depended on him, and much else besides. . . . To be honest, as far as art goes, it isn't people that have interested me lately but, rather, energy. States. Magnetic fields. Freaks of nature. What's left of people? Just the pod. To be on the safe side and avoid entanglements, you designate them by their first name or with a single letter. You slip in some little detail as a reference point—and that does the trick. But you're sadly aware in advance that, no matter how much you outline and sketch, any character, even the most hopeless case, will elude hypothesis, true description, even his own photograph. Like smoke from a chimney. Like an unfinished cigarette, tossed to the wind . . .

The smell of something burning. Smoke. Chestnut trees. My neighbors are burning leaves. I am free of nostalgia. It is autumn here in France. Autumn is the same here as at home in Russia. Leaves are burned, preparations are made for winter. Except that you sigh deeply, and breathing's a pleasure. September. The Silver Age. Emigration.

Even if they allowed me to return with a guarantee not to kill me (as I sometime fantasize) and to let me write what I want, I probably still wouldn't go back. I'd rather make a trip to Iceland. Or Greece . . . That night when the cellar window was kicked in by a boot was a turning point. But the soul still isn't so sure. Russia clings to it like a burr. I'm not budging. If the soul wants it so badly, let it fly to Russia in a dream and refresh itself. Then, afterward, it can tell me what it saw and correct me if I've gotten something wrong. . . . And isn't that the reason—the impossibility of returning—that gives rise to memoirs? . . .

In 1947 a Frenchwoman came to study with us third-year students in the Lang and Lit Department. She was the first Frenchwoman we'd seen in the flesh, and in those distant days the only foreign woman enrolled in a Soviet institution of higher learning. Her father, a naval attaché, had supposedly expended considerable effort—going through the Ministry of Foreign Affairs all the way up to Molotov—to win his daughter the exceptional right to study on an equal footing with everyone else, to attend lectures and take examinations, to further her already quite advanced Slavic education, which she had received, funny though it may sound, in Paris, in an institute that was under the ambiguous aegis of "Oriental languages." We did not think of ourselves as part of the East and even viewed this as a form of slight discrimination on the part of the bourgeois West. What did they take us for—Turks, Chinese? Does that mean we all look alike to them? So, let them become more closely acquainted with us. Closer, closer! . . . No cold cyclone was yet blowing full-force from Siberia toward fair Europe. Or else we hadn't noticed it yet. After the war we dreamed that the whole world would be open to us. And we were glad to be in contact with this unique foreigner who had descended to earth on a diplomatic parachute. And Helene, as if doing what she was supposed to, entered our enchanted house, fearless as Cinderella. . . .

The surprising thing, as I recall, was that no one in our circle was suspicious of her or hostile to her. There was no feeling of distance. Everyone seemed secretly in love with her. She aroused respectful curiosity and restrained admiration in us all. Moreover, her manners and appearance utterly refuted our preconceived social and political ideas: there was nothing bourgeois about her. She dressed modestly—much more modestly, I suppose, than she might have. Not like a diplomat's daughter. The clothes she wore to the university always had a certain threadbare elegance to them. Still, she trailed a sort of invisible train behind her through the university and on the street. Theoretically that train could be represented graphically as "FRENCHWOMAN," the lacy letters becoming smaller and smaller, "Frenchwoman," "frenchwoman." . . . To this day I see her in those fleeting sounds. . . .

There are natures—or so it seemed to me at that time, because of her contrast to us and because of the singularity of her ethereal presence in our ingrown little world—that, unbeknownst to and independent of themselves, bear the traits of their country or nation. In such cases, a person's very individuality and character become a sign or, to put it better, an expression of that person's inward tie to his geographical homeland, a celestial symbol of his place of origin on earth. One way or the other, Helene was and still remains in my mind the expression of something spatially greater than her own soul—a fairy, a puff of light-blue smoke, a luminous emanation, the result of her being part of France by birth. . . .

Strange as it may seem, I came to know her in the Marxism-Leninism course, where she somehow stood out all the more vividly in our eyes. Come on, how could a foreigner be so intent on fathoming a doctrine that we, in our heart of hearts, were already a little sick of, though it continued to play its obligatory role as a privileged possession, a consistent world view accessible to us alone, a view, we were taught, that was very well constructed. Later on Helene was almost the death of our poor teacher of Marxism; after passing the course with flying colors and answering all the thorniest questions, she modestly confessed at the end of her exam that, personally, she still retained her idealistic views. What?! To have an excellent grasp of Marxism and still remain an idealist?! I think they lowered her grade for that.

To tell the truth, at first I too was somewhat flabbergasted when she said of herself, "I'm a Catholic." It was not that I doubted her right to her own French ideology and the faith of her fathers or forefathers. It was just that the word "Catholic" sounded as remote as the word "catacomb." Yes, yes, at one time in history there had been monasteries, Jesuits, the Inquisition. . . . But how was I to put the two things together, the term "Catholic" and her vivacious face, her kindness and humor, her indisputable interest in and liking for contemporary Russia? At the time the fact that I was a believing Komsomol member may have seemed just as remote and improbable to her and as difficult to reconcile with my taste in literature and my adoration of Picasso and van Gogh, which over the years already had clearly begun to predominate in my intellectual baggage. Yes, I too suffered from a split in my values until all that came to an end, ideology collapsing under the blows of Zhdanov's attack. But somehow or other, until that time, all this cohabited quite nicely under one roof with my Komsomol conscience and my concept of a highly elevated revolutionary morality, one ready, if need be, to sacrifice man temporarily for the sake of his future, universal resurrection.

Once Helene and I were friends, we discussed all this openly and fervently; fortunately, neither of us tried to win the other over. That would have hardly been possible. We exchanged views, or, to be more precise, we exchanged the directions of our thoughts and feelings were taking, not under anyone's influence, good or bad, but just from the painful bumps we experienced along life's hard way. And no matter how much she revealed the truth of Scripture to me, I could not comprehend her invisible God, just as the moral purity of the revolution may not have been completely intelligible to her, no matter how much I crucified myself trying to explain it. . . . The culture or spirit of a country that attracts you in and of itself is a different matter for people like us. France assumed the same form in her stories as it would later on, when I saw it for myself. To confirm that impression, all I had to do was leave my country.

Helene, Mariya, and I drove out past red brick Toulouse through the summer fields that ran down the hillsides. Everything was exaggeratedly soft and smooth to the eye. Both the dampness of the rounded lines and the feeling of space enclosed, as it were, within the limits of the eyeball itself gave rise to a rare, gratifying sense of landscape that we have experienced only in France. Compared with the Russian plain, the horizon here is still quite wide but more spelled out, spherical, limited, regulated. Space is laid out like Giorgione's sleeping Venus, and the flora recalls her breathing in a long sleep. . . .

Eyes bulging like a barbarian's, I devoured those contours, those well-tended fields and vineyards combed with a hard comb like a woman's hair. You were aware of the body of agriculture, overcome by sleep in the sun. And in your own body you could feel the weight of the centuries, and mortality. But, regaining possession of your faculties, you observe that you're not just looking to the right and left but absorbing and assimilating the landscape; what you see is gradually changing you. You're not the same person you were yesterday because of what you've seen. And it may well be that the landscape is not surroundings or an environment at all but a sap that automatically enters the makeup of the tribes inhabiting a place since earliest times, the heirs and descendants of the land that had raised and nourished them like an extension of itself. How strange to recognize oneself in the faces and customs of others, who were brought into this world by the same sleeping mother! And how much power must the earth have if its surface can become our flesh and blood. . . . We are rooted in what we have seen. We grow into the landscape. And we are no longer ourselves but the rocks and the trees; one look is all it takes. And in dreams we lead the dead who still flutter above us into those gentle contours. Look! Remember this! . . . So that sooner or later we all can settle into the contours of the hills . . .

Back then my sense of Helene's kinship with her sunny land was probably reinforced by the art books she used to bring me from France. I had never seen anything more beautiful in my life. The Shchukin collection was closed after the war, a decision rumored to have been made by Klim Voroshilov, who, accompanied by Alexander Gerasimov, had visited the museum, which had by then fallen out of favor. The most innocent early Impressionists were considered sorties by frenzied international reaction. . . . And then all of a sudden, "Here, for you," and I'm holding a book on Cézanne! And what a Cézanne! Even S., a connoisseur of such things, went wild with delight at the sight of that dazzling book: "Well, fortune has smiled on you, Andrei! . . ." Meanwhile, having come to know S., Helene in her generosity also gave him a volume on van Gogh as a present, an absolutely incomparable van Gogh, all beauty and pain. Where could you hide from the frightening blue of his skies, his vases of flowers? From those eyes lodged splinterlike everywhere in the canvas under the guise of brush strokes? The reproductions seemed strewn with tormented eyes where the caustic pupil drowned in the artist's iris. Was it possible, I wondered, that even over there in France such unbearable pain could be concentrated in the earth and the air? . . .

Now, walking idly past book stands in Paris, I glance with indifference at the spate of folios for sale at bargain prices, cheap, second-rate editions of that fabled wealth which in the Moscow of my youth I alone possessed. Apparently, while I was making my way here, those books were multiplying in immense quantities. But art always exists in the singular. . . .

For my part, I wanted to give Helene a gift of the best of Soviet Russia's relics, and dragged her to Duvakin's special seminar on Mayakovsky. The seminar leader, Victor Dmitrievich Duvakin, a senior lecturer with a boxer's bulldog jaw and a head that resembled a hedgehog bristling with fury, was the kindest of men, a great scholar of Mayakovsky, and had more enthusiasm for the thorny field of education than I was ever to encounter again. To this day, when asked about my training in literature, I answer with pride, "I studied with Duvakin! . . ." I will not, however, touch on certain other aspects here, to avoid causing an old man harm, as already occurred once before, in that ill-fated courtroom where, scorning the danger, Duvakin rushed to my defense. He paid dearly for that—he was permanently dismissed from all teaching. . . .

In my time his Lit Department seminar was truly the last refuge for twentieth-century poetry, which was increasingly subject to pogroms and prohibitions. But in his efforts to save what was left of poetry, Duvakin was greatly aided by Mayakovsky, a powerful patron whose golden palm of undisputed superiority somewhat protected our oasis from the drought. One way or the other, those who had been close to him took cover under the shade of Mayakovsky, while a pleiad of other mighty heroes slept the sleep of the dead; any one of them could have contended with Mayakovsky, that last Mohican of the revolution—all you had to do was quietly and unobtrusively pretend to be acquainting yourself with the primary sources. It was all there! . . . Malevich, Tatlin! . . . What horror! . . . Not horror, my dear, but a counterrelief! . . . And transrational language, a miracle of heaven! . . . Did you know that Lunacharsky compared Mayakovsky's play *Mystery Bouffe* with German Expressionism? . . . You're always slinging it. . . . Go ask Duvakin if I'm slinging it, ask him! . . . Whitman, Veraeren, Rimbaud . . . Petya, have you read Benedict Livshitz's *The Archer with One and a Half Eyes* or haven't you? . . . But wasn't he an enemy of the people? . . . But he was a friend of Mayakovsky's! . . . And what about Meyerhold? . . . He was a friend of Mayakovsky's too. . . . But wasn't he an enemy of the people? . . .

But he was also a friend of Mayakovsky's! . . . I don't want to know anything about any of that! Do you hear me? I have no desire to! . . . But someone else did, and after digging deep, would crack mockingly à la Khlebnikov: "Cheepchurp! Cheepchurp! . . ."

Even after my time, other lovers of poetry entered Mayakovsky's work there as if gathering mushrooms: picking a Pasternak, a Tsvetaeva, an Anna Akhmatova. . . . We didn't even have seminars on Blok or Sergei Esenin! Mayakovsky was the sole refuge for them all. And even though Mayakovsky had shown them no quarter in the legendary past, he now towered above us as their sole delegate on that scorched earth, and even seemed to protect them a little. Thank you, Uncle Volodya!

One time his broad hand even shielded me when the newspaper *Komsomolia,* posted on the main wall in the university, attacked me point-blank for studying Khlebnikov, in a huge editorial entitled "Who Does Andrei Sinyavsky Work For?!" The author, a boss in training, sounded the alarm, saying that in a seminar report on Khlebnikov I'd given last year I was actually working quietly and covertly for the Anglo-American imperialists. . . . By then the cold war with the West was going full-force, and this activist had obviously decided to eliminate me as a potential rival for a graduate slot. But he overrated his strength in impugning Mayakovsky's honor, and word soon came down that he was to be considered a cosmopolitan, even though he was quite innocent—it was all because of his Jewish surname. . . .

But the arrow of fate did not pass me by either, for we pay for everything in life, and the signs placed in front of us almost from birth tend from time to time to burst into crimson flame, like signal lanterns in mines, warning others of the danger a person contains. ?!—first the question mark, with its serpentine head bent like a surprised girl, and then the exclamation point, a direct hit on the dot. And from then on, from that memorable first mention in the wall newspaper under the menacing headline "Who Does Andrei Sinyavsky Work For?!," the jealous Russian-language press flared up at me with vigilant regularity, be it in *Izvestiya, The Literary*

Gazette, the magazines *October, Ogonek, Anti-Aircraft Defense,* or the émigré publications *Kontinent, New Journal, Our Country, The Sentinel.* . . . Everyone is at his post. Guarding the borders. Even after thirty or more years, that article in *Komsomolia* will finally overtake me, striking me from behind like a bolt of implacable lightning. And where can you find a lightning rod now? Mayakovsky has remained in Moscow, in Duvakin's disbanded seminar. . . .

Now, at this remove, it's difficult even to imagine how much Mayakovsky meant to us in the dawn of youth. Righteous and indomitable, he had the fire of the revolution's initial phase smoldering in him alone, he who would commit suicide, and those echoes introduced a note of devotion and nobility into our one-track Komsomol bravado. We did not study the propagandistic elements of his work. All that went without saying, parenthetical at best, overshadowed by the fact of his heretical personality, which had shaken all the pedestals and monuments. I don't know what Stalin had in mind when appointing that rebel to the position of the "best and the most talented poet in our Soviet epoch." The epoch had long since parted company with Mayakovsky. Mayakovsky was not in power. Mayakovsky was a mutiny in our midst. For a great many people "it all started" with Mayakovsky.

In memory of the ringleader and "drummer" of the revolution, our seminar would sometimes meet outside the classroom, over a bottle. And since we still hadn't learned how to drink properly, we'd stay sober till dawn of the next day. Going around in a circle, each of us would recite poems in his own fashion, a ritual that would last the entire night. That was what I would now define as a rite invoked to galvanize the force of poetry, which was also present in the darkening blue of the windows. We did not read poems, we lived them, with everything we had. The poets would change as we went around the circle, first Blok, then Gumilev. The vodka would be all gone after the first glass, but our shamanistic incantations never ceased. . . .

Meanwhile, things had begun to go out of joint for me. My

dreams were not the usual run, and they came in dense cloudlike shoals, though even now, after all I've been through, I still don't put much stock in dreams, and I put even less back then. . . . For example, I'd dream that I was standing in a clearing and looked like a well-shaped poplar, despite the fact that, to be blunt, shapeliness was never one of my strong points. Kittens would be playing and frolicking on the grass at my feet. In the dream I loved those kittens and found them very endearing. Departing from the dream for a moment, I will mention in passing that my future wife fell in love with me because, to kill time while waiting outside to walk her to work in the morning, I would play with one of the kittens in her building. But ten years before this, in that dream, the exact same kind of ordinary little tomcat began playfully climbing up me, higher and higher. I laughed and petted it; meowing pitifully, it kept climbing under my hand, up along my green canvas boots and the cotton field shirt which I invariably wore after the war, its little claws already sinking into the white skin of my chest to a point where I could feel it, and then it made a sudden leap to my throat, trying to bite through the skin. Irritated, I grabbed it painlessly by the scruff of the neck—it was still just a kitten—tore it free with some effort, and flung it a good distance away. But by then the rest of them were hanging clustered on my Adam's apple. Before you could get one off, another one was at your throat. By then they were squealing on your face, their little claws covered in blood. I tore them off and flung them away, tore and flun . . . , tore and flun . . . tore . . . flun . . . toreflun. . . .

I battled with them all through the long night. Later on I would read in dream books and be told by people experienced in these matters, who challenged my skepticism, that it was a bad sign to dream of cats, whereas dogs meant friends were coming. Even now, here in France, it still makes me happy to dream of a dog—friends are coming! I can feel the happiness right there in the dream. Unfortunately, when I wake up, no friends have come. . . .

The majority of such dreams stem from a rather simple popular etymology. Cats evoke craftiness, deceit. "Wine" and "crime" sound alike and go together. And wine may be even worse than cats. . . . So it turns out that it is not dreams that govern us but words. . . .

In that connection, allow me to tell another dream, one that also proved prophetic but belongs to another part of my life, and for that reason I have to skip ahead a little.

On the night before my arrest, I dreamed that I had come home from a lecture to find my house full of strangers. Our dinner table had been extended to its full length and was literally covered with goblets and glasses of red wine that for some reason looked tart. Not a pure red, more the color of Bordeaux. There were crimson circles around the glasses, like those around eyes after heavy drinking, as if, sparing no expense, the wine had been poured generously, brimming over onto the tablecloth. And, to my delight, Stalin was seated in the middle of the table. As if he were waiting for me. The Leader's expression was stern, displeased. He didn't look at me. Silent but glowering. This was many years after his death. No one was drinking, but the servants kept pouring wine. And in my dream I thought: God, I'm no longer the master in my own house, and now he can do whatever he wants with us, with my son, with my wife, who was standing pale in the doorway. . . . They could do anything. . . .

But let's get back to reality. We had a disabled war vet in our department. Not just one but a few, which was in keeping with the postwar situation. Healthy men were at a premium. Besides, who had any thought for literature in those days of hunger? Only girls. That group of disabled war vets, peasants by origin, with nowhere to go now, remained aloof, clad in iron. While we toyed with poetry, they hobbled through the exams the same way they hobbled on their prostheses, and formed a small group apart based on their unhealing wounds, black bread, and, if luck was with them, strong drink. I think they had some contempt for us, the cream of the department, the Komsomol, the diligent girls, Mother's little darlings dizzy over Pushkin, and for that entire marble university with its bronze statue of Lomonosov; their main interest was how to survive on next to nothing and make their way in the world in the not-too-distant future, despite their own primitiveness. They simply had other things in mind. . . . Still, one of the disabled vets stood out from the rest and showed greater promise. He was tall, and his face would have been attractive if it hadn't been scarred. Despite his injury he wrote, and wrote well, on Saltykov-Shchedrin, working under Ellsberg. Part of his cranium seemed to have been sheared off by a shell fragment, so that when talking with him you were always involuntarily aware of his thick, wrinkled, but still-transparent skin, which for minutes at a time would seem to pulse with a reddish light where his temple should have been. No matter how much you tried not to notice it, you could not take your eyes off that signal of a scar, placed on him like some sort of warning. As indeed it was: it wasn't long before a jealous lover killed him with an ax, a barmaid he'd moved in with and who was supposedly a beauty. But it wasn't enough that she murdered her lover for no reason at all. To compound the horror, she hacked him into little pieces, which she put in a backpack and took with her on a commuter train, finally to throw them away in a woods outside Moscow. . . .

I saw him for the last time, a few weeks before the incident, in a dream on an empty square at night, or perhaps he and I had intersected in parallel dreams. Seeming tipsy, his scar glinting, he said to me: "I've been meeting you in my dreams a lot lately, Andrei, and you're always with the same person. You go around Moscow at night with a girl in a light-blue dress. And the other guys in our group have also seen you with her: on the Sofia Embankment or near the Kremlin, on Kamenny Bridge. . . . After midnight, maybe even after one. You're out walking with her pretty late. . . ." In the dream I knew whom he was referring to, but it made no sense at all, because I was never out walking with her or anyone else at that hour of the night back then; if I happened to be out wandering the city at night, I was usually alone, composing poetry. All the disabled veterans must have been seeing things, or else they had confused me with someone else. He, however, kept pressing the point, and, to prove it, he named the place where our paths had crossed; truly, for an instant I could see myself from without, on the Sofia Embankment and then on Kamenny Bridge, as if all that had actually happened the day before and had actually been seen by him. I was in the company of a light-blue, phosphorescent, and, needless to say, young creature. But I couldn't make out exactly who that person was. I didn't notice anyone beside me at that moment on the bridge. They could see her, my light-blue friend, but I couldn't. I was walking alone, calm as can be, muttering poems to myself.

> I accomplished very little:
> and all my days
> squandered on scandal.
> And I didn't save a cent.
> The same way walls
> break up space
> crosswise
> to the horizontal.
>
> In the houses are men
> smiling like Abel,
> Mute stones
> at the borders,
> And everything so decorous
> and everything so correct,
> And nowhere for me
> to escape to. . . .

And there was another one, also in the Imagist style:

> I'll sit down. I'll smoke cigarettes.
> I'll give away and sell all I can.
> And if I feel drawn to the stars and space,
> I'll go to a brothel instead.

Yes. I'll never believe in sincerity,
Your sincerity of average prices.
Better to walk in the rain, as if under fire,
your proud head the target.

Better to love the naked squares,
The green of fences, the laces of shoes . . .
The homelessness of all these days,
The third decade of hunger. . . .

Later it became clear that somewhere behind a wall, the wall of my soul (?!), a double had long since taken up residence and was keeping an implacable record of my entire ideological breakdown.

He established the even and the odd.
The birth rate, the death rate. Income and expense.
He understood that I was simply an echo
Of a verse almanac published in 1913.

He understood that I'm an epileptic,
The vestiges of someone's depths. . . .
And today he sentences me to death
For lack of any more humane means.

Calmly I go to meet my punishment:
The first line of a new chapter! . . .
But, then, why aren't you cheerful—
you a so-called life-loving man? . . .

The only interesting thing about these poems is that they do not correspond in the least to who I am. I did not go on drinking sprees or to brothels, which, to the best of my knowledge at the time, did not exist in Russia. But I did smoke like a fiend. That's a fact. I borrowed the line about the vestiges from Blok: "We are the forgotten vestiges of someone's depths," a subtle hint that we had been cut off forever from the lovely poetry of the Silver Age. And I don't think I was an epileptic back then either. . . . But youth, you know, loves to embellish. Oh, how often we die and are resurrected in youth! But, alas, when we're old we can't bring that off very often at all. . . . To make a long story short, I was playing the Decadent a little, for which I was condemned by the "life-loving" person who I think was the positive hero of Soviet literature at that time, and whose unshakable optimism I had begun quietly hating, probably because I hadn't fully detached myself from it. . . .

But to hell with psychoanalysis! That's not what matters! Immersed in words as I paced through Moscow, I had not noticed who was walking beside me. But the disabled veteran could read my mind. The signal light on his forehead winked like a conspirator. "Watch out!" he said. "That foreign woman won't bring you any happiness. You're out walking hand in hand with your death. I decided to warn you. . . . Watch it!" And he was drunk as can be. . . .

The next morning I spent a long time wondering what it all could possibly mean, as if I had actually been accompanied by a charming, invisible, light-blue woman, asking myself who she might be. Helene and I did not take walks through the city at night together; our occasional walks were only during the day. And I would have known in the dream if she were Helene. But what other foreigner could it have been, then? Death? Was it time to get packing? . . . Why not? And why does death have to assume the traditional guise of an old woman? Maybe death is a girl, a young friend who walks hand in hand with us through life, quietly warning us, alerting us: Watch your step! Hold on! It's not time yet! . . .

However, an ill fate was in store not for me but for that unfortunate disabled veteran of whom I have already spoken. On the surface at least, nothing happened to me. I was just summoned once to the district draft board to meet with a comrade in civilian clothes who had an office of his own and whose purposes, though murky and mysterious, were obvious to all. But for the sake of clarity I will summarize the general features of our three dialogues, which, of course, took place over a period of time, a little less than a year.

First dialogue. Yes, yes. So, you're in contact with a foreign woman? . . . No, why? We're not against it. . . . It's just that . . . Why break it off?! On the contrary . . . You mean you don't understand? . . . What do you mean, what are you saying! You have an excellent reputation in the Komsomol. . . . Are you a good Soviet or aren't you? Are you a good Soviet or aren't you? Are you a good Soviet or aren't . . . I don't recommend that. . . . I'm not demanding any . . . Stop, we know everything about you. . . . What, are you afraid? . . . Explain that! Does that mean that there's something to hide about your contacts? . . . But you don't have anything to be afraid of! . . . Let's look at it another way. . . . Didn't you say yourself that she has a positive attitude toward Soviet Russia? . . . And how does she feel about the Americans? . . . Negative? . . . Aha, you didn't talk about that. You didn't feel like talking about that? . . . Forget it, that doesn't interest us. . . . Where'd you get that idea? . . . Just . . . In a friendly way . . . As a precaution . . . What do you mean spying? . . . We can see for ourselves. . . . Look at yourself in the mirror. . . . But this is a friendly relationship . . . purely friendly. . . . All you have to do is keep it going. . . . Are you a good Soviet or aren'——? What?! Don't you think we're human beings too? . . . Sign here that you won't disclose anything that . . . Don't worry, we'll find you! . . .

Second dialogue. It's been a while, quite a while. . . . And are you making any headway in your intimacy with the woman? . . . Your what? Your seminar? Ha-ha! . . . Listen, we know what's going on. . . . And by the way, the White émigrés also love Russia. But which Russia? There's a difference. . . . Aha, so she's apolitical, is she?! . . . Give me a straight story here. . . . Good Sov—— or aren't . . . Who is she working for? . . . What does that mean? . . . Her father's an attaché! . . . What, you don't underst——

what an attaché is? . . . They're intelligence. . . . You can tell by the rank, the post. . . . And we're counterintelligence. . . . I was in the Finnish war, the Mannerheim Line, I assure you. . . . Reactivate the relationship. . . . On a more intimate . . . What do you mean, you can't do that? . . . What do you mean, you have a fiancée! . . . I have a wife and two children. . . . But if my country needed me . . . But can't you court her a little? . . . No, I don't insis—— Yes, yes, we know what those Catholic women are like. . . . And she's met your old friend S., hasn't she? . . . That's fine, fine . . . Couldn't be better . . . But I have another question, a purely personal one. You're working on Mayakovsky. . . . Is it true that Mayakovsky uses the unprintable word "whore" in a poem?! . . . Really, three times? . . . Let me make a note of them. . . . And so it was "I'd rather serve pineapple juice to whores in a bar. . . ." What wandering dog? . . . These are just details. . . . And the second time? . . . Say it again, one more time. . . . "The poet, like a one-ruble whore, sleeps with any words that comes by. . . ." That's going too far. . . . That's too much. . . . And from our best and most talented poet! . . . And the third time? It really was about the Five-Year Plan? Aha! "Where the whore, the hooligan, and the syph——" Thank you, thank you . . . Still, it's very rare. . . . You don't recall anything similar in Esenin, by any chance? . . .

Third dialogue. So, you're going to meet her in Sokolniki Park tomorrow. And it's tomorrow that you're going to propose. . . . No . . . we don't need that. . . . Just make an old-fashioned proposal, offering your heart and your hand. . . . Why are you smiling? . . . Girls always like that. . . . She's a Catholic! You said so yourself. . . . The rest's no concern of yours. . . . Leave it to us. . . . At best you'll marry her—in name only, of course. And at worst . . . What does your own fiancée have to do with anything here? No one will ever find out. . . . Andrei! If your country calls on you . . . You'll come out clean in the end. . . . It's not your problem what happens to her when . . . We can see what kind of a lover you'd . . . But for now you have her affection. . . . For some reason she doesn't feel for S. . . . Anyway, tomorrow . . . You have only yourself to blame. . . . Every word of yours . . . What?! That's news to me! Consider yourself mobilized. . . . When your country is in danger . . . What do you care about her future? She'll be gone after all this! Do you understand—long gone! . . .

I went reluctantly to Sokolniki Park the next day. I was struck by how littered and shabby that famous park looked. Even though the terrible heatwave of 1948 had only just descended upon us, broken bottles, crumpled paper, and eggshells caught your eye everywhere. . . . That may have been an aberration on my part. I had already experienced other distortions of reality. Recently I had noticed that I was leaving whitish tracks that looked like lime on the living-room floor. Godamnit, I thought, I must have stepped in something again! I'm tracking up the place like a sloppy house-painter! But a look revealed there was nothing on the soles of my boots. A broom didn't work on the mess, nor did a brush. So I began using a wet rag and a pail of water. No luck! A disaster! It was whiter than ever! Must be oil paint! Mama would come home from work tired and have to wash the floor. . . . All of a sudden the tracks yielded to pressure and vanished. I was standing back to admire my success when, a moment later, those little devils reappeared on the wet floor, twice as bright as before. Was I suffering from delirium tremens, of all things? . . . Then it occurred to me to look out the window. I was jubilant! It was the sun! It was the sun making even strips and perfect circles on the floor. At some deflected angle. And the passing clouds either kept wiping out the streaks like a floor polisher or gratefully restored them. Sometimes, you know, it's a pleasure to learn that it was not your fault, wasn't dirt, wasn't lime, but the sun that was to blame. . . . But it was just the opposite there in Sokolniki Park. Even the light seemed to lie on the grass and bushes like a layer of white alluvial dust. Like lead, not lime. Hurling down heat, the cloudless sky was turbid and noxious, replicating my state of mind. Too many people were out in the park relaxing on that early-summer day; stretched out, sunbathing or napping, traceries of shadow on their newspapers, they looked like lifeless rubber worms. From time to time they would crawl to keep up with the sun, still maintaining the inert placidity of worms, which only heightened the oppressive disgust I felt for everything. No one but Helene had a soul that day. . . .

A proverb says that another man's heart is a dark place. That isn't true. With rare exception, other people's souls, if, of course, souls exist, are crystal-clear. I don't mean the personality but the soul, which may not even be connected to a person. A man kills and deceives but his soul stays pure. And for a time it lives its own independent life. And sometimes it can inspire you to goodness. I read somewhere about a saintly ascetic in a cave who prayed for the murderer who had come and announced that he was there to kill him. And he did in fact kill him, though only after the prayer. But that ascetic was clearly not praying for himself, and certainly not for that cutthroat, himself already a dead man, consumed by sin and vice, like a worm-eaten leaf. He was praying for the salvation—strange words, they make me stumble—for the murderer's soul, which in all likelihood was as plain as day to him. Why should the poor soul perish for its owner's transgressions? And he really wasn't so much praying as cleansing that soul. He did everything for it that he could in those final preparations. Then he kissed him on the mouth: Kill me! . . .

And it was then that I seemed to see it for the first time, the soul. Helene's took the form of a small oval body or cloud; it looked like an infant in white swaddling who, unlike a child in the womb, was in an upright position, head up, not in its mother's stomach, but in her chest, reaching for her face. The soul shines through. You cannot see that in yourself. There's too much darkness in you. But there, in the depths of matter . . . That little icon . . . That final candle burned before the Lord God. . . .

I don't know where such thoughts come from. Is there some reservoir in us? I didn't believe in God back then. Not in the least. And I didn't acknowledge man as having any kind of special soul. I experienced no religious impulses, having only the foggiest ideas about religion, nor did I experience any of the savage hostility toward religion typical of Russian atheists. . . . It was apparently just that I'd come up against insuperable limits. To entice? Betray? Kill? Even if it wasn't with my own hands. But kill? No, that is beyond our powers, and far from everyone is capable of it. . . .

And I began hurriedly explaining it all to her. In sequence. "Now, I'm going to tell you a terrible secret, Lenochka. . . ." While confessing to her, I kept expecting her to jump up and run away howling. And then, of course, the arrest, the firing squad . . . I had it all worked out in my head. At first she didn't seem to understand—what kind of country she was in, who that raving man was sitting in front of her like a rabbit on dirty grass, or the role of deliverer that our mutual friend Seryozha was supposed to play in all this. And it must have been because she didn't understand that she smiled twice during my invectives against a love feigned on assignment from State Security, marriage on orders from the Motherland, after which a foreign woman automatically falls into the dangerous embrace of Soviet citizenship, and then they would torture her, I swear, they would torture her. . . . It may have actually sounded comical. Pretentious. A person reveals his tenderest feelings, all the while repeating: We have to stop seeing each other or else you'll be killed. Kill? Fall in love? . . . But I was in no mood for laughter. . . .

She grew worried: "Let's get out of here, Andrusha. . . ." And in fact a man with a newspaper was creeping toward us just past the bushes. He was creeping along on his back, belly up, and, despite all the discomfort involved, pretended he was still sunbathing and reading his paper, an issue of *Culture and Life,* containing a new resolution on depraved composers who were polluting Russian music. . . . We moved to a different spot. And while the man with the newspaper was changing position, and since no one else had crept over to us yet, we, as I recall, kissed. And it was then that I noticed that she was still with me, sitting or standing or walking with me down a path in Sokolniki Park— which is a park in name only and in fact is no more than an outhouse of bushes and plucked trees that have no idea why they're growing there, and whose bark can be peeled by anyone with a will to—instead of running away from me with the superstitious horror of a distinguished foreign woman, racing to her father and mother, begging the ambassador: "Save me! Save me from this abomination, which is without limit if my best Russian friend is also an agent assigned to ruin me, as he himself just confessed! . . ." But she kept on walking with me as if she were beginning to become loving and demonstrative, from a distance after a fictitious breakup caused by all the horrors I poured out. And, you'll pardon me, we kissed a second time.

Oh, Lenka! Now, when I remember all this, I think it was only a miracle that saved me then, the miracle of your trust in me, your believing what I told you, as I rushed again and again to explain it all from the beginning. And you were wrong to argue constantly, saying, apparently on Christian grounds, that man has the power of choice and is therefore free. At the critical junctures, the soul has no more power of choice than we have a choice of our children or our parents. And I was not acting of my own free will when I informed you of the plot against you, even though that may have been the most serious crisis in my life, after which it was emotionally impossible for me to return to the ranks of moral and political unity with the Soviet people and Soviet society, placing my hopes in the initial purity of the revolution. Think of it like this. What if you were ordered to murder a child in the name of the highest moral ideals. Would you be making a choice there— to murder or not to murder? And afterward wouldn't those very ideals seemed slightly bloodstained, to put it mildly, not with our own blood, not with the proletariat's, but with the blood of others, of innocent children, the more of which you see, Lenka, the longer and closer you look at our valiant, bloodstained banner. Oh, and those songs: "Our banner waves over the world . . . ," "We will go to our suffering brothers, we will go to the starving . . . ," "To a battle bloody, holy, and just . . ." You know, even now, as I'm finishing this novel and sighing from time to time, purely physical sighs, I hum those songs to myself to lift my spirits. "March, forward march, nation of workers! . . ." Those marching songs were beautiful! . . .

Yes, freedom is painful—not freedom of choice (there is no choice), but freedom of solitude in a world where you are compelled to live (and I wouldn't have chosen any other), one you love nonetheless and in which you are rooted. Even though they say I called Russia a bitch, Russia is my mother, Lenka, and it was so beautiful and just in my eyes when I was starting out in life. . . . And, remember, when you and I parted in Sokolniki, having said everything that needed saying, we thought we were saying goodbye for good, forever (you in France and me in Russia); then I went on my way, walking the length of the city, and I kept thinking that people on the street were staring at me, pointing at me: Look, an enemy of the people, there goes an enemy of the people. . . . And that has stayed with me to this day, as if I were still on my way home from Sokolniki Park, walking the length of the city. No, those aren't pangs of conscience but a feeling of some ultimate isolation from people and society, a terrible sense of being an outcast, something hardened criminals feel, even though my crime at the time was being unable to force myself to be an accomplice to murder. Some part of my mind kept insistently asking: But aren't you a good Soviet? Yet another part would bark back: Leave me alone, I'm just a person, nothing else, not an enemy of the people. . . .

Many years would pass, and somewhere outside Suzdal I would wander by chance into a little church that had survived by chance and was still functioning, and a fluffy little old priest would ask me, in an imperious tone, taking my measure from head to toe, "Where are you from, servant of God?"

"Moscow," I answered automatically before I could gather my wits about me. And so does that mean that I too, I too am like everyone else? . . . A servant of God, and that's all there is to it. And we don't need any other title or office. . . . For there is no better title, no designation more precise. . . . At long last. No one's servant. Only God's . . .

But that was to happen later on, whereas that day in Sokolniki Park I was constantly afraid she hadn't fully understood. I thought that everything depended on the slender thread of her understanding, all we had to cling to. She would not betray me, of course, just as I would not betray her. And without any hope of our meeting again, she would take with her a love, scarcely born and never to be, ashes, grave dust in her heart. It wasn't for me to instruct her, a Catholic, in those fine points. . . . But how were we to act on stage, in public, miming a final rift? Helene had one inborn failing: she was incapable of dissembling.

Yes, Helene, you and I worked out a fictitious account of what had transpired in Sokolniki Park. Word by word. Step by step. Matching cover stories. And not all that fictitious either, if you think about it. Our tender friendship had indeed collapsed beneath the blows of brute reality. I was to be blamed, but remember, Lenka, the initiative was yours. The vulgar pressure I brought to bear on you, that bewildering attempt to marry you, almost by force, and thereby, through deception, to turn you into a Soviet citizen, all this seemed so monstrous to you, so morally indecent, that moral indignation compelled you to break off relations with me. . . . Here she took my side—"Andrusha, you don't have to say that, about its being morally indecent. That's not true. . . ." O my God! She was still searching for the truth. "A ray of light in the kingdom of darkness." And there I was instructing her in deception and nothing but deception. We have to, Lenka, we have to! Those bastards, those patriots of the Motherland should only know how indecent it all really is. That in the end you even grew suspicious of me, your best Russian friend, suspecting me of the vilest acts because of them. . . . It sounds funny, but I had even argued with them about patriotism, me, an enemy of the people. The image of Soviet Russia they were presenting to the world! It was shameful. They should stop whoring around! . . .

"What does 'whoring' mean?" she asked, curious about that unfamiliar Russian word. I explained what it meant, more or less, and she blushed. I don't know if French has any adequate equivalent. I don't think two people can really curse each other out in French: the language is too aesthetic. I also wanted her to feign slapping my face like some enraged Diana as we spoke. But she would not go that far, and she may have been right. It wouldn't have been in character for her. Musn't overact . . .

All right, then. The script was ready. The roles assigned. But now the question was how to play them plausibly. Enact them. Make them real. And what guarantee was there that we'd succeeded in deceiving the secret police about our little tête-à-tête? A third person was absolutely necessary. What we needed now was an informer. . . .

Unfortunately, she did not like Seryozha, without knowing quite why herself. A duly courteous foreigner, Helene was pleasant to him. But I had already observed that certain women required no cause to find him unbearable. He was affable, handsome, talented, educated, intelligent. . . . But they put up a brick wall with him, nothing got through. They shied away from him like the devil from incense. For example, my own mother could not stomach him: "Get rid of him, drop him!" Even when we were children. At first I thought this was just her maternal fear of the "decadent" phase I was supposedly going through—because of some bad outside influence, as she put it. A mother always thinks her good little child is running with a bad crowd because of someone's pernicious influence. Why couldn't the child himself be no good? Yet, later on, when . . . But I'm always getting ahead of myself. . . .

My ear was to the receiver of a black telephone, and at least every thirty seconds a voice as abrupt as a stopwatch would announce the present whereabouts of the person under surveillance—Helene. There was no screen. But, trained as a direction finder in the army, I could visualize a dark grid along which a pale speck moved making a dotted line—Helene. I've had occasion to examine the cardiograms of ships and airplanes, but this was the first time I had seen a device that could keep an individual from slipping out of sight, from hiding in the middle of a city in broad daylight. They were following her, of course, but like that! I had never dreamed that Moscow could be strafed like that. That all those blocks of stones, barriers, girders could be seen clean through, X-rayed, the human body the only cavity in the stone. There wasn't the slightest chance to escape or elude them.

She came out onto Yakimanka Street.

"Attention! She's come out onto Yakimanka Street!" said the voice on the telephone in a tone of command. "You know what the script calls for—a reconciliation. With no talk of marriage. We'll put that aside for now. Friendly relations are to be re-established. Is that clear? A chance meeting . . . Attention! Yauza Street! The Shock-Worker Cinema! . . ."

The voice broke off. I too paused and, through the tense silence, seemed to hear people on the phone, at what must have been headquarters: "This is seagull!" "This is eagle!" "This is hawk! . . ."

"Attention! Get ready! She's crossing Kamenny Bridge! . . ."

I could see that bridge, which is immense and seems made entirely of stone if viewed from above. And a minute human bacterium was slowly creeping across it. Tell me, what could she do if her every step had been watched and plotted? . . . Listening to the telephone, I could see Helene, oblivious to it all, adjust her purse on its leather strap, switch her poor raincoat from one arm to the other, and then continue on her way across Kamenny Bridge, heading in my direction. May God let it dawn on her, may she have the sense to dash away down the embankment in time, toward the Moscow River, so that we don't run into each other, and are not reunited. . . .

"Attention! She's heading toward Frunze Street! Quick! Leave for the rendezvous point! Make running into her seem accidental.

No hurt feelings. You understand the scenario? Prepare to close in. I'll repeat the coordinates: she's heading for Frunze Street from the Arbat. All clear. Full speed ahead! Good luck! . . ."

This was followed by a short click, and then the line went dead.
. . . Feeling shaky, I went outside, now aware that, no matter what a person did, he could be seen clear through—from above, from the side, and from behind. He could be controlled, directed by radio. They had shoved me out with a parachute the way they sometimes do with paratroopers—with a kick in the butt. Was it war? It's always war for them. They couldn't exist without war. I floated, sailing over Moscow, desperately trying to figure out where I would land and how to get the two of us out of trouble again. . . .

All the same, I did not think then that the world we are born into is evil and insane, nor do I think so now. Beneath all the evil, I see paradise on earth. After all, each of us, literally each of us, comes into the world with the desire to give happiness. We are not avengers or murderers, but emissaries from paradise. . . . Even Cain . . . You'll laugh, but his intentions were good, ha-ha. . . . Oh, I know, I know, but his intentions were good! But what is their source if the evil done is irreversible? Do you think that the ideal is somewhere off in the distance? No, it's not, it's right here, underfoot. And we walk all over it. And what is the source of all our impulses to escape from time to heaven, from society to a golden age, whatever you choose to call it? That comes naturally to us, that clouded, anxious prevision of beauty. Otherwise, why would we even think about it? . . . Flowers and birds are signs of paradise on earth. The elephant. Every last animal. Why is everything so interesting, wherever you look, that it seems a shame to die? . . . Children are signs of paradise. Look how pure their faces are. Children are innocent. And we always place our hopes in them: They'll make us happy! They will! They're innocent! They'll restore paradise on earth! Or at least the memory of paradise? . . .

We almost collided at the end of Frunze Street. She rose out of the ground like a post as I flew full speed ahead around the corner on my assigned route. "Helene?! Is that you?! Fancy meeting you here! . . ." I was almost howling, waving my arms, as if twitching from electric shocks, to express my amazement and happy confusion ("Don't even think of smiling! There's nothing to be happy about! It's a setup! We're being followed . . ."). "I'm so glad to see you, Helene! I was just running over to the Lenin Library, and all of a sudden . . . !" ("Were you able to tell S. what you and I agreed on? Were you? . . .") I succeeded, I hope, in lending my intonation and gestures that obtrusive artificiality, that conspicuously foolish archness that say straight out that we are playing it as farce when the director wants melodrama. Let them see if they want the kind of actor I make. And it was beneath that clatter of hooves and the kettledrums of exclamations that the prompting had to be done: "Don't be afraid, child! Don't be afraid! . . ."

But she was not in the least afraid, standing there like a post in front of me, all in blue, and bright as a May noon. An angel, no other word for it. Her apparel, as always, was extremely modest— the wings of a dragonfly—and matched my idea of heaven. Her face was lit by a smile that could only have been real. In vain I told her through clenched teeth that it was my job to smile ingratiatingly and hers to frown and pout and, recoiling, to walk away from me while I continued to fawn and play up to her. We would make up, but not right away, not before I had renounced my dishonorable motives. None of it made any impression on her. Incapable of dissembling, she was still all smiles.

"Goddamnit!" I thought aloud. "What a team, a devil and a baby."

"And who's the devil?" she asked seriously.

"Me, of course. You're a babe in the woods here. You act like an angel. . . ."

Then she broke into tears. But that was even better, I thought. They might pass as the tears of a woman furious that her trust had been violated. And, taking her timidly by the elbow, as if trying to persuade her not to be angry and to stop quarreling, I led her away from the square.

Military in its bearing, Frunze Street seemed almost deserted. I had not spotted anyone tailing us. Could that artsy beret and cane over there be "eagle" or "seagull"? I doubted it. Just an ordinary person. Flatfeet don't go in for berets. I didn't even bother to look at the military people. They had business of their own. . . . Aha, finally, there he was, our man, you could spot him a mile away. His hat somehow sat too straight up on his head and suited him the way a saddle suits a cow. That wasn't a hat he wore on his head but a fort, a mausoleum. Newspaper in hand, reading intently, he stood like a lump of pig iron in the middle of the empty, clean-shaven asphalt. His interest had suddenly been caught by an editorial on culture, and he was engrossed—fine by me. I think the newspaper did not so much serve him as a shield or camouflage as lend him the emotional assistance he needed to blank out and fuse with the clean asphalt. He wasn't hiding from us, he was distracting himself from his own image. He seemed deeply immersed in his own absence. And this was a good thing: the sight of the detective calmed me at once. He loomed like a lighthouse in a world without form or boundary.

"So, did you go see Seryozha? Did you tell him we quarreled? That marriage was completely out of the question? . . ."

We walked back and forth past the man tailing us, never coming too close to him but never going so far as to lose sight of that landmark; otherwise he would be replaced by another interceptor, of whom we were not yet aware. It's always best to keep your enemy in view. . . .

Of course they had seen each other. She had been to S.'s house that very day, in the late afternoon, and, her face covered with tears, she had told him the whole story, putting in everything the recipe called for. She was full of complaint and indignation. And then what happened? Her faithful confidant pleaded with her not to be upset. He had offered no arguments. Despite all the evidence. So what, you had a tiff, make up, make up! I hadn't said what I really meant, she'd taken me wrong. And he insisted so vehemently that we begin seeing each other again that she had not been surprised in the least when we came within an inch of colliding on that square. . . .

Oh, foreigners and their charming diligence in learning expressions like "within an inch of" with which they correctly ornament their laborious version of the local tongue ("not surprised in the least"), and which always make my ears prick up whenever I hear them. But, even after mastering my native language with commendable purity and innocence, do they understand, those foreigners, the meaning of being tailed, denunciations, prison? And what do they see of Russia through their calibrated and stylized lenses? . . .

"Don't rush to make up with me! Don't rush to make up! Or else we'll fall into another trap. . . . Do you think Seryozha believed you? Did he go for the bait? So much depends on him, we can tell a lot by how he acts. . . ."

"Of course he did, Andrusha! I cried so much! And I tore you to pieces!"

She burst out laughing. Can you imagine, she burst out laughing at everything that hung over us and all Moscow and even at what wasn't even there. But was she truly aware of what was going on if she could still laugh about it? . . .

"He went for it, Andrusha! He went for it!" the Frenchwoman suddenly exclaimed with all the fury of a Russian peasant woman. "And I've seen it for myself—he's a provocateur! . . . Let's get out of here, Andrusha!" She tugged at my sleeve. "To the museum, if you want, or the zoo . . . Look, where's your, what did you call him, flatfoot? . . ."

She formed the difficult word "flatfoot," even savoring it tenderly. I looked around. And, indeed, while she and I had been having it out, the initial tail had melted away. That meant some other "eagle" or "hawk" was tailing us now. But I couldn't pick him out of the crowd. A bad sign. It really was time to be going. . . .

What should go here instead of an epilogue? When she and I met, at various times and, as it so happened, in various countries and cities, she often recalled those ordinary words: "Let's get out of here, Andrusha!" As if we really could have. It was only Stalin's death that allowed us to jump from the enchanted circle. But while still in that circle I had already decided that—despite all evidence to the contrary—I would be getting out of it as a writer—and what to write, how, and for whom, the circle itself whispered all that to me. Helene agreed to send my works to the West when the occasion presented itself, and this she did a few years later. And that was the end of the long path that had begun for me in Sokolniki Park. "Let's get out of here! Let's get out of here, Andrusha! . . ."

It remains for me to say a few words about Vienna. What benefit did I derive, what has remained in memory from those three days in Austria in 1952, where I'd been ferried by a military plane? Practically nothing. The Bristol, a residence hotel. A marble Johann Strauss, in a realistic tailcoat, sawing away at a marble violin: "The priest fucked a Tartar, and the Tartar fucked the priest." He was surrounded by diving naiads, half naked, marble: "fucked priest, fucked priest" . . . On the sidewalk by the statue, I bought a pair of green sunglasses to heighten my incognito, as if I were a tourist from overseas, and also to make the whole thing seem utterly implausible, happening underwater. "The Tartar!" thumped Strauss. "The priest, the priest!" seconded the naiads.

We hung around Vienna, in the occupied zone, I and the two scowling supermen assigned to me, waiting for Helene. She had written me that she was planning a trip to neutral Austria, and I replied, saying what I'd been ordered to—that as a doctoral candidate I was being sent to Prague to oversee the Russian archives and, while I was there, I hoped to find a good reason for dropping by Vienna. But at the last minute I managed to insert the innocent word "must" into the telegram (You must come, I said, I'll be there on such and such a date)—which meant the exact opposite, as she and I had arranged in advance in the event of any such dire emergency.

I was afraid! I didn't know what they would do to her. They

had not informed me of the purpose of the mission. A worm. Bait. A lacquered lure, I had been cast from a great distance into deep extraterritorial waters but was still under the jurisdiction of our armada. Not a man, but a dilapidated scarecrow, a sack full of hay dust wearing a brand-new suit of clothes, bought the day before at Mostorg, who, in twenty-fours hours, without a passport, ticket, or visa, had been shot by cannon to the moon, chilled to the bone, in an empty bomber, accompanied by two men, sitting on sheets of bare iron—they couldn't be called seats—across from the bare fuselage. What was I there for? For what purpose? Kidnapping? Abduction? To enlist her services through blackmail? God help me. . . .

It was a little bumpy over the Carpathians. My first time in the air, I had no faith in the wonders of flight. I thought the clouds through which we flew were not as soft as they looked but were composed nearly entirely of potholes and ruts through whose smoking craters earth loomed darkly. And it did not feel as though we were soaring through the heavens but only on our way to crashing into the earth in a fiery explosion.

My companions were tight-lipped, all business. In the lobby of the hotel reserved for Soviets and other bloc members, they set me aside like a coatrack and began a discussion in a worried half-whisper with other men in civilian clothes, as faceless as they were, but more restless. There were Soviets everywhere you looked. Outside, they wouldn't let me a step away. We walked a great deal, combing the city like a three-man army patrol. The one in charge had a plan. First: a little recognizance, a thorough study of the locale. Second: since the Parisienne might already have slipped past the cordons and be merrily waltzing around Austria's hospitable capital, we could nab her right on the street. Keep your eyes peeled! This is war! . . . But—and this made no sense whatever—they kept getting stuck in front of display windows. They would stand there with their hands in their pockets, rolling pensive eyes, and could not be budged. They gazed at ladies' undergarments. A motorcycle that resembled a fat ant. Thin-spoked

bicycles with handlebar mustaches. Suitcases made of hippopot-
amus hide. Handbags of spotted snakeskin. Brassieres—scaffolding
for breasts—a style for every taste. A male mannequin with the
strong-willed chin of a Viking . . . The two of them whispered
back and forth like conspirators, and though they were almost
inaudible, I caught on soon enough: "Cheviot!" "Tussore!"

I wanted to go to an art museum. I said: This is Vienna, after
all! Once in a lifetime! What are we going to do in there? they
replied. But then, after thinking it over: You think your friend
might be in there? . . .

There was no one inside. Tourism was a little off, needless to
say. Some of the canvases were missing. One, two, three, and you'd
seen everything. Blank squares where frames had been. They'd
either been taken out of harm's way or else been requisitioned.
But they still had some Bosch, Breughel, tapestries. . . .

The mountaintop had nice curls of forest, and the knights stood
nicely at its foot. There's one thing I don't understand: how were
the old masters able to take needle and thread and turn their own
times—bad, probably cruel too, and perhaps quite oppressive—
into the magnificent superiority of art? What was that gift, that
sense of woven fresco, which beckons our eye back and forth from
art to life? Just exactly what are tapestries? we might ask. A magical
force turned into playful embroidery? The weaver's jolly shuttle
darts back and forth. Here even the Passion is so artistically executed and so unlike reality that we feast our eyes on it, instead
of feeling shame or pain at the horrifying crime being committed
before our eyes. Is this because the masters saw past suffering and
death to that which comes after? Doesn't the hope of resurrection
work its way into all art, no matter what its subject? Or the pledge
of resurrection? The promise? And isn't that art's principal means
of vanquishing reality? Art is stronger and more enduring, and, if
you will, more alive, than destructive life. That is why it is both
healing and always moral, but independent of foolish morality.
. . . There is no art without love. Love is at the basis of art. And
that is why art reaches for the heights. And death, well, death is

only a condition for creation. An indispensable condition. But in the end how magnificent Christ bearing His burden is, even here, in a tapestry, resurrected for his walk to Golgotha. . . .

Then my escorts grew fidgety. "Why are you hanging around in front of that dirty rag so long? Are you playing for time? Let's go! Out! . . ." And then back to the show windows and their moving lips: "Cheviot," "Wool," "Cashmere," "Staple . . ." I noticed that no one else so much as paused to sample those idle pleasures of a courteous civilization. The locals rushed by on errands of their own. Wearing knee socks, shorts, Tyrolean hats with mocking, freedom-loving feathers. Somehow Russians, the Soviet Union made me feel embarrassed. Where we were from and who we were was written all over us. The Austrians seemed to disdain us, took pains not to look at us, and sidestepped us, pretending we didn't exist. But they worked for us, they worked for us everywhere! . . . Dismembered by Allied troops, teeming with spies, the country, to my horror, was supplying the Soviets accurate information on the arrival and departure of all foreigners. Twenty-four hours a day, names, times, at train stations, at the hotels and pensions—now, that's a staff for you!—including, I think, customs, the main post office, the telegraph office, the harmless police department, and the American-enemy zone. Our fugitive had not yet figured in any of those lists.

O God, I cried, may this cup pass from me. Don't make me a hunter, a beater in this hellish hunt. It was ridiculous—unbaptized, rootless, and suddenly there I am praying: Have mercy. . . .

It is true that, when I was around five or six, I did for a time fall into the absurd habit of pulling my blanket over my head to make a little shelter so no one could see me crossing myself before I went to sleep. Not knowing the details and rules of the ritual, I figured it best to reproduce that magic sign randomly, using the theory of probability, starting from my left shoulder, moving to my stomach, my forehead, this way, that way—one variation had to be right. Even my mother, for all my boundless trust in her, had no idea about the church I had improvised out of my ignorance. Other reasons aside, I kept this nook of primitive ambition from her, because I was ashamed and unable to put it into words—for me at that time, God, in some inscrutable way, had fused with the image of my mother, merging into her features. I firmly reminded myself that God, unfortunately, did not exist. But my mother was there with me, and that was beyond any refutation. It was impossible to imagine anything better than her love. And for want of God, I, the heretic, prayed to my own mother. But I didn't ask for anything; content with the infantile happiness of being near to her, and stealthily crossing myself before falling asleep, I would place myself under her blessed shadow, which for some reason already fell upon me from heaven. . . .

When leaving for Vienna on special secret assignment, I had grossly deceived my mother, saying I was off on a Komsomol trip to nearby Kharkov for a few days. Some kind of a summer conference, I no longer remember on what. I didn't want to burden her. She'd had enough, with my father being arrested in December, his fate remaining unclear until the next autumn. My two escorts probably considered him a hostage against my disappearing while in the West. But I wouldn't have, no matter what. Even if I were alone in the world, even to be free as the wind, I still wouldn't have done it. Other plans and plots were fermenting in me. . . .

I did not, however, speak of my father's fate in prison with my zealous guardians. Steel doesn't commiserate. I was cut off. No go! And the one who held the condottiere's reins in the Vienna expedition showed me how pitiful it was to attempt any glimpse into that netherworld. I don't know what rank he held, and now I have only the foggiest recollection of his inscrutable face (I remember nothing but his small, cruel mouth), but he must have been up there in rank, since his assistant, who clearly played second fiddle, introduced himself as a major. But I saw neither of them in their regalia. On the earth's shaky surface they operated like the faint outline of some newly designed battering rams that, for the time being, were being kept under wraps. Big men, pushing fifty (or so it seemed to me as a young man). One, an athletic type with the glazed, almost inlaid eyes of a statue, was already completely bald. Only whitish feather-grass fluttered on his ebony skull, accentuating the chiseled power of his handsome swarthy brow. . . . A month before the trip to Vienna, his boss (or we could call him the Chief), the one with the small mouth, informed me that he had familiarized himself with the details of my father's case and could authoritatively say that my father was a dangerous political criminal, a traitor to the Motherland—he gave me his word of honor on that. . . .

Covering our trail, we did not leave Austria by plane but by train, supposedly for Prague, though our actual destination was Chop. This was, of course, a new trick, part of the competition with American intelligence if it, working with the French and Allied command, had decided, at insane expense, to track my mythical itinerary, having the same sources of information at its disposal— the hotels, the police, customs, train stations. To my mind, that would have been a venture as pointless as our own presumptuous and excessive raid. On the way to the train, our open car made an extra little detour off the highway to avoid any hypothetical roadblocks or unwanted conjecture, passing what appeared to be a fashionable resort with swimming pools filled with marvelous dark-green water under a pale-blue sky and flanked by nearly naked, golden odalisques reserved for millionaires passing through town. They're lying around like they were at home, mumbled the Chief with odd hostility, without looking at them. But the bald one, sitting up in his seat, grinned benevolently at that unusually vast rookery of women. "All those European women, and us with no binoculars! . . ."

The train, however, packed with military people, discharged or on leave, seemed entirely Soviet to me. Everyone was a little tipsy, and we had barely picked up speed when you could hear the sound of glass breaking. People were tossing empty bottles out the train windows, aiming them at poles along the way. There wasn't a soul in sight along the train line—people were hiding wherever they could from this military convoy, and for several hours running we seemed to be traveling through a deserted land to the accompaniment of endless salvos of broken glass. I reflected sadly on the savage destructive instinct that is part of man, and which I had not encountered before, except for the peals and reverberation of war's ominous echoes.

Why does a strike battalion, smashing through the front line in the vicinity of a women's camp, kill the guards and then immediately race in and rape the applauding women prisoners, Russians, Ukrainians, Poles, and Croats, whom they had saved from death? Those women would have willingly gratified their liberators, and there'd have been plenty for everyone—this question was shamefacedly posed by a participant in the affair, a peaceable, bashful boy from a patriarchal village. But no! They had indiscriminately and publicly disgraced every last one of them. Without even really wanting to. Just as part of their wild running start and charge. Their hearts' desire was not a woman's caresses but a continuation of the attack. Those poor wombs were new battlefields. . . . The force propelling the soldiers was evidently too strong, too irresistible!. . . . And now, seven years after the battle's end, I could hear something of the same sort in the clashing, smashing symphony (if you lost yourself in it) of bottles shattering against the stone walls through which our careful convoy wove its way, shuddering warily at junctions. The wheels seemed to slide and skid in the crash and gnashing of ground glass. In a downpour of slivers, a clinking requiem, we moved through an alien and merciless land, Austria under Russian occupation. . . .

I, however, as usual, overlooked a great deal in my hasty diagnosis, or else, influenced by a moment of melancholy, I distorted the picture as a whole, and though I practically didn't open my mouth the entire way, the fourth person in our compartment, who had no connection to us, an air-force colonel, his hair a distinguished gray, offered a corrective to supplement my perceptions. "Friends, there's no need to worry about those bottles that once held the fruit of the vine. They don't turn in bottles here. So our boys can enjoy themselves to the hilt. They're celebrating a happy ending, the rest they've got coming, the promotions they won in the army, and by competing in marksmanship on what you might call ground targets (heh-heh). That's a tradition now, since the war. They always do that here when they're leaving the country. What can you do? They've been bored, they've missed Russia and freedom. Serving abroad is no pleasure for a Russian. But, with rare exceptions, you don't have to worry about any drunken brawls on this stretch of the trip. And there's mostly officers in our car anyway. Disciplined, enterprising, well-mannered, well-trained people . . ." And he began explaining the garrison system to us, its strict isolation, far from the thickly settled areas, as if hidden from view and at the same time on view to tight-fisted Europe. He spoke of the local ways and customs—just sickening to the likes of us. They don't have enough spice in their life. They don't know how to have a really good time. They don't enjoy life. And they don't get the point of life, they don't know why the fuck they're alive, if you'll pardon the expression! They're just passing time. And such poverty of ideas and spiritual aspirations . . . Oh, it makes you sick to your stomach when you've been here as long as I have! . . .

And as if to confirm his judicious observations, in the increasing intervals between the bottles, now missing their targets, and the colonel's garrulous guffawing, I caught cries and snatches of conversation from all over the car, which here, for brevity's sake, I will quote verbatim:

"For all the harm it does you, vodka still gives you strength. And the swill they drink in the West! It's too sour and almost zero proof; it weakens their civilization. . . ."

"Morally! Morally! . . ."

"Our soldiers were tempered by that freeze-up in '42! . . ."

"They get a lousy winter there in Austria! . . ."

"That used to happen where I come from on the Volga! . . ."

"I got in the bathtub and the water in it was warm, warm! . . ."

"It's too bad the Viennese woods are in American hands; I didn't get to see them. . . ."

"We look out and there's an old woman on a bicycle, we almost hit her! . . ."

"The climate's all wrong here. They call this nature! . . ."

"People are tight-fisted here. I go into a drugstore and ask: *Haben Sie* . . ."

"They call this a village? The houses are made of stone. Not only that, they got brick roofs!"

"I don't care what you say, the Danube's a beautiful river. . . ."

"Of course, they have a very high level of consumerism. . . ."

"That's not so. Don't exaggerate, Lieutenant. Our cameras—I own one of the latest models—can hold their own with the Zeiss. . . ."

"But the watches! The watches! . . ."

Unintentionally, I glanced over at my stone-faced escorts. They weren't smiling. Or had they had their ears talked off by our cheerful air-force colonel, who, as he told us, had been with the quartermaster's department since they started dismantling Germany's technology at the very end of the war?

"They're very polite, but you can't really talk with them! . . ."

By analogy I thought of Rex, a fierce dog brought back as war booty from Germany to a large and already well-furnished Moscow apartment, who probably would simply have died if an interpreter the owner knew hadn't dropped by unexpectedly and started speaking with it in German. The enormous German shepherd, formerly owned by a Gestapo man, crawled over to its savior's feet, whining like a puppy, and sprawled on the rug in front of him, its bare, defenseless belly up. The new owner had to sell that priceless creature to the interpreter for a song. It's tough on a dog to lose touch suddenly with the leash of human speech. . . .

"No, I'm not a pilot! I'm an aviation engineer! But now I'm a humble quartermaster, a steward," said the colonel, holding forth,

detachment leader's searching gaze on me, studying my features
for what seemed the first time, squinting as he puffed on a Kazbek
cigarette. After studying me for a minute, he chewed confidentially
on his cigarette with his lips, as if whispering to himself, and then,
leaning closer to me, said in a tone of disapproval:

"You're tenderhearted."

"Where did you get the idea I was tenderhearted?" I had a
somewhat edgy impulse to stand up for my own dignity as a man.

"There was one detail. The way you toss your cigarettes in the
ashtray. You don't toss them. You place them in the ashtray. You
don't smoke them down to the end. And you don't stub them out.
You feel sorry for them, don't you? . . . That means you're tenderhearted. . . . But me, I'm cruel! This is what I do with a
cigarette!"

Snatching the smoking Kazbek from his mouth, he crushed it
between his fingers, literally wringing the neck of the poor butt,
with a few brisk twists. I didn't understand the meaning of this
drunken act. But what can you do? There's a great deal about
their way of thinking that eludes me, and to this day I can't fathom
the ultimate goal of our entire venture, which struck me as foolish
and pointless. The woman they had hunted with such initial ardor
and intricate plotting had escaped them unharmed, unworried
about her reputation and at peace with her conscience. Without
having lied or taken fright. She had escaped the closing noose with
her life, thank God. . . .

All right, I had made it clear to her whom she was dealing with
and what dangers our meeting held. But the Chief did not make
much of a secret of his mysterious connections with certain extremely influential circles (I'm afraid he was liquidated after Beria's
fall, or else he retired; I never ran into him in any camp later on).
He did not flaunt those connections, of course, and behaved re-
spectably, reasonably; still, any child could see who it was inviting
her and me to the Prater for a ride on the ferris wheel said to be
famous throughout Europe, or for the three of us (minus the bald
one) to take a boat ride down the blue Danube. Or who ordered

the dry wine in the hotel restaurant. The comments made by both sides at dinner were comically transparent:

"Abstract ideas won't save mankind. . . ."

"I don't agree . . . ," said Helene.

The tall, narrowed-necked bottle of vermouth on the table looked like a model of a torpedo. The mineral water fell into the crystal goblet with a murmuring clatter, the kind you'd probably hear in the Caucasus Mountains as a cavalcade gallops down a stony trail. Then, once again, lazily, without any pressure:

"Abstract ideas won't save mankind. . . ."

"I don't agree. . . ."

He was hardly trying to convince her. They're not that naïve. He was most likely affecting a grandee's distracted and magnanimous intimacy, while our striking little group, in a corona of gleaming silver and glass, was, unbeknownst to us, captured on film by the bald one, who spent those hours working behind the scenes. With the long-range aim of possibly someday presenting Helene and her father with an ultimatum. The Soviet logic of detective films: since they're all on film sitting side by side, and in a smoky restaurant—they must be in league! But no ultimatum was presented in the years to come; the film was a waste, the trap all for naught. Oh, those romantics of espionage and crime! Still, I am afraid that the Chief was removed from his post . . .

Meanwhile, evening had fallen. Sated, my drinking and traveling companions struck on the idea of a card game but, indifferent, never having held treacherous cards in my hand, I slid over to an empty seat in the compartment's cozy gloom and sipped my cognac from my cut-glass there. In those days I was still a stranger to strong drink, and I remember being pleasantly surprised by the thick transparent wall that immediately sprang into being around my head. Everything passes through that lens and seems perhaps even finer and more distinct than usual, but you yourself are trapped within the glass. Then I understood the etymology of the folk expression "to be under glass." Isn't that why drunken people sometimes become loud and keep hammering at the same point again and again, making abrupt gestures at those around them? There, under glass, they have a heightened sense that their replies are not getting across, and they have to struggle to make their point. In that sort of state, however, I, unlike most people, never become rowdy or seek closer communication but quickly withdraw into that glassiness, for purposes of contemplation. A lesson taught me by those damnable escorts of mine . . .

What kind and gentle faces they have, peaceable passengers, whiling away the evening like children but without any great excitement, slapping their jacks and kings down softly. Why had I been so upset, what unforeseeable event had I tried to anticipate? Why I did beseech Helene to register with the French command? A person who's registered has less of a chance of disappearing. The two of them swore a blue streak. As soon as Helene and I could speak in private, I urged her to leave Austria soon. Bizarre— no sooner were we together than we were rushing to part. But it was also out of the question for her just to turn around and leave: suspicion would have fallen directly on me. . . .

Oh, how they laughed that last night when, after seeing her to the train, I returned downcast to the hotel and, with a crushed look, informed them that in my opinion she had guessed what was up, had figured out the Chief's role in that waiting game, and that was why she had left in such a hurry. Then I became truly frightened—this time for myself. They were laughing, as if they saw right through all my efforts to save her and had only been lying in wait to catch me red-handed. Those guffaws resounded too long, too loudly, and too hollowly to be taken as natural. After performing their chuckling duet, they seemed to change their approach. My troubled state of mind at that moment can be most accurately expressed by quoting from a novel written exactly twenty years later by my seven-year-old son. At an early age he began writing novels that abounded in superb lines and fast action, and I could never think of anything better than Egor's "And, putting three pistols to his head, they took him off to prison." That was what I felt lurking behind their picturesque good humor.

. . . Their laughter broke off as it had begun, on command. Then the Chief said to me without smiling:

"What made you think that she was telling you the truth? Why couldn't she be working with us? Behind your back . . ."

He gave me a long and enigmatic look. I just shrugged my shoulders. The burden was off me. The trick hadn't worked. It was all clearly as fake as the criminal charges against my old father, whom they had under lock and key. They're in the habit of sowing mistrust between people. And they must have been trained to laugh like that too. Just in case, for future reference, to keep you constantly intimidated. There was nothing to laugh at there. Except perhaps the dismay on my face . . .

Now, on the way back to Russia, I no longer thought I'd be picked up as soon as I returned. The score would be evened at some later date, but for a time I could sleep in peace. Otherwise they wouldn't have fooled around playing cards like that, normal as could be. They wouldn't have wasted expensive cognac on me. They wouldn't have let me sit alone and unwatched in the wonderful dim corner of the compartment, where, my face unseeable, only the expression in my eyes revealed my heart's glad peace, timid hallelujahs on my lips. . . . Still, how wrong and unfair of us if, when in mortal danger, we pray for mercy, and then, once the trouble is past, we go on living happily, expecting new bounty, as if that were the way life was meant to be. And we keep asking for more and more! . . . Meanwhile, everything, absolutely everything—the air, the water, the earth, and the night sky—is given to us as an advance, which we usually forget to repay, feeling no gratitude for all that is closest at hand.

"Thank God! Thank God!" I whispered, and at once assailed myself: Don't take God's name in vain, don't use God's name when you pray. . . .

I felt a flame, a diabolical flame, issue from my mouth. It must have been the unfamiliar cognac flaring up in spontaneous combustion. The night rushed in imperiously through the half-opened window, bearing a wave of dark air, slightly rancid with the smell of burned coal, which only made it seem purer. Air furious and inexhaustible in its purity! And the sound of the locomotive's whistle racing toward us as it bore us away into the night . . .

I looked over and saw that, having had their fill of drink and cards, my good companions were snoring away on their berths. I hadn't even noticed when the game broke up. It was time for me to turn in too, but I kept putting it off, delighting in the solitude that had come to me as a gift and ran parallel to life, all-consuming and no longer real to me. . . . It's marvelous how sleep makes everyone equal, without distinction as to historical importance or purpose, rank or title. In nothing else are we so much alike as in that universal inclination to sleep. Are you prepared, you ask yourself, to be like everyone else? Of course, I reply, and like the beasts and the trees too, but by then your eyelids are closing. Goodbye, I'm leaving for parts unknown; how can you tell where you're going in that clatter of wheels? . . . But the night does not sleep; the night stands guard over sleep and it creates, drawing light and fire from the gathering dark and air from the plants poisoned by the fumes of the day. If not for the night, we would not know the starry heavens, the lights on the other side of the river, trains, or the air. And that drawn-out melancholy train whistle which I know from my past, my youth . . . That's what I'll regret leaving most—the night air and locomotive whistles—this thought flashed through my mind for no reason. Of everything I've done in life, I'd say the most superb thing was sleeping out in the fresh air. I did that in my childhood, on hay, on the little terrace in Rameno— my destination now—or, bliss itself, with my father, my mother, my wife, or my son—under the open sky. You inhale deeply and sail away as you exhale; asleep, you keep breathing in the scent of the grass, the stirrings of the leaves, and the chill of the night that pierces your old sheepskin coat. If you half open one eye, the stars are so bright they come streaking down at you. Sleeping in the open air, your conscience is clean as you hear a train passing on the far side of the ancient woods, the locomotive whistling at the Batraki landing, out past Syzran. And you say thank you, thank you to everything, despite all the delirium of the day. And you scarcely sleep, but only breathe in the purity of the night, which streams into your chest all by itself, liberates you, becoming your thoughts, becoming you. I don't remember anything. Only the air. And the distant parting hoot of a locomotive in the night . . .

Paris, 1983